The Flame of Ram

THREE RED LIONS

The Flame of Ram

ISRAEL I. COOLEY

HILGREEN PRESS

To my wife, Kimberly.

Thanks for not letting me give up.

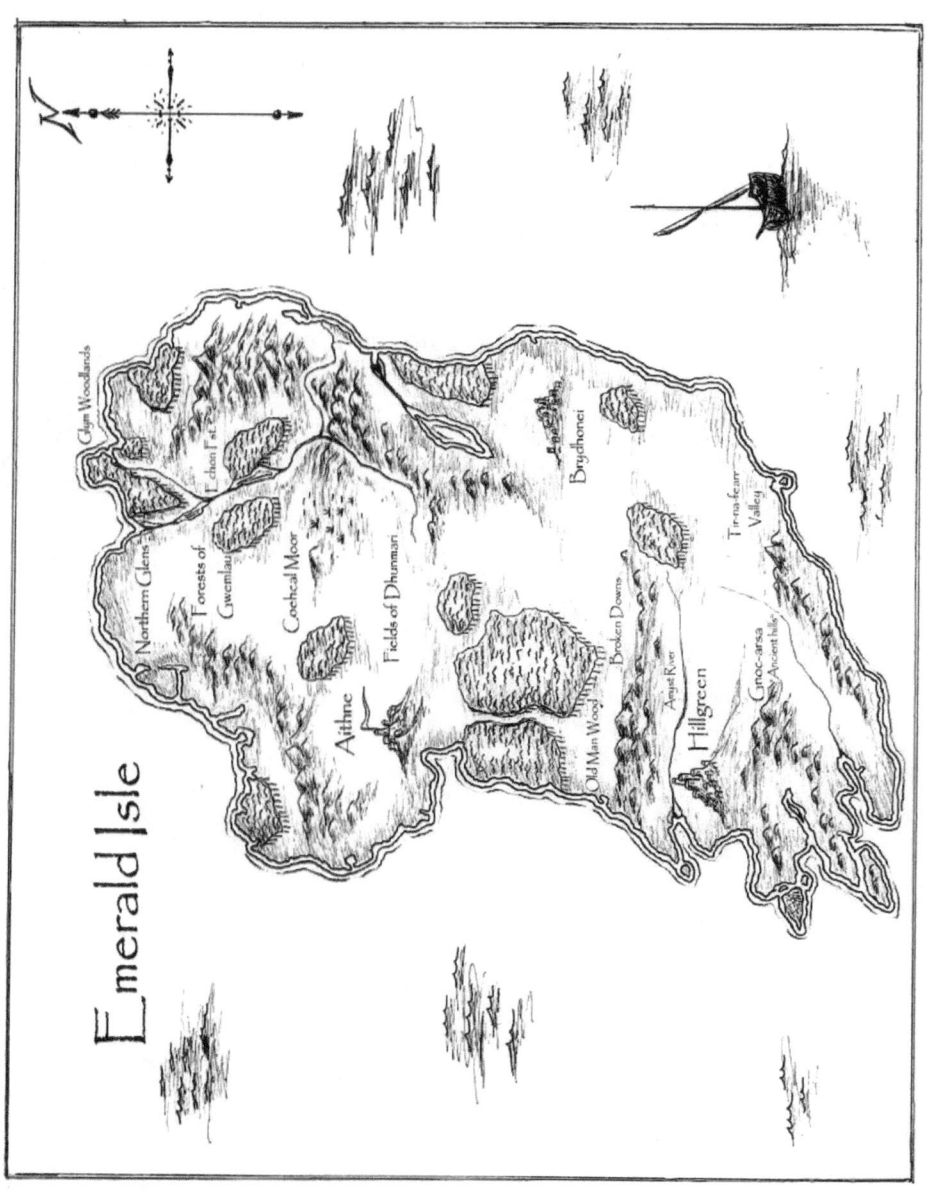

Emerald Isle

Glen Woodlands
Echon Forest
Northern Glens
Forests of Gwenlland
Cocheal Moor
Fields of Dhumian
Aithne
Brughonei
Tir-na-fearr Valley
Broken Downs
Old Man Wood
Argel Riss
Hillgreen
Cnoc-airsa
Ancient Isle

Prologue

R am stood on the crown of a small hill just outside his village. The sky glowed orange as the dull yellow disc made its final descent into the red waters of Erythraean, the western sea that surrounded his island home. It would be dark soon. He turned his gaze toward the black forest line that rose up a stone's throw to the southwest. Coldness crept slowly down his back. The fear that settled in Ram's gut washed over him again. It became a great weight, straining his features with weariness.

He looked back over his village and considered whether their punishers would come again tonight. And even as he tried to find some hope, in his heart he knew the answer. They would come.

Ram's father, Arland, had long ago united the people of their island. He ruled them well. Perhaps he was not known for his great wisdom, but the strength of Arland's arm was legendary among the people. He was a good and honest leader, and their people prospered until the coming of the Aletae.

Arland often told Ram of these Aletae. They were the mighty rulers of the White Isle, a great island kingdom, which lay some seven days across Erythraean to the southeast. It was said that they were descendants of the god Nethuns, half human and half god. Ram's father described them as being huge in stature, more than an arm's length larger than himself, with skin as white as bone. And if the stories others told could be trusted, they lived well beyond the normal life span of men.

Arland saw their power with his own eyes and knew there could be no victory against them. And so, he reluctantly joined the throng of other rulers, some from lands he had never even heard of, who were bending their knee to appease the powerful Aletae. The imposed tribute was a heavy yoke, but one their people under Arland's leadership had quietly borne as agreed. Year after year the treaty was satisfied, and life continued without further strife. This year, however, when the warm south winds began to blow again, the emissaries of the Aletae had come to collect an additional tribute.

The usual payment of silver and goods were still expected, but this year the Aletae required an extra tribute to be paid out of the children of each village. Over two hundred children were demanded under the new tribute of souls, as their overlords now called it. Ram's village alone was to deliver up fourteen of their children. Arland flew into a rage at the unthinkable demand and openly refused. He was the protector of his people. To allow their children to be enslaved was a fate worse than death. The Aletae, nevertheless, would not be denied.

An ancient curse was released upon the rebellious villages— demons that took the shape of beasts. The people called them Sargaroth, the dogs of death. Their reign of terror began not more than a fortnight ago during the darkest part of the night. The Sargaroth had come from the woods and attacked Ram's village without warning. His father was one of the first to be killed.

Ram had heard of these dogs of death since early on in his life. From the time he was a child, the older boys in their village tormented those younger than themselves with stories of these nightmarish creatures. They always were just that: children's tales. There was no such delusion anymore. Although Ram was still not sure what they were, it was now horribly certain that they were real.

It was clear to all that these Sargaroth were sent to do the bidding of their masters, the Aletae. Now that his father was gone, it fell to Ram to lead his people. But what could he do? The Sargaroth could not be stopped. The first time they came, anyone unlucky enough to be in their path was killed outright. Their long, blade-like claws cut down the men with unimaginable speed. They never saw the death that came to them. True, for Ram's father, it was different. He and a few of the bravest warriors made a stand in the village square when everyone else fled. They tried to defend the people from these dogs of death, but to no avail. They were cut down as quickly as those who ran. At least they died with honor.

Since that first attack, the Sargaroth came many times. Each time it was the same. They came under the cloak of darkness, killed any that resisted, and took one child. Ram wondered when they would stop. They'd already taken thirteen, but the required tribute of souls for their village was fourteen. His stomach twisted with the hopelessness he felt as he looked back over the village. Would they stop at fourteen?

The horizon began to glow bright orange and red as the blue sky above deepened into shades of azure. How could such beauty exist together with such fear? Ram looked back over his shoulder toward where the forest line was now invisible in the encroaching darkness. Something different began to rise up within him. To be sure, fear still surged through his gut. But from somewhere deeper inside, he began to feel a rush of anger. Someone must stand against this evil! If they continued to do nothing but protect their own, they would all fall.

It was with a renewed sense of purpose and courage that Ram turned back to his village. He passed the outer holdings, which were dark and boarded up from the inside. The rest of the village was the same. All signs of life had receded deep into hiding. Every dwelling and workshop appeared dark and abandoned. Ram ran to his own home and banged on the door. The noise sounded unnatural in the lifeless village. The wooden door opened slowly, and the apprehensive face of a young woman appeared from the dark inside.

"Ram! Where have you been? The darkness is coming!"

Ram entered without speaking and strode to the corner of the room. He bent and picked up a wooden torch and brought it to the hearth. He began lighting a small fire.

"What are you doing?" Ram's young wife was exasperated. "The rest are already waiting in the lower level! We must join them," she urged.

"There is time yet," Ram replied quietly, but with more resolve than he felt.

"If you light the fire...they will know we are here," his wife implored.

Ram turned quickly and snapped back with more anger than he intended. "I will hide no more!"

A look of shocked hurt passed over his wife's face. He immediately regretted the harsh response. He reached for her and tenderly sat her down in a chair. He knelt down in front of her, lifted his hand to her cheek, and looked directly into her eyes. "I will hide no more."

He hesitated, and then continued more quietly, but with a surge of emotion that welled up in him suddenly. "No more, Este. They know we are here *already*. We cannot just sit by and hope that our house will be avoided tonight. We must fight, Este...or it may be one of our children this time."

"Others have fought back. They are all dead now," Este said as tears began to roll down her soft cheeks. Ram felt her pain. Her older brother was one of those killed defending Ram's father. Ram likely would have died as well but for his absence when the first attack came.

He stood and pulled his wife into his arms. "If we do not fight back, then we might as well already *be* dead. I will not suffer my children to live under this shadow of the Sargaroth," he said, looking back into Este's hazel green eyes. He continued in a softer tone. "I would see the children dance and sing again, rather than cower in a hole in the ground."

He slowly released his wife, reached for the torch, and held it into the small fire. The flames leapt to the pitch as he pulled it back and put out the hearth fire. He turned to his wife one last time.

"Keep the children hidden. If I do not return"—he paused while casting a quick glance around the home of his childhood—"leave this place forever!"

Ram turned abruptly, picked up his sword, and stepped through the door. Half running and holding the torch in his left hand, Ram did not take long to reach the village square. A brief survey confirmed what he already knew would be true. It was empty. He quickly moved to where the alarm bell hung. He grabbed the rope to pull, but a new wave of fear caused him to hesitate. What was he doing? Did he want to die? The soft crackling of the burning torch in his hand was the only sound that reached his ears. All was eerily quiet. The darkness of the night was deepening. There would be no moon tonight.

Ram's eyes fell to the spot where his father had been left to die. Rather than fear, Ram once again felt anger surging within him. He grabbed hold of the rope and began to pull it. The first few clangs sent a thrill of shock through his ears. At first there was no response. Ram continued pulling the rope. The warning bell filled the air with an unnatural clanging.

After he thought no one would answer his summons, a door across the square slowly opened. A bearded face peered out.

From somewhere further down the square came a hissed shout. "What are you doing, Ram?"

Ram continued to pull the bell rope. Another door down the square opened slightly, but then quickly shut again. The bearded man from across the square stepped out from behind his door. He looked carefully in every direction but made no further move. Ram looked in his direction but continued ringing the bell. Another man apprehensively approached from the eastern side of the square. Ram stopped pulling the rope, and the last few clangs slowly faded into the deadened night air. He stepped up onto the nearby raised platform. Two more men came from directly behind where he now stood.

"What is the meaning of this foolishness?" one of the men demanded.

Safnon, the man who spoke, was one of the elders of the village, and despite his obvious fear, he still carried an air of indignant superiority. He continued. "Have you gone mad? The dogs of the Aletae may come at any moment!"

Ram snapped back, "And what if they come? Should we let them overtake us hiding in holes?"

Safnon did not like the insinuation in Ram's voice. He clamped his lips tight and refused to answer.

Ram turned to the man who had come from the eastern side of the square. "What say you, Mark? Should we hide or fight?" Mark had been his friend since childhood, and Ram always knew him to be ready for a good fight.

"How can we fight...them?" Mark held out his hand as though in supplication. He continued with frustration. "I cannot fight what I cannot see. I do not like hiding, but these things cannot be killed. They are demons!"

There was a hushed agreement among the few gathered to Ram.

"They are not demons." The bearded man from across the square appeared from behind them. "I have seen them before," he stated without emotion.

The man was a metal worker who had lived in the village for less than a year. He had no family and kept to himself for the most part. He continued. "It is said that the Aletae gave them the cunning of men, the bodies of jackals, the mouths of ravening wolves, and the strength of bears. No, they are not demons. They are worse. They are real!"

"If they are real, then they must have a weakness," Ram answered. "They must be able to be killed. We must fight them! "Ram's voice betrayed none of his own misgivings.

"We?" Safnon spoke up again. His tone was incredulous. "There are only five of us even stupid enough to leave the safety of our homes on such a night."

"Safety! None of us are safe this night! My father—" Ram began, but he was cut off sharply by Safnon.

"*Your* father died on the very spot you now stand. It was his foolish actions that brought this curse down upon our heads in the first place!" Safnon spoke as though Ram were a rebellious child.

Ram glared back at him. "I would rather die like the hero my father was than live like the coward you—"

Ram's voice, now thick with accusation, was silenced by the sudden and bone-chilling sound of a howl. It was similar to a wolf's, yet with a harsh, deeper quality unlike anything canine. It was an unearthly sound. The four men stood frozen and completely silent. After a moment it came again, but it was distinctly closer this time. Without another word, Safnon turned and fled back toward his well-prepared hiding spot. The other man who came with him joined his hasty retreat.

The bearded man looked up at Ram. "If they do have a weakness, I have never heard of it." With that the man turned and slowly walked back into his house and shut the door. Ram watched him go and then turned to look at Mark, who was caught by a moment of indecision.

"Ram, I would... I mean I do not know what..." Mark fell silent but implored Ram with his eyes.

Ram relented. "You are newly married, Mark. You must go to your wife. She will need your strength tonight." Ram desperately wanted someone to stand with him, but he knew he could not ask such a sacrifice of his friend. Mark nodded, shame filling his barely visible features. He turned slowly and moved back through the square and soon disappeared into the night.

Desperate thoughts began to assail Ram from every corner of his mind. What could he do? He must do *something*! He looked across the square in the direction where the forest lay. Another howl revealed that his time was short. The darkness became suffocating. He spun around with an increasing level of panic and looked for some plan of defense. In his growing state of confusion, his foot caught on the ledge of the platform, and he fell forward into the dusty street. He lost his grip on the torch, and it spun into the dirt a few feet away. It sputtered and dimmed, but did not go out.

As he lay with his face in the dirt, the sudden feeling that he was no longer alone washed over him. It was an uncanny sensation that someone, or something, now waited in the darkness just behind where he had stood a moment before. He slowly looked toward his torch. It was within a long arm's reach. He carefully placed his hand on the handle of his sword.

He noticed that he lay next to the village fire pit, which was still full of unburned wood and branches. Ram took a deep breath and with one fluid motion reached with his left hand for the torch while also pulling up the sword with his right. He rolled toward the fire pit and sprang to his feet in a half-crouched position.

Whatever it was that Ram expected to see was not what met his eyes. There, standing on two legs like a man, was a hideously unnatural creature. It had the elongated jaws of a wolf, but its head was much larger and its eyes blood red. Its entire body was covered with long, dark, matted hair. As it looked at Ram, deep gasps of hot breath filled the night air with clouds of steam. Ram locked eyes with the abhorrent thing and cried out in spite of himself. His first instinct was to throw down his weapon and run.

He took a hesitant step backwards and raised the torch higher and outward toward the beast. The monster's reaction was immediate and unbelievably swift as a long arm snaked out and knocked the torch into the air above Ram's head. A low menacing growl came from deep within the creature. Ram swung out desperately with his sword. The blade directly hit the creature's midsection, but it merely glanced off the thick hide. Ram looked up at the Sargaroth with astonishment as its clawed hand reached out and grabbed him around the neck.

Ram slashed at his enemy with all the strength he could muster. The blows that would have felled ten men seemed useless against the Sargaroth. Ram began to gasp for air as he was lifted off his feet. He dropped his sword and grabbed the beast's arm with both of his hands. A short distance behind Ram, the pile of branches and wood in the fire pit suddenly sprang to life with flame ignited from the torch. The wood was dry from sitting in the hot open air, and the flame quickly roared into a full blaze, jumping well above Ram's head. The Sargaroth jerked violently away from the sudden light created by the fire and released its grip on Ram's neck.

Ram sprawled back onto the ground next to the fire, gasping for air. His sword lay where it had fallen, at the edge of the fire pit. Hot flames licked at the double-edged blade. Ram grabbed for the sword's handle and slashed backward at the beast with blind desperation. Instead of simply bouncing off the impenetrable hide as before, the blade of the sword, which momentarily still carried small pieces of burning brush, slashed through the middle of the monster's chest. The cut was not deep enough to kill, but its hide hissed wickedly. The unnatural creature screamed with such intensity that Ram took an involuntary step backwards. The thing turned and vanished into the shadows.

It took Ram a moment longer to realize that he was alone once more. He stood in stunned silence, trying to understand what had just happened. The roar of the fire filled his ears. He turned slowly and looked at the flames and then at the sword in his hand. A thick, pungent, black liquid still bubbled and hissed across the surface of the blade. Strangely, the silver metal of the blade itself glowed with a hint of red and yellow light that danced slightly as though a fire now burned inside of it.

From somewhere across the square, a woman's scream pierced the air. Ram sprang to his feet and reached into the fire pit for another torch. He looked at the still-glowing sword blade in his right hand, then turned in the direction of the scream and ran to Este.

Mock Battle

One Thousand Years Later

The day was hot. The sun was already high above, burning with relentless indifference. Serigant stood next to his older brother, Pharigant. They both held a stout wooden sword in their right hand, and a small, round, plain wooden shield in their left. Eighteen other boys about their age stood all around them in the middle of the hardened-dirt training yard. Serigant blocked the sun as he looked up to his older brother. "When will they let us back inside? It's hot out here."

Pharigant returned his look. "It will be different today," he replied sympathetically. "The older boys will come for us soon. "He put his hand on Serigant's shoulder. "Stay close to me. I will do my best to keep them off you. Just remember no one knows who we are. To them, we are just new trainees who need a beating. They will give us no quarter."

Serigant was younger than the normal initiate, but he had begged to be admitted to the warriors' training school two years early, along with his older brother. Their father, King Pharin, let out a robust laugh at Serigant's insistence, ruffled his hair, and said, "Now that is *just* the way I would have it too." It was the king's specific instructions that his sons be given no special treatment. One day, he reasoned, they would need to be strong enough to rule a kingdom, and he would not have anyone make it easy on them. As such, their royal titles were hidden from everyone except the master of training, who was in fact their uncle, Malen.

All new trainees were first required to endure a period of initiation before beginning their training. The initiates were subjected to all sorts of stamina and hardship trials during this period. It usually lasted several weeks, finally culminating with an all-out battle against the older trainees. The combatants, of course, were armed only with wooden swords, shields, and crude helmets.

The purpose of this final trial was to make the initiates face the very real pain that came with defeat. This mock battle inevitably ended with the initiates being beaten mercilessly by the older trainees. Although the swords were really not much more than blunted sticks, and even with the protections afforded by the small shields and helmets, most initiates were covered in bloody bruises when the horn sounded, ending each battle. The older trainees were constrained by only one rule: anyone knocked to the ground was eliminated from the battle.

Today was the last day of the new trainees' initiation. Serigant swallowed hard, but he nodded his understanding back to Pharigant. Just then, there arose a loud battle shout from the perimeter of the training yard, and fifty older boys of varying ages ran from the surrounding buildings, all of them brandishing wooden swords and shields, somewhat larger than what the initiates carried.

Pharigant pulled his younger brother closer behind him and made ready for the inevitable charge. "Remember, stay with me!" he said over his shoulder. Serigant, whose eyes were slightly wider than before, nodded nervously.

The rest of the initiates instinctively backed away from the menacing group of older trainees until they had formed a tight ball. Their attackers had painted their faces and bodies in wild strange patterns, only adding to the initiates' growing sense of panic. The expected attack, however, did not come right away. Silence descended over the attacking force as they waited for some unknown signal.

The sun reached its highest point in the sky and burned with hot intensity. Sweat poured down the young boys' faces and burned their eyes as they fought to control their fear. The sound of a loud battle horn filled the air as the trainees who surrounded them charged from all sides at once. Those initiates who gave way to panic paid the battle price first. Three or four threw down their swords and tried to run, finding too late that there was nowhere to go. Their cries and screams were silenced, as they were quickly and brutally smashed to the ground by the onrushing attackers.

Just as the main wave of attackers reached Pharigant, he spun to his right and swept his wooden shield low toward the legs of the first assailant. The older boy let out a cry and went down. He completed the spin by swinging his sword high, catching the next nearest attacker on the helmet with a loud crack, knocking him to the ground.

The battle swirled all around him. He looked quickly around in an attempt to find Serigant. His younger brother stood not three paces away, fending off two older boys and holding his own for the moment. Three more attackers jumped at Pharigant as he quickly defended against the first to reach him. He slashed a downward stroke at the boy's sword, pinning it to the ground as he smashed upward into the unlucky boy's face with the flat of his shield. Blood spurted from the older boy's nose as he crumbled backwards to the ground.

The other two attackers were more wary. They came in slowly, circling Pharigant. Two other rather large trainees joined the encircling maneuver. Pharigant looked toward his brother just in time to see him receive a nasty knock on the shoulder by one of his assailants. Pharigant rushed the attacker, who was between Serigant and himself. The move was unexpected, and the older boy backed up, only to lose his footing. He stumbled and fell, yelling in anger at his own stupidity.

Pharigant jumped to Serigant's side, quickly overcoming the attacker on Serigant's left. Four more assailants jumped to the attack. The two brothers fought desperately. All around them was chaos. Shouts and screams filled the air. More than half of their fellow initiates were already down.

A particularly large youth with a cruel face similar in appearance to a pig suddenly jumped in front of Serigant. The other trainees seemed to pay him some level of deference. He pointed at Pharigant, and six of the larger trainees ran to the attack, the sheer blunt force separating him from Serigant's side. It was all he could do just to keep from being overwhelmed by the onslaught.

The pig-faced boy laughed with glee as he bore down on Serigant with powerful smashing strokes. Another assailant ran into Serigant from behind and knocked him to the ground, but the cruel young man did not stop his attack, continuing to hit him with a twisted brutality. Pharigant saw his brother's plight and shouted his name, but could not break through to reach him. A loud whoop sounded above the fray of the battle, as another initiate, a boy about the same size as Serigant, jumped in front of the much larger pig-faced trainee. The initiate's wooden sword was a blur as he smashed his opponent's shield with a flurry of strokes.

The older youth was taken off guard by the sheer ferocity of the attack and stumbled backward, almost losing his footing. He bellowed with fury as he regained his balance and made ready to charge the upstart who dared challenge him. Serigant's unlikely protector stood over him, already bleeding from a dozen gashes, with a look of determination well beyond his years. Three more attackers joined the pig-faced youth. They abandoned themselves to their rage as they charged the young initiate. They would take extra pleasure in giving him the beating he had coming. Serigant, who was too weak to stand, held up his sword. The young boy took it and charged the oncoming assailants.

As they met, the initiate jumped with his feet out in front of him, pushing the nearest assailant to the ground. He rolled over and was back on his feet with cat-like reflexes. The other attackers turned on him all at once. His two swords were a blur as he met them. The older youths were clearly not prepared for someone of the younger boy's skill level. He quickly disarmed two of them, leaving only the pig-faced trainee, who yelled with frustration at his ineffective companions.

The large youth raised his sword above his head with both of his hands, making ready for a massive crushing strike. No one had ever stood against his full power before. His face twisted in a cruel grimace as he swung down. The expected crunching sound, however, never came as the smaller boy deftly reflected the blow to the side and with a spinning motion swung back around and connected his right leg with his opponent's backside. The force of the older boy's swing, encouraged along by the initiate's leg, sent him staggering forward. Unable to regain his balance, he fell in quite an inglorious manner over one of his companions still sprawled on the ground, landing face down in the dirt. The horn sounded again, ending the mock battle.

Across the training yard, only two initiates remained on their feet. Pharigant pushed his way through those who had just moments before been trying desperately to defeat him. Now that the battle was over, he met with no more resistance. In fact, the older boys saluted him with a sign of respect as he broke through their circle. It was rare indeed that any initiate lasted through the entire battle on their feet.

He looked across the yard, trying to find Serigant. The other initiate who had come to Serigant's aid was helping him up. Pharigant ran to the spot. "Are you all right?" he asked with concern and out of breath.

"I... I think so." Serigant spoke through clenched teeth. He was badly bruised and bleeding from a nasty gash on the upper part of his nose.

Pharigant turned to his brother's helper. "Thank you," he said simply.

The young initiate shrugged his shoulders as if his aid had been worth very little. "I was trying to find that big fellow since the horn first sounded," the boy said, extending his hand to Pharigant. "My name is Lanthir."

The Emerald Isle

Thirty Years Later

B ryn stood waist-deep in water beneath the new dock as waves gently rolled around him. It was cold, and a shiver ran up his back. His examination of the work revealed what he already knew he would find. It was solid and would last for many years. He and his brothers, Aedan and Llew, had done well. And even though their father, the king, would be pleased with the results, Bryn found little satisfaction in the accomplishment. He had grown numb inside, and the sensation began to take hold of him.

An ocean-born breeze ruffled his flaxen-colored hair. He lifted his nose to the air and breathed in deeply. It smelled of salt and the sea. He looked toward the other side of the dock and gently placed his hand over the small leather pouch that hung around his neck. His eyes glazed over, captivated by a memory of what once was and could never be again. It was a memory that would destroy him if he did not find a way to bury it once and for all. He was never one to openly show his heart. And even now, only the deep pools of dark brown in his eyes hinted at the grief imprisoned there.

Several curious seagulls landed on a nearby boulder that protruded from the water. Hopping closer toward Bryn, they squawked loudly, hopeful that his presence would mean an easy meal. He stirred from his reflections.

"I am not fishing today," he said. Amusement crossed his mouth without touching his eyes. "I have spoiled you these past many days!" he chided with mock seriousness. Turning his attention back to the far side of the dock, he carefully began picking his way across a bed of submerged rocks piled in the water under the dock.

After reaching the nearest pylon, Bryn leaned out as far as he could over the deep-water drop-off and grabbed hold of the lowest cross support. He easily pulled himself out of the coldwater and up onto the wooden beam. It felt good to use his muscles and shake off the cold bay water from his legs. It was a short climb from there to the spot he had chosen.

He reached for the leather pouch that hung around his neck and lifted it free. He paused a moment, considering the small pouch again.

After a long moment of indecision, he gave in and began opening it. He turned it upside down and gently shook out its contents onto the palm of his hand. A thin golden chain fell loosely against his strong fingers. Clasped to the middle of its length was a small creamy white stone set in a design of golden knots. He reached down and carefully picked up the smooth white stone and turned it slowly back and forth. The light was poor under the dock, but a ray of bright sunshine poured through the wooden planks above. He held the creamy white stone into the light. It flashed with multiple colors, as though a fire kindled inside it.

He continued to stare at its beauty for some time, but his mind held a different image captive. Kelsi was a girl like none he had ever met before. He was never one to care about the whims of any female. But with one look, Kelsi was able to dictate Bryn's emotions as easily as a queen commanded her court. She would tilt her head slightly to one side with her long, fiery red hair hanging freely about her neck and smile in a way that made his knees feel weak.

A cloud covered the sun high above, casting a shadow over the white stone and Bryn's memory. It was the most unique gemstone he had ever seen. He had discovered it at the market one day when looking for a new knife. A certain merchant from somewhere far to the east had shown it to him when nothing else he was selling interested Bryn. He knew the moment he saw it that he must give it to Kelsi. As it turned out, he was no great negotiator. The merchant, on the other hand, immediately saw his fish on the hook. The cost was great, but even now Bryn knew he would have happily paid twice the price for it.

The shadow above grew darker, and its gloom filled his mind. He closed his hand over the gem and carefully placed it back into the small leather pouch. He looked above and to his right. Seeing the place he had chosen earlier, he reached up and loosened a small block from a protected shelf under the deck boards. He had carefully selected the spot and secretly prepared it during the building of the dock. He stood and cautiously placed the pouch as far into the small chamber as possible and replaced the block. Turning back to the large timber pylon nearest the chamber, he took out his knife and carved a small *K* on it before making his way back to the shore.

Bryn climbed out and changed into dry breeches. He sat down on a rock that jutted out over the water and ate an apple along with a lump of sharp-tasting cheese. The sun shone bright in the western sky. The earlier clouds that had covered the light had all but vanished. The warmth felt good on his smooth skin after the coldness of the bay water. Golden rays poured over the distant sea and down through the small inlet, brightly illuminating the village of Aithne that filled the valley beyond. It was a sight that brought a measure of hope back into Bryn's heart. Perhaps not for his own happiness, but for the others he knew and loved.

He considered his brothers. Aedan, Bryn's older brother by two years, always knew the ways of wisdom. Building the dock in such cold, deep waters presented several challenges, but Aedan found solutions to every problem. Bryn believed there was nothing that could hide its answer from Aedan. He was the sort of man that others were drawn to. He had a natural-born authority that was neither contrived nor arrogant. Aedan was not just a leader by birth and certainly not by ambition, but simply because others chose to follow him.

Bryn, on the other hand, was always more than willing to let Aedan lead. It allowed him the freedom to pursue other things. There was never just one thing that ever captured his interest. It was, rather, discovery and the desire to explore that drove him to seek adventure. Although he had gained renown throughout his father's kingdom, it was never what he sought or wanted.

People called Bryn heroic, and in truth, many sought to be like him. He always noted, however, that very few of them ever tried to actually follow where he went. No matter; Bryn preferred his solitude. He heard the songs that were sung in the halls of the land. The Tales of "Bryn and the Bear" and "The Dragon's Breath" were common favorites among the people. It did not seem to matter to anyone that they were greatly overdone. For Bryn's own part, he simply wished to be left alone.

And then there was Llew, the youngest of the three. Often enough, a younger brother is caught in the snare of chasing after the glory of those older than himself. And by doing so, they often fail to attain the unique glory of their own gifting. It was *not* so with Llew. He was as natural to his gift as it was to him. Llew had a strength born of compassion that was beyond physical power. Many said that he was winsome; others described him as magically charming. But to Bryn, the simple truth was that Llew had heart. Where it was true that men would follow Aedan and wanted to be like Bryn, it was equally true that they wanted to stand *with* Llew.

Bryn stood from his perch on the rock and looked back over the valley. From the Elder's Hall to the smallest fisherman's hut, Aithne's appearance was practical and yet carried a warm sense of hospitality. The village was nestled in a bright green valley that opened directly into one of the many natural harbors that made up the western coastline of their father's island kingdom, the Emerald Isle as it was called. Bryn was glad for the time he and his brothers had spent here. It brought some measure of peace back to his mind. He always favored the open air and ease with which these villagers enjoyed life.

Covering his eyes against the bright rays, he turned back to the west and surveyed the large hills and cliffs surrounding the bay. The Emerald Isle was a kingdom like no other. Its green hills rose straight up out of Oceanus' depths like gems set amidst a sea of sapphire. It was an abundant, well-forested land, full of sunny glades and laughing brooks. There was a kind of magic about the Emerald Isle, its flowing hills arrayed in rich colors of brilliant green. Most who looked upon it once, forevermore longed to return. Bryn could not help feeling as though what he loved most about the Emerald Isle were the very same things he saw in Kelsi.

Again Bryn drank deeply of the fresh ocean breeze that filled the harbor. It was a good day, and he was glad for the solitude. He knew that he and his brothers would soon be returning home and leaving behind all chance for seclusion. The rest of their work crew had already been released days ago. Nonetheless, the day was still young, and Bryn felt refreshed under the rejuvenating warmth of the golden disc above.

Llew sat on a wooden bench beneath a large, ancient oak tree. A group of children sat in rapt attention all around him. He was telling them the story of "Bryn and the Bear" and had just jumped off the bench in imitation, startling many of his keen listeners into squeals and excited giggles, when he first noticed a rider approaching along the south road. Even from a distance, the king's messenger was easily recognized. Llew paused his retelling of the tale. He turned and called to Aedan, who was deep in discussion with the village elder. The interruption caused several loud groans and complaints from the children who were impatiently awaiting the end of Llew's story. When Aedan did not seem to hear, Llew called again.

Aedan was ever able to find simple yet right solutions to the problems presented to him. So it was that the leaders of the smaller, and in truth many of the larger, holdings readily sought out his advice. Aithne's elder, who was a short, slightly robust, ruddy-faced fellow named Flan, had been explaining a minor dispute between himself and the elder of a neighboring village. Apparently, the two villages shared usage of several fishing weirs located centrally between them. All wanted access to the obvious benefits of the weirs, but frequent disputes between the clansmen as to who was failing in their duties of upkeep had grown more intense of late.

Flan had just finished his rather lengthy and overly detailed description of the problem when Llew interrupted him with his shout. Aedan turned his gaze toward the direction Llew was indicating and saw the rider. No further explanation was needed. "Have you seen Bryn?" Aedan called back.

"He was down by the dock the last I saw him," Llew responded.

"Good, you meet the messenger and I will find him." Aedan had already begun walking away when he looked back and noticed disappointment move across Flan's face. Aedan turned back shortly and said, "If it were up to me, I would set aside time each spring for the men of both villages to come together and work on the upkeep of the fishing weirs."

Flan's look of hopefulness that reappeared at the beginning of Aedan's advice just as quickly disappeared when he heard it. "But my lord," he implored, "how can I convince the other village to do their share of the work? That has been, in fact, *the whole* of the dispute." It was less a question than a frustrated conclusion.

With a slight twinkle in his eye, Aedan hesitated for a brief moment before patting Flan on the shoulder. "You are looking at this joyous occasion all wrong!"

"I see nothing joyous about mending the fishing weirs," the elder retorted.

A slightly confused expression crossed Aedan's face. "I suppose not by *itself*," he said slowly, and then he paused reflectively. "But I should think that a feast would be considered a joyous occasion by anyone lucky enough to be invited."

The look of disappointment on Flan's face was now replaced by one of total bafflement. "What feast is that, my lord?"

"Why the very same feast you shall declare and host at the conclusion of the work."

Flan was thoughtful for a moment as he tapped his right forefinger against his lips and rested his free arm across his protruding midsection. "That's it!" he exclaimed. "The promise of a feast should bring more than enough men running to the work."

Satisfaction crossed his face, but as Aedan turned to go, the realization that such a yearly feast would mean a significant cost began to wrinkle Flan's brow again.

Aedan turned one last time to face the elder as though he read his mind. "Oh, one last thing, Flan, if I know Bartimus at all," referring to the neighboring village's elder, "he will be quick in claiming the rights to hold next year's feast. I should not be surprised if his claim is made known well before the food from this year's feast has a chance to grow cold. Especially when he sees the acclaim your feast will surely bring to you."

Flan had the look of a man who had just defeated a gang of thugs single-handedly. The prospect of solving the problem left him feeling lighter than he had in months. And what did it hurt that he may receive some local acclaim for his generosity? He was not a proud man, but after all, one cannot tell others what to think.

With that, Aedan turned back toward the dock. Bryn was easy enough to find, and little explanation was needed from the king's messenger. Their father summoned their return. Within the hour, they said their good-byes and began the journey home.

The Old Man in the Woods

The lands south of Aithne were remote, lonely regions where few people lived or traveled. It was a wild and beautiful land with vast tracts of ancient forest through which the king's highway meandered. There was, of course, the occasional trader or merchant headed for the coastal villages. But for the most part, Aedan, Bryn, and Llew traveled alone.

The dark and thickly leafed forest that flanked the road on both sides was alive with many known, and some unknown, creatures. There were plentiful deer, boar, and bear, which when they could not be seen were usually heard crashing through the underbrush not far from the roadway. The trees grew tall for as far as the eye could see across the softly undulating hills, and a stream would occasionally dance down through a carpet of brilliant green moss to cross the road. The first day of the brothers' return journey was under warm and sunny skies. The call of the raven and laughter of brooks rushing over the moss-covered, rocky terrain were never far from their hearing. There was little reason for conversation, and so the day passed on quietly until the sun was close to the tops of the tree-lined horizon.

It was then that Llew, who was riding in the lead, stopped his horse and turned toward the woods on his right. The others came abreast of where Llew sat his horse.

"Is all well?" Aedan asked.

Llew was squinting his eyes in an attempt to better focus on something in the woods. He scanned the short distance into the forest back and forth several times. It was a spot where two hills met, creating a natural, sharp breach between them. It was not large enough to be called a valley, but rather more of a gully.

Llew's face wore a puzzled expression.

"Llew?" Aedan asked again.

Llew looked to his brother with a slight look of distraction. "I guess it was nothing."

"*What* was nothing?" Aedan replied, unsatisfied with his younger brother's vague answer.

"Well"—Llew paused momentarily, trying to find the right words—"I could have sworn I saw the face of a man. Right there. In the wood." He looked to his brothers a bit sheepishly. "I can see nothing there now. It might have been the shadows playing tricks on my eyes."

Bryn looked toward the cleft between the forest hills, but he said nothing. The place was just like the rest of the forest they had ridden past all day long, thick and deeply shadowed.

"What did this face look like?" Aedan asked.

"Ancient, like the old oak at Aithne," Llew responded without hesitation.

The others glanced quickly back at Llew as if to question whether they heard him right. All of them knew the stories of the Old Man in the Woods. The versions of the tale were many, but all of them had a common, and quite murderous, theme.

Long ago, when the Emerald Isle was young, a good and wise king ruled the people. As the story went, the king took up a quest, which required him to journey to a distant land. Before leaving, he called his two sons to him and gave them equal charge over his kingdom during his absence. Not long after his departure, however, the younger son arose, murdered his brother while he slept, and seized the wealth of the kingdom for himself. For many years, the usurper ruled his father's kingdom with self-serving greed and violence. One day, the good king returned home to find his kingdom much changed. The people now lived in poverty, and sorrow had replaced their joy. The king sought an answer from his son, but he was abused and flung from the king's hall in shame. When the people of the land saw how their king had been treated, they arose and overthrew the usurper. For the murder of his brother and treachery against the kingdom, his father pronounced a curse on the son. For all the long years of his life, the walls of his prison would be the brambles and thorns of the forest, never more to live with men or in the dwellings of men, but to live on and on until the forest was no more.

Over the years, the tale of the Old Man in the Woods became more and more murderous. Whenever travelers went missing or were found dead in the forest, it was blamed on the Old Man in the Woods. They were just stories, but stories that endured.

Aedan covered his eyes and looked toward the sun. "There isn't much time before we lose the light. I, for one, would not like to stay the night here. If someone *is* hiding in these woods, I would prefer to put as much distance as possible between us."

With that, the brothers turned their mounts back to the roadway and gave them their heads. Although that night passed without further incident, Llew grew more restless as they continued through the next day. Aedan tried several times to alleviate his younger brother's agitation, but without success. By the time they made camp the second night, Bryn had become visibly more watchful. Aedan noticed Bryn's watchfulness and asked if he had seen something.

"No. But I feel it. Someone, or something, is out there." He indicated vaguely toward the forest to his left. "They stay just beyond sight, following, waiting for an opportunity to strike." Aedan nodded. He already noted that even the horses were tense and alert, and he'd learned to trust Bryn's gut when it came to the forest.

That night they made camp close by the roadway. Normally, they would have chosen a spot less visible. The Emerald Isle was, for the most part, inhabited by good and decent people. But, as in all places, there were those who would take any opportunity for quick profit. On this night, however, it was the forest that concerned them the most. Having the openness of the roadway at their back granted a measure of comfort toward the prospect of getting some sleep.

It was well after dark when they stopped for the night. The moon was full and gave good light to the roadway itself, making the task of gathering wood a bit easier. Plenty of old, dry wood was ready to hand, and it was not long before they had a good-sized fire lighting the night. It would serve well to keep any curious predators at bay. Even so, all three of them knew it was not wise to look directly into the flames for too long. Eyes that become accustomed to the bright light of a fire cannot see into the surrounding darkness, and the forest walls would be dark enough without added blindness.

The first and second watches of the night passed slowly as the brothers lay with their backs to the open road. They remained quiet and still as though asleep, yet each of them held his sword under his blanket and watched the forest wall. A breeze stirred the trees and thick undergrowth, with random fitful gusts giving the night a tense feeling. The fire burned down but still contorted with each wind that passed through its burning embers.

Something moved in the night not far from their camp. The noise it made was cleverly masked by the sound of the leaves being moved by the wind. But unlike the randomness of the leaf chatter, there was an unnaturally deliberate quality about the sound. It could almost be felt more than heard. The slow, even pressure of a foot pressed against the forest floor, and then nothing more. Then it would come again. This process went on and on into the third watch of the night and then stopped. Though they strained their ears to listen, no further movement could be heard. The wind all but ceased, and an unusual silence settled over the forest.

Llew, who was stretched out to the left of his brothers, slowly turned his head to look toward them. His neck felt tense, and the lack of sleep was beginning to take a toll on his senses. He could not see their faces clearly in the darkness. Yet even though his brothers appeared to be asleep, he knew they watched the tree line not five paces away. He turned his head back toward the encroaching forest on his left. All was as it had been a moment before. He eased his head back a bit more, trying to relax the tension out of his muscles, but something nagged at him. Something was out of place, but he could not think of what it was. He looked back to the brush line at his left, and again could see nothing amiss.

A slight movement near the far edge of his vision drew his attention. It was near the roadway where the ground was dark but completely open. It did not seem possible that any danger could approach from that direction without ample warning. He squinted his eyes, wondering if he had really seen anything at all. Not more than five large steps from where he lay, he noticed a patch of ground that was slightly more elevated than the rest. In the darkness it did not look particularly out of place. Patches of dirt and even small rocks could be seen covering the small mound. He convinced himself it was a natural formation when it moved again. It was less of a movement than it was a shifting of its shape.

He tightened his grip on his sword and peered at it intently. His eyes carefully scrutinized its edges and surface. Near the end closest to him there was a woody protrusion, almost like a curving root that broke through the surface of the ground. Suddenly his blood went cold as he realized what he was seeing. It was, in fact, a hand grasping the midsection of a rudimentary bow. The bow was held almost flat against the ground, the tipped end of an arrow pointing directly at him. The hand appeared to extend directly out of the mounded earth itself giving the horrible impression of someone crawling out of a grave.

There was no time to react or move. The bow was drawn taut, and Llew knew he was caught in a trap with no escape. At that distance, his unknown enemy could not easily miss. He braced himself for the impact, but he was met instead by a loud crack and a flash of bright light. Something whistled by his face close enough for him to feel the air move, and then he was on his feet, running to the attack. He would not wait to face another wicked arrow in the dark. Aedan and Bryn were only a step behind as Llew reached the spot where the assailant hid. The mound was gone, and they could hear the sound of something crashing through the underbrush with great speed.

Aedan placed his hand on Llew's shoulder. "Are you all right?"

Llew nodded and took a step toward the forest line. Aedan held his shoulder a little tighter. "The forest is his domain. It would not be wise to challenge him in the dark on his own ground." Aedan was right of course, but Llew could not bring himself to turn away from the blackness of the forest wall. He didn't see more than a glimpse of their enemy, but Llew knew it was the Old Man of the Woods. The stories were not only true, but Llew had also come dangerously close to becoming a permanent part of them.

"What is it, Bryn?" Aedan asked with a note of concern in his voice.

Bryn stood with his back to his brothers, staring into the darkness on the far side of the road. He indicated the other side of the road with a slight nod of his head. "Someone is there…just inside the tree line," he spoke quietly. The three of them stood mute for a time, watching the darkness." At first, Llew thought he could see a lighter spot in the otherwise black forest wall. But if anything had been there, it was gone now.

After another long moment, Aedan spoke. "It will be light soon and I do not believe any of us will find sleep in what remains of this night. I say we ride on and make an early camp once we have left the forest behind." The others quietly agreed as the dark sky above began spitting down a soft, cold rain.

The Hooded Man

By midday the sun had broken through the gloom of the morning. Warmth and bright sunlight greeted them as they finally rode free of the dark, forested regions and climbed into the sharp, broken hills beyond. The light poured across the ridges with a soft, golden green hue, causing their spirits to rise. It was late in the day when they reached their next campsite.

A short distance from the roadway, a small, hidden cleft in the hills with a pleasant little waterfall provided an ideal shelter from the weather and prying eyes. It was a spot they knew well and had stayed many times before. It did not take long to care for the horses and get a fire going. All three of them were exhausted from their all-night vigil, and the prospect of bedding down early was welcome. Llew sat quietly next to the fire as Bryn began slicing pieces of pork into a small frying pan. Aedan stood at the small waterfall, refilling their drinking pouches. As the refreshingly good aroma of sizzling meat started filling the small cleft in the hills, Llew replayed his near escape of the night before in his mind.

It did not make any sense. He had been caught as surely as night follows day, yet he had escaped completely unscathed. He had faced battle before, with both men and creatures, but never with the sure knowledge of his own impending death. It was more than unsettling. Something deep inside him was triggered. A sense filled his heart and mind that his life was lost and then returned by something or someone yet unknown. Llew knew he was dead to rights, but for the flash of light that blinded the eyes of his unknown enemy at just the right moment. He was saved by the smallest of degrees. The question he could not now escape was, who had returned his life?

"Are you all right?" Aedan asked as he sat down next to Llew.

Llew searched for the right words to explain his internal struggle. "There was a flash of light last night…right before the Old Man's attack. Did you see it?"

Bryn remained silent and turned another piece of the sizzling meat over.

Aedan thought for a time before answering. "In truth, I had closed my eyes to better listen for approach. I saw nothing, but I did hear what sounded somewhat like a single clap of hands together. Bryn, did you see a flash of light?"

Bryn looked from Llew to Aedan before turning his head slightly back and forth to indicate he had not.

"How could you *not* have seen it?" Frustration clouded Llew's features. "It was bright enough to light the whole of the night."

"Perhaps the camp fire flared in the wind, or you saw a flash of lightning. It did rain," Aedan offered without conviction.

"I know lightening when I see it!" Llew snapped.

"I don't doubt you saw something," Aedan replied softly. "I'm just not sure what. That is all I am saying." After another short pause, he added, "We are all tired, and as for me, I am having a hard time remembering getting off my horse only moments ago, let alone what took place last night. Perhaps we would feel better with a bit of food in our stomachs and some sleep."

Llew let out a silent sigh. He was tired as well and could understand their reluctance. He knew what he saw and how close death had been, but it would be hard to explain it to the others. Perhaps Aedan was right. A long night's rest sounded good. There would be no fear of attack this night. The horses would alert them to any approaching danger. The constant dancing of the small waterfall provided a peaceful background as they finished their meal and drifted off to sleep.

Llew awakened as he lay in his bedroll. How long he had slept he could not be sure. The night was cool but not uncomfortably so. He lay still, staring up into the cloudless night sky and trying to decide what had stirred him. A small gust of wind brought the embers of the fire alive, causing it to pop and sputter. Looking around the camp, he could see nothing out of place. The horses were resting peacefully and gave no indication for alarm. Llew turned over onto his side. The fire still burned enough to cast light around their small camp. Everything appeared fine, but Llew couldn't get past the thought that something was different. It was not that anything felt wrong, but only that something had changed and he could not put his finger on it.

He stretched his arms a bit and began turning back over when he realized with a start what it was that he had missed. On the far side of the fire sat the cloaked figure of a man. What surprised Llew was the fact that this discovery did not give rise to any feelings of apprehension. He was not sure how, but he simply knew that this man was not a threat. Llew glanced at his brothers. They were both sound asleep. He looked back at the strange visitor. The man's face was completely covered by the large hood that covered his head. The hooded cloak, which must have been white or a light tan color, reflected the dim firelight in a way that made it appear to be softly glowing around its edges.

"Will you come and sit with me?" The question surprised Llew. He did not recognize the man's voice, but there was a quality about it that made Llew feel at peace. Llew stood and walked to the fire and sat down without speaking. Now that he was closer, he realized this man was much larger than he had guessed at first. Many questions swirled through Llew's mind, but he felt as though he should not speak until he was given leave to do so.

"What would you ask of me?" The man's voice carried a quiet generosity.

Llew hesitated, not knowing how to ask what he wanted to know. "It was you in the forest last night, wasn't it? I mean, somehow you made the flash of light that saved my life."

"I did, but you already know that. What do you really want to ask of me?"

The man was right, but his confident assurance puzzled Llew. "Why? I mean why did you save me?"

"I have saved many."

Llew was not satisfied with the answer. "If you had not intervened with that flash of light, the Old Man of the forest would have killed me. The others may not have seen it, but I know what happened." Llew paused, but the man did not respond. "What I mean to say is I owe my life to you."

The man remained silent. Llew struggled through the emotions of his own heart. To say he owed his life to this complete stranger, or to just say thank you, somehow felt inadequate. "No, no, what I really mean to say is that my life *is* yours." It was out before Llew could even think about what he was saying. His own words shocked his ears. Who was this man that he had just pledged himself to? His mind screamed he was insane to give such a pledge to a man whose face he could not even see. However, his heart had never before known such peace. He exhaled slowly, releasing himself to the moment.

The man reached down into the fire and picked up a stick that remained unburned. He snapped the small branch in two pieces. "Anyone can break a stick such as this. But who can put it back together again?" The man waited for a moment, then he ran his hand over the stick. Llew could not believe his eyes; the break was completely healed and the stick was perfectly rejoined. The man handed the branch to Llew. "A token for you." Llew took it and examined it carefully. There was no evidence of the break. He applied a little pressure to it. It was strong. Llew was still studying the branch when Bryn awoke.

"Are you all right Llew?" he asked.

Llew looked toward Bryn and then back to the hooded man. No one was there. Llew now sat alone by the fire. He glanced around the camp, but there was no sign the man had ever been there. Llew rubbed his hand across his face. "Yes. I guess I just couldn't sleep." Llew responded somewhat distractedly, before realizing he still held the stick in his hand.

"You need to sleep. We will leave early enough."

Llew nodded his agreement and moved back to his bedroll.

The brothers woke early the next morning under dark gray, clouded skies. The wind was fitful and spat a drizzly rain at them as they donned hooded riding cloaks, mounted their horses, and continued the last leg of their return journey. The damp morning hours passed slowly as they rode along the king's highway in silence. Llew did not mind the lack of conversation. It gave him time to think about his encounter with the hooded man.

Who was he? Now that he thought about it, the question hadn't even occurred to him while they talked. He was real enough, of that Llew felt sure. But there was something different about him. Why did he not make himself known to all three of them? Why hide his face? There were plenty of questions, but few answers. Llew reached his hand inside his cloak and felt the small branch he had tied there. Yes, he knew it was not a dream.

As they drew nearer to home, the morning rains lessened and the air around them lightened. A wispy fog rolled over the hilltops and settled into the valleys as a light mist gently cooled their faces. They passed a bend in the road, and the land before them opened onto a scene of such grandeur that even they, who had seen it many times before, paused to simply take it in once again. There was a wide view of the harbor beneath the ancient walls of the Emerald King's castle. It had been built high upon a hill, which overlooked both the southern and western seas. The large, blue-gray stones of the walls completely encircled the whole of the hill's crest and towered high above its summit.

The castle itself was bigger than some of the larger settlements on the Emerald Isle. Due to the prominent look of the hill and its brilliantly shaded grasses, the settlement that grew up all around became known as Hilgreen. It was truly an amazing sight to behold. To look upon Hilgreen and the king's castle was to look upon a city within a city. Out of the hills north and east of Hilgreen flowed the mighty river Amyst. Its hues of deep blue and turquoise only served to brighten the green of the surrounding valleys and hills. Amyst flowed wide and deep as it wound through the valley plane, which flanked Hilgreen to the east, and emptied into the harbor far beneath the castle walls.

The horses whinnied with excitement and tossed their heads back and forth, urging their riders onward. They knew home was close and that a fresh bait of oats would be waiting for them. Aedan held his mount tightly as he looked to where the harbor met the sea and noticed a ship sailing into its mouth. Its sails gleamed white in the bright light of a late morning sun, which had now completely broken through the gloom of the morning. He pointed toward the ship. Bryn and Llew looked toward the spot he indicated.

The sight of a ship arriving in the harbor below the castle was not a noteworthy event. This ship, nevertheless, was extraordinary. Most vessels of their day were small, practical, and made for work, not beauty. The ship that now sailed through the mouth of the harbor was both magnificent in size and unique in design. Never had they seen such a vessel. There were at least two levels visible above the waterline, and it cut the smooth water of the bay with grace and speed. As the ship turned its prow toward the docks, the main sail, located between two smaller ones, caught in the wind. Three brilliant red lions could be seen stretched across a rich, white background. The three of them stared on in silence.

After a few moments, Aedan broke the quiet. "Father is waiting."

Without reply, Bryn and Llew turned their horses back to the road and followed their brother.

The Waking Dream

The Emerald King stood at one of the many windows in his castle overlooking the harbor far below. He wore a golden, tan-colored tunic embroidered with encircling green knots at its edges. His feet were, according to the way of his people, wrapped simply in leather sandals tied high up his brown leather breeches. Crowning his dark golden hair, he wore a simple gold circlet set with a single large emerald. Despite bearing the wisdom of many years, he still possessed much of the strength and agility of his youth.

He watched the ship cross the deep bay beneath the castle walls. Truly his shipwrights had worked a miracle. It was large, but its lines ran smoothly through the choppy inlet waves. Continuing to stare out the window, he remembered the first time he had seen this ship. Late one night, as he lay awake upon his bed, something happened to him that he still did not fully understand. It was an experience he would not soon forget, something the wise men of his country called a *waking dream*. The familiar surroundings of his private room suddenly began to fade. Before long, the walls completely vanished and he found himself standing on a grassy hilltop enshrouded in a dense cloud of fog that swirled all around him.

The darkness of the night became the gray of an early morning. A vague illumination flashed within the low-hanging cloud that engulfed the hill. Each flash was followed by a low, muted rumbling that reverberated through the heavy air and vibrated through the ground as though a storm raged in the distance. He stood peering into the heavy fog for some time before it began rolling away, very much giving the impression of a door being opened to a corridor.

He quickly followed it at first but then jerked to a sudden stop. A realization swept over him that he stood on the brink of a great mountain cliff. Waves crashed harshly against the rocks far below, and a stiff ocean-born wind raced up the face of the cliff to sweep past him.

The light flashes and rumbling noises intensified, and the king became aware of a presence moving in the surrounding fog. Out of the cloud where the light flashes and rumblings were most intense, a voice spoke so quietly that he was not sure he really heard it at first.

"Look across the waters. What do you see?" the voice said. It was deep but gentle, and although many long years had passed, he knew he had heard it before. When he had been a boy of but twelve summers, he was awakened one night to the sudden awareness that he was not alone. The voice that spoke to him in his waking dream had also spoken to him then. The king was never told the name of the speaker, but the wonder of his presence and the wisdom of his truth left no room for doubt. In his heart, the king had always known that he had received his calling from the Creator God himself. From that time on, he devoted his life and his reign to the calling he had been given, and to the one who gave it.

As a boy, it had been difficult to explain the fullness of this experience to others. To simply describe with words what had happened always felt inadequate. For in the sound of the voice he heard the thunder of a thousand waterfalls along with the song of the meadowlark rejoicing on a summer day. It was not that it imitated any such earthly sound. Instead, it was as though all that was beautiful and majestic in this world reflected what had already existed in the sound of that voice.

In his waking dream, the king remembered looking out over the waters toward the horizon as he had been instructed. To his surprise, he could see across the distant waters and past many islands to the furthest reaches of the west. His sight was drawn to a mighty land of far mountains and vast plains. He could even see that its inhabitants were strong and noble.

"I see a far land with a fair and mighty people," he answered.

While he still spoke, darkness began to cover the distant land. The voice in the cloud spoke once again. "All who trust in their own strength will fall into darkness."

"What will happen to this people?" the king asked.

No answer came. And as suddenly as he was brought to the grassy cliff, the king found himself standing in utter darkness. The closeness of the air and the hardness of the floor under his feet suggested that he was no longer under open skies. Strangely enough, it felt very much like he stood in the heart of some mountain, deep within the earth. Although the air smelled of filth and dank mold, it was the darkness that was the most oppressive. It was not so much an absence of light, but a sensation that the inky blackness was itself a malicious living creature.

Before long, the heavy darkness lifted slightly, allowing him to see a little of his surroundings. That is when he saw the man for the first time. He was sitting not more than ten paces away from where the king stood. The man's head was hung low over his knees. Even though a small amount of dull light shone through an iron grate high in the roof above, the place remained very dark. He guessed it was some sort of dungeon. Besides the iron grate above, the only other opening in this pit was a large, jagged crack located in its far corner. Something about this black fissure made him feel uneasy. There was nothing specific about its appearance that should have lead to such fears. It was, rather, an unnerving sense that something terrible would crawl out from it.

The king hesitantly looked away from the fearful crack and back at the man. Even now, as he remembered the waking dream, he could see him in his mind. Everything about the man spoke of nobility. True, his cloths were of an odd design, like nothing the king had ever seen before. It was clear, however, that they were expensive beyond ordinary means, and despite the filth of the pit, the cloth shimmered ever so slightly in the dull light.

The man lifted his head, raising his eyes to look right at the king. There was something familiar about his face. The question of the man's identity flooded back into his mind. Who was this man? Should he know him? No, he still felt sure he had never met him before. But something about the man remained strangely familiar.

The king quickly made to see what aid he could give the prisoner, but before he was able to take one full step, everything changed once again. The man vanished, the darkness was gone, and he once again stood on the grassy cliff edge. This time, however, there was only a light misty fog, but not as heavy as before, and the sounds of thunder were gone. He turned and looked around him in every direction, but he found no sign of anyone in the mist.

"What am I to do?" he asked loudly. "There *must* be a reason for showing me all of this!" He tried once more, but the only sound to meet his ears was that of the waves far below. When it seemed there would be no further answer, he dropped to his knees and bowed his head. "I do not understand, Lord," he prayed.

After another long period of silence, and after he had given up all hope of receiving an explanation, the voice spoke to him again. He did not actually hear it this time, but instead he felt it. Like receiving a nudge from someone standing next to you. Without hearing anything, he simply knew that he should stand and look to the west.

The darkness still covered the distant land. It had grown even darker than before. He found his eyes being led away from the enshrouded land. Without really understanding why, he was curiously drawn to the sea a little to the south, where the waves were high and driven by strong winds. Through the crashing and tossing of the waves, a soft green mist began to rise. A few rays of golden sunshine broke from a small window opening in the dark clouds above to dance upon the waves. When it reached the green mist, it lit the particles of water in a way that made them look as though a million emeralds had been flung into the air.

Out of the sea's green mist came a ship. Its appearance was so sudden it caused the king to catch his breath. A pure and bright light surrounded the ship as it cut through the dark sea. And there was something else. He glimpsed something moving across the ship's deck.

At that moment, however, the ship sliced through another large crested wave and disappeared behind a veil of green ocean spray. The king strained to see it again. Then, as abruptly as before, the ship smashed through the veil and was there before him. At first, he saw nothing on the ship's deck. But as he continued to watch, what looked oddly like a lion came into view. In fact, there were three lions. All three were a deep shade of crimson red. He watched as the ship descended upon the dark enshrouded land, and its light pierced through the dark veil. Wherever the light shone, the darkness fled. As the darkness retreated from the light, the vision began to fade. In the briefest of moments, he found himself once again looking at the familiar surroundings of his personal chamber.

The king knew he could not ignore the obvious calling of the vision. It was given for a purpose. And so, he ordered the building of the ship. Long after the waking dream had ended, the ship of light in all of its smallest details remained clear in his mind. He knew it would be a marvel, for no ship like it had ever been see nor heard of in all their part of the world.

Now the time of completion had arrived, and he found himself unable to turn his eyes away from the distant waters. He continued to stare blankly out the castle window. The sparkling blue of the sea stretched on as far as the eye could see. Restless waves rose and fell on the swell of a rising tide. Many times his thoughts were drawn to what lay beyond those distant waves. He often considered sailing off across the seas himself. Yet, a king's place is with his kingdom, and he knew this task was appointed for others.

Turning away from his thoughts, he noticed that his personal advisor had arrived and was waiting quietly at the far end of the room. "Ahhh, Martin! Have my sons arrived then?"

"They have."

Martin had served the king since before Aedan, Bryn, and Llew were even born. Yet he still carried the presence of a man half his age and a strength that spoke of one born to be a leader of men. In truth, Martin was far more than an advisor. There was no one the king trusted more.

"Good. I will await them in the great hall," the king said.

Aedan, Bryn, and Llew knew this meeting with their father was to be anything but usual from the moment they arrived. Waiting servants quickly took charge of stabling their horses. Other servants began pouring into the yard bearing piles of fine clothes. Water basins appeared from nowhere. Aedan made to protest this unusual treatment. But before he could even finish his words, a rather large serving woman named Matilda began to tug and pull at his riding cloak with a very determined look in her eyes, mumbling something about the king's orders. It quickly became clear that their father had already overridden any authority they would normally have possessed.

Aedan, in an attempt to salvage what remained of his dignity, pointed at Llew, who was likewise being assaulted. "Llew, how is that injury? You know, the one you received on the road." It was a rotten trick, he knew. But Llew was younger. He would recover faster from the humiliation.

Matilda clucked her tongue and pressed her hands against her cheeks in concern. She and the other serving maids abruptly abandoned Aedan and Bryn and rushed to Llew's side in a panic of concern. Llew, who was neatly trapped, watched as Aedan and Bryn grabbed their fresh clothes and disappeared into the stables.

"This is not over!" Llew yelled.

It did not take long for the dust of the road to be completely washed away and for each brother to be transformed into the princes they were. Clad in finely quilted leather breeches and brilliantly colored tunics, they were escorted through the inner gates of the castle. Aedan turned to Llew as they walked, and he smiled and slapped him on the back. "Well, brother, it looks like Matilda and her *washlings* wasted no effort."

Llew, who at first did not share in his older brother's humor, shrugged off the jest with a good-natured smile at his own expense and asked, "Why the special treatment?"

"Someone important has probably come," Aedan replied.

Bryn considered his brothers' thoughts but gave no response other than a slap across Llew's shoulder. Their attendants continued to lead the way through the castle's halls until finally coming to stand before the two large oaken doors of the Great King's Hall. In front of each door stood one of the king's warriors, each dressed in fine leather armor, holding a silver tipped spear in his right hand, with a scarlet cape draped over his left shoulder.

The guards turned aside in unison, and the doors began to open. The Hall within was lined with row upon row of warriors from the king's war band. Every clan's chieftain and his lady stood quietly behind the warriors. Sitting on the throne, dressed in a deep yellow robe fringed in green and bearing an emerald-encrusted crown, was the king. All was silent as Aedan, Bryn, and Llew came forward and knelt.

The Journey Begins

A warm south wind blew gently as their ship flew across the western seas. Bryn stood at the rail, gazing across the endless waters. Neither he nor his brothers had ever ventured so far from their father's realm. On occasion they had been sent to neighboring kingdoms as ambassadors, or visited the island villages under their father's dominion. A fortnight into their journey, nevertheless, and Bryn watched as the last familiar landscape passed finally from view.

He had always loved the sea and everything about it. The boundless waters carried a sense of adventure all their own. Anything could be out there waiting for them. Yet the dark depths also carried bitterness for him. They had taken the one thing he loved most.

Somewhere northwest of the Emerald Isle, the ship carrying Kelsi had been lost. The reports said it had sunk in a storm. There were no survivors. Even now, the hard reality of this memory was unreal to Bryn. It was like a bad dream, but even a bad dream ends in the morning. From this sorrow there could be no waking. A sense of panic began to rise in the pit of his stomach as the unhealed wound threatened to burst open. He fought back the encroaching pain, forcing it deep down inside once more. He would not return to this memory; he could not.

Bryn forced his mind back to their journey and its purpose. More than a month had passed since he and his brothers entered the Great Hall in answer to their father's summons. They had experienced the grandeur of royal gatherings many times, but they had never before been the focus of one. After kneeling before the throne, their father, towering above them and with outstretched arms, spoke the ancient blessing of their people.

May the golden gift of heaven be upon thy brow;
Let righteousness and mercy go before thee;
Hold faithfulness at thy side and truth all around thee;
Be steadfast in spirit against the enemies assault; and
Follow the true and narrow path and none other.

The king recounted his experience with the waking dream to all in attendance. His voice resounded throughout the Hall in the chanting style of their people. To Bryn, time itself stood still until the last golden strains of his father's voice echoed throughout the Hall. It was a strange tale to be sure, but no one doubted the truth of it. That it was symbolic most understood, but none could guess its meaning. No one had been more surprised than Bryn when his father turned to him and his brothers and pronounced them to be the three red lions.

Martin, who was standing at the king's right hand, held out an exquisitely carved box made of a rare mahogany and covered in strange designs.

"My sons, do you accept this charge?" the king asked.

Aedan stepped forward first. Llew and Bryn followed their brother's lead, but with somewhat less comfort. Bryn never liked large gatherings, especially if any attention was to be placed on him. As they knelt before their father, he opened the carved box to reveal three beautifully crafted golden rings. Each ring was set with a single emerald, the symbol of their father's kingdom.

Preparation for their journey began immediately. Much to their surprise, their father and Martin had already readied most of what would be needed. All that remained for them was to plan their route. Maps and charts were studied, restudied, and studied again, many times followed by discussions that lasted long into the night. Then, after two weeks of planning, their father pronounced the quest ready to begin. Bryn remembered Llew questioning him about what ship they were to sail on. With a conspiratorial glance, the king replied, "Follow me!"

Bryn and his brothers were led in the direction of the harbor, and as they followed their father, more and more people joined them. First was Martin, who always knew what was going on and never needed an explanation. Next, Rand, the captain of the king's war band, appeared behind them. Soon, a handful of others were also following, and before they reached the castle gates, their numbers had grown to more than twenty.

As the group drew closer to the harbor, the crowd of curious onlookers swelled into the hundreds. Bryn remembered walking along with his attention focused on the gathering crowd, when Llew came to a complete stop directly in front of him. The memory of the embarrassing collision brought a small measure of mirth back to Bryn. He was ready to chastise his younger brother, until he noticed that Llew's attention was completely fastened on something before them.

Following Llew's gaze, Bryn realized with astonishment that in the upheaval of the last weeks, he had completely forgotten the ship he and his brothers first glimpsed entering the harbor on the day of the king's summons. Yet there before them, anchored a short way into the harbor, it waited. It was beautiful, a work of craftsmanship not seen in this part of the world. To call it a masterpiece seemed somehow less than it deserved. Even without its splendid sails hoisted, none could take their eyes from it.

Their father leapt onto a nearby loading platform, and declared out loud, "Behold 'True North'!"

Bryn let the name roll off his own lips. It was a good name, and it was well matched by the strength and dependability of the ship's deck he now stood upon. Lost in his thoughts and looking out across the endless waters, Bryn failed to note the arrival of another at the rail next to him.

"It's a beautiful day, is it not?"

Taken by surprise for a brief moment, Bryn glanced to his right only to see the familiar face of Martin scanning the distant waters. Martin was unlike anyone Bryn had ever known. His hair was as black as a crow's feather, and the features of his face spoke of quiet strength. Yet it was Martin's eyes that either captivated or unsettled anyone his gaze fell upon. They were a striking shade of amber, laced with varying hues of golden yellow.

Looking back toward the gently rolling ocean, Bryn quietly agreed as one whose thoughts remain distant. It was as beautiful a day as could be had, he supposed.

"Unless I am far wrong, you have more on your mind than the view before you," Martin gently coaxed. There were few who could hide from Martin's uncanny ability to see into the deepest parts of the soul.

"I was just wondering why the things that happen to us, happen to us and not another."

Martin stood in silent reflection for some time. Then, after Bryn was sure that nothing more was to be said, Martin replied in a distant and far-off voice. "We are seldom given to know why we suffer, or are chosen to a task. Yet we can trust he who does the choosing has not failed in the choice, *nor* allowed his chosen to suffer needlessly. Some pains must be faced before they can be healed." Coming to himself once again, Martin turned to Bryn. "As for tasks, it is far better to be about their completion, than to wonder why they came to you."

Few understood the wound that Bryn carried deep within himself. He hid it well. And in any case, he did not know how to express what was inside, even to those closest to him. Martin was different. He not only knew most things without needing to be told, but most often also had the answer. He knew Martin was right, but that did not make it any easier. Bryn never shied away from any hard path, but he would rather face the pain of a thousand battle wounds than delve too deeply into his own heart.

After another period of silence, Bryn turned to Martin and asked, "What about you, Martin? What do you seek on this journey?"

"Like you, I hope to help those in need." After a momentary pause, Martin added in a somewhat more reflective tone, speaking more to the wind than to Bryn, "and find redemption for myself."

Martin's answer puzzled Bryn. It had not occurred to him that Martin might have a personal stake in this quest. He was always there for Bryn and his brothers. In many ways he was like a second father to them. Bryn just assumed that Martin had come along as an advisor. Yet there was something deeper in his answer, and Bryn wanted to question him further, but the moment's opportunity quickly faded as Martin was called away by Berand, the ship's navigator. When sailing across the open sea, there is always work to be done, things to be fixed, or decisions to be made, and seldom time for leisure.

Over the next several days, Martin, Aedan, Bryn, and Llew, along with the rest of the ship's crew busied themselves with the work of sailing. As the days passed, each of the brothers showed themselves to be fine and worthy sailors. Much to Berand's good humor, all three also proved to be excellent navigators, whether by day or night. The passing of each day saw True North sail further into the unknown west and away from everything familiar.

As the eldest brother, the mantle of ship's captain fell to Aedan. His first action was to establish a council of advisors made up of his brothers, Martin, Berand, and Rand, the captain of the king's warriors. The council met at dusk every day to discuss the day's progress and the continued journey into the unknown. It was after one such meeting that Bryn found a private moment to talk to Llew, who had gone out on the open deck to take the first watch of the night.

"What brings you out into the night's air?" Llew asked.

Of the three brothers, it was Llew that appreciated conversation the most and always found a way to place others at ease. Back home, it was said that the mere sound of his voice could coax honey away from a hungry bear.

"I like to breathe the open air before taking to my bunk. It helps me sleep," Bryn replied.

A moment of silence passed as the night air blew gently across the ship's deck. The brilliant white sails flapped in the light of a full moon, and the soft sounds of wave crests slapping against the ship's hull could just be heard.

It was Llew who spoke again. "How long do you think it will take to reach where we are going?"

"Hard to say," Bryn said. "Judging by Martin, it may be as much as six to eight weeks, depending on the wind." After another pause, Bryn asked, in a tone that suggested he didn't care about the answer, "how do you think Martin knows so much about where we are going?"

"I'm not sure. I assumed he and father studied the charts and maps more closely than I. Why?" Llew paused and then added with growing interest, "Do you believe he's been there before?"

There was another contemplative pause before Bryn answered. "It is true that no one knows more about ancient and rare maps than Martin, but all the ones I have seen are partial at best and based on legend more than anything. Yet Martin seems to know our direction without even consulting maps anymore."

He continued. "There is something more, something in Martin's manner of late. There have been moments when he stands at the deck's rail, when he believes he is alone, and speaks to the wind with words I cannot understand."

"You mean a different language," Llew interrupted.

"Yes, but no ordinary language, I mean, not the sort of words that you would expect to hear ordinary people using."

"I'm not sure I know what you mean."

"The words he used sounded grand beyond normal conversation, almost as though they had power and strove against some unseen enemy," Bryn said.

"Have you asked him about it?"

"No, there has simply not been the opportunity. But when the right time comes, I will ask him."

The Pit of Voices

S erigant sat with his arms resting across his knees. His prison was deep within the very mountain that served as the foundation for his own castle. Over the many centuries of its existence, this black hole deep in the heart of the mountain had become known as the Pit of Voices. It was said that those unfortunate enough to be thrown into it were so close to the realm of the underworld that they could hear the voices of the dead.

Very few of those who descended into its depths ever came out alive. None, to his knowledge, had ever emerged with a right mind. Its walls, floor, and ceiling were made of seamless chiseled rock. The only exception, other than the entrance grate far above his head, was a large, jagged crack in the floor, about the width of a man's waist.

Serigant hadn't sat long upon the throne of Illyrium before his demise. His coronation as king was a bittersweet day. The death of his father, King Pharin, in a hunting accident left Serigant with a heavy weight of grief and responsibility. He had never aspired to be king. As a boy, he always rested in the fact that his older brother Pharigant would hold that duty, but that was not meant to be. With the disappearance of his brother years ago and the death of his father, the kingship passed to Serigant.

Not long after his coronation, however, he was brazenly accused of attaining the throne by the murder of his father. Serigant was incredulous that anyone could take such a baseless accusation seriously. Perhaps no one would have but for the fact that it came from Malen, Serigant's uncle. He had no evidence, just lies. But against all reason, the people believed Malen. It made no sense, but he was quickly, without even a hearing of the evidence, found guilty.

Something had changed in Illyrium since his father's death. A heavy cloud descended over the land and robbed them all of their peace and many of their reason. Few rallied to Serigant's defense when his own palace guards came to arrest him. Not even Lanthir stood with him. Since the time they were boys, Lanthir had always been there for him, but now he stood with Malen. Of all people, Malen!

Serigant stood stiffly to his feet and peered through the entrance grate above. The dull torchlight from the jailer's room flickered through the single opening. It was not much, but Serigant found that this light, no matter how weak, soothed his beleaguered mind and kept madness at bay. After tiring, he dropped back to the dark floor. His thoughts returned to the day of his arrest. He seldom thought of anything else since being shut in this pit. He ran through the events surrounding his father's death and his own imprisonment over and over again. His mind always settled back onto one image: Lanthir standing at Malen's side.

"Even you, Lanthir! Why did you not believe me?" Serigant groaned aloud. Yet no one heard. The only human contact he had came in the form of a mute prison ward that brought him a ration of food once a day. He looked forward to this momentary connection to another human being. There were times now when Serigant thought he could hear the whispered accusations of the dead. Like a hint of the evil tempest to come, the voices assailed him with torment and fear.

When the voices came, Serigant would muster his remaining strength, lift his hands, and recite every prayer and blessing he could recall. Yet with each passing day, his strength waned. He knew it would not be long until it failed completely. It was not death that he feared, but the slow decline into insanity that was now so inevitable.

It was late in the afternoon when Lanthir and a small handful of his most trusted men mounted upon the finest war horses in the land and road into the courtyard at Ryathidon, the ancient palace stronghold of the king. Ryathidon was a magnificent vision of royal splendor. From its dominating towers, which flew the royal blue banners of their people, to its exquisite gardens and pools arrayed in the most exotic of colors, it commanded the land to the west and ruled over the seas to the east. It was the center of power in Illyrium, the name of that land, for more than a century. It did not come to power through military conquest.

The strength of Illyrium, much the opposite, was in the union of the people that inhabited its vast plains and cities. They were always of one mind and purpose for as long as there were records of their exploits. And their king had always been a mighty king. Lanthir was the king's own champion, a position that brought him great honor. The warriors he traveled with were no ordinary fighting men. They were handpicked and specially trained in the arts of war. Each of these men was not only deadly but also vowed to serve Lanthir to the death.

Through a cloud of dust, Lanthir quickly dismounted and strode resolutely toward the inner gate. He was quick of temper, but he was able to control it where ambition or friendships were served. Today, however, his surly mood gave way to outright anger, a direct result of the rigors of unwanted travel and a dusty road. His dreams were dark and disturbing of late. Something was nagging at him, stealing his rest. But he could neither remember what it was, nor forget its nagging at the edges of his conscience. As he approached the entrance, the gate ward, a mousy man who overly enjoyed the power of his duties, made to stop Lanthir.

"Declare your purpose!" the man spat as he extended his arm in a warning to stop.

But before the unfortunate man could utter anything further, Lanthir grabbed him by his tunic and threw him aside and over a nearby cart of goods, which a local merchant was holding for inspection. The unlucky horrified merchant shrieked as he scrambled to salvage and reassemble the mess that had once been his well-organized cart. A dog tied to a nearby post erupted into a violent torrent of barking and battled against the chain that secured it. Turning to his men, Lanthir barked his order to remain in the courtyard and be ready to leave upon his return.

Inside the castle walls, the air was thin and dank. The atmosphere of the palace had never felt so close and heavy to Lanthir before. His lungs began to burn as he stomped up the stone steps toward the council chamber. The palace was always so open and free under King Pharin's reign. No matter. What of that! If Malen wished to live in such conditions, that was his concern. What did one expect from one who pursued the dark arts? Lanthir never put any stock in things such as spells and magic. He always trusted in the strength and skill of his own arm. It was the speed of his hand that ever won the day, not high-sounding words. All such things ever accomplished were the muddling of his brain.

Upon reaching the door to the council chamber, Lanthir lifted his clenched fist to pound on it. He intended to not only announce his arrival but also emphasize his displeasure with being summoned. As he raised his hand, however, a quiet yet clear voice came to Lanthir from all directions at once.

"Come in and be seated. Your arrival is not overly late."

Lanthir's bewilderment began to undermine his resolve, so he simply entered and threw himself down into one of the many chairs surrounding the large table at the center of the room. He removed his riding gloves and slapped them unceremoniously onto the table with a glowering look upon his face. Malen sat with his back to Lanthir at a smaller table on the far side of the dimly lit chamber. Piles of parchments were scattered across the surface of the small table, and Malen's head was bent in review. Yet despite Lanthir's loud squirming and occasional grunt, Malen sat unmoved.

Lanthir never was a patient man. Patience was to him a thing more suited to servants and women. A few moments more were all he could stomach before he began to rise and turn toward the door.

"Sit!"

It was a command that was not to be denied, so Lanthir collapsed back into his seat and, with a little more confidence than he now felt, replied, "Have I been summoned, merely to be ignored?"

It was then that Malen first turned to face Lanthir. Since the time he was a boy, Lanthir had felt uncomfortable around Malen. He never liked to admit fear of anything, but Malen had always been the exception. Lanthir was a child of only ten when they first met. It was the beginning of his warrior's training, when the sons of noblemen and those of lesser bloodlines lucky enough to be sponsored by benefactors were specially selected for future leaders of the king's own war band.

Lanthir's father was one of the most influential noblemen in the land, and as such, his place among the trainees was assured since birth. That was where he first met Malen. He was different back then. As king Pharin's half-brother, Malen was given charge over the instruction of young warriors. From the very beginning, there was something about Malen's gaze that could make a person shrink from within. He was, nevertheless, tall and strong of limb and carried a commanding physical presence that, whether you liked him or not, did inspire confidence and respect.

While much of the day-to-day training was left to others, Malen had a practice of selecting the best trainees for a special honor. These young men would receive extra training and extra privilege from Malen's own hand. King Pharin always encouraged such distinctions as were fitting to those who excelled in their training. Pharin's two sons, Pharigant and Serigant, were, included in such an honored selection. Yet despite the nobility of their birth, Pharigant and Serigant were truly the best of the best. Only Lanthir ever surpassed them in anything. No one could ever handle a blade like him, except for maybe Malen himself.

Ah, now those were days to remember, Lanthir thought. He and Serigant were inseparable. Even though Lanthir always triumphed in personal combat, Serigant more often than not bested him when strategy was involved. The thought of Serigant made Lanthir's stomach uneasy and tight as he sat waiting for Malen to reveal the purpose of his summons. When they had come to arrest Serigant, Lanthir had done nothing but watch. He would have gladly given his life to defend his sword brother, but not for murdering his own father. The evidence was plain. After all, Malen had more than proven the charge. Lanthir searched his tired, aggravated mind in a futile attempt to recall just what the evidence of guilt was.

"What do you know of Tharrus?" Malen asked. The question took Lanthir off guard.

"Tharrus? It's a dung heap of an island! Do you wish to move your palace to a more suitable location?" Lanthir's tone was both mocking and impatient. Yet Malen showed no signs that he even noticed the insult.

"Have you been there before?" Malen continued with an even tone.

Lanthir, who was beginning to feel small at having his insults so ignored, did not reply immediately.

"Come now, it is an easy enough question."

Lanthir looked at Malen hesitantly and with a growing uneasiness. Somewhere in the courtyard below, the churlish laugh and abusive language of the gate guard drifted through the open window.

"You know I have. My father was a good friend of Peleg, King of Tharrus. I visited many times as a youth. Why?" Lanthir answered, suddenly feeling cautious.

Malen turned back to his parchments stretched across his desk. With a dismissive gesture, he ignored Lanthir's question and continued speaking. "I will presume you know the strength of King Peleg's forces then. Take your warriors and as many other soldiers as you deem necessary and bring King Peleg to me in chains."

Lanthir could not believe his ears. "You want me to do what?"

An Unusual Fog

A month into their journey, and True North's crew had not seen land in over a week. The last few days, however, were seasonably warm, with a strong breeze blowing out of the southeast.

Today as on most other days, the rich white sails were gently flapping in the wind. The azure blue waters of the western seas and the frothy white-capped waves slid past as True North neatly sliced through them. The combination of the balmy weather and the roll of the ship's deck lent themselves to a lazy atmosphere aboard True North. Could a day be more perfect? The question would have been normal enough for anyone else reflecting on such beauty, but for Martin it held a mocking note of irony. As much as he had tried to fill each day of their journey with work, he still found the newly awakened accusations of his past never far away. More than twenty years had passed. He convinced himself long ago that his flight from home was best for everyone.

Convincing one's mind, nevertheless, is very different than finding peace in your heart. In his dreams, he still saw the faces of those he left behind. Would they believe his reasons were right and just? If Martin had not fled, he may have finally given into the darkness that sought him. Had he chosen the right course, or simply saved himself?

He looked across the waters to the southwest and inhaled the fresh ocean air deeply. His attention was drawn to a large eagle flying just a short distance south of them. He had noticed it following them sometime ago, but thought very little of it until now. The great bird appeared to be tiring. With one last effort of strength, it pushed forward, swooped down, and came to rest on the ship's prow.

"I wonder what has driven you so far from your home. It is good you found a perch to regain your strength." Martin felt his spirit rise slightly as he spoke to the bird. "I think you and I have something in common."

The eagle sat upon its new resting place and examined Martin with unblinking eyes as the constant wind ruffled its feathers. It was true. They had both found a resting place away from the weariness of their flight. Martin's journey was no less desperate. If this bird had not found True North, it surely would have tired and fallen into the sea to its death. The Emerald Isle had been such a place of refuge to Martin. It was a place like no other and was a balm to his wounded soul. The air itself gave him strength. He would be perfectly content to spend the rest of his days on the Emerald Isle in the service of the Emerald King.

Martin always loved the search for knowledge. He was taught from an early age that the path of enlightenment was the greatest thing in life, and so he, above all his peers, had mastered learning about the known *and* the unknown. His success was almost his undoing. There is a knowledge that leads only to destruction and slavery. It was on the Emerald Isle that he first understood that the search for truth is far different than the mastery of knowledge.

The spray of the waves descended upon Martin in a mist of refreshing coolness. For twenty years he had been given peace. Now he knew the time was rushing toward him when he would once again have to face the fears and failures of his past. The life he had made on the Emerald Isle would soon meet the life he had fled, and the ensuing crash would forever decide his future and the future of those he loved.

Martin sat back against a large wooden water cask, which was strapped to a post a short distance away. The laziness of the day began to take its full measure on him as he succumbed to a moment of light slumber. His eyes had barely closed when he heard Aedan's shout. It only took a moment for Martin to join Aedan and Bryn at the ship's helm. Aedan pointed to the northern horizon. A widening bank of ominous-looking fog was rolling out of the north, but it looked as though it might miss them if they kept on their current bearing.

"That is strange for these weather conditions," Martin said.

"Better sound the warning bell, just to be safe." Aedan spoke to Bryn without taking his eyes off the dark line. The warning bell produced immediate results, with sailors and warriors running to their appointed stations and tasks. There was a brief moment when Aedan, Bryn, and Martin all stood silent watching the horizon to the north. Strangely enough, the dark wall on the horizon appeared to have shifted its course and was now heading directly for them. As it drew closer, they could make out an odd greenish tint to the dark fog.

Martin turned and spoke. "That is no ordinary fog. There is something evil at work here. I can feel it." Llew arrived just then, slightly out of breath after running up from the stores below where he had been assessing their supplies.

"What's going—"

But before Llew could even finish his question, a blast of icy cold wind broke across the ship's deck with such an unearthly sounding screech that it gave all who heard it a chill that shot along the spine and caught in the throat.

Aedan turned quickly to Berand, their navigator, and ordered a course of south by southwest with all possible speed. Berand turned quickly and barked out Aedan's order to the rest of the men. The ship's deck was again transformed from the silence of men at attention into an ordered rush of crewmen running to tasks and the sound of instructions being shouted. The crew worked with an efficient calmness. It was in this hour that their experience and skill became quite evident. Each man worked with confidence and speed. Each movement was fast, but efficient. It was clear why they were specially chosen to join this crew.

This flurry of activity continued on a pace for an hour as they tried to outrun the fog. Llew, who joined the crew in their labors, spoke encouragements to all as they continued their efforts. The three red lions bulged under the power of the gale as the winds were caught and the sails were made taut. At first, they all but flew across the waters, and the crew took heart at the sight of clear blue skies to the southwest. A few men even broke out into song as they worked. A short time later, however, another cold scream of wind, even stronger than before, sliced through the song, silencing all aboard the ship. Berand, looking over his shoulder at the approaching fog, called out that it had shifted its course and was again heading directly for them with increasing speed.

After another half an hour, the scream of the wind became a constant attack against the courage of all. Llew could see the growing panic in the eyes of the men around him. There was something unnatural at work here, and they could feel it. All of them had experienced bad tempests and dark fog before, but this was different. Llew's attempts to reassure the men were now lost amidst the hideous raging sounds of the gale that began to sound more like the tortured wail of a living creature than wind. Nevertheless, Llew continued to move among them, placing a reassuring hand on a shoulder here and there and adding his strength to various tasks.

"It is no use!" Bryn shouted through the wind's howl. "This same vile wind that we try to catch drives the fog upon us!"

Looking back to the north, Aedan quickly turned and gave the signal to pull in the sail. Martin and Berand, surprised by the order, looked at him with questioning eyes.

"Do it!" Aedan ordered. "Then turn into the fog! I would rather face whatever it is that seeks us than be caught in the backside while *running*."

The emphasis he placed on his last word and the grim set of his jaw were not lost on those close enough to hear him. The terror they were running from seconds before was now something to be faced rather than fled. After the orders were passed from man to man, the whole crew began busily reversing their course. The sails were brought in and the oars were made ready. Before long, True North was inching forward under the ship's oars directly toward the onrushing darkness.

The fog grew darker and the howl of the wind increased as it came on. It is true that any fog can be dangerous at sea in unknown waters, but this fog carried its own terror. Fear reached out from it with icy fingers, grasping for a victim as though it were a living beast. In the chaos of the screeching wind, Bryn noticed that Martin was standing at the ship's prow with his hands upraised. Although Bryn could see Martin's mouth moving, all his words were lost upon the shriek of the wind.

The fog devoured the length of sea between them as it raced toward True North. Bryn could see the mounting apprehension in the eyes of the men around him. Even the veteran warriors began to show unusual signs of wavering. Still, on came the darkness. And then, it was upon them and all became silent.

Morviana

At Aedan's order, crewmembers were positioned around the ship's perimeter. Each man was given a lamp for whatever illumination it would provide. None needed to be told the importance of such a precaution nor the danger of crashing into rocks or other ships.

What had been bright daylight only moments before became the inky darkness that normally comes of a moonless night. Not only did the wind abruptly vanish upon entering the unnatural fog, but the hideous howling that followed was gone. The men stopped rowing in unison as though they had received a silent signal. All was quiet, too quiet. Those aboard True North found themselves straining against the silence to catch even the slightest stirrings of sound. One of the younger sailors leaned over and whispered to a nearby friend, "What we lis-nen' for?" The whispered question sounded unnaturally loud, and his friend recoiled as if it had hurt his ears.

"I don' know!" he hissed back.

"Be quiet!" A third man standing nearby ordered under his breath.

Aedan shook himself out of the spell of silence that held the entire ship in its grip and gave the order to continue steady forward progress. The oars began dipping into the murky waters once more and the ship moved slowly through the darkness. Aedan noticed Bryn standing at the rail a short distance away and moved to join him. Bryn turned and silently acknowledged his approach.

"Can you see anything?" Aedan asked as they both peered into the dark greenish fog.

"No." Bryn's answer betrayed none of the growing apprehension he felt.

Aedan was about to say something more when the silence was broken by a shout further down the starboard side of the deck. Aedan left Berand at the helm while he and Bryn made their way forward through the fog. Although they moved as quickly as possible, both took care not to appear overly concerned. Nothing steals the courage of men more than the sight of their leaders giving way to fear. Although in reality it only took a few moments to reach the spot, moving through the soup-like fog was slow and arduous.

Aedan and Bryn arrived to find a cluster of men engaged in eager but hushed conversation. They were pointing into the fog off the ship's starboard rail. Upon seeing Aedan and Bryn, several of the men tried to speak all at once in an excited rush, clearly afraid of something they had seen. Llew now also appeared from behind Bryn with a questioning look on his face. Aedan held up his hand for silence.

"What has happened?" He spoke with a quiet confidence that had an immediate calming affect. One of the men at the forefront of the group spoke first.

"Your Lordship, me and Renny"—the man pointed to a nearby companion—"was just standin at the rail, like ever-one else. When there she was! Right there in front of us, out of no-where it was. Then she was gone!" All the men looked from the speaker to Aedan as though he held the answer to the mystery.

"Aric, isn't it?" Aedan addressed the man who had spoken up.

"Yes, Your Lordship."

"Aric, what was it exactly that you and Renny saw?" The calmness with which Aedan spoke was more than he felt.

"Well, sir, it was snake-like. That is, I saw somthin' that was scaly and sorta shiny." Aric looked to Renny for his agreement.

"Well, Renny what did you see?" Aedan continued.

"I don' know 'bout no snake, sir, but it was the eyes I seen!"

"Eyes?" one of the other men blurted out, forgetting his place. Bryn looked at the man with disapproval.

"Go on." Aedan encouraged Renny to continue.

"Just that! I saw em glowin-n-th' fog. Like burnt coals, they were!"

This latest revelation caused a murmur to ripple through the men that stood close by. When it became clear they would get nothing further from the men, Aedan, Bryn, and Llew encouraged them to continue their vigilant guard and then moved off out of earshot to discuss the development.

"Have either of you seen Martin?" Aedan began.

"I can't see anything!" Llew replied.

"I saw him standing at the prow before we entered the fog," Bryn said. Aedan turned his head toward the front of the ship.

"You're right, Llew. I can't see five paces, let alone the prow. Bryn, go back to the helm and see what aid you can be to Berand. Make sure Rand and his warriors stand alert. We need to be ready for anything. Llew, you continue your support here to the men. I fear their nerves are already spread thin. I will go and find Martin."

The others nodded and moved off, while Aedan turned toward the front of the ship. He moved slowly through the veil of fog that now began to smell of rotting seaweed. Every few paces or so, he could just make out the glow of a lantern held by one of the men at the ship's rail. As he grew closer to the prow, he stopped to listen, hoping to hear some evidence of Martin's presence. But there was nothing but silence, so he continued forward.

The slightest of stirrings off to his right caused Aedan to unconsciously glance in that direction. At that exact moment, out of the thickness of the fog directly in front of him swooped a dark shape. Aedan threw himself to the ship's deck as he heard what sounded like the cry of an eagle. As he hit the deck and rolled over, there was a rush in the air just above him, and Aedan felt a stabbing pain as something ripped into his right shoulder. A thick dark form disappeared into the obscurity off the ship's rail. And then, from out of nowhere, Martin was kneeling by his side with his sword drawn and ready.

"Are you hurt?" There was a quiet urgency in Martin's voice. He was close enough for Aedan to see that his face was furrowed with concern.

"No...I think I'm fine. What was that?"

"I'm not exactly sure. But it's been watching and waiting ever since we entered this fog," Martin replied. He then added as he looked up to scan the surrounding darkness, "I think it might be prudent to draw the men back from the perimeter where possible."

Aedan quickly agreed as Martin helped him to his feet. It didn't take long to spread the word to draw back from the rail. The crewmen were more than eager to abandon the isolated perimeter. As Martin and Aedan approached middeck, Llew came up out of the murkiness.

"What happened? We heard a commotion. Is everyone all right?" he asked.

"There is something out there," Aedan answered. "Re-form the men. I want the oars manned with three crewmen each. Let's see how quickly we can get free of this fog. Have Rand's warriors form two lines, one facing port and the other starboard. Let's get out of here as soon as possible."

Llew nodded in reply.

"Martin and I will join Bryn and Berand. Here, sound an alarm should anything happen." Aedan handed Llew a horn with a gold-tipped mouthpiece. It had been their father's since he was a boy and was passed on to Aedan as the eldest. Llew nodded his ascent as Aedan and Martin disappeared in the direction of the helm.

Peering through mindless, hate-filled eyes, Morviana watched and waited. Slowly she moved through the murky darkness around her prey, looking for the exact moment to strike. Hate and an unquenchable hunger were all she felt. Only the strongest powers of darkness could have roused her from slumber in the uttermost depths of the sea. And it had. Now she would have her revenge!

She could see the puny men skulking aboard their ship. She could taste their fear and her hunger grew. Yet Morviana hesitated. There was something that disturbed her, something that undermined her resolve. There was a strength that warred against her. It was an illumination, a light that made her recoil. For the briefest of moments, she almost decided to forgo the battle and return to the depths and slumber, but the dark malice that had awakened her tightened its grip and returned her thoughts to hatred and cruelty. She must kill! She must devour or be tortured further by the powers that drove her.

Morviana saw the solitary figure of Aedan moving slowly toward the front of the ship. She poised herself for the quick deathblow. Yet even as her terrible fangs sliced through the spot where he stood but a moment before, Morviana, that vile sea serpent, knew her victim had escaped this time. She retreated back into the black void to wait.

Aedan and Martin rejoined the others at the helm. It was then that Martin noticed the red stain growing on Aedan's shoulder. "What's this? You're hurt," Martin spoke with growing concern.

Bryn and Berand turned and looked at them. Aedan, having forgotten about the pain he felt in his shoulder as he dove onto the deck, looked at his arm, somewhat surprised himself.

"It's probably nothing, just a scratch. I had forgotten it until just now," he answered without conviction.

"Nevertheless, it needs to be examined," Martin insisted as he began to remove the torn part of Aedan's shirt around the wound. There was a ragged gash across the lower part of his right shoulder. Martin's face was set in a grimace as he finished his examination.

"That will need to be properly cleaned, and as soon as possible," Martin spoke and then looked at Aedan for his agreement. Aedan simply nodded. "By the look of that wound, whatever it was that attacked you almost achieved its ends," Martin continued.

Aedan looked back toward the front of the ship. "I thought I heard the cry of an eagle," he said. "It came at me out of the fog."

Berand, still puzzled, interrupted. "What happened? I can't hear anything in this dead fog."

Berand continued. "Did you say you were attacked by an 'eagle'?"

Aedan, with a slight feeling of distraction, drew his attention away from the front of the ship and looked back at Berand with questioning eyes. "Attacked by the eagle? Of course not, if not for that eagle's warning, I would be sleeping with the fish right now!" He answered.

Martin was intrigued by this new revelation, but he kept his thoughts to himself.

"Then what gave you this?" Bryn spoke as he reached out and pointed at Aedan's wounded shoulder.

"I'm not sure, but whatever it was would have had more than *this* little taste." Aedan paused momentarily to indicate his wound and then continued. "If that eagle had not warned me first."

The Killing Strike

Llew moved among the men from one side of the ship to the other, speaking in quiet, even tones. His voice held a note of carefree confidence. The unnatural temptation to fear that now held True North's crew in its unrelenting grip did not diminish. Even the warriors under Rand's command shifted uneasily. Every man's eyes intently scanned the surrounding fog. They all knew that a fight was coming. It was inevitable now. Yet their enemy was an unseen terror. There was not a man among them that was unwilling to die for his king. But unknown danger causes uncertainty. And uncertainty in battle is deadly.

The next few hours passed slowly, and the constant tension began to take its toll. There was no indication of the fog lessening nor any sign of their enemy. The air was heavy and smelled foul. Many of the men began slowly giving in to the kind of dullness that comes from focusing too long and intently on any one thing. A few of the men, strangely enough, even began fighting back yawns as their attention and reflexes glazed with lethargy. *Another hour*, Llew thought, *and their unseen enemy would be able to simply pick them off one by one as they slept.* He stirred himself to shake off the growing heaviness in his own limbs and thought to speak with Rand, who was standing a few paces to his left.

Llew had just turned and begun to speak when he suddenly stopped midspeech and gazed intently into the fog directly behind Rand. Whether there was some imperceptible change in the fog or he had actually heard or seen something, he was unsure. But something attracted his attention. Something was there, just beyond the rail. Rand noticed Llew's unusual behavior, and he began to ask whether all was well. Llew held up his hand, continuing to peer past the ship's rail with a new intentness. The dense air held a tension that gripped the muscles in Llew's neck. He could hear the blood pounding through his ears in a drum-like cadence that followed the beat of his own heart. After a while, Llew realized he was holding his breath. He softly exhaled.

Had it been his imagination only? It was certainly possible that his senses had simply been tricked by the constant weight of tension. He almost convinced himself that it was nothing when he saw it again. Although it was only at the edge of his vision this time, he was sure the movement of something large displaced the fog. Llew looked to see whether Rand had also seen it. Rand, still standing in the same place as before, now looked directly off to Llew's left.

Few things ever unnerved Rand. He had proven himself in battle more times than he could or cared to remember, but it was never for the thrill of battle or the glory of victory. Rand followed his duty wherever it led him. Why worry about consequences? You either lived or died at the end of the day, but the only real question Rand ever thought important enough to consider was whether he lived or died with honor.

Rand caught Llew's gaze, and as though some silent signal passed between them, he drew his sword. All his warriors followed his example, leaving only the slightest whisper of sliding metal against leather sheaths to be discerned in the muted air. Something could now clearly be seen moving in the fog just off the ship's port. An order was passed quietly from man to man to be ready. The men began shaking themselves out of the tiredness that wore at them over the last few hours. Everyone's attention was now keenly drawn to the object now easily seen moving through the fog to port. The heavy fog lifted slightly, making it easier for the men to see each other.

"Can you see it anymore?" The question came from Rand, who was standing, sword drawn, next to Llew as though he intended to defend Llew from any host of enemy no matter what shape they took.

"No. It has vanished once again," Llew said.

The trick could not have worked any better. She allowed herself to be seen and then quickly moved around the ship to the other side. Morviana could already taste the delight of her deception. What pitiful creatures. *It was almost too easy*, she thought with disdain. It was her time now. She would feast upon them and finally satisfy her unquenched hunger. With all the stealth and speed she could muster, Morviana—that ancient monster of the deep, full of hate and hunger—attacked!

While the men's attention was drawn to the other side of the ship, her fangs sliced through the air with a speed that was unthinkable. Her first victim never even saw from where his death came. Screams and shouts filled the air as men tumbled over each other in a vain attempt to get away from the reach of her awful fangs. Morviana relished in the chaos and struck again. Another of the men fell, never to move again. The water in the sea around the ship boiled from her excitement.

A piercing sound blasted through the air, momentarily causing Morviana to recoil, as the darkness began to recede, somewhat revealing the ship's strange illumination. Two of the puny men actually ran out at her. They meant to fight her! Her! The foolishness of their arrogance made Morviana's anger burn. This act of folly would be their last. In a fury of rage, she attacked again.

The attack came so fast. It was with utter disbelief that Llew turned to where the screams tore the air. With Rand at his side, Llew let go a blast on his horn as he ran to the fight. He could feel the anger rising up in his throat as his feet pounded across the solid wooden planks of the ship's deck. How could he have been so stupid? He knew he had underestimated his enemy, but he vowed under his breath that he would make the thing pay dearly for its deception.

They could now clearly see the vile creature of the deep. It was hideous beyond their imaginings. A murky dark gray, its giant, scale-covered, snake-like body coiled in and out of the water. Blood dripped from its fangs as it made ready to strike again. The wretched serpent let loose a screech that shook the very deck under Llew's feet. Still, he did not give ground but stood and made ready for the assault.

The monster struck with a blinding speed. Llew had only enough time to shift the shield strapped to his left arm before the awful jaws slashed toward him. His reflex saved his life. The force of the blow was largely absorbed by the shield, which now lay smashed and useless on the ship's deck.

Llew was knocked into the air, landing breathless on his back in a pile of ship rigging. He grasped for his sword, which had been knocked from his hand by the sheer impact of the attack. But it was nowhere to be found. A hot pain stabbed through his shoulder, and Llew realized that he could not move his left arm. He looked back toward the creature to see that Rand and several of his warriors were forming a defensive half circle in front of their attacker. They sheathed their swords and now stood waiting with lances in hand.

A dozen sailors who had fled at the monster's initial attack were now rejoining the fight. They saw Llew's courageous stand and rallied to his defense. Armed with small throwing harpoons, they waited behind the defensive perimeter set up by the warriors. The creature hesitated. Her eyes glowed with a ghastly luminescence.

The next attack came as a feint, and one of the sailors lofted a small, clumsy, harpoon-like spear at her head. It didn't even come close to its target. Sweat streamed down the men's faces and stung their eyes as the fight continued. The air remained heavy and stagnant as they labored to breath in the stifling heat. The creature's stench was horrid and burned their eyes and nostrils.

Now with the battle engaged, all stealth and secrecy was abandoned by their foe. She feinted once more in the direction of the warriors to her right, and then without even the slightest pause smashed into the men on the opposite side. Two warriors were knocked sprawling to the deck, but a third man's lance pierced the scaled neck and stuck fast. Before the unfortunate man could release his grip on the spear, Morviana contorted upward, resulting in the warrior being flung and lost into the dark waters on the far side of the ship. The sounds of her anger thundered into the battle. Morviana struck again and again, with a bloodlust that was relentless. Rand's warriors were being quickly overcome.

One man was pinned to the deck under Morviana's gaping maw, and he would have been torn to pieces but for the reappearance of Llew.

Without a shield or the use of his left arm, Llew saw the man's plight and knew he was the only one close enough to help. Shouting as he charged, Llew thrust his bone-handled dagger into the side of the creature's neck right under its jaw. A thick black liquid spurted from the wound, and Morviana jerked back with a terrible hissing sound.

Llew helped the man up as they both retreated back from the fight. The small wound only infuriated Morviana more. She turned her wrath back toward the retreating men. But before she could continue her attack, a javelin cut the thick air as it flew toward its target. The throw was a direct hit, but the weapon simply glanced harmlessly off her scaled body.

Morviana turned to face her new attackers. A group of sailors led by Aedan and Martin armed themselves with shorter throwing spears and were now coming to the aid of their shipmates.

Llew watched as Martin took aim and let fly his javelin. It too flew straight to its mark, but unlike the first spear, it smashed the scale and pierced deeply into the serpent's flesh. Morviana, reeling from pain, abandoned all caution and flung herself at the new attackers. But as she swung down to meet them, a wild whoop pierced the air somewhere above Llew's head. He glanced up just in time to see the muted shape of a man flying through the air. He slammed into the side of the serpent's head. Somehow, instead of just sliding off into the dark waters of the sea, he was able to grab hold of the slimy, seaweed-like hair, which covered the crown of the creature's head. The sheer impact of the collision surprised Morviana enough to cause her to break off her attack.

She hesitated in her confusion. Llew could see the man struggling for a better hold.

Some of the warriors, led by Rand, began thrusting their spears at the serpent in order to distract her. Their ploy worked just long enough for the unknown man to pull himself to the top of the creature's head. It was then for the first time that Llew could see him clearly enough for recognition.

"Bryn!" Llew's shout broke from his lips before he realized he had even shouted.

He rushed from his place of relative safety back toward Rand and the others just in time to see Bryn straddling their enemy's head as though he was merely riding a horse. With a mighty heave, Bryn plunged his sword deep into the top of Morviana's head. A split-second later, the point of Bryn's sword was clearly visible, protruding from the base of the serpent's jaw. With a strange, metallic, hissing sound, the creature of the deep violently jerked from side to side, hovered for the briefest of moments, and then crashed back into the dark waters from whence it came.

As their defeated foe hit the surface of the sea, its death throes caused such a tumult that True North was quite suddenly lifted up on one side, knocking many of the men off their feet. The force of the shock wave rapidly pushed them away from the battle scene. The strange and morose silence that preceded their battle now returned. Morviana, the horror of the deep, was dead.

Llew regained his feet and ran to the ship's rail and shouted Bryn's name again. His call died in the thick air and was met with complete silence. Aedan and Martin quickly appeared at his side.

"How far do you think we were pushed?" Aedan asked in an urgent tone.

Martin continued to scan the fog-covered waters. "It could not have been far," he said.

"Yes," Llew agreed, "but from which direction were we pushed? In this fog, every way looks the same to me. Our direction was sure to have been shifted by the waves." Llew continued. "Let me take one of the ship's lifeboats and run a loop around our current position."

Aedan looked doubtful. "We would take too great a risk losing you in this fog, even at such close range."

"Besides," Martin interrupted, "by the looks of your left arm, you could not even hold an oar, let alone climb down into the boat." Llew made to protest, but Aedan held up his hand for silence as he bent his head to one side. Martin and Llew looked to Aedan questioningly.

"The waves. They are still rippling against the ship's hull!" He quickly grabbed one of the nearby lanterns, tied a rope to it, and began lowering it over the ship's rail. When the light reached close enough to the water for them to see the waves, all three peered downward.

"That way!" Martin stated as he pointed forty-five degrees to port.

Aedan ordered the nearest boat to be lowered into the water. "Tie the end of a length of rope to the ship's rail and to the lifeboat. I will not have anyone else lost at sea."

The sailors named Renny and Aric made it to the closest lifeboat first and began making the necessary preparations for its launch. The canvas boat cover was collapsed, twisted, and covered in sea slime and debris from the deadly battle. They immediately began to yank and pull at the canvas covering the boat, trying to clear the mess as quickly as possible. The canvas was stuck on something. With one great effort, both Renny and Aric pulled with all their might as it came lose. Something banged against the bottom of the boat, and they heard a low moaning sound. Aric looked quickly at Renny and began untangling the mess of canvas as he yelled over his shoulder.

"Cap'n, Cap'n! Over 'ere! Someone's 'ere!"

Aedan, Martin, and Llew ran as quickly as they could to the spot of the commotion. They arrived just in time to see Aric and Renny reaching over the side of the boat as the back of a flaxen-haired head came into view. Renny was yelling something in an excited but quite unintelligible tone, when they finally pulled the man out and onto the ship's deck. Bryn, having been flung from Morviana's head in her last convulsion, had sailed high through the dark fog and miraculously landed just over the ship's rail onto the soft canvas stretched over the lifeboat. Five feet more or less in either direction and he would have been smashed onto the ship's deck or plunged into the sea.

Bryn shook off Renny and Aric's grasp and tried to step forward, but he simply fell onto his hands and knees as his brothers and Martin rushed to support him.

"Are you injured?" Martin asked quickly. The men all gathered around the area and were being led by Berand in rousing cheers. Bryn stared back with a dazed look in his eyes. Blood trickled down his face from a gash just above his right eyebrow.

"Did we win?" he asked with a weak voice.

Valentus

A dozen ships filled the harbor below the rocky outcropping where Valentus lay watching. He was puzzled. Why were they here? A fleet of smaller transport boats ferried heavily armed men and horses to the wide shoreline below him. Why would anyone want to invade Tharrus?

From his high vantage point, Valentus could see the entire view to the west. The sun stood high in the sky. It was already beginning its arc toward the western horizon, toward the lands of Illyrium across the sea of Erythraean. *The ships must have arrived hours ago*, Valentus mused. It was clear these warriors were not friendly. If they were, they would not be coming ashore in such a remote region.

Valentus felt a rush of excitement rise in his chest. Nothing interesting ever happened to him. From sunup to sundown, his life was tending his uncle's sheep and goats. He did not know his uncle or cousins very well. In fact, it was hard most times for Valentus to feel any real family connection to them. He was grateful for the place they provided, but he knew it was charity more than anything. He did not remember his father or mother. They had died when he was a babe and left him in the custody of the man he now called Uncle.

The only thing he had left of his parents was a small metal pendant he kept on a leather strap around his neck. It wasn't much, but it reminded him that he once belonged somewhere. His uncle was not an unkind man, but he valued hard work. So when Valentus came of age, his uncle placed him over the flocks. A job that meant he often spent more nights under the open skies than under any real roof. The loneliness was intolerable at times.

There was seldom much chance for human companionship. Once, every couple of weeks, his uncle would send a man with supplies. And there was the occasional drifter or traveler who happened upon Valentus, stopping in hopes of a shared meal. Otherwise, there was just the flock. Although he was nearing his seventeenth birthday, he could count on his hand the number of times he'd actually seen a girl over the last few years. In his daydreams, he saved many beautiful ladies from certain death, but reality was much less glorious.

His last real encounter with a girl was at the harvest festival just last year, and it would be some time before he forgot it. It was the first time his uncle allowed him to attend such an event. The night air was filled with music and the laughter of those pursuing merriment. The aroma of meats sizzling on the open spits mixed deliciously with the smell of freshly baked, sweet breads and a dozen other specialties. Five minutes into the celebration and Valentus was in simple awe. He had heard of such celebrations, but every description fell quite short of the real thing.

For most of that night, Valentus wandered like a wide-eyed child through the throngs of merrymakers and past the many tents and booths, each one offering its own unique entertainment or tasty delicacy. After passing one rather large tent filled with men robustly indulging themselves in foaming mugs of ale and mead, he caught the hint of a sound different from all the rest. It was a soft, undulating song coming to him on one of the lilting breezes.

Valentus would always remember that night and what happened next. The moon shone brightly across the festival grounds as he searched for the source of the song. It was a melancholic sound and Valentus could feel the loneliness of the hills in it. It came from a small, nearby knoll. He strained to hear it better. The other sounds of the festival that at first delighted Valentus now became disruptive and irritating to him. He pushed faster through the crowd until he reached the hill.

At the top, he found a gathering of listeners sitting around a small, wooden stage that stood in a recessed depression. The effect of the hilltop depression was much like that of an amphitheater. A girl sat toward the front of the wooden stage on a simple chair. She cradled a small harp-like instrument from which soft notes were being crafted. A medium-sized fire blazed directly in front of the stage, and several torches burned around its perimeter.

Just then the girl began to sing again. Her voice was even more beautiful than it sounded from down below the hill only moments before. Several more songs filled the night air before Valentus realized he was still standing while most everyone around him was sitting comfortably.

When the song ended, the girl stood and bent her head to the crowd's cheers and whistles. This was the first time Valentus really got a good look at her. Standing in the light of the fire and torches, her fair features were well illuminated. She could not have been any older than Valentus himself. Clad in a blue dress and cream-colored shawl, the dark locks of the singer's hair hung about her slender shoulders and shimmered in the dancing light. Valentus, who could hardly help himself, openly stared at her.

The singer turned and looked right into his eyes. He was so unnerved by the look that he unthinkingly stepped backward, without taking into account the slight rise of the slope behind him. He lost his footing on the ever-dampening grass and landed square on his back with a loud thump. Much to his embarrassment, the people around him chuckled at his unfortunate clumsiness. The singer was gone by the time Valentus regained his footing and composure. Although he wandered the festival grounds the rest of the night, hoping to catch another glimpse of the girl, she was nowhere to be found.

Over the next six months, he spent every spare moment daydreaming about the singer. When he sat and watched the flocks during the day, he could still hear the lingering notes of her songs. When he closed his eyes at night, he saw her, standing in the firelight. But as each day passed, dreams became harder to dream. His life continued to revolve around the sheep. Each day was just like the last; nothing ever changed. It had never bothered him before, but now, for some unfathomable reason, the loneliness was deeper, the night was longer, and the heat of the day dragged on and on, until today.

It was not that Valentus misjudged the seriousness of the scene before him. But even the momentary excitement of danger was somehow preferable to the extended periods of loneliness and boredom that was his life. Perhaps he was being given a rare chance to change his destiny. This was his chance to do something heroic. A thrill of excitement shot through him at the thought. No one else would know of the presence of these invaders, not in this remote place. He would be the one to sound the alarm and save the kingdom, but how? He had no horse and did not expect supplies for another week.

He turned away from the rocky edge and looked back to the northeast. It was a full day's walk back to his uncle's estate, but he must sound a warning. He considered the sheep. He could move faster without them, but they would be left unprotected. He hesitated for a moment with indecision, until he made up his mind. No one could fault him for leaving his uncle's flock, not at a time like this. The sheep would have to fend for themselves for now.

Malen's Nightmare

Malen walked down a narrow, dark corridor. He held out a small candle for light with his hand extended just above his own head. It barely lit the way, but Malen preferred not to draw any unwanted attention. A serious misgiving grew in his mind. But he asked himself why. All was going according to his plans. So why should he let doubt nag at him?

The corridor wound around several corners and continued on straight for another twenty paces before coming to an abrupt end at the entrance to a small room. Malen hesitated and looked back over his shoulder before entering.

He forced a tepid grimace to break across his rigid face. Word of the inevitable victory over Tharrus was expected any day, and as soon as his reluctant stooge Lanthir completed the conquest, the next part of his plan could begin. The thought of what he would find on Tharrus sent a tingle down the back of his neck.

He held the candle a little higher as he reached toward the wall on his right for a cleverly hidden release lever. Malen's grimace hardened back into a frown as the door, which was completely invisible a moment before, began to swing inward. He continued to walk down another dark hallway.

His thoughts drifted back to the source of his misgiving. Every night for the last two weeks, his sleep had been tortured by the same recurring nightmare. *There was really nothing to it*, Malen thought. Yet despite his best attempts to ignore it, worry continued to plague him. Every night the dream was the same.

He found himself standing alone on a stone balcony. As he looked to the east, a great bird of prey filled with the brightness of the sun would appear over the horizon. The wings of the bird moved with such strength that the darkness around it shuddered. The creature would come closer, and as it came nearer, its wings and tail feathers began to glow brilliant red. A light emanating from some unseen source surrounded the creature.

It was of such a burning purity that Malen would shield his eyes against the stinging pain it caused. The blinding brilliance of the great bird was so intense it cast him to the hard stone floor and caused him to lie prostrate before the light. After a few moments of painful fear, he would awake in his own bed covered in cold sweat, his ears still ringing with the distant echo of the great bird's cry.

The nightmare began to wear at Malen's nerves, and after a few days, he resorted to the dark arts for a solution. There were none alive who ever attained his level of knowledge. *Perhaps one came close*, Malen mused with something akin to a pang of regret, *but that was long ago*. Pharigant, Malen's nephew, had shown real promise. Together they could have ruled the world. What's more, if Pharigant still lived, Malen would not now be stuck with that imbecile, Lanthir.

Malen, nevertheless, did master the dark arts beyond anything he and Pharigant once dreamed possible. It is true that they would not have referred to them as the dark arts. They simply sought knowledge. *But what of that*, Malen thought. *Knowledge is simply another word for power, if used correctly*, he concluded with a sneer. He simply used knowledge to gain power. It did not take Malen long to realize the dark arts could afford untold opportunities for new knowledge and greater power. There were certain sacrifices to be made, but it was his willingness to endure such things that led him to the Book of Knowledge, his greatest discovery.

Malen continued to follow the secret hallway until it intersected with a spiral stone staircase branching off to the right down into darkness. The hallway itself continued straight ahead. He held up his candle and peered down the hallway. Assured he was not being followed, Malen turned to the wall on his left. There was a lantern hanging on a hook. He lit the lantern, then blew out his candle and placed it on a small shelf next to the hook. Turning back toward the stair, he began the long descent toward the lower levels beneath the surface. As he continued downward, the walls changed from cut and fitted block to the solid, chiseled rock of the mountain, and the air became increasingly cold and damp.

The Book of Knowledge opened a new world to him. True, it was Pharigant who had first happened upon the fragment of the Book, but only by mere accident. It was Malen who unlocked its great potential. Therefore, it was his by right. It was *his* discovery.

Pharigant had made it his custom to escape to the old ruins of the original palace library whenever a free moment presented itself. It was a lonely place where others did not go any more and the only place where he could find solitude. Malen found the place to be a dirty pile of rubble and never understood its draw to Pharigant. How was he to know the value of the treasure that lay hidden there? Much of the book was either too damaged to be of value, or simply missing. The fragments, however, were still readable and quickly became more valuable to Malen than the whole of Illyrium. At first, it made little sense to either Pharigant or Malen. The language was ancient, but their experience with other resources of similar age made its translation slow but possible. It told of a garden and its keepers, a heroic race of ancients called the Aletae.

At first, the nature of this "Garden of the Aletae" and its plants seemed nonsense. They translated phrases such as "the frozen thorn, which weaves its web of song." But it was the references to the "dark paths of discovery" that proved to be the key unlocking all the rest. This may have been the undoing of his young apprentice. The Book of Knowledge described a ritual, which must be completed for anyone to discover the hidden paths. Pharigant should never have attempted it by himself. Malen alone possessed the necessary experience.

The ritual carried much pain and sacrifice, but its accomplishment brought unexpected delight to Malen. For nine days and nights, he tortured his own body, following his interpretations of the ancient ritual. One misstep and he would be dead, which he knew was Pharigant's fate.

By the end of the ninth day, Malen succeeded and gained the ability to free his mind from the constraints of his physical body, a practice allowing him to wander the dread paths where only the disembodied could walk, the "dark paths" of the Aletae. In theory they could lead him anywhere. Unfortunately, they were wound together like a great maze. Without a map, you may stumble upon anything, but never find the one thing you were looking for.

Malen, with much effort, eventually gained a near-perfect understanding of the ancient language of the Aletae. With his increased knowledge, he recognized many mistakes in his and Pharigant's earlier translation of the fragment. It did not say "*frozen* thorn," but rather "*ice* thorn." Unfortunately, the portions of the Book of Knowledge giving the location of the Garden of the Aletae did not survive. The discovered fragment, however, did provide two very important things—it gave a clue to where a map could be found, and it also led Malen to one of the garden's plants. The Aletae planted the Ice Thorn in several places as a means of controlling their enslaved peoples. Much to Malen's glee, the salvaged fragment contained references to such locations, which were known to him. It took a little effort to piece the clues together, but he eventually found this plant using the dark paths.

It could not be uprooted and relocated, but he was able to harvest its seeds. He himself secretly planted and cultivated the thorn until it finally reached fruit-bearing maturity. Its resilience was amazing. Now that it was fully grown, it no longer needed protection from him.

This thorn was not like any other tree in this world. Very few, indeed, were able to resist the power of the thorn. A few miserable wretches tried to defy its unusual powers and were quickly disposed of. One fool even tried to cut the thorn down. His body, or what was left of it, probably still hung from the tree's branches where he was caught and trapped. Malen smiled to remember how long he sat watching and laughing at the man's predicament.

Its fruit was unique, to say the least. It was not like the variety of fruit that most trees bear. That is to say, it was not a thing to be plucked and eaten. Rather, it produced a sound. Malen liked to think of it as music, but in reality it was more of a low vibration barely audible to the human ear.

How easily most men are led, Malen thought with scorn. *They are oxen with empty heads. They exist to be used by those with knowledge and power*, he mused. All it takes is a key to unlock their thick skulls. And Malen possessed that key in the ice thorn. Its "music," as he called it, caused most who heard it to fall prey to its master's suggestions. And that is exactly how he used it.

Malen's thoughts returned to his recent nightmares as he continued to descend the stone stairs. It was to the dark paths he turned for an answer to this torment. Although he had told himself a thousand times it was nothing more than an ordinary dream, he could not shake the unrelenting sense that it portended an imminent threat.

Thus, he walked the forbidden paths, but despite his searching he could discover nothing of the bird of light. He did, nonetheless, discover *her*. In the deepest darkness of the eastern sea's depths, he found her coiled in slumber. Who could tell how many ages of the world she slept there undisturbed? But now, that malevolent queen of the deep, Morviana, would serve him. Just to look upon her terrible strength and imagine the horror and destruction awaiting anyone unfortunate enough to fall within her coils filled Malen with a perverse glee. His new pet should be more than enough to protect against all enemies, real or imagined, coming from the east.

The stairs finally came to an end, opening into a cave-like chamber with rounded, uneven walls. To the left ran another tunnel in a direction away from the stairs. Directly ahead stood an ancient door of blackened iron. The air was damp and musty, adding to the sense that this place was ancient beyond reckoning. Malen moved to the door and lifted a heavy iron latch. There was a dull scraping sound as it moved and a clank when it finally came to rest. Although the door looked heavy, it moved with little enough effort, and Malen stepped through it.

The hulking form of Ranf, the keeper of the pit, met him.

"I presume all is well with our guest?"

Ranf simply nodded.

He neither liked Malen, nor disliked him. Ranf just did as he was told. He served whatever master was in charge. His loyalty was not to any man, but simply to the order that existed in his life. Whoever was in charge told him what to do, and he did it. That was the only comfort he had ever known.

Malen walked over to the rusted metal grate in the floor that led to the Pit of Voices. He hesitated for a moment longer as he stared through the grate bars into the utter darkness below. There was no sound.

Malen turned to Ranf who waited a short distance away. "You are sure he still lives?"

Ranf simply nodded his head again.

"Open it."

Ranf slowly bent his great hulk, got hold of a large iron ring attached to the grate, and pulled.

Serigant sat with his head collapsed against his knees. He did not move or make a sound. Malen spoke evenly at first, but when there was no response, his voice grew louder.

"Serigant!"

Still there was no movement, so Malen reached down and pushed at the captive's shoulder. There was a slight stirring.

"So at least you live!" Malen said. A slight look of satisfaction crossed the rigid features of his face.

Serigant's head began to slowly lift. His once noble face was now covered in a matted beard, and his hair hung in long tatters over his eyes.

"Do you…*know* me?" Malen asked as he stepped closer. There was a long pause while he waited for an answer. Since none was forthcoming, he continued to talk. "It *is* too bad. About the need for all of this, I mean." He waived his hand vaguely around in an attempt to portray something akin to sympathy.

"It was never your kingdom I wanted," he said, as though it should have been an obvious conclusion. "I wanted your allegiance. And I will have it still! I will have all their vows before I am done. All the little kings shall come and bow down to me."

When there was no response from Serigant, Malen turned and headed toward the stone stairs that led to the iron grate. Halfway up the stairs, he stopped abruptly. Malen could have sworn he heard Serigant mumble something. He turned and looked back at him, squinting through the darkness of the pit. Though barely audible and spoken as though it was part of a lyric, the words came to Malen.

"See how the great bird has taken flight."

A cold sweat broke across Malen's brow, and a knot tightened in his stomach. He turned quickly and fled back the way he came.

The Storm

Martin stood at the rail of True North. He held his arm out and slightly upward. A tightly wrapped leather bracing adorned his forearm. It was another clear, sunny day at sea. Their narrow escape from the sea monster was truly a harrowing experience, but several days of clear blue skies and gentle winds were a balm to them all. They mourned the loss of three good men, but things could have been far worse.

A high-pitched whistle flew easily from between his teeth and lips, cutting high upon the wind. He waited a few seconds more and whistled again. For a moment, there was no response. And then, from somewhere high above True North came the answering call that he had been waiting for. A smile flashed across his face as his eyes narrowed their focus in the direction of the sound. The eagle dropped from high in the sky above as it made its approach. Martin marveled at the grace and control of its descent. The distance between them disappeared with astonishing speed. At the last possible moment, when it appeared certain the eagle would simply fly right past him, its wings came up and out, and it deftly perched on Martin's forearm. The great bird gripped the protective leather bracing with surprising lightness. These same talons, now gently resting on him, could just as easily tear his flesh to the bone if the eagle so desired.

A voice spoke from behind Martin. "You have gained his trust. And so quickly!" It was Bryn who approached.

"He is magnificent, isn't he?" Martin spoke without taking his eyes from the eagle. He reached into a pouch that hung at his side, pulled out a small fish, and held it out. The eagle turned its head and looked at Martin momentarily. Then it snatched the fish with its beak, lifted its head upward, and swallowed it down whole.

"I suppose it helps to have an endless supply of his favorite food," Martin mused as he reached a gloved hand slowly toward the eagle's neck feathers and slowly stroked with the backside of his forefinger.

"Maybe. But I think he stays because of you," Bryn replied.

Martin glanced over his shoulder at Bryn as if to question his meaning.

"What I mean is, I think you two are the same. Both of you could soar far above all of this"—Bryn waived his hand about him in an inclusive gesture—"but neither of you choose to go your own way. You have chosen to serve the Creator and His way."

Martin hesitated momentarily and then turned back to feed the eagle another small fish. Bryn noticed what almost looked like a wave of shame pass over his mentor's features. Darkness quickly clouded Martin's eyes. Bryn, misunderstanding Martin's sudden change in expression, thought to undo whatever he had said to cause this reaction.

"I am sorry, if I have misspoken, I only meant to say that—"

Martin turned back toward Bryn. "It is not you, Bryn. I am simply not the man you think I am. And although I thank you for your kindness, I am neither worthy of your praise nor admiration."

Bryn watched with a confused look on his face as Martin walked away.

Over the next few days, Martin became unusually quiet and withdrawn. When he did speak, it was more often to issue a rebuke. Several of the crewmen began to comment on his poor temper. Few of them indeed escaped a quick tongue lashing for the smallest infraction. Bryn considered approaching Martin again, but then thought better of it. He knew Martin would explain himself when he was ready and not before.

Two more uneventful days passed aboard True North as they followed a course into unknown waters. Toward the end of the second watch of the night, Aedan came to relieve Bryn at the ship's helm.

"Is all quiet?" Aedan asked. Bryn looked upward, toward the night sky, and shrugged.

"No stars. It'll be a dark night without moonlight. Might even rain," he responded. Just then, the first few drops of rain began to hit the deck around them. Aedan began putting his rain cloak on. As he angled his arm back to put it in the sleeve, his face grimaced with pain. Bryn's eye caught the reaction.

"How is the wound you received from the sea serpent?" he asked with a note of concern.

Aedan did not respond immediately, but he turned his face toward the dark skies for a moment. "Hopefully we will pass through this weather soon," he said as if to change the subject.

Bryn nodded his agreement, but pressed his question. "Has Martin examined your wound recently?"

Aedan replied with a slight amount of irritation in his voice, "Martin has enough on his mind and does not need to worry over an infected scratch."

"Infected? How long has it been infected?" Bryn pressed for a direct answer.

"You are worried over nothing, brother." Aedan's tone of voice changed once again, now reflecting a carefree attitude.

Bryn put his hand on Aedan's shoulder opposite the wound. "Let me take your watch tonight, you should have Martin examine the wound."

Aedan smiled broadly. "Bryn, I am telling you that I am fine." In order to further his point, Aedan flexed his arms and moved them up and down. "There, you can see I am as strong as ever. But if it will ease your mind, I will seek out Martin in the morning."

Bryn hesitated. "You will alert me if it gets worse?" he questioned in earnest.

"Of course, and if you're not careful, I shall use this scratch as an excuse to get an extra shift of sleep at your expense." Aedan prodded Bryn with a look of amusement. Bryn's concerns eased somewhat as he relented.

"If this weather turns for the worse, send someone to get me," he replied.

Aedan smiled and nodded in response as Bryn turned to go.

Several hours passed as Bryn slept below decks. His sleep was sound, and he did not notice the extra swaying of his hammock. His dreams took him far away from the ever-rolling deck of True North to a place where he walked the paths of a hidden tropic jungle. He did not wander without purpose, but rather he followed a girl. He did not know her, but she beckoned him to follow and he did.

It was the most real dream he ever had. It was not real in the sense of being clear or day-to-day practical. It was rather quite the opposite. It was a rush of the wild wind; the beating of his heart. She was there and then not, but he knew he was being beckoned to follow, and so he did. Without understanding why or how, he simply knew she was trying to show him something.

One moment she was there ahead of him, and the next she was gone. He slashed at the thick undergrowth with his sword. He pushed faster and faster until she was there, right in front of him. He stopped and silently caught his breath. She made to push back a thick tangle of vines as she motioned for him to look. He stepped closer, but as he did, he felt something shake his arm. With a sudden jerk, he turned over in his hammock and looked into the desperate face of Aric.

"Beg'n yir pardon, but all han's t' deck."

"What is it?" Bryn asked, sensing the note of urgency in the sailor's voice.

"It's a bad' n! Worse'n I ever seen!" No more needed to be said as they both hastened toward the main deck. The sound of the storm grew as Bryn and Aric climbed up the stairs. Bryn opened the door to the upper deck, and the force of the wind slammed it back and knocked him into Aric. They regained their footing and pushed with both their shoulders against the door. It opened abruptly, and a wave of water hit them in the face. Bryn caught his breath, wiped the stinging salt water from his eyes, and made for the ship's helm.

Aedan, still in the same spot Bryn had left him earlier, was fighting to keep the ship's course. Martin stood beside him, shouting orders into the wind. Lightning flashed across the length of the sky, and Bryn momentarily caught a glimpse of the seas around True North. They crested a wave the size of a small mountain and were heading straight down the other side at breathtaking speed. The lightning lit up the skies like noonday. Each wave seemed to grow in size and looked to be their sure destruction. But Aedan's arm remained strong and the ship's prow cut true and each monstrous wave was hit head on and ridden straight back to the top. Berand took it directly upon himself to join and lead the men responsible for pulling in the sail. In such a storm, those responsible for climbing the rigging to pull in the sail and secure it often never saw the blue sky again. But so far, under Berand's skillful watch, not one sailor had been lost.

Every man not aiding Berand was busy manning the water pumps below deck under Llew's supervision. Llew was not much good up on the main deck with his arm still in a sling. His shoulder had been dislocated during the battle with the sea serpent, and although it was not broken, it would take sometime to mend. So the task of the ship's pumps fell to him.

These pumps were of a unique design, never seen before on the Emerald Isle. Martin had designed them based upon similar pumps he had seen during his travels far to the east early in his life. They were made of a wooden cylinder that sloped downwards into the lower parts of the ship's hull. Inside the cylinder was a screw-shaped piece of wood. When turned, it forced the water up and out the top. Martin had worked the design in such a clever way that the men could turn the screw from the side of the cylinder and the water would be pumped out holes toward the floor of the upper deck.

True North was given eight of these pumps, four on each side. Until this night, they'd found no need to use them. All eight were now in continuous use with the men each taking a shift at the turn levers. Even with all of them in operation, the sheer amount of seawater coming over the rails was beginning to overtake them.

One hour passed into the next, until time became a blur. There was no morning sun to signal the beginning of a new day. Only the darkness of the tempest rent by lightning filled the sky. The crew continued to take shifts manning the pumps and helm. Those who were relieved from duty huddled in a corner below decks, wondering if the next wave would bring their watery grave. The noise was a constant roar broken only by the occasional popping and groaning of the hull. The grinding and relentless crashing of the storm upon True North tore at their nerves for another day and night as it drove the ship before its fury.

And then, as quickly as it had come upon them, the anger of the tempest caved in upon itself and the wind began to sputter and spit before gradually coming to a complete stop.

The driving torrents of rain first softened into a light, soaking downpour and then became an occasional drop here and there. The seas around True North eased back into their normal cadence and rhythm. But the most beautiful thing to the men was the sight of golden sunlight bursting over the eastern horizon, causing several of them to break into spontaneous songs of celebration. Others, simply too exhausted to move, dropped to their knees in thanksgiving. Aedan, Bryn, and Martin stood silently watching the sunrise. The inviting warmth of the golden light brought a soothing, almost dreamlike peace. Every eye looked to the east, soaking in the redemptive light that transformed the dark waters into a deep turquoise. The songs initially begun were now quieted as the men stood silent.

It was Aedan who first pulled himself from the stillness of the moment in order to take count of how they'd weathered the storm. He spotted Berand sitting wearily on a crate below the main mast and called to him. Despite his lack of strength, Berand made a surprisingly quick review of their losses and the damage to their ship. His report was brief, yet covered anything important.

The ship itself proved amazingly resilient and suffered no significant damage. The force of the wind and waves, however, brought significant water into the ship's holds. Although the presence of the pumps most likely kept them afloat, they were unable to keep ahead of the water intake despite being in continual operation throughout the storm. Berand hesitated and cleared his throat before continuing his report. Although most of their food supply could be salvaged, a large portion of the freshwater supply was contaminated by the sea and undrinkable. His voice held no emotion, but the seriousness of the statement was not lost on anyone who heard it.

Aedan quickly called an emergency meeting of the council. They met in the captain's quarters so they could talk more freely. After everyone was seated, Aedan began with a question directly to the point.

"How long will the water last?" he said.

"With rationing, we may stretch it to five or six days." Berand responded with slow deliberation.

There was a quiet moment as the other council members came to grips with the gravity of Berand's answer. They all understood what it meant, and nothing further needed to be said. To any man at sea in unknown waters there are many terrors, but few as practical and understood as running out of fresh water. It was really quite simple. You either find a way to replenish it, or you die from the slow, relentless torment of thirst. When at sea, there were precious few ways to replenish a water supply.

"Martin, what's your best guess as to the nearest land?" Aedan asked.

Martin stood up and walked over to a nearby cupboard. He lifted a latch and opened one of the upper doors. He pulled out an old scroll map, tattered and brown at the edges, brought it back, and began to unroll it on the table. After a brief overview, Martin pointed to a spot on the map. "We were about here, when the storm hit. And I believe we were about one week from an island called Tharrus. But now..." Martin shrugged and tapped his finger on the map. "Now, my best guess says the storm has pushed us some distance to the south." His finger slowly moved to a spot on the map where no landmasses were indicated. "The only real question now is how far we have been pushed off course." Martin finished and sat back down.

"That storm could've easily blown us two weeks to the south. We'll never reach this... this Tharrus, before the water is gone and we are all dead!" Berand spoke in a tone of exasperation.

The table was quiet again. It was Llew who spoke next. "The ocean is filled with unexplored islands. I say we correct our heading and pray that the One who sent us lead us true. We have perhaps a week of rationed water, if we are careful. And who knows, it may rain again. We could try to gather more when it does."

Aedan seized on Llew's optimism. "Good, Llew and Bryn, you organize the men. See what can be done to catch any rainwater we are blessed enough to receive, and Martin will be in charge of rationing our existing water supply." Bryn and Llew left immediately to begin their tasks. Aedan, Martin, and Berand stayed longer in order to consult over what direction would be most hopeful in making landfall and finding fresh water.

Poison

Three more days passed since the storm had contaminated most of their water supply. Despite Bryn and Llew's efforts at hanging out tarps and placing empty barrels on the open deck to catch rainwater, there was not even a cloud in the vast blue sky. The wind, constant until now, all but completely vanished. The brilliant white sails of True North sagged limply. It was as though the fury of the storm had been so complete that all the winds on the sea simply blew themselves out.

When it became apparent the wind would not make their search for land a simple matter, the men were put to the oars. The council, after much deliberation, decided that the best direction was directly west. South would take them too far off course, and north, Martin strongly believed, would find them nothing in time to help their need. So for the last three days, each man aboard True North took his turn at the oars and waited for his ration of water. The sun beat down upon them without mercy, heating the lower decks where the oars were located like an oven. The men were rotated frequently to avoid heat exhaustion.

Bryn was at work on the oars as the sun was setting and slowly disappearing over the western edge of the ocean. He looked out the oar window. The great yellow disk that tortured them unsympathetically all day long was now paying for its arrogance as its heat was doused in the black depths of the distant waters. Bryn sneered at the dying disc and put his muscle into the rowing motion as if to challenge the tyrant of the sky. It was a slow and weakened Renny that tapped him on the shoulder.

"Beg'n yer pard'n sir. I'm feelin up t' me shift now."

"Are you sure?" Bryn replied, feeling loath to pass his seat and burden on to any other.

"You've done two shifts already, and I'm as good's I'll git."

Bryn reluctantly stopped and slowly pulled himself from the hard rowing bench. Every muscle in his body felt numb and useless. He stood and rubbed his arm. Instead of going to his bunk, he climbed the stairs to the main deck. The open air felt good compared to the heat below decks. He glanced up toward the helm where he expected to see Aedan taking on the first watch of the night. There was no movement in the dying light. He decided it would not hurt to check in with his brother and discover what progress they'd made that day. He turned and walked over to the short stairs leading to the helm. It took him much longer to climb them than it had a week ago.

He reached the top and scanned the deck. At first, Bryn did not see anyone. His first impulse was to think it odd Aedan would leave his post without finding a replacement. But before he could puzzle over this for long, a soft, muted groan drew his attention to the deck not far away. The night was coming on fast, and deep dark shadows already covered the deck. Bryn strained his eyes against the encroaching darkness and thought he saw something move.

"Aedan?" A burst of adrenaline pulsed through Bryn's heart as he rushed to his brother. Bending down, he grabbed under Aedan's shoulder and rolled him over into his arms. "What's happened?" Bryn felt a knot tighten in his stomach.

Aedan's eyes flickered open slowly and lethargically. His voice was a distant whisper, but it still carried a carefree attitude. "Bryn, I was just resting my eyes..." He tried to gesture with his hand, but it just fell back to his side. "Musn't let the men see me resting while they...so faithful." Aedan's voice sounded as though he whispered from an ever-increasing distance.

Bryn, who many times before faced the prospect of his own death with unflinching courage, now felt a surge of panic grip and hold in his throat. Aedan was always there for Bryn. It was not that Bryn relied upon his advice, like so many others, or that many words ever even passed between them. But for all of Bryn's life, Aedan was there. He had already lost Kelsi; he could not lose Aedan too. Bryn could feel his brother's life slipping away, and it felt as though his own guts were being wrenched apart again. He turned his head toward the main deck as a cry for help tore from his throat.

It only took a moment for Bryn's alarm to produce results. Aedan was quickly carried into the captain's cabin and laid across the table, where a deeply concerned Martin began his examination. Under the light of a large lantern, he gently cut at the cloth of Aedan's shirt above the right shoulder. He used a small pair of scissors he retrieved from an enclosed shelf located over the captain's desk. After making a complete circuit, the sleeve was gently pulled off of Aedan's arm. The wound from the sea serpent was a ghastly pale color with a black hue at its edges, and it oozed a pungent liquid. Aedan's shoulder was swollen, but instead of looking red and inflamed, it had a strange greenish pallor to it.

Martin quickly put his hand to Aedan's head.

"Is there any fever?" a concerned Berand asked.

"No," Martin answered with growing concern.

"But that must be good, right?" Berand continued, looking for any hopeful sign. Martin stopped and looked into Berand's uncomprehending face and back to Bryn and Llew.

"No fever means no infection, and if there is no infection, there is only one other probable answer for the condition of Aedan's wound." Martin paused, but the others still did not seem to understand the import of his words. "Poison!" he spat as though the word tasted bitter. "The vile sea serpent poisoned him."

"But why has it taken so long to affect him?" Llew asked.

"There are many different types of poisons, Llew. Some act quickly while others are slow in their effect."

Bryn, who was quietly listening to Martin's conclusions, spoke the question they all now thought. "Can it be stopped?" His voice cracked with the emotion he fought down.

Martin looked directly into Bryn's eyes. He could see the pain that was hidden to the others. He looked away before answering. "The beast was ancient and its poison uniquely evil, but we will do all that can be done! With the Lord of heaven's aid, the creature's bite will be overcome." As Martin stopped speaking, he looked back toward Bryn and the others. He knew his attempt to quell their fear had failed. Although his words were spoken with confidence, Martin's eyes betrayed his own misgiving. Without looking away from Bryn, he half-turned toward the others and spoke again. "Berand, there are some medicinal herbs and salves in various sized flasks in my quarters. I need them."

Berand turned on his heel to go, hesitated, and with a nervous inflection in his voice, asked, "Which ones should I bring?"

Martin responded with a tone that was calm enough, but now betrayed an edge of iron. "Bring them all. And Berand, I need them *now.*"

Berand closed his mouth with a new determination and all but ran from the captain's quarters.

Martin turned to Llew. "Get some water and boil it."

The captain's quarters quickly broke into a quiet yet busy commotion. Everything Martin needed was quickly assembled on a table next to where Aedan now lay. True to his task, Berand quickly returned with every flask in Martin's quarters piled into a large leather bag.

Martin deftly began mixing herbs and salves together. He held one bottle up to the lamp's light for proper identification and then replaced it with another. This continued on into the night.

As the others rushed about their tasks, Bryn just stood at Aedan's side and said nothing. The others moved around him without notice. His face betrayed nothing of the anguish that tore at his insides. He would gladly have given his life in pitched battle many times over in exchange for that of his brother. But here was an enemy with which he held no power or sway. He looked into his brother's face and saw the pallor of death begin to grow there. Bryn choked back the bile rising in his throat.

Martin finished mixing the contents of several bottles into a wooden bowl. He moved back to where Aedan's still body lay. He glanced at Bryn and noticed his ashen face. Turning his head to the far side of the room, he spoke over his shoulder. "Llew, bring the water."

Martin proceeded to thoroughly clean Aedan's wound. After another brief examination, he produced a small, thin knife and began to reopen the wound in various places. The lack of reaction from Aedan worried those who watched. There should have been pain, a lot of it. A black liquid began to ooze from the incisions. Llew aided Martin in keeping the wound clean as he continued to probe and make new cuts. This process continued for some time before Martin reached for the wooden bowl. He carefully applied a thick coating of the paste to the entire surface of the wound and around its perimeter. Lastly, after Martin was satisfied that all was done that could be done, a bandage was applied. The affects of the ointment were almost immediately visible. The strange pallor in Aedan's face lessened as a hint of color arose.

Martin spoke with a tired voice. "Bryn, Llew, we will need to watch him, and that bandage should be changed with a fresh one applied every couple of hours. Unfortunately, I have only enough supplies to make a few more bowls of the healing ointment."

Bryn, for the first time since Martin began talking, quickly looked directly into Martin's eyes. "How long until it runs out?" he asked.

"About midday tomorrow."

"Can it be replenished?" Llew asked.

"Of course... if we find land. All the plants, thank the One God, are quite common."

Without saying another word, Bryn turned toward the door and walked out. The rowing had come to a complete stop when Aedan was discovered and the crew alerted by Bryn's cry for help. Most of the men stood idle here and there across the deck in small groups, waiting for some word of their beloved captain. Not too few of them, including Rand, were waiting directly outside the door to the captain's quarters.

The moon was full, and its light reflected brightly off the ocean's surface. The night air was still, and True North's sails still hung lifeless. Bryn paused, looking into the men's faces that stood waiting, and then walked directly to the stairs and down to the oars. He abruptly sat down and began straining against the heavy oar. It was dark beneath decks, but lanterns provided just enough light to see by. Bryn's muscles burned with exhaustion, and his face broke out with sweat. Rand and several of his warriors were the first to join him.

"C'mon then!" Rand shouted to the others. In a few moments, the oars were slicing through the dark waters and True North was gliding across the placid western sea at a very respectable speed. The sailor named Renny put his hand on Bryn's shoulder.

"Begin yer pardon, but we need a navigator." Renny pointed upward.

Bryn hesitated. He could feel the men's concern. He had already worked at the oars longer than any one should in this heat and with little water. He never liked the idea of quitting anything. But he could already feel a lightheadedness setting in and knew he would shortly be more hindrance than help. Bryn nodded and gave up his seat. There was little to do as navigator. Their heading was a nonspecific westward direction, and the stars shone bright in the cloudless night sky. Anyone of the men could have easily maintained their present course under such conditions. Bryn, despite his growing exhaustion, forced his eyes to search the western horizon for land. If by some act of sheer will he could make land appear, they would have found a continent by now. Yet all that met his unrelenting gaze was the calm, dark waters.

A couple of hours into the second watch of the night, a bedraggled Llew approached Bryn.

"I've had some rest now. Let me take the helm," Llew said.

Bryn looked at him and then silently returned his gaze toward the sea.

"I know we must find land, but you cannot make it happen all alone. The Lord of heaven directs our course. He will be our help!" Llew urged.

Bryn looked skyward for a moment and then returned to his vigil.

Llew's frustration began to grow with his stubborn brother. "Do you hope to save Aedan by achieving your own pointless death?" he blurted out with growing impatience.

Bryn snapped his head back toward Llew. "If need be!" His eyes flashed with anger.

Llew could see the pain behind the anger in his brother's eyes. He softened somewhat. "Bryn"—he paused—"and when we find land, what then? Will you have the strength to help us search for what we need? What help will you be then?"

Bryn stubbornly turned his back to his younger brother. But Llew's words were true, and Bryn knew it. He looked down, and his body slumped slightly as he softly exhaled. "You are right, of course," he said apologetically. And then with more conviction, he turned, looked Llew directly in the eyes, and took hold of his forearm. "You will let me know the moment land is sighted?"

"I will!" Llew said resolutely.

The quarters below deck were humid, and the air was dank and close. Bryn paused briefly as he entered his room. He was sick of being locked away within the confines of the ship. A feeling of imminent failure mixed with despair warred at him as he let his eyes wander over the interior contents of the room. His gaze fell upon the journal he was keeping. He walked over to it, reached down and opened the book to his last entry.

"The storm has spoiled much of our fresh water supply. We will seek heaven's provision and do whatever else we can, but if the wind does not come..."

His last entry left off without completing the thought that now became Aedan's doom. If the wind did not come, they would not find land in time to save him. In truth, they would not any of them be saved.

True North was the greatest ship Bryn ever had the pleasure of sailing on. She was larger and could move faster with less effort than any other vessel he'd ever heard of. Her every movement was graceful. It was a thing of beauty to behold. A year ago he would have paid any cost for a chance to sail upon such a ship as this. She was a true Empress of the Sea. Now, he just longed for solid ground under his feet and the wind on his face. Without wind, a ship on the seas becomes little more than a prison.

Bryn moved slowly across the small room and sat down on the edge of his bunk. With his elbows planted on his upper legs, he let his head drop into his open hands. Despair began to grow until it was a thing to be felt, a darkness that grasped into Bryn's soul. Combined with the heat, dehydration, and exhaustion, this new attack began to steal what inward strength Bryn still possessed. He softly groaned as the torment of fear began to grow. Bryn was not like other men. He did not suffer from fear. He always just pushed his way through. But now, there was no way through, and it was his brother that would be lost.

He fought to keep the deep emotions at bay, but the weight of the darkness only increased, and he began feeling as though his insides were being ripped apart. He coughed back bile as it rose into the back of his throat. His heart pounded as though he fled from a hound of hell. A cry burst from between his clenched teeth.

"Lord of heaven! Help me!"

It was the first time he ever called upon another for help. The despair in his own voice surprised Bryn. His pounding heart slowed somewhat, and the air felt a little lighter. He collapsed back onto his bunk, and blessed sleep began to wash over his torment. As he faded, Bryn vaguely recalled hearing a quiet voice whisper in his ear, "All that trust in their own strength will fail."

Follow Argolis

Bryn awoke with a start to the cry of a great eagle. Gone were the walls of his quarters aboard ship. Instead, he lay on what felt like wet sand. And instead of the beating rays of a hot sun, soft refreshing droplets of rain moistened his dry face. It was full day, but the sun was softened by large, puffy, white clouds. A few of the clouds were dark enough to carry the blessed moisture that now renewed his strength. Bryn looked up and noticed the shape of a bird flying high above him.

He slowly stood to his feet and looked around, realizing he was apparently on some secluded beach. True North was no where in sight, but it was the sound of running water that caught his immediate attention. Bryn turned sharply to his right. There, about a stone's throw away, was a bubbling brook running down to the sea out of the jungle tree line of what he now presumed was an island.

Without thinking about the strangeness of his situation, he turned and ran to the stream. Upon reaching it, he splashed in and fell to his knees and began gulping in the sweet-tasting liquid. He had never tasted such delightful water. Strength and energy flowed back into his beleaguered body. He lay down in the stream and let the healing water wash over him. After a few wonderful moments, he sat back up, wiped the water from his face, and looked toward the jungle. Perched on a branch at the edge of the tree line next to where the stream emerged was the great bird that had soared overhead moments before.

Bryn stood and slowly walked toward the tree. When he reached the place, he could see the feathered creature was, in fact, an eagle. The great bird looked at him for a moment, then turned its head and flew back into the upper branches of the jungle canopy. Bryn watched for a moment. A strange sense that he should follow tugged at his senses.

He slowly began pushing back the jungle growth, stepping over broken branches as he went. Progress through the confused tangle of vines and undergrowth was difficult. After a few minutes, Bryn paused to peer at the canopy high above. He could not find the eagle. His eyes scanned the tall trees. Bright shafts of light broke through the upper branches and pierced the cover below, looking more like great spears of flame than sunshine. Although dark shadows enveloped much of the jungle, small islands of green shone wherever the spears of flaming light fell.

Bryn followed the bubbling sound of the stream as closely as the thick undergrowth allowed. Water dripped in a steady shower from the high branches as the rain continued to fall far above him. A foggy vapor rose sparsely in patches all about the hot jungle floor. Somewhere ahead, an eagle's cry sounded in the muted air. It seemed to Bryn as though the sound came from another world, piercing the veil into his own. He turned his head and looked to his left. Not more than ten feet away stood the young woman from his earlier dream. She wore a long, pale yellow mantle. The locks of her hair shimmered golden in one of the shafts of light that fell upon her. Bryn stood still, afraid if he moved she would disappear.

"Who are you?" he asked.

She did not respond. He tried again.

"What is this place?" He waved his hand about him.

The mysterious girl just looked back at him in silence. There was no fear in her face, nor any caution. If anything, her face wore an expression of curiosity. After what seemed much too long, she spoke.

"What is it you fear?"

Her voice did not hold any accusation, but rather genuine sympathy. The question unsettled Bryn, and he lowered his eyes to the ground. He could not bring himself to open his heart. Instead, he looked around briefly and then back to his visitor. For the first time, he considered the strangeness of his circumstances.

"This is a dream, isn't it," Bryn concluded softly. The eagle's cry sounded again from somewhere above them. The young woman tilted her head up as though she listened to someone speaking. She looked back at Bryn.

"You must follow Argolis," she spoke as though answering an unspoken question, and turning abruptly, disappeared into the thick undergrowth. Bryn quickly looked after her.

"But wait! What does that mean?" He half-ran through the dense jungle toward the spot where she'd aptly disappeared. There was no sign of her. She had simply vanished, leaving no sign she was ever there.

Bryn turned quickly in the opposite direction and yelled. "Who is Argolis?" In his frustration, he took three large strides in the direction she had disappeared. The ground gave way, and he lost his footing. He grasped at the plants and roots all about him in a panicked attempt to stop his fall. He slid with ever-increasing speed toward an edge now only a few paces away. His fingers dug and scraped into the slick spongy turf, but nothing slowed him down. A heartbeat later, Bryn was falling through open air with a feeling of vast openness all about him.

He awoke with a sudden upright jerk only to find himself back in his bunk aboard True North. The air below deck was still stale and stifling. He listened for a moment. Everything was just the same as when he first laid down. His mind raced back to what he now knew must have been a dream. *It had been so real*, he thought. Strangely enough, he felt completely renewed in his strength. His thirst, which became a constant companion, was gone. He slowly moved to the side of his bunk to collect his thoughts.

Follow Argolis. That was what she said. *But who is Argolis?*

Bryn's thoughts were confused. He rose from his bed and slowly made his way back to the open air of the main deck. The sun was already beginning its climb up the eastern horizon. The heat was also increasing. Bryn looked up at the great white sails, only to have what he already knew to be true confirmed. There was no wind. He located Llew and Berand in a discussion at the helm and walked toward them.

"Bryn! You look as though your sleep has done you well," Llew answered. Berand and Llew, on the other hand, looked just like the rest of the crew, bedraggled and worn thin.

"Has there been any word on Aedan?" Bryn asked.

"No change," Berand answered, who had just come from the captain's quarters and was about to relieve Llew as navigator. Without further comment, Bryn turned toward the stairs and the oars beneath deck. He replaced one of the men who looked like he would fall over at any moment. Bryn's muscles felt good as he pushed at the great wooden oar. The ship's progress had slowed considerably from the night before. The men were simply at the end of their strength.

As the sun rose higher in the sky, the heat continued to climb. Somewhat before midday, the men at the oars began giving into exhaustion. One by one, they stopped rowing. Bryn saw the futility of continuing at the oars. A few of the men had collapsed onto the floor. Others still sat at their oar, but they stopped trying to move it. Bryn, being the only one aboard who now possessed any strength, stood and walked back up to the open deck. He paused and then knelt down in supplication to heaven. He did not cry out loud. There was no waving of arms and hands. He just bowed his head and silently began to seek the One God's mercy. As he knelt, all his heart poured out in earnest prayer.

If any help would come, it must now come from above. Their strength had failed them. Bryn knew that the condition of the men would not improve without help. The water supply might keep them alive a short while longer, but it would not renew their strength. There simply was not enough left. His father had once told him that it was a king's duty to provide for his people, but it was also his right to determine how to provide.

The Lord whose help he now sought was also a king. In fact, his father called him the King of all kings. This great King created the very sovereignty that upheld all true kings. He would provide a way where there was none.

Bryn's knees began to burn. He heard movement from somewhere behind him. He shifted his position somewhat and glanced to his left. Those men still strong enough to move about had joined him on their knees. His heart surged with the sight as he renewed his vigil.

"Great King of heaven!" he prayed out loud. "We are your servants. We seek your help that we might do your will. Only show us the way."

Silence met Bryn's petition. Time dragged on without any sign of deliverance. The sun now reached the top of its unrelenting arc. Many of the men slumped to their hands or simply fell to their faces. Bryn was about to abandon his vigil in order to provide a ration of water to those not strong enough to rise, when the cry of an eagle drew his attention to his right. Martin's feathered companion alighted onto his perching post. He looked right at Bryn as if to draw his attention. Bryn almost looked away before he noticed something hanging from the bird's beak. He looked closer. There was something slender and greenish protruding from each side of its beak. He slowly stood and walked closer.

"Hello, my friend. Where have you been?" Bryn spoke softly. He was not at all sure that the eagle would let him get much closer. He took another couple of steps. The eagle looked at him and waited. Bryn was relieved when he finally reached the bird without it choosing to simply fly away.

"What's this you have?" Bryn asked, slowly extending his hand palm upward. The eagle hesitated a moment, dropped his head down toward Bryn's hand, and deftly dropped its mysterious cargo. Bryn examined the object.

"It's a small branch!" he spoke with quiet excitement. It had several green, leafy protrusions to show that it had been growing until very recently. Bryn looked back over his shoulder and yelled to Berand who was still at the helm. The eagle, with a flurry and rush of wings, lifted off into the blue skies above True North. Bryn quickly turned back to follow the great bird with his eyes. When he had fixed its position and direction of flight, he turned and ran back to the helm.

Berand looked at Bryn with a tired but questioning look as he took the stairs three steps at a time.

"Berand! We must follow Martin's eagle."

"Follow the eagle?" the puzzled navigator questioned.

"Yes, look at this." Bryn jutted out his palm with the twig in it. Berand took a moment to wearily look at the object. As its significance dawned on him, his eyes widened and a small smile broke across his features. With his newly found excitement, Berand's strength was briskly renewed.

"Look alert, you men on deck below!" Berand shouted through cupped hands. He then reached over to the signal bell and began to vigorously ring the alarm for all hands to deck. The signal took some time to produce the desired results. The men, weak and lethargic, began looking toward Berand. Those below decks took a moment longer to begin stumbling out onto the open deck, Llew and Rand being among them.

Once the men had formed somewhat of an assembly, Bryn held out his hands and spoke with a loud voice. "Men, Martin's eagle has found land!" It took a moment more for the significance of his pronouncement to sink in.

"Did 'e say lan'?" one of the crewmen croaked.

For more emphasis, Bryn held out the small branch. Hope slowly began to seep back into the men's expressions. There was a rush of excited statements and questions. Bryn once again held up his hands to gain their attention.

"But without the wind, we must gather our strength for one more push at the oars."

Several men groaned, but the choice between death and life was evident to all.

Llew's once golden voice, now hoarse, cracked as he spoke. "Where is the eagle now?"

"He flew off to the southeast," Bryn replied.

The men moved to the rail's edge with surprising speed, searching for land. The ocean waters stretched on as far as the eye could see. Before disappointment could steal their new strength, Bryn called them back. He let each one of them handle the small branch. It was evidence enough to convince most of the men that their hope was not misplaced. Llew urged them to follow him to the oars. Under their new bearing, with Berand at the helm, True North slowly began moving south by southeast.

Despite their new hope, the men would not last long at the oars without some change in the weather. The heat's intensity only worsened as the men tried to find untapped hidden strength from somewhere deep inside. Bryn made his way to the captain's quarters to check on Martin and Aedan. In his excitement at discovering this new hope, he almost hadn't noticed Martin's absence. Bryn knocked softly on the cabin door, opened it, and entered. After the brilliance outside, it took several moments before his eyes adjusted to the dim light within. There was as light stirring in the corner. He squinted his eyes and could just make out Martin sitting in a chair.

"Martin, it's Bryn," he said softly. There was no response. "Martin, is all well?"

Still there was no answer. Bryn moved toward the table and found the lantern. He lit it and held the lantern toward where Aedan lay on his bunk. There appeared to be no change. Aedan's breath was low, but even.

"I have failed," a shadowed Martin spoke.

Bryn turned toward the unmoving figure still sitting in the chair. "He looks to be the same...there is still hope," Bryn encouraged.

Martin seemed not to listen, but continued on speaking. "It is only a matter of time now. Without the wind and land, I have led you all to your death." The gloom in Martin's voice could be felt as well as heard.

"Did you not hear the news?" Bryn asked. "Your bird has brought us hope in the form of a small twig! With the help of your healing salve, Aedan will make it until we find land and then—"

"And what then!" Martin snapped. "The salve only delays the poison, it does not heal." Martin's tone was filled with exasperation. "All I do is delay the inevitable and even that has come to an end. The salve is gone. It is all gone, and Aedan will die because of me!"

Martin was defeated, but Bryn did not believe Aedan was the true source of his struggle. As serious as it was, Martin knew the salve would run out from the very beginning. And although Aedan's condition was bad, it had not worsened from what Bryn could tell. In truth, Martin's gloom had been building for many days.

"Martin, what is it? What else is bothering you?" Martin did not answer, but only continued to sit in his darkened corner. When it became obvious he would not be of any help, Bryn turned to leave the room. He hesitated for a moment and then placed the small branch on the table before turning once more for the door.

Martin continued unmoved for some time before turning to examine the item Bryn had left for him. He slowly reached to pick it up, but he stopped as he got a better look at it. His heart started to beat faster. There was something about this twig. Martin searched his memory. The woody part of the small branch had a reddish hue. Its few leaves were small, round, and green. There was a cluster of tiny, blue-colored berries protruding from under one of the leaves. Martin gently lifted it up and turned it around under his scrutiny.

"Could it be?" he wondered out loud.

At that moment, an excited shout could be heard coming through the open window facing the deck. "The wind!"

Search for the Garden

Malen sat at a table in his private chambers. A manuscript lay open in front of him. Its extreme age was obvious by the tattered edges and yellowed brown color of its pages. A stack of new vellum sheets sat on the table next to the ancient book. Malen's eyes were shut. Anyone seeing him might have presumed him asleep if not for the rhythmic tapping of his right forefinger on the stack of newly pressed pages.

He opened his eyes and stood abruptly. His chair slid backward a small distance, and he quickly strode to the other side of the chamber where stood a tall dark oak bookshelf. His eyes scanned the numerous volumes until they came to rest on a large black book with gold-colored binding. Malen reached out with his left hand and pulled it from the shelf. In golden ink lettering across the front, it read "A History of the Tharusians."

He crossed back to his chair and sat down. Many other books sat in various piles across the remaining part of the table. They were all in some way concerned with Tharrus, the island kingdom neighboring Illyrium. It was not until many years after his and Pharigant's first translation of the Book of Knowledge that Malen discovered a mistake. A small mistake, yes, but one that shaped every minute of every day since its discovery.

The fragmented Book of Knowledge spoke of the Garden of the Aletae. Many of the references, unfortunately, were partially broken off or unreadable due to the book's deteriorated condition. The raw excitement Malen originally felt at discovering the dark paths of the Aletae and the ice thorn carried him for many years. Eventually, his initial success began to cloud with the frustrations of being unable to discover more. Although he already knew more than any other mortal now alive, the realization that there was more just outside his reach gnawed at him.

It was just over a year ago that, quite by accident, Malen stumbled upon a key to perhaps the greatest mystery presented by the Book of Knowledge, the very location of the Garden of the Aletae. He was reading an account of the kings of Illyrium. His interest piqued when coming to the story of his grandfather, King Tathin. As the story went, King Tathin was an old man on his deathbed when a miracle was performed and he was healed. Malen recalled hearing something of the tale as a youth, but had never given it much thought, until now. After all, he was no longer a young man by any standard. Of course, he was still faster and stronger than most, but of late he felt his strength and energy lessen. What does all the knowledge and power profit you after death? Unless...? He was not even sure what it was he sought at first.

Malen, after a feverish search, finally found a resource that recounted the miracle of Tathin's healing in more detail. It was, however, not at all what Malen had expected to find. There was really very little to it. To Malen, nevertheless, it was the beginning of the solution and the rekindling of his vision of vast and limitless power. After reciting the story of the aged king's exploits, the account ended with a brief yet intriguing conclusion. The final entry stated,

Almost gone were the days of the king, when came there a man of Tharrus with the power of the life plant and raised him up to the golden years.

The clear reference to the "power of the life plant" was the first thing that caught Malen's attention. His and Pharigant's translation of the Book of Knowledge contained a reference to the "power of the *plant's life*." They took this statement as merely a reference to the resilience of the garden's plants. This new and independent reference, however, gave Malen another view on the content of the Book of Knowledge. It did not say "the power of the plant's life"; rather, it said, "the power of the life plant, or *plant of life*." So there it was. If he could find the Garden of the Aletae, he would find a plant with the key to eternal life.

At first, the realization that he still did not know how to find the garden's location bore down on him like a crushing weight, until his attention focused back on the scant reference to King Tathin's healing.

"When came there a man of *Tharrus*..." It was to this final clue that he desperately clung over the past year. He poured over every resource he could find concerning Tharrus. He devoured each text as though it was a banquet set before him, until he found the link.

There was a "man of Tharrus" who was reputed to have the power to heal, so the records revealed. But he was really no man of Tharrus at all. He was, in fact, altogether foreign to Tharrus until he made it his home later in life. The shock to Malen was the man had not died that many years ago. But where was he actually from, this man of Tharrus who had the power of the life plant? Several of the historical references placed his origin in a place referred to simply as "Atala," which translated into "the White Isle," a place Malen had never heard of.

It had been just a few months ago that Malen, thinking he'd run into another dead end, found the next link in his chain. After receiving a shipment of old manuscripts from his source on Tharrus, he discovered another reference to the White Isle. The resource was also a fragment of extreme age. Very little could be deduced of its origin. It's content, however, was all that interested Malen. It described a stone map with the location of Atala, which appeared to be located somewhere beneath King Peleg's palace on Tharrus.

King Peleg, who never liked Malen and certainly did not trust him, would never give him the kind of access he would need to discover the stone map. The solution was really quite simple. Peleg would need to be removed. All the small kings would serve him eventually anyway. So, Lanthir was unleashed. Even now, Malen awaited word of the successful conquest. He wanted to make sure all was ready the moment word came. So he spent every waking moment pouring over his resources. He now knew more of the history of Tharrus than any Tharusian currently living.

There came a soft knock at the door to his chambers.

"Enter, Lisnor," he commanded.

Malen projected his voice by the secret arts he discovered. It was really nothing compared to his other powers, but it helped to keep his servants awestruck. Lisnor was a different type of servant. Lanthir, whose skill with weaponry was needed for its obvious uses, was loyal only to his own notions of honor. Lisnor, on the other hand, was selected for his level of devotion. He didn't just serve Malen; he worshiped him.

It was not long after Malen's discovery of the dark paths and the ice thorn that he decided to replace his prize pupil, Pharigant. The problem was, no one person possessed all the weaponry skills combined with the mental prowess that so defined Pharigant. Malen's answer to the problem was to divide out the necessary skills. Lanthir would serve as his puppet champion, while Lisnor would become his new pupil. In some ways, Lisnor was actually better for Malen's plans than Pharigant would have been. Perhaps Pharigant was *too* talented. Yes, Malen was forced to consider that his prized pupil may very well have had the potential to best the teacher. Lisnor, on the other hand, was religiously devoted to Malen, not to his own search for knowledge.

Over the last few years, Malen began a new type of training program. He personally selected those individuals who could be transformed into a sort of order of devout zealots. The only real difference being that he, Malen, was the object of their worship and devotion. He called this new order "The Lawless." It was a title that reinforced a notion that the general laws and morality of society did not apply to them. They had but one law. If followed, it exempted them from all others. That one law was obedience to Malen. As a special mandate, the members of their order were made guardians of the Ice Thorn. Although it really needed no protection, the close proximity to the thorn kept the members of the Lawless easily led by their leader.

Lisnor opened the wooden door and entered Malen's chambers with his head bowed low. A wicked-looking, self-inflicted scar stretched from his left eye upward across his forehead. It gave his face a twisted, menacing look.

"Word has come?" Malen asked.

"Yes, my lord. Your armies have defeated the Tharusian rabble." Lisnor's voice carried no emotion as he spoke. "Your ship awaits in the harbor."

"Good. Make ready to leave within the hour. I will require you and five other members of the Lawless to accompany me." Malen never looked up from the volume in front of him. Lisnor turned and left the room without further reply. Malen finished writing the last entry onto the new vellum sheets bound in leather casing. He looked back to the volume on the history of Tharrus and cast it aside onto one of the discarded piles of resources. He reread the last entry in his compilation of clues.

Beware the northern forest reach, where in the darkness daunting death sleeps.
In Escalon's ancient prison hole, ancient demons there we keep.
The emerald amulet holds at bay, those unholy dogs of the Aletae.

The short rhythmic verse came under the subtitle of something called the Sargaroth. Malen held the lyric in his thoughts a moment longer, then closed the leather bound pages and placed them in his satchel.

Wandering the Forest

Valentus was nearly out of breath and strength when he finally emerged from the forest that flanked the hills of Perginton, the chief city of Tharrus. He leaned forward on his shepherd's staff, stopping momentarily to rest. This was his first clear view of the sky in more than two days. The sun had nearly completed its arc toward the western horizon. Not much daylight was left.

For nearly a week, Valentus climbed hills, crossed fields, and pressed through tangled forests. There were roads that would have been easier to travel, but they wound around to the west before turning north to Perginton. With the use of a horse, the road would have been far more preferable. Valentus, nevertheless, had no horse and so decided on the more direct route across country.

The paths he found at first were relatively easy to see and walk upon. But all too soon, they became faint and over grown, eventually disappearing altogether. Valentus chastised himself many times for not choosing the easier road. The last two days were the worst of all as he stumbled through brambles and thickets so dense he wondered whether he would ever make it out the other side. When he finally broke through the last group of thorns and looked up to see the light streaming through the edge of the forest, a deep sense of relief washed over him.

The sleeves and leggings of his already well-worn clothes were now torn and tattered. His arms and legs were scratched and bleeding. Finally free of the forest, he raised a weary hand to shield his eyes from the direct light of the setting sun. Hills covered the landscape to the west as far as he could see. His food was gone, and the ache of hunger that awakened him early that morning now became constant. He reached up and wiped the sweat from his brow. Much to his excitement, directly to the north rose the walls of Perginton. There was another ridge that blocked most of the view, yet the towering heights of the city could just be made out in the distance. The sight of his destination had a wonderfully renewing effect on his strength.

One full day from the time he first stumbled upon the invaders, Valentus reached his uncle's estate. Much to his surprise, his uncle, cousins, and all male servants of fighting age had already been summoned to Perginton. Apparently, a warning was already raised. The women remaining behind were practically buzzing with the horrible excitement of it all. Valentus was puzzled. He was sure no one else would have discovered the invasion in such a remote region.

A surge of disappointment quickly replaced his earlier thoughts of heroism. As usual, the important events of life simply passed him by. He felt cheated. Not only was he not the one to deliver the important news, he was also left behind. He was of fighting age, after all, and it was just as much his right to be called to battle. The injustice of having his one chance for glory cruelly taken away crushed Valentus. To add to his misery, not one able horse was left. They took them all.

His first instinct was to return to his flocks and the lonely hills where he could simmer in humiliation. It was the life he knew, and despite the monotony, there was always comfort in the familiar. But after packing a few supplies, he felt something strange rising up in him. A sense of determination like nothing he'd ever felt before overtook him. Should he allow himself to be left out again?

As he considered this question, it also occurred to him that maybe he had been left behind by accident. After all, the news must have come as quite a shock to his uncle. They would not have had time to consider Valentus. Yes, he felt sure his uncle would want him to join their efforts in defending Tharrus as soon as possible.

Valentus made his provisions ready and then climbed a nearby hill. He looked to the south where he knew his flocks grazed and then back to the north. There was a moment when he was unable to start upon the path. All that he knew was behind and only the unknown lay ahead.

Now, as Valentus stood at the edge of the forest and looked upon the towers of Perginton in the distance, all the doubts that had plagued his decision at first were banished. In his mind's eye, he envisioned the glorious reception he would receive from his uncle and cousins. There would be glad greetings all around. He would be slapped on the back and given a warrior's welcome and perhaps a meal. Thoughts of food made his stomach ache.

Then, in a flash of horrible reality, he wondered whether anyone would really care at all that he came. Or even worse, perhaps be angry with him for leaving his duties. He would not be able to bear the further humiliation of being told to return to his uncle's flocks. He fought down his doubts and began the final leg of his journey. He walked another ten feet, climbing the gradual slope before him. A shadow passed overhead. He looked up to see a large bird fly high above. He paused a moment as several more passed by.

Valentus continued on. Something began to war at his sense of order. He glanced around, trying to find what was out of place. The wind was gusting from the south and pushed past Valentus as it whipped up the slope. The uneasy feeling that assailed him began to grow. At first he could not discover the source of the misgiving, until it finally occurred to him. A sound was growing in the background of his hearing.

At first, he had not noticed it, but now, in between the sound of the gusting wind, he could hear a confusion of noises. It grew as he climbed closer to the crest of the rise. Valentus felt apprehensive without quite knowing why. His pace slowed as he neared the top. The sound became a din of cackles and squawking. He reached the crest and blinked at the sun, which was now lower on the horizon. Its rays still shone over the ridge to the west of the city, hitting Valentus directly in the eyes.

The plain below Perginton was situated in a way that covered it in a deep shadow. The dark plain looked as though it moved in some sort of strange cadence. Valentus strained his eyes to focus on the scene as he began the descent.

The sun's rays finally dropped behind the western hills, and the wind all but vanished. It was the smell that first and suddenly attacked his senses. He had plenty of experience with the butchering of animals and knew the smell well. It was the stench of blood that came to him with the disappearance of the wind.

His eyes began to adjust to the shadowed plain around him. The realization of what he was looking at washed over Valentus in a wave of panic. Dead bodies littered the valley floor in every direction. It looked as though an army had been slaughtered. The dead lay where they had fallen. Men and horses stretched in their unnatural poses of death. The strange sound and motion Valentus first noticed was produced by a large number of carrion birds that now danced to their grisly feast. Valentus turned and stumbled over his own feet, falling in his panicked rush to escape the hellish scene before him. He vomited several times over the ground. Gaining his feet once more, he turned and fled back over the hill he had just climbed. He ran until his lungs burned with the exertion. He reached the edge of the forest and continued his headlong flight into the heart of the wood. Brambles tore anew at his flesh as complete darkness descended. He ran until he could run no longer then collapsed and slept where he dropped.

Without a fire, the night chill made it difficult to sleep. Valentus eventually was able to burrow under enough of the leaves blanketing the forest floor to gain sufficient warmth. Although he slept, recurring scenes of horrid death and birds with gaping maws dripping with blood tortured his dreams.

The day was already well underway by the time Valentus awoke with a startled cry. He looked in every direction, expecting the ghosts that so haunted his dreams to materialize now in the daylight. The vivid memory of what he'd witnessed brought tears to his eyes as he tried to choke back his erupting emotions. Despite his best efforts, Valentus broke down and wept.

Sometime later, he began to wander deeper into the forest. He had no specific direction other than away from the horrors behind him. The trees grew thick and tall. Many of them were draped in garments of moss and vines. The forest floor became more broken. Hills and ravines of various sizes gave it a wild and tangled look. Valentus walked for most of the morning until he came to a brook that wound around the base of a small knoll. It was here he first considered it would not do to simply wander this forest forever.

Two days had passed since he'd eaten anything close to an actual meal. He was used to foraging in the wild and knew he could find wild berries and roots here and there to pacify his angry stomach. It would not be long, though, until something more substantial would be needed. He sat down on the spongy turf at the edge of the bubbling brook and let his mind go back to what he had witnessed at Perginton.

What had happened? If they were warned, how could the destruction have been so complete? He could only guess. There was now, most assuredly, no reason to continue his mission. He reached down and removed his leather shoes and let his feet dip into the refreshing cool water. He supposed there really was only one course left to him. He would go back to his uncle's estate and await their return.

Their return... He now considered the possibility that his uncle and cousins may not come back at all. What then? What would be left for him? For the first time in his life, he feared the loss of his stable little world. It may have been lonely and terribly boring, but it was secure. It was all he had ever known, and now that all his foolish dreams of heroism and glory were shattered, he longed to return home.

It occurred to him then. Why not return anyway? Even if his uncle's estate were owned and run by someone else, they would still need a shepherd. The most obvious choice would be someone who already knew the flocks and where best to graze them. Besides, it was most likely at least one of his relatives would return.

It did not take long to decide upon the only course Valentus now considered open to him. He dried his feet, put his shoes back on, and stood up. Until now he had paid little attention to his direction. He made a quick survey of the surrounding forest. From where he was standing he could see that the brook ran out of a small valley enclosed by several hills and ridges. He glanced upward to see if the sun could be located. The towering trees blocked any direct view. Instead, the diffused light poured through the leafy bower to produce a muted illumination of the ancient forest.

The valley, he guessed, ran somewhat to the southeast. Following the stream would provide the advantage of a ready source of fresh water. And in any case, the sounds of the tumbling water did tend to put Valentus more at ease. With a new determination, he began walking again.

He followed the brook as it wound in a gentle arc across the forest floor. Moss carpeted its overhanging banks and the rocks that littered its bed. If it had not been for the events that led him to this place, he could have marveled at its beauty. The moss, appearing everywhere, was a brilliant, almost fluorescent green. The brook rolled gently over its smoothed stones in a singular fluid motion. It had the look of an ancient forest where the veil between myth and reality became thin. As he walked, he envisioned a world of fantastical creatures: fairies dancing by moonlight and trees that would awake to walk the forest paths. He had heard of such things as a young boy and always fancied they could be true.

The day progressed toward evening, and the air became cooler. A fog began to rise and swirl around the water currents. Valentus turned his thoughts toward finding some place to bed down for the night. He followed the stream until it ended in a small dell snuggled between three sharp slopes. At the other end, a waterfall poured over a smooth rock ledge and dropped into a pool. This looked as good a spot as any to spend the night. He looked around for anything that could be used for a makeshift shelter. Not far away from the pool lay a tree that had fallen in some recent storm. The mossy turf was uprooted with the tree providing somewhat of an enclosure.

Dusk was quickly turning to darkness by the time Valentus had made a small, cheerful fire to fend off the night chill. There was plentiful dry wood in the forest, and it took little effort to gather enough to last the entire night. He always carried a flint fire starter in a small leather pouch tied to his belt, and he was glad for it now. The mossy ground of the dell provided a soft if lumpy bed of sorts. He sat next to the fire and held his arms around his stomach, trying not to think of his growing hunger. The night grew darker, and a fitful breeze caused the flickering fire to cast eerie dancing shadows across the sides of the hills and trees. Valentus built up the fire and wrapped himself in a small blanket he always carried.

He often lamented the lonely nights spent tending his flocks, but the loneliness of those times could not compare with what he now felt. He was truly alone and deep in the heart of an unknown forest. At least the sheep and goats provided some companionship. He would frequently talk to them and often felt as though they actually understood what he said.

The sounds of the night had never bothered him before this night. The breeze that played with his fire was not enough to visibly move the trees. Instead, it made their branches imperceptibly rub together with just enough strength to cause awful creaking and squeaking sounds. The continual sound of the small waterfall was just enough to mute all other sounds, making them harder to recognize. Valentus furtively glanced from one side of the dell to the other. The earlier beauty of the place had been subtly replaced with the sense that it was haunted. Somewhere, a night bird sounded its displeasure over his unwanted presence. He pulled himself a little closer to the turf-covered roots of the fallen tree and closed his eyes.

The night passed slowly, and Valentus woke early the next morning. The fire had burned down to gray ash. He considered restarting it, but there was really very little reason to do so. After all, he had no food to cook, and the warmth of the day was already removing the night chill. He looked around the glade for any sign of food that could be gathered. There were no berries to be seen. He did find a few mushrooms growing near the other end of the fallen tree, but they were not of any variety he recognized. He knew enough never to eat a mushroom he could not readily identify. For now, he would continue to hunger.

It only took him a few moments to make ready to move on. In order to climb out of the dell, he would have to cross the brook. He picked a likely spot and waded in. The water was cold against his skin and made him hurry his pace. He quickly reached the other side. Climbing out, he paused briefly to examine the ridge surrounding the small dell. It was steep but could be climbed without much caution. He found a small animal trail that opened at its base and followed it. Various animals must have used this trail for ages to reach the pool. The footing was solid, and Valentus was able to reach the top easily enough.

He stopped to look back over the glade. Its mysterious beauty and allure returned with the light of day. Gone were the dancing shadows and whispered threats of the night. He realized he actually regretted leaving this place.

He turned and began walking away when he glimpsed something off to his left. There, imprinted into the ground by a small stump, was the impression of a boot heel. The moss that covered the stump was torn and smudged as though it had been sat on. Valentus looked back toward his camp and realized with a shock that someone had been watching him. He continued to search the area and found several more tracks leading away to the northwest.

Thoughts of horrible, wild men with long, scraggly hair wearing animal hides and carrying wicked, rusty knives jumped into his mind. He nervously glanced around, thinking his unseen watcher might still be close by, waiting for just the right moment to spring on him. For years he had heard stories of wild hermits inhabiting the older places, who frequently resorted to cannibalism when other sources of food were scarce. And then it occurred to him that he had never heard of any wild men who wore boots. He relaxed for a moment before considering that perhaps his watcher was actually one of the invaders. But why would a single invader be out here in the middle of this forest? It did not make any sense. Valentus, still looking over his shoulder, decided to angle more to the east, away from the path taken by his unseen watcher.

He walked only a short while before discovering a fairly large patch of blackberries. Despite not being able to shake the continual feeling of being watched, his hunger got the best of him. The blackberries were small but plentiful. He picked and ate them with hungry abandon. Reddish black juice stained his fingers as he greedily gathered as many of the berries as possible. He would gather a handful and then stuff them all into his mouth at once. Soon the stains that adorned his hands also covered his mouth and chin. He finished eating every berry ripe enough to enjoy and not too few that were not before wiping his mouth. It was not a meal, but it cut the sharpness of his hunger.

He turned back toward the southwest and began walking again when a fairly large man abruptly stepped from behind a tree not two paces directly in front him. Valentus felt his throat tighten as his breath caught. He turned to flee, but another man appeared out of nowhere to block his only escape. The first man reached out his arm, palm forward.

"Now, son, don't do anything rash! We just want to ask you a few questions."

Valentus's eyes had the look of a wild animal, every muscle tense and ready to spring away. He looked to his right and saw the thicket where he had just been feasting. As the men moved in closer to grab him, Valentus threw himself with all the speed he could muster into the midst of the brambles and undergrowth. Something hard hit his head and all went black.

Captured

It was dark when Valentus woke up. He lay on his right side stretched out across the open ground. His own blanket lay loosely around his shoulders. The trunk of a fallen tree sheltered his front side.

At first, he had no recollection of where he might be or how he came to be there, but as he tried to sit up, his head began to throb with sudden pain. Groaning softly, he raised a hand to his head. A strip of cloth was wrapped snuggly around it. As he felt the cloth, he brushed over a large bump on his forehead. The pain of touching it made him wince, and the memory of his encounter with the two men flooded back into his mind. Every muscle in his body tensed again, ready to spring into flight at the slightest provocation. Lying with his face inward toward the fallen tree, he could see nothing to reveal the circumstances he now faced.

He lay absolutely still and listened. The sound of falling water and the occasional crackle of a campfire was all he could make out. The waiting only served to increase his tension, causing his head to throb more. He desperately wanted to turn over and see if there was any way to escape. But the fear of who or what awaited him made Valentus hesitate.

"Are you hungry, lad?" The sound of the man's voice nearly made Valentus's heart stop beating. He held as quiet as possible, hoping his captor would think him still asleep.

"There's no use play'n possum with us boy! We know you're woke up." It was a different voice than the first, deeper and gruff-sounding.

"I was hoping to have help eating all this bacon." It was the first man who spoke again in a voice filled with genuine regret. *He did not sound like a villain*, Valentus thought. But the sound of the second man left him feeling less sure. His voice did tend to produce images of hairy, wild men with blood-dripping knives. The smell of frying bacon wafted over Valentus's shoulder, causing strong hunger pains to return with a vengeance. His resolve to continue the ruse of being asleep began to wane.

"Give me the rest of that there pig belly. If 'n that youngsters guna stay shy, well, I say let 'im!" The words sounded as though they were spat rather than spoken. The fear that the brutish sounding man might eat all the bacon finally made Valentus's decision for him. He slowly turned over, pain pulsing through his head with every movement.

Sitting next to a small fire were the same two men that had assaulted him in the blackberry thicket. One of them was considerably larger and better dressed than the other. He wore the kind of clothes a nobleman wears into the forest while hunting game for sport. The smaller man was quite hairy and wild-looking, much as his voice suggested, and carried a nice-sized pouch of a belly. Valentus did not like the look of him. Several large strips of meat sizzled on a pan balanced low over the flames of the campfire. A small plate stacked with already cooked bacon sat on the ground next to the fire. Valentus's eyes locked on the treasure trove of meat, and he licked his lips despite himself.

The bigger man laughed. "Well, don't be shy, lad. Help yourself!" He indicated the plate of steaming bacon.

The smaller man donned a disappointed scowl as Valentus reached down, picked up the plate, and began eating. "You go right on then, boy, what'd you care if we ain't et since firs' light," he complained.

"Mr. Bonfire, is that any way to treat a guest?" said the first man.

Valentus couldn't be sure in the dim firelight, but it looked as though mirth played at the corners of the bigger man's mouth and eyes as he spoke.

The smaller man looked sharply back at his companion. "Mr., is it? After all I dun...Mr. Hmpf!" With that he crossed his arms and turned away from the fire on his stump.

After gorging himself on a considerable amount of the delicious meat, Valentus thought better of his bad manners. He slowly placed the plate back near the fire and began furtively glancing around his surroundings. It only took a moment to confirm what he already suspected. He was back in the very same glade where he had camped the night before. The man called Mr. Bonfire caught the movement from the corner of his eye and quickly turned back to the fire while rubbing his hands.

"I gess you et yer fill then." He smiled and began eating the remaining bacon without further need of invitation by his companion.

"We seemed to have started off on the wrong foot this morning. My name is Archimere," the bigger man said, completely ignoring Mr. Bonfire and looking directly at Valentus as he extended his right hand.

Valentus was puzzled by the friendliness of his captors. For the first time, perhaps encouraged by the generous behavior of the man called Archimere, he felt angry. "You attacked and captured me, and now offer me your hand in friendship?" Although he intended an angry tone, full of just accusation, his voice cracked instead and sounded a bit shakier than Valentus had hoped.

"Hold on now, lad. Who's been attacked and captured?" Archimere let his hand turn upward in a questioning gesture. Mr. Bonfire momentarily stopped chewing and just looked at Valentus, grease dripping down his beard. Valentus looked back with a puzzled expression, unsure of how to answer. Archimere's expression softened again.

"Look, lad, we tried to tell you this morning that we meant you no harm. We just have to be careful with anyone unknown who is wandering in this part of the forest."

Valentus slowly put his hand to his wounded forehead as if it provided the proof of his accusation. After all, what kind of friendly inquiry begins with a serious knock to the head?

Mr. Bonfire nearly spit out the entire contents of his mouth with laughter. "You gone and done that yerself, like a durn fool." The small man was laughing so hard he had to hold his protruding stomach as though he were in pain.

Valentus's face began to burn with embarrassment without fully understanding what Mr. Bonfire meant. If he was jesting, it was more insulting than Valentus liked.

"What my rude friend means is…" Archimere paused and gave a look of disapproval to Mr. Bonfire who continued to laugh so hard Valentus though the might fall off his stump. "When you threw yourself into the thicket, you had the misfortune of finding one of the many large rocks that are scattered across these hills. You were out cold most of the day, as you already know."

"I knew you would probably be hungry when you finally woke up," he continued. The big man had a winning way about him. He had a manner of speaking that made Valentus want to trust him. But there were still questions needing answers.

"Who are you and why do you live in these woods?" Valentus was beginning to feel more at ease and able to speak his mind. The two men just looked at each other as though a fresh wound were touched. Mr. Bonfire stood and walked away from the campfire. Archimere stared into the flames of the fire as though he looked at something far away.

"One week ago, I lived in a fine house in Perginton. Then word came of an invasion force, and the army was mustered. We marched out in righteous anger at the audacity of the invaders from Illyrium. Why would the men of Illyrium invade Tharrus? We have always been friends." Here, Archimere paused with an expression showing he still did not comprehend the answer.

He picked up a stick and poked at the coals of the campfire.

"Our warriors faced each other for a full day without attacking. We had the superior numbers and a good defensive position, so we waited for the enemy to move. But they would not come. Why? Many of our men, incensed by the arrogance of the invaders, begged for the order to attack. Then at dawn on the second day of battle, the enemy's left flank attacked. We were ready for them, and the invader received the worst of it, falling quickly back to their own lines. Then the Illyrians attacked on the right flank with the same result. These minor clashes continued throughout the second day. On the third day of battle, our king watching from the tower, seeing we had gained the upper hand, ordered a full attack. The men were eager to crush the enemy. Our soldiers hit them hard and pushed them back toward the harbor where they had landed."

At this Valentus interrupted. "But they landed far to the south of where the battle took place."

Archimere looked hard at Valentus for a moment, then back to the fire. "The invaders we were fighting came from the bay of Perginton. But as we were to find out, they were not alone. As we pushed the invaders toward the bay, a cry arose from our rear ranks. A second much larger war band had come in secret from somewhere to the south. They smashed into our rear rank without warning or mercy. All turned to chaos. Those in the rear never even knew what happened. They were slaughtered by the dozens before they could even turn to defend themselves.

"The warriors under my command, all mounted, were located on our right, furthest from the flanking attack. We were able to exploit the weaker lines of the enemy in front of us and punch a hole through them. Some of our men escaped back into the city behind its protective walls from a smaller gate on that side. My men defended the escape of all who were near enough to reach the city. Few enough made it back."

Archimere, still staring into the flames of the fire, stopped speaking for a moment. Valentus thought he saw a pained look pass over his features before he began recounting his story once again.

"Nevertheless, our retreat to safety did not last long. Perginton had not been threatened by invasion for a hundred years, and as such, we had not reinforced the gates. It was only a short time before they began to splinter. King Peleg ordered me to take the remnant of our war band into the forests to wage a resistance. He knew there was no longer any chance for direct victory. The enemy numbers were simply too great.

"That was three days ago and here we find ourselves. We hide in the forest, while the enemy holds the city and our king."

Archimere spat into the fire to emphasize his distaste with the conclusion of his tale. The big man sat quiet for sometime. Then he abruptly looked back at Valentus with a momentary look of distrust. "How did you know of the enemy that landed to the south?"

Valentus squirmed under the sudden change in scrutiny. He slowly recounted his discovering of the invasion force while tending his uncle's sheep, and how he came to be wandering through this forest alone. His only hesitation came when trying to explain why he had fled into the forest after discovering the two-day-old battlefield on the plains of Perginton. When his story was done, Valentus hung his head, feeling the shame of what he thought his new acquaintances would surely believe to be cowardice. Much to his surprise, Mr. Bonfire silently appeared back at the campfire and sat down on his stump.

"There's no shame in it, boy. You dun what we all dun! There ain't no glory ner bravery in lookin' on the dead." Mr. Bonfire slowly shook his head. "Well, anyhow, you gone an' showed 'nuf courage by what you dun in comin' here." He paused, looked at Archimere, and then looked back to Valentus. "I'm proud ta know ya, boy." He reached out his hand. Archimere smiled at his friend's decisive action.

"What's your name then?" Archimere asked.

"Valentus"—his voice cracked again—"my name is Valentus." He extended his arm and took Mr. Bonfire's hand. For the first night in a long time, Valentus did not feel lonely. The noises of the night and the dancing firelight were all peaceful now. The water fell gently over the falls in a merry cadence as the night birds softly sang Valentus to sleep.

Deeper into the Forest

T he next morning, Valentus followed his new companions deeper
into the forest to the north. The two men moved quickly and
quietly over near-invisible game trails, finding hidden ways through
dense thickets that at first looked impassable. It was all he could do to
keep pace with them, and much to his surprise, even the shorter and
fatter Mr. Bonfire moved like an agile wildcat. In fact, he appeared to
serve as a guide of some sort.

The terrain began to rise as the day went on, and the shadows
began to lengthen again. They stopped twice for a few bites of dried
meat the others carried, but as of yet, there had been no suggestion of an

actual meal. Valentus began doubting whether he would ever again have anything substantial to eat.

All in all it had been a strange day. From the moment they broke camp early that morning, there was little more than a word spoken amongst them. They just moved out and kept moving, until Valentus felt as though his legs would simply give out. As best as he could tell, their direction was intentionally changed in wide, sweeping arcs from time to time, until all hope of knowing their direction was gone. Valentus could not help feeling as though his guides where attempting to throw off his sense of direction. Did they still distrust him? Whether they trusted him or not, he was rapidly beginning to resent the grueling pace without the chance for any food or a rest.

Just as Valentus was about to complain, they stopped at the base of another substantial forest ridge, which was an amassed tangle of fallen trees and brambles. The light in the wood was fading quickly as it does in all ancient forests, and the two men paused to examine the thick wall of thorns and branches. They were searching for something, but for what Valentus no longer cared. He abruptly sat down on a nearby log and tried to stretch out the sore muscles of his tired legs.

Only a moment passed before Mr. Bonfire gave a low whistle. Valentus glanced up to see him pointing toward a spot in the thicket wall. Archimere was nowhere to be seen. Valentus let his head drop with the effort of standing back up. The stiffness in his muscles punished him for his decision to relax, and he groaned as he regained his feet once more. He looked back toward Mr. Bonfire only to discover him gone. Valentus looked in every direction, but he could see no sign of either man. A quick surge of alarm filled his chest as he ran to the spot where he last saw Mr. Bonfire.

The bramble thicket was a mass of dark, tangled thorns taller than a man. It looked impassable for anything but rabbits and foxes. Valentus thought that it would be just his luck to be abandoned by his new companions and hopelessly lost to boot. He continued to look in every direction, thinking Archimere and Mr. Bonfire must have gone further down the ridge way. A stick snapped somewhere behind him, and he spun back toward the bramble wall. Off to his right, he noticed the trunk of a large tree looming in the ever-darkening forest. Its base was as wide as four or five Mr. Bonfires. Yet there was something about a dark patch that seemed to protrude unnaturally from this side of its trunk.

Valentus leaned forward as he peered at the spot, trying to make it out better. It did not look like it was actually part of the tree, but rather something just beyond it.

He took a slow step closer and peered into what he now believed was an actual opening in the dark thicket, big enough for a man to walkthrough stooped over slightly. As he began a closer examination, an owl hooted somewhere behind him, drawing his attention over his shoulder. The owl, resenting Valentus's intrusion into his hunting grounds, flew off in agitation. Valentus smiled and turned back to the opening. Mr. Bonfire was standing directly in front of him. Valentus stifled a cry at the abrupt reappearance of his strange companion.

"What kep' ya, boy?"

From what Valentus could see of Mr. Bonfire in the twilight, his normal scowling facial expression was now more of a slight smile or amused grimace, as Valentus thought of it. The only time Mr. Bonfire was without his usual scowl, he reflected, was when he was mocking Valentus in some way.

"Ain't sceer'd a boogie men, air ya?" Mr. Bonfire openly laughed.

"N-no, you just surprised me a little," Valentus said, while feeling quite foolish and none too pleasant toward his new acquaintance.

"Foller me." Mr. Bonfire paused and stifled another laugh. "If ya ain't soiled yerself."

Valentus did not have long to dwell on his dislike of Mr. Bonfire before the man turned and, just as abruptly as he had appeared, vanished from sight. Valentus bent down and clumsily stepped into the apparent opening in the bramble wall. At first he could see nothing inside the tunnel. He tentatively stepped forward and directly into the thorn wall on the other side of the tunnel opening. He backed up and waited shortly for his eyes to adjust to the darkness inside the hidden passage. It was still very dark, but he could just make out what appeared to be a turn in the tunnel. Right after the small opening, it turned sharply to the left.

Valentus followed the turn and then continued on through the tunnel, which was much longer than expected for the fact that it wound back and forth several times before it finally exited past another great, ancient oak. The path on the other side wound up the ridge between large boulders that littered the hillside. Although not much could be seen in the dark anymore, Valentus considered that a person could ascend to the top of the ridge almost completely undercover. He and Mr. Bonfire finally caught up with Archimere, who was waiting behind one of the larger rocks toward the crest of the ridge.

"All seems well," Archimere said as they approached. "I will signal our arrival."

Archimere reached inside a cleft in the rock and pulled out what looked like a small bell in the failing light. He held it up and rang it once and then replaced it and waited. From somewhere further up in the rocks, another single bell rang softly in the night air. Archimere stood and began up the trail once more, signaling them to follow. They shortly came to the top of the rocks where Archimere stopped. A dark figure stepped slowly into the path.

"Is that you, Archimere?" the man whispered softly.

"It is. Mr. Bonfire is here as well."

"I know. I could smell him before he entered the bramble path," the dark figure said with a note of jest in his voice.

"Hmpfh, that you, Rafe? I should box yer ears, an' learn ya to respek yer eldars!" Mr. Bonfire's words were harsh, but Valentus could hear the smile behind them.

They followed Rafe out of the rocks onto a grassy plateau. The sky above them was clear, and the stars shown brightly across its vast canopy. The great trees of the forest grew all around the meadow like a protecting wall, but they did not encroach on it. Toward the center of the meadow sat a melancholic pool. A small grove of birch and ash trees, none bigger in circumference than the size of a man's leg, surrounded the pool. In all his days, Valentus had never seen such a magical place. It was simple in its beauty but breathtaking in its peaceful melancholy.

They continued across the high meadow. The pool was black in the dark of the night, but it perfectly reflected the constellations above as though it was a large mirror revealing the heavens. The reflected light was magnified as it softly illuminated the surrounding silver birch and golden ash trees of the grove. The grass that covered the rest of the meadow was now replaced by a soft, mossy turf, which only added to the feel of the place. Valentus could hear the sound of running water and was not surprised to find a brook emptying out of the far side of the pool where the ground sloped gently downward.

They followed the brook to a place where it disappeared over a smooth edge into darkness. Rafe walked up to the edge and turned to the left and appeared to float downward as he descended on some invisible path.

When Valentus reached the edge, he could see the clear outline of a stone-cut stairs. The black water of the brook partly fell and partly danced down a steep, rocky wall to his right, plunging into a frothy pool smoothed in the rock before cascading out the other side into a darkness Valentus could no longer see through.

They continued down the stair for another three flights before it ended between two large standing stones that presented an imposing gateway through which Valentus could now see the flickering glow of firelight. They passed between the standing stones onto a large flat rock that jutted out over another smaller meadow. Out across this second meadow, Valentus could see a dozen campfires surrounded by various sized tents. He could see men sitting by the fires, while others walked here and there. Due to the large rocky escarpment that crowned the portion of the ridge directly above them and the forest that continued on below them, this meadow was completely sheltered from prying eyes.

It was not long before they were completely surrounded by those excited for the return of Archimere and any news he brought of Perginton. Valentus was surprised to discover that many women and children were there among the men. He later learned that the warriors who came into the forest had brought their families with them. Valentus was quickly introduced and, much to his relief, welcomed heartily by one and all. For the first time in his life, he felt a part of something important and could not stop smiling despite himself.

Archimere was just asking Rafe to find a place for Valentus when another small group approached. Valentus, not used to so much attention, was growing tired of smiling and being gawked at when he turned away to avoid this new group's curiosity. He turned and found himself face to face with the woman of his dreams. Not merely the type of woman of his dreams, mind you, but quite literally the very same girl he had daydreamed about ever since seeing her at the harvest festival hosted on his uncle's estate. It was, in fact, the singer.

The dark locks of her hair hung gently over her shoulders as she looked directly into Valentus's eyes. Her lips parted slightly as though she might speak, but then changed her mind. Valentus's heart beat like a team of horses pounding up turf. There was no mistake. Even though he had seen her but once before and only for a brief moment, it was the singer. She was even more beautiful than he remembered. The light of the fire danced in the depth of her amber green eyes, as she measured Valentus for some unknown quality. All else around him became faint, and Valentus realized he had stopped breathing, when Archimere came up behind him and clapped him on the back. The sudden contact made him jump.

"Valentus! Let me introduce you to my sister, Alenia." Archimere, still resting his arm on Valentus's shoulder, looked at him with amusement.

"It is good to make your acquaintance, Valentus. Welcome to Escalon," she motioned with her hand to the surrounding forest. The sound of Alenia's voice was soft but confident as she dipped slightly and extended the back of her hand out toward Valentus, who just starred at it, unsure of what he was to do.

Archimere glanced at Valentus and quietly cleared his throat. "When a lady extends her hand to a gentleman, it is customary to accept it."

Valentus looked at Archimere with momentary incomprehension before realization broke over his features. Although his cheeks felt as though they were on fire, he quickly reached out and took Alenia's hand as he bowed his head. He had never felt anything quite so delicate and soft before, and he thought his heart would crash right out of his chest. Even though the touch was brief, the memory of it lingered on into the night.

The White Isle

The sun had barely moved a hand's breadth across the sky since Bryn's discovery of the branch carried by Martin's eagle. As he looked around at the men, he was amazed at how hope could revive the hopeless.

A short time ago, most of them could barely walk, let alone work. Now that land was in sight, a few even attempted singing as they prepared for the inevitable landing. Some of the men stood at the rail, refusing to take their eyes from the clear view of the rounded and jutting coastline. It was as though they thought it might vanish along with any hope of survival.

Argolis, for that is what Bryn now called the eagle, was nowhere to be seen. Bryn reflected on the fact that if not for Argolis's timely arrival, True North's crew would have continued rowing in the same direction, never knowing they had just passed their best hope of survival. They had only to change their course back to the southeast a short distance before sighting the coastline they now thanked the Great God of heaven for.

Once the shoreline was sighted, True North changed course again and sailed back around to the west and north of the protruding point of coastline. Bryn and Llew stood by Berand as he piloted in closer to land. As they came around the point, the shore stretched inward in a half moon shape for some distance before arching gently back out to another point. The sands of the beach and the rock cliffs that rose out of the jungle in the distance had a peculiar lightness that shone bright white when the light of day hit them.

Bryn put his hand on Berand's shoulder. "Here will be fine. Llew and I will take a party ashore right there." He pointed off to the right a little where a small but vigorous stream broke through a dense jungle wall and rushed down into the sea. Bryn turned to Llew. "Would you see to a party large enough to re-provision the ship's fresh water supply and anything else useful that can be found?"

Llew nodded his acceptance, but noticed a look of something akin to excitement in his brother's eyes. He paused then responded with a question. "Are you not coming?"

"I am." Bryn hesitated and looked over Llew's shoulder toward the men on the deck below them as if his response was non consequential. "I will be exploring the island. In their weakened state, you will need all the men able to help with the re-provisioning. So I will go alone."

Llew made to object to the notion of his brother wandering off by himself in a strange and unexplored jungle.

Martin appeared from behind them and interrupted. "I think Bryn is right, Llew. But he will not be going alone. Rand and I will be with him."

Llew was relieved, but he now saw a distinct look of disappointment in Bryn's face. He remembered seeing such a look before when they were younger. Bryn was a boy of about twelve summers when he found a hidden cave with a secret pool. He would often visit it, but always alone. One day, his father asked him to take Llew. Bryn would never go against his father's wishes, and Llew felt as though he had intruded on something very personal.

Martin didn't seem to notice, however. His countenance was near miraculous in its improvement from the past couple of days. The strength and intensity of his gaze returned, and he no longer wore the gloom of defeat, but seemed to carry a newfound confidence.

Llew asked, "What of Aedan? Does he not need your continued care, Martin?"

"All I can do for him is done. My supplies are gone." Martin turned and pointed to the shore. "Whatever help he is to receive now, must come from there." It was then that both Bryn and Llew noticed that Martin held Argolis's small branch in his hand.

Martin continued, "Aedan is stable for now. We must seek heaven's help for him… and I believe we have been led here for that very reason."

It did not take long for several landing parties to make their way to the shore. After each of the men were allowed time to refresh themselves, most were set to the task of preparing barrels for fresh water, while others were sent in small groups to search for food. Only Berand and a skeleton crew remained aboard ship with instructions to keep Aedan comfortable while the rest searched the island. Bryn issued orders that the first boats to return with provisions would relieve those left aboard. Martin felt it important that everyone get a chance to walk on solid ground and wash in the fresh water.

Bryn, who was aboard the first boat to make the shore, now stood next to the fast-moving stream and shielded his eyes from the sunlight. He looked up into the tree line of the jungle for Argolis. There was no sign of the great bird. It was uncanny how much this place reminded him of his dream. It was the same; the stream, the shore, the jungle line, everything. Martin and Rand approached and came to stand beside him.

"Well, Bryn, where should we begin?" Martin asked.

Rand finished strapping on a long sword that hung over his back. Bryn looked back at him and noticed that while he had left off his heavy leather armor, two more short swords hung from both his sides. Rand noticed Bryn's appraising look.

"I like to be prepared, my lord," Rand said by way of an answer.

The heat of the day reached its peak as the sun hovered halfway between its midday position and the horizon. Bryn turned, without speaking, and followed the stream back into the tropical forest. Martin and Rand followed close behind. The jungle was dense with vines and undergrowth, and the sounds of men working on the beach all but vanished when they broke through the jungle forest barrier. The way was somewhat better by the banks of the stream, but their progress, nevertheless, was slow.

After walking for some time, the drumming sound of rain could be heard in the canopy high above. It was not long before the green foliage began weeping and dripping fresh droplets. Soon the water ran down in a thousand cascades all around them. The heat of the jungle air, mixing with the cooler rainwater, began forming wispy clouds of steam that rose and swirled at their feet. Although they could still see well enough, it was considerably darker in the jungle than it had been on the beach. The air around them glowed with a soft green tint as the sunlight above could not break through the crowded canopy, but it did shine with enough intensity to illuminate through the great, leafy branches high above.

Their progress was far too slow for Bryn's taste. His sense of expectant urgency was growing along with his frustration at their slow pace. They would have been able to move more quickly, but for Martin's slow and detailed search of plant specimens. As the light grew slightly fainter, Bryn pushed them onward.

"Lord Bryn, shouldn't we consider returning to the shore before we lose the light?" Rand asked as he breathed hard under the unrelenting humidity.

"Just a little further in!" Bryn snapped with an impatient tone.

Martin looked at him. "Bryn, it would be unwise to continue too long in one direction away from the shore and our supplies. Rand is right. Dark will come early here."

Bryn continued pushing his way through the undergrowth, which grew well above their heads. Martin was about to challenge Bryn with more authority when they suddenly broke through the dense tangle into a fairly open glade. Rand caught his foot on an exposed root and plunged headlong into the shorter fern that covered the jungle floor. After helping Rand regain his feet, Martin turned quickly toward Bryn. The rebuke was almost on his lips, when he noticed Bryn standing completely still, facing forward away from himself and Rand. A quick look around the small jungle glade revealed a wider bend in the stream where it made a sharp turn to their left and disappeared into the dense jungle again. The wide bend formed a small pool directly in front of them. Martin walked forward and placed his hand on Bryn's shoulder.

"Bryn, is all well?"

Martin noticed that Bryn's eyes were fixed forward. It was as though he had seen a ghost. Martin scanned the scene and almost missed what had so captured Bryn's attention. As his eyes swept more slowly across the jungle glade, a shock of realization swept over him as they fell to rest upon her. A slender young woman sat on the far side of the pool. She had not noticed their abrupt intrusion into the solace of her small clearing. The stream bubbled and chortled with just enough sound to mask the noise their entry must have made. The young woman sat with her feet in the softly swirling water of the pool. Long, golden hair hung past her shoulders in small, plaited braids. She wore a light, silvery green dress that blended in with the colors of the jungle in the most amazing way, which was why Martin had not seen her at first.

The small, wispy tails of steam clouds still floated up from the moss-covered floor. The rain had stopped its drumming in the canopy above, but water still flowed down in miniature cascades all about them. All three of the explorers stood transfixed with the scene that met their eyes. Rays of golden sunshine broke through the branches high up in the treetops to throw themselves like spears of flame into the greenness of the glade, just like in Bryn's dream, or whatever it had been.

The girl, who could not have been any older than Bryn, froze as her eyes came to rest upon the three men. For a brief moment, it looked as if she might take flight. Yet before she could act upon her impulse, the cry of an eagle sounded from somewhere above them.

She stopped and looked up into the trees. The three men followed her gaze to find Martin's eagle, Argolis, not far from where they all now stood. The girl looked back at her visitors with the curious expression one gets when appraising something's worth. It was her next look, however, that took Martin most by surprise. When her eyes alighted upon Bryn, she paused and Martin could swear that a look of recognition flittered across the girl's delicate features. He looked back at Bryn, whose expression continued to be intently fixed on the young woman.

"What is your name?" The sound of Bryn's voice was unnatural in the serenity of the glade. The girl did not answer but instead stood to her feet on the opposite bank. Her dress glimmered with the movement, and she turned slightly to look back up at Argolis. The great bird looked back at her and called out again. To Bryn, Martin, and Rand, it was almost as though the eagle talked with the girl.

"If you please, my lady, what is the name of this place?" Bryn took a halting step forward and held out a hand as he spoke. There was a note of desperation in his voice. Bryn simply wanted the girl to speak. It did not matter so much what she said, but just that she spoke. For from the moment they had sighted this land, Bryn struggled between a certainty of knowing he would meet this lady and an unknowing of whether she was a phantom or flesh and blood. The girl returned Bryn's look with eyes that could have seen straight through to his heart. There was no trace of fear in her expression.

"This place is called Atala, the White Isle." The girl's voice was light and beautiful. It had a lilting quality that bespoke the gracefulness of the speaker. "It is good that you have heeded my call and followed Argolis." She looked straight at Bryn as she spoke.

Bryn was silent for a time. There were more questions than could be asked, and he feared missing what was important. He almost forgot the presence of the others when Martin broke the stillness of the glade with his own question.

"Pardon me, my lady, but do you live nearby?"

The girl looked from Bryn to Martin. After a brief but curious assessment, what she did next greatly surprised all three men. She gracefully bowed her head in the manner of a servant addressing a king and said, "My lord is welcome here on the White Isle. My dwelling is not far."

Bryn, who now also stood starring at Martin, had a look of astonishment on his face. He always had the greatest respect for Martin and honored him, as a teacher should be honored, but this young woman just paid him the homage of a king. As amazed as Bryn was by this turn of events, Martin appeared almost as though he had been hit in the gut.

"My lady, you pay me too great an honor, for I am but a servant of the great King." Martin, despite his calmness, could not completely mask his own bewilderment.

"Even the greatest king does well to serve Him," she answered with a tone of acknowledgment.

"Have we met before?" Martin's question only served to puzzle Bryn even more. Why would he contemplate such a possibility? Just then, Argolis's cry filled the softness of the glade. The girl cast a furtive glance at the jungle around them.

"It will be dark soon. We cannot stay here. You must follow me closely, for the way is narrow." The girl was already moving toward the jungle wall on the opposite side of the glade before the men could respond.

"Wait!" Bryn spoke quickly, not willing to lose her like he did in his dream. The three men found a spot in the stream where they could easily cross to the other side. In the dying light, nonetheless, it was difficult to locate where the girl stood waiting. Against the deep green of the foliage, her garment made her nearly invisible. In fact, if not for her golden yellow hair, they might have passed right by and never known it.

The light in the jungle was all but gone when they left the small clearing and followed the young woman onto a well-hidden path that led away in the opposite direction. The men found themselves having to run to keep up. The girl moved like a gazelle, virtually leaping down the pathway. In spite of her remarkable speed, she made no noise. They continued on this way for sometime before she came to a stop. Bryn, Martin, and Rand almost fell over each other in their attempt to avoid colliding with the young woman. She waited for them to regain themselves, before pointing toward the path ahead. In the deadened air of the hot jungle came the sound of a blood-chilling howl from somewhere not that far behind them. Rand looked at Bryn and Martin.

"What was that?" he asked.

Both Martin and Bryn looked questioningly at the girl. She was neither surprised nor afraid. Yet when she spoke the name, it was distasteful to her. "Sargaroth!" she answered before deftly disappearing around the trunk of a tall straight tree that stood hard against the north side of the trail.

Bryn looked back at the other two and then quickly stepped up to the tree and followed the girl around it. The darkness of the jungle gave way to a brilliant setting sun across a vast valley. The last rays of molten gold poured over the jungle horizon on the distant side of the valley. Bryn, used to the darkening forest, shielded his eyes. The grandeur of the scene before him was stunning.

The four of them stood on a narrow trailhead between two tall lampposts of an unusual spiraling design. They overlooked a vast and deep chasm of a valley, which was further broken by ravines and hills.

The jungle grew right up to the edge of the rift and then fell sharply away several hundred feet to the bottom of the wide valley below. Far away on the opposite side of the broken valley stood another wall equally as high as the one they now stood upon. Some distance to the south, the horizon rose in the pointed peaks of a rugged mountain chain. To the north the valley sloped downward toward a wide bay, which opened directly into the sea beyond.

It was not, however, the expansiveness of the scene that most surprised the men. The entire valley floor was covered with the ruins of a once great city made entirely of white stone. Now, in the dying light, the very tops of the highest buildings still reflected the oranges, yellows, and magentas of the brilliant setting sun, giving it a most dazzling appearance.

Aayliyah

Another tortured, inhuman howl sounded in the jungle behind them, closer than before. Bryn could not help looking back over his shoulder. The darkness was now so complete that nothing could be seen past the first layer of undergrowth. Rand pulled his long sword off his back and stepped closer to the jungle wall, ready to defend if needed.

The young woman gave him a quizzical look. "Your sword cannot stop them."

There was no fear or chastisement in the words. They were simply spoken as a soft conclusion and held a note of respect for Rand's bravery. Instead, the girl turned to one of the lampposts, reached down its side, and lifted up a slender, silver-colored rod. She made a movement with her hand, and a small flame appeared at its upper end. She held the flame up to each lamppost. The men now saw the usefulness of the strangely designed lanterns. They reflected the light of the flame in such a way that both intensified it and caused it to fully illuminate the trailhead.

They followed the path a short way downward until it came to a stone stairs cut from the cliff wall. Another set of lamps stood on either side of the stairs. The girl lit them as well. A howl slashed the air so loud it felt as though the beast was upon them. All three men now held their swords and stood facing what they were sure would be an imminent attack.

"Do not fear. They will not come," the girl said.

"A thousand apologies, my lady," Bryn said, "but I think whatever it is has already come." Bryn looked intensely at the edge of the jungle just beyond the trailhead and thought he could see the form of something huge standing just beyond the light of the lamps. Its presence created a sense of menacing dread not there a moment ago.

"They will not come. They are afraid of the light." The girl looked back at Bryn and then the others. "Come, our way will be slower in the dark."

The confidence in the young woman's voice despite such apparent danger puzzled the men. They cautiously turned away from the jungle to begin their descent, casting furtive backward glances.

The oddly shaped lamps were positioned in equal intervals along the stone stairs, and the girl stopped to light each one. The descent took longer than expected. It was full night before they finally reached the bottom. An ornately carved stone archway stood at the foot of the stairs. A lamp was attached to each side of the arch with several more positioned higher along its top. The girl lit the lower ones, and by some hidden device, the upper lights also flared with flame. Once through the archway, she motioned toward several handheld lanterns. They were made of the same silver-colored metal as the lampposts along the stair. Once lit, they brightly illuminated the ruined buildings all around them.

They walked through the ruins of the great city in silence. The ancient age of the place was evident by the moss that clung to the stone, yet many of the larger buildings appeared mostly intact. Martin paused next to one particularly impressive structure, which had words chiseled into the rock face above its large doorway. The wooden doors were long gone, and the dark opening looked a bit like a gaping mouth ready to swallow them. Martin held his lantern higher.

"My lady, can you read these words?" He pointed toward the chiseled letters.

The girl stopped walking and looked to where he indicated. "It is the language of the Aletae," she answered.

Bryn thought he saw a shadow pass over the young woman's face.

"Yes, I have been taught, my lord." Again, the girl bowed her head in the fashion of one addressing royalty.

Bryn waited for Martin to ask what the words meant, but instead he turned away from the building and continued to follow the girl. Bryn shrugged and turned to join them.

The moss-covered street, which was made of the same white stones, now turned and began ascending up one of the larger hills that covered the valley floor. Before long they came to a small bridge covering the expanse of a dark rift in the valley floor. The bridge was also made of white stone and arched gently over to the other side where the street continued to wind upward between rows of smaller stone buildings.

After some time walking, the street entered into a circular courtyard before continuing farther up the hill on the other side. In the center of the courtyard stood a large circular fountain. Amazingly, water still shot out of its center and from several other side porticoes to splash into the pool at its base. On the south side of the courtyard stood a manor-style house with large pillars and a balcony across its front. The girl turned and walked up to it. Unlike most of the other buildings, this one's door was still attached and working properly. She opened it and disappeared inside, and soon, light from inside the building shone out through its round windows. Then she appeared at the doorway once more, motioning them to come.

"You will stay here tonight," she said. "I have left food for you there." She pointed to a table in the middle of the room.

Martin, thinking he misunderstood, responded, "We will accompany you home to your family before taking any rest."

"I alone live in the White City," the girl said simply and moved out the door.

Bryn turned quickly. "Surely you do not mean to stay alone tonight, not with those creatures out there!"

The girl stopped and looked at Bryn with a soft smile on her face. "Leave your lanterns burning. We are safe in the city." She turned and began walking through the courtyard.

Bryn, afraid it might be the last they would ever see of her, blurted out, "But we don't even know your name!"

She paused, turned back to them, and said, "I am Aayliyah," then continued walking away.

"We must stop her and convince her to stay here with us." Bryn's voice held a note of frustration.

Martin looked after the girl as she passed the fountain and continued up the hill. "Bryn, she *lives* here *alone*. I do not think one more night will make a difference. Besides"—he paused and turned back to Bryn and Rand—"I do not think she is afraid." Just then an eagle's cry filled the night air as Argolis swooped down and past the girl as she disappeared around a bend in the street.

Rand, who had been silent until now, spoke up. "Do you think the rest of the men are in danger from these…Sargaroth creatures?"

Martin looked at Bryn for some indication of his opinion, but Bryn still stared after the spot where Aayliyah was last seen.

"Our men will not venture into the jungle after dark, and they will have campfires. Whatever these beasts are, they appear not to like the light." Martin turned to the table where the food was laid out. "We can give them no better help this night than our prayers. We may as well eat and rest. We will discover more of this place in the morning."

The girl named Aayliyah had left them a variety of soft breads that tasted of honey and a pitcher of water mixed with the sweet juice of some fruit. All in all, it had a wonderfully refreshing affect after their exhausting exploration in the hot, humid jungle. The men were surprised to find benches covered with pillows made of an odd-feeling fabric that was quite comfortable.

"I must confess I do not like the feeling of this place," Rand said.

Martin looked surprised by Rand's admission. "I have never seen such a grand city. Why, in its day, it must have been far greater than even Hilgreen!"

"To be sure," Rand replied, "it is vast in its greatness. But there is something else. Can you not feel it? A heaviness, like something evil took place here, or lived here once."

Bryn, who had not yet settled down on his couch, turned his gaze toward the door facing the courtyard. "I feel it too. But it is more the wariness a hunter senses when he has become the prey." He paced back across the open room. "Something evil still lurks here, and I do *not* think a young girl should be left alone." The emphasis he placed upon this last statement drew Martin's attention.

"Yes, in truth, I too have felt it. But it is not the same danger as what lurks in the jungle." Martin paused, as if considering it for the first time. "I felt this same forewarning of hidden danger once long ago. It was not a peril to health or body, but rather to the soul," he concluded and then closed his eyes as though his answer should be sufficient to quiet Bryn and Rand's concern.

None of them slept well that night. They were comfortable enough with Aayliyah's thoughtful provisions, but that was what left them unnerved. How did she know they were coming? The food and beds she left for them must have been prepared earlier that day, before they met her in the jungle. But there was something more. Aayliyah said she was alone, but all three of the men felt another presence, something or someone with malevolent intentions. It was like Bryn's old hunting instructor used to tell him. A true hunter will always feel the presence of the bear before he sees it. In truth, there was a mystery in this place vacillating between good and evil. The night, nevertheless, passed without incident.

It was during the early hours of the morning that Bryn first awoke. He lay still for a moment, listening for what, he did not know. A sound stirred his senses and continued to tug at him. He sat up and looked over at his sleeping companions and then around the large, open room. It was still dark. He lay back down on the coach and listened for some time before hearing the sound again. It was a whisper so quiet, he wondered if he imagined it. A short time later, however, it came again.

"Lord Bryn," the voice called from the dark courtyard outside.

Bryn's first thought was Aayliyah was calling to him, and he quickly stood up and walked to the door facing the courtyard. The inky darkness of the night was fading slightly into gray, but he could see no one. Cautiously, he continued outside for a better look. He briefly considered waking Martin and Rand, knowing it was the wise thing to do, but something inside held him back. He wanted to speak to Aayliyah alone, if only for a moment. Bryn was not a selfish person. It was just that he liked to do things on his own. Besides, she called to him, not the others.

The early morning air felt crisp against his face as he performed a careful search of the courtyard. As far as he could tell, no one was there. He decided to return to his bed, and he was halfway up the steps to the manor house when he heard the call again.

"Lord Bryn!"

The voice sounded urgent. It came from around the east side of the building. Bryn quickly walked past the great pillars and around the corner of the house. Set back a ways was another much smaller structure. In truth, it was little more than a stone shed. Bryn hesitated as he scrutinized it from where he stood. The sense of foreboding from the night before returned. He moved slowly closer.

"Come, Lord Bryn." The voice was more insistent.

This time Bryn could tell it came from inside the building. He walked closer and noticed that a strange plant grew in a round circle all about the structure. Upon a closer inspection, he thought it looked similar to the branch Argolis had given him. The ring of plants completely blocked the pathway to the door.

He stepped over them, but as he did a surge of apprehension washed over him, more distressing than the earlier warning he'd felt.

He reached for the door and lifted a simply designed release latch. The door was, again, much like the door of the manor house, in relatively good condition when compared to the ruins all around him. He pushed gently, and the door swung open without resistance or sound. The building's interior was not what Bryn expected. There was no floor to speak of, but rather an opening where a stone stairway descended into blackness. *It seems to be a gateway to a cellar or some underground storage area*, Bryn thought.

The apprehension he felt did not lessen. The sky lightened to a soft gray behind him. He looked back toward the courtyard, almost deciding to return to the others, when he heard the voice again. It was much clearer this time and sounded like that of a woman. It possessed an alluring quality, but it lacked the softness of Aayliyah's voice.

Bryn peered into the black stairway opening, noticing a faint silvery glow emanating from something further down the passage. His heart still pounded its warning. Again, he decided to go wake up Martin and Rand, but before he could turn away, the voice became a cry for help.

"Help me, Bryn! Help me!"

Bryn forced down the rising caution and began descending the stairway. He could not turn away from any person who called out for help, especially a woman. The air grew colder the further he descended. Walls of perfectly cut square stones flanked him on both sides. There were none of the signs of age so visible in the ruins above. There were no cracks or crumbling, not even dust. Bryn continued slowly.

The silvery glow emanated from some source beyond the landing at the bottom of the stairs. It was an odd illumination. Instead of spreading out and banishing the darkness the way natural light did, it hung in the air toward the top of the passage. Bryn crouched again and bent his head forward to look down the passageway just beyond the landing. The floor was too low to receive much illumination from the higher up glowing light, and Bryn could not make out anything clearly.

He slowly straightened and made to take the last few steps, but he stumbled on something unseen on the darkened steps. Pitching forward, he fell face first onto the landing with a thump. His sword, which hung from a belt around his waist, clattered against the smooth stone floor but held fast. Peering back over his shoulder, he saw a small shadowed shape on the floor by his feet.

He slowly sat up and reached back toward the object. It was square and heavy for its size, and he held it up higher for a better look. It was a box or flat chest of some kind, about the thickness of Bryn's forearm. He could feel a latch and keyhole on the flat hard surface and several smooth, small bumps covering the container. In the poor lighting, he couldn't make out much detail so Bryn stood up and set the flat chest onto one of the steps, careful to note its placement. He turned and looked back down the passageway. The strange silver glowing continued for some distance until swallowed up in the darkness. Upon closer examination, Bryn discovered that the strange glowing light came from the top row of stone blocks lining the hallway walls. The lower rows remained dark.

He began walking down the corridor, careful not to lose his footing again. The thought occurred to him that the door above was locked from the outside, which meant whoever called to him was trapped or imprisoned down here. He stopped and instinctively placed his hand on the hilt of his sword. The sound of someone walking came from down the corridor. He squinted his eyes against the darkness but saw no one. The sound stopped.

Bryn knew he should return to his companions, but there was some mystery here and he intended to discover its source. Looking back over his shoulder toward the stairs, out of the corner of his eye, he saw movement down the hallway in front of him. He quickly turned back just in time to see the gray form of a woman disappear into the wall on his left further down the corridor.

The Underground City

A wave of cold shock passed through Bryn's mind. He strained his eyes against the dull, glowing light. All was completely still in the gloom of the corridor. He hesitated, expecting something more to happen. But there was no further sign of the strange apparition. It was a woman, of that he felt sure. She was visible for only a brief moment, but Bryn was left with a strange mixture of excitement and apprehension. Something about the woman intrigued him. Who would be down in this forlorn underground passage? Aayliyah claimed to be alone in this ruined city.

Bryn continued moving toward where the woman vanished. It was not far, but he was cautious. His footsteps sounded unnaturally loud as they echoed in the passageway. He reached the spot only to find another hall branching off to his left. It was much like the first passage, but Bryn noticed the glowing blocks now covered two of the upper rows, giving a little more light. The floor of the side passage slanted downward. He followed it for some time before coming to a small platform.

On one side of the platform, another stairway led downward, which in turn also ended in a platform and another stairs. At the bottom of this final stairway was a small chamber with a single door at the far side. The door was slightly ajar, with a much brighter light coming through the partial opening.

He moved to the small doorway and looked through, surprised at what he saw. A vast hall filled with the silvery, glowing light stretched on beyond Bryn's sight. It was a city beneath a city. Yet there were no dwellings of any kind that Bryn could see. Instead, there were hundreds of great statues and stone monuments rising up across the hall. There were narrow streets of sorts, which outlined each monument in a square, giving Bryn the feeling it was a sort of giant maze.

He walked toward the nearest statue, which was at least twice his own height. It was the image of a great warrior with his left foot resting on a boulder and his arm upraised lofting a great sword. The warrior's face reflected strength, but Bryn noted cruelty in his eyes and expression. Across the narrow lane to Bryn's left stood another warrior statue. This one rode a great warhorse. The horse wore a fierce snarl as it charged some unknown enemy. Both statues were made of white marble and glowed silver in the strange light. To his right several more statues dominated his view.

There was something about this place that made the hair on the back of Bryn's neck prickle. All his senses warned him of danger. He looked back toward the stairway door, which yawned black only a short distance behind him. The sight of it helped to calm his growing nerves. It was strange after all. Why should he feel so apprehensive? He had seen nothing to be afraid of. Turning back toward the statue of the rider, he glimpsed someone disappear behind the base of a monument just beyond where he stood. Quickly he ran to the spot and looked down the already empty lane. He hesitated in another moment of indecision, not wanting to venture too far from the doorway back to the surface. In a maze of this magnitude, he could easily lose himself for days.

The sound of lilting laughter came from somewhere not far ahead to his right. He moved down the lane and crossed at the base of another oddly shaped monument. The laughter came again, but from his left now. Bryn changed direction, moving more quickly. Hearing the sound of water splashing in a steady cadence, he stopped and tilted his head to listen. The laughter had stopped, so he continued on toward the sound of the running water. It was not far.

Standing alone in one of the many square courts surrounded by the paved lanes was a large round pool and fountain not much different from those in the city above. On the far end of the square stood another statue, the imposing figure of a king sitting upon a throne. It was larger and more prominent than any of the others Bryn could see. It was unique in that the robes covering the figure appeared to be real cloth. They were bright purple and flowed from the king's shoulders to his ankles. Bryn found this odd, but he did not have long to consider it.

Sitting on a stone bench on the far side of the pool facing the statue of the king sat the woman. She wore a shimmering silver dress almost metallic in its sheen. Her hair was long and black. Bryn walked slowly to the bench without speaking, and the lady appeared not to have noticed him. Her face was turned upward toward the kingly statue, a look of rapture on her face.

"My lady, is all well with you?"

The lady, for lady she obviously was, turned to look directly into Bryn's eyes. She was beautiful. Her exquisite features took Bryn by surprise, and he swallowed hard.

"My Lord Bryn!" She spoke with a sudden smile that for some unknown reason made him feel a surge of pride. "You are *most* welcome here." Her emphasis brought a mixture of discomfort and yearning to Bryn.

He did not understand the war going on in his mind. It confused him. Not being a proud person or one given to self-satisfaction, his thoughts were being filled with a level of arrogance he would have otherwise despised. He tried to clear his head by shaking it back and forth. Bryn looked back at the woman and was not sure what to say.

"Do you need help?"

She did not answer at first, but she tilted her head as though listening.

"You called for me? Did you not?" Bryn tried to prompt a response.

"A hero was needed and a hero has been found." The lady's answer was more of a riddle than anything.

Again, Bryn felt pride swelling up inside. She turned toward him and lifted her hand to his arm. Her movements were fluid, and Bryn could not help feeling his heart beat faster. The feel of her skin was soft but oddly cold.

"The king has long awaited a worthy hero. You are his chosen."

Every time the lady spoke, Bryn felt an inexplicable rush of excitement. Her voice was unlike any other, beautiful and bold. Yet as wonderful as it sounded, something was missing. It made no sense to him at all, but the feeling persisted.

The lady raised her soft white hand to Bryn's cheek and looked deep into his eyes. "*I* too have waited long."

For a moment, Bryn felt as though he would do whatever this lady asked of him, if only to please her. Scenes of glory began to flash through his mind. Riding a great white stallion and charging a line of warriors who quaked at his approach, he lifted a great sword high above his head and loosed a battle cry, filling the air with thunder. He crashed through the warrior's feeble-looking line with a terrible fury, utterly smashing his foe without mercy or remorse. The enemy fled before him as he again lifted his battle cry.

Bryn jerked as he came back to himself and heard the sound of his own voice echoing away in the vast underground hallway. Embarrassed to realize he held his sword outstretched above his head, he quickly sheathed it and turned back to the lady. He expected to find her embarrassed or at least shocked by his unseemly outburst. However, she was not even looking at him. Instead, her gaze was upon the king, and she was on her knees in a posture of worship.

The warning in Bryn's heart now began to pound in his ears. He felt like a rabbit caught in a snare. He glanced quickly around to locate the door back to the surface, but he could no longer see it. As quickly as before, another scene of glory flashed through his mind. He was standing on a balcony dressed in kingly robes, and a crowd of thousands, even tens of thousands, now stood below him waiting with expectation. He raised his fist high in the air, and with one voice, the people's cheer filled the air. He smiled with horrible arrogance as he soaked in the crowd's adulation.

Snapping out of the vision and back into his right mind, the self-indulgent smile still clinging to his face, he cringed as a surge of panic swept through his stomach. Something was happening here he did not understand and could not easily fight. The lady was still on her knees, but was now raising her hands in supplication to the statue. Bryn heard her softly chanted words, but he did not understand them. A cold sweat broke out across his forehead. All the intrigue and curiosity that lured him to this place fell away. He looked quickly around, trying to get his bearings, and then turned sharply back to the lady.

"I will leave this place at once. Will you come with me?" He gave her a last chance for help, if she truly wanted it. He held out his hand to the woman who still looked upon the statue.

She gave no response.

"My lady, you should come with me." He beckoned her with his outstretched hand.

Still, she did not respond, but continued looking intently upon the statue.

Bryn grew more impatient and snapped, "It is nothing but stone!"

The woman's features suddenly hardened in response to Bryn's statement. Her eyes turned so cold Bryn thought he could actually feel the temperature drop all around him. Slowly she turned her eyes toward Bryn and there was a look of malice that was not there before. After a brief moment, however, her demeanor changed once again, becoming as light and beautiful as before.

"Lord Bryn, surely you jest?" There was dismissive laughter behind her words. "His throne may be made of stone, but the king is not!" She turned back to the statue and bowed her head again.

Bryn looked on, not sure whether to be angry or to feel pity. It was obvious to him the lady must be mad. He looked out across the hall, and as far as he could see, stone statues rose, one after another. *Now* what should he do? He could not very well leave a crazy woman down in this place alone. Yet it was becoming quite clear she would not be easily convinced to leave this place either.

He turned toward the statue and looked up at it out of disgust more than anything. The white stone features were amazing in every detail. Bryn had never seen such workmanship. A real and quite magnificent gold crown sat upon the king's head. It was encrusted with many gemstones. The figure sat in a state of repose, with his eyes closed as if he were in deep consideration. He looked back toward the crown. Something did not seem quite right.

He considered this for a moment before deciding it was the king's hair. It was not like other statues. Individual strands could be seen and the level of skill it must have taken to accomplish such a craft was amazing. There was, however, something else. The hair was white, but not the same shade as the rest of the statue. Bryn's eyes narrowed as he considered this new discovery. He turned momentarily to glance at the woman still kneeling beside him. She was chanting softly in some unknown language.

Bryn slowly exhaled and looked back to the statue. Horror filled his heart when he realized the king's eyes were no longer closed, but now looked directly into his own.

The Aletae

What sorcery was this? Bryn could not believe what he was seeing. The statue's head moved slightly downward as he looked upon the lady next to him. Bryn could not help staring wildly at the thing as it raised its right arm toward her. The woman stood to her feet and kissed the outstretched hand over and over again. Bryn continued to stare at the king as the truth now flooded over him. This was not a statue made by human hands but a creature, like a man but not a man.

The king slowly stood to his feet and stretched as if waking from a long sleep. His skin was as white as the stone all around them. He reached for something hanging on the other side of his great stone throne. A sword as tall as Bryn slid from its hidden sheath, and the king held it out in front of him. An expression of maliciousness crossed his large features as he examined the sword, then he turned back to Bryn and the lady.

"I have slept long, waiting for my champion to arise." His voice unnerved Bryn. It was deep and hard. The authority it carried was unmistakable. He looked directly at Bryn. "Kneel." It was a command not to be denied by anyone who loved life. Bryn, nevertheless, stood a bit straighter than before. A flash of angry puzzlement flashed across the king's white features. He looked back to the woman, who was already on her knees. She in turn looked at Bryn with an expression of alarm.

"You must kneel," she said nervously.

The determination in Bryn's face only grew.

A small wave of panic swept across the woman's face before she regained her original demeanor. She quickly stood and moved deftly to Bryn's side and raised both her hands to his cheeks.

"My love, this is what we have always wanted," she spoke alluringly.

Despite having never seen this woman before, memories of the two of them planning this very moment began flooding into his mind. He shook his head in an attempt to clear it once more. Nothing made any sense. Everything was muddled. A strong desire to please this lady flooded over him again.

How easy it would be, he thought, *to do whatever she asks of me*. To simply live within her embrace would be all he needed for happiness.

As if in response to his thought, she slid her arms around him and squeezed gently. The scent of flowers and incense filled the air around him. Oh, how he wanted to give in. All he must do was kneel. It was a small thing she asked, after all.

Something deep inside him still resisted. It was nothing more than a note of conflict, but it would not desist. It irritated him. Why could he not just release himself to this lady and her king? Heroic visions began to play across his mind again. He turned toward the king.

"Kneel!" the command came again.

Bryn, forcing down the warning that held him back, looked at the lady. She examined him with a hungry anticipation. Slowly he began bending his knee, and as he did so, his right hand came up across his chest. A flicker of green light distracted him. He glanced down to see a golden ring set with a single emerald on the first finger of his right hand. The image of his father handing him this golden ring came back into his memory. He froze with his knee still only slightly bent. What was he doing? The words of his father's blessing echoed back to him. "Follow the true path and none other."

His allegiance was already given to the High King of heaven. He could not, nor would he, give it to any other. Shaking his head briskly, he straightened and stood fully erect.

"I know not what goes on here, but I will *not* swear fealty to you nor bend my knee!" There was no give in Bryn's words.

The woman cringed violently and pulled away from him. She glared at Bryn with a hatred he never experienced before. The king's face did not change, but for a slight darkening of the tone of his skin, if that's really what it was. The change that came over the lady, however, caught Bryn by complete surprise. She now stood a head taller than Bryn, and her hair turned gray with streaks of white. She hissed at him and gave him a menacing grimace. Two prominent fangs now protruded from her mouth. He shuddered to think of what he had almost succumbed to.

"No one will resist me and live! Kneel before me or die," the king said, lifting his sword.

The choice was plain, and the danger quite real, but Bryn was not one to shrink from any threat. Everything was clear again, and he would not budge. He pulled his own sword from its sheath but, before he could even raise it, the woman's arm snaked out with blinding speed. Grabbing it by the blade, she ripped it from Bryn's grasp. He stepped back out of surprise more than anything. He had never been disarmed in such a way before.

She grabbed Bryn by the neck and squeezed. He gasped for breath and tried to free himself, but the strength of this... this thing was too much for him. He could feel darkness starting to encroach on the edges of his vision, when the woman shrieked and dropped him. He fell to his knees, choking and wheezing. The woman screamed and writhed in agony. The king dropped his great sword, which clanged onto the stone floor and threw his hands before his eyes to shield them. Bryn struggled back to his feet, trying to discover what had saved him.

Standing on the far side of the square, Aayliyah held her hand up and out in front of her. She was holding something green, but Bryn could not see what it was at that distance. She would come no closer, but called out to Bryn instead.

"Come quickly," she called again. There was urgency in her tone.

Bryn did not need any further encouragement. He was already running to join his unlikely rescuer. She continued to hold out her hand as she turned and pointed back to the doorway, which was now clearly visible. They both made a hasty retreat up the long stairway and down the dark corridors until Bryn could at last see the patch of natural light coming down the stairway leading to the surface. Here, Bryn paused as Aayliyah continued up the stairs. She looked back down at him with a questioning look.

"Wait, there is something I must find," he said in response.

A look of understanding crossed her face mixed with some small regret. "I am sorry. Your sword cannot be reclaimed without great and unnecessary peril."

"No, it is not that. There is something else here. I found it earlier."

As much as he appreciated his sword, Bryn would not even consider trying to reclaim it. He felt the dark steps until his hands hit upon the square box he had tripped over earlier. He picked it up, held it under his arm, and quickly followed Aayliyah up the remaining stairs.

The rays of the morning sun were just breaking across the top of the jungle to the east of the ruined city. The brightness hurt his eyes at first, but he was so glad to see the natural light again. There was warmth in it that refreshed the soul.

Aayliyah did not stop until she crossed over the row of plants that grew in a circle around the small building. Bryn followed her to the other side where they both paused to catch their breath. He glanced sheepishly at Aayliyah, ashamed of how easily he had been ensnared by such evil. Bryn thought he could see disappointment in her face as she glanced toward the opening to the underground hall.

"I am sorry, Aayliyah. I should not have..." Bryn let his head drop slightly, trying hard to find the right words to redress his failure. What could he say? He was not one to seek personal glory, but down there he almost gave into something horrible. He looked back down at the ring on his hand and wondered what his father would think of him.

Aayliyah turned to look directly at Bryn. She appeared perplexed. "The fault is not yours," she quickly concluded. "*I* should have warned you of the Aletae. I did not think they would act so swiftly."

Bryn glanced quickly back at Aayliyah, not willing to let himself off so easily. "I almost gave into *them*!" He spat out the last word with distaste.

Aayliyah shook her head. "No, Bryn. You resisted them to the death. No one could have done better."

Bryn turned away sharply, letting his frustration show.

Again, Aayliyah looked momentarily puzzled at his reaction, before understanding swept across her features. "I see," she said more to herself than Bryn. "You have never been defeated in battle before."

Bryn felt ashamed and could not look into her eyes. He knew that but for her timely arrival, he would be dead now, or worse. She reached out and put her hand on his shoulder. Her touch was nothing like the woman's in the underground hall. Instead, it was warm and caring, and Bryn felt an immediate restorative balm wash over him.

"Bryn, you were *not* defeated." It was stated as a simple truth, but there was empathy in her words. "Few can resist the power of the Aletae. Those who do are victorious, *not* defeated. They have reason to rejoice, not feel shame."

As Aayliyah finished encouraging Bryn, she glanced down and for the first time noticed the square object he still carried under his arm. She caught her breath and slowly reached for it. Bryn, not sure why she reacted so, handed her the object. It was a carved wooden box two handbreadths in length and width. The wood was dark and aged, and it was heavy enough for Bryn to guess it was not empty. Several jewels were inset into the wood on the top panel of the box, and there was a keyhole on the side.

"Where did you find it?" she asked without taking her eyes from it. Her expression now turned to one of wonderment.

"Well… I sort of stumbled on it down there." He pointed back toward the stairs, remembering his unceremonious discovery of the box. "It was just sitting there, not hidden in any way." Bryn's curiosity was growing. "Why? What is it?"

She did not answer immediately, but continued to examine the box. Her eyes fixed upon a line of strange rune-type markings stretched across its front. Bryn guessed she understood the markings based upon the growing excitement in her eyes.

"Aayliyah?"

She looked from the box back to Bryn and hesitated, as though judging whether he could really be trusted with her secret. For a moment, Bryn was not at all sure he would pass her scrutiny, but then her face softened once again.

"I believe it contains an ancient book of stories. But I have only heard of it. I have never seen it. My father used to tell me of it and the stories it contains, those that were passed down anyway. It was lost long ago, and like my father and grandfather before him, I have searched for it most of my life. It is said to contain the very words of life."

She hesitated once again and then, with a pained expression, slowly extended the box back to Bryn. "You found it. It is yours now." Her voice was tinged with a soft hint of sorrow.

Bryn took the box and carefully turned it over. Carved in the wood of its back were two small trees. Even though he would like nothing more than to find out what the book contained, if it was a book, he knew no one would take better care of it than Aayliyah. He extended it back to her. "Thanks, but I don't think I will find much time for reading. I give it back to you."

"Truly you are noble," she said with wide-eyed gratitude.

Despite himself, Bryn smiled at her reaction, before turning away to look at the eastern horizon. The light from the rising sun was intensifying over the rim of the jungle wall. He ran his hand through his hair, still trying to understand what had happened in the underground hall. *What were those things down there, and why were they seeking him?* He turned back to Aayliyah who was still gazing with joy at the small box in her hands.

"Who are you really, Aayliyah, and what were those... things down there?"

She was silent for a moment before answering. "Like my father and his line before him, I am the guardian of the Plant of Truth."

Bryn waited for her to continue, but she apparently thought her answer was sufficient.

"What is this... Plant of Truth?" he coaxed, trying to find out more.

Instead of answering, she held out the small, green twig she was carrying and gave it to Bryn. It was the same leafy plant Argolis brought to True North. Bryn looked over at the row of plants ringing the small stone building. For the first time, he noticed they were all the same plant. He was about to continue questioning Aayliyah when he heard Martin's call.

They found Martin and Rand in the courtyard by the fountain. Aayliyah quickly disappeared into the manor house as Bryn explained the morning's events. Much to Bryn's surprise, Martin offered him no chastisement.

"You said Aayliyah puts high value on the contents of a box you found?" Martin rubbed his jaw as he spoke, expectancy filling the features of his face.

Bryn, noticing Martin's unusual demeanor, answered with a question. "Why? Do you think it is important?"

Aayliyah reemerged from the manor house carrying a platter of the unique but delightful food from the night before. Martin's eyes remained full of questioning excitement, but he held his tongue as she approached. She brought the sweet breads to each of them, starting with

Martin. After they were served, she set the plate down on the fountain wall.

"My lady," Martin said, not able to wait any longer. "I know that this is your home and must have been for some time." He paused and tapped his finger against his chin. "But does anything prevent you from leaving this place with us?"

Aayliyah bowed her head in a submissive gesture. "I am the last of my father's line. It was for this very purpose and time that 'Ram of the Flame,' our forefather, was entrusted with the Plant of Truth. I have waited many years for Adoil to come. I will go with you."

The three men exchanged questioning glances. Aayliyah's explanation, as always seemed to be the case with her, left more questions than answers.

"Who is Adoil?" Bryn asked.

"Adoil is the ship that carries creation's light. It was prophesied during the days of Ram that Adoil would come at the end of our line. When one who is lawless arises and tries to seize the power of the Garden for himself, Adoil would come."

Rand, who up to this point did not have a clue as to what was happening, perked up. "I believe she means True North," he spoke with excitement. Something finally made some sense to him. Both Bryn and Martin simply looked at Rand, who promptly sat back down on a bench by the dancing fountain.

"Good!" Martin said eagerly. "Then we shall return to True North... ah... Adoil, together." He paused again. "As Guardian of the

Plant, is there anything that prevents you from collecting some of it to bring with us?"

Aayliyah, still holding tightly to the box containing the Book of Stories, smiled back at Martin. "I have already prepared it." She pointed to a pot sitting on a bench at the entrance to the courtyard. A medium-sized plant grew in it. She turned back to Bryn and said, "Do not fear for your brother."

Bryn, continuing to realize there was far more to Aayliyah than met the eye, looked to Martin as if to ask whether this plant could really save Aedan. Martin did not speak, but only nodded his head slowly in assent to Bryn's questioning look.

It only took a few moments to gather Aayliyah's things. Bryn and Rand carried her packs, while Martin quickly took careful charge of the plant. They waited in the courtyard while Aayliyah briefly returned to the manor house and retrieved a long, tapered item wrapped in a mixture of leather and cloth. She walked over to Bryn and held it out in a gesture of gratefulness.

"A gift worthy of your courage," she said simply.

Bryn reached out with uncertainty. He knelt down and carefully unwrapped it. The glint of silver metal made him blink. A sword like no other met his eyes. It was simple enough in its design, but the length of its metal blade danced with subtle light, almost as if it burned with an inner flame. Its hilt was inlaid with three small, red rubies on each side. He hefted it and felt its well-balanced weight. This was not just a sword, but also a companion to be valued in its own right.

"It is the sword of Ram, my forefather. Use it as he did and his sons after him. Use it to defend the defenseless and to see justice done upon the wicked. If so used, it cannot easily be overcome. The Sargaroth know and fear it." Aayliyah spoke with an appreciation for the sword the men could easily understand. Bryn inclined his head in acceptance. What could be said to justly honor such a marvelous gift?

The Stone Map

T he large ship swayed under a restless breeze as it entered the
expansive bay adjacent to the western walls of Perginton. It was a
hot day, and the wind was welcome. From this distance, the high walls
of the city appeared normal enough. Nothing could be seen of its recent
violent overthrow. The harbor was busy with commotion as small boats
ferried men and supplies back and forth.

Lisnor looked beyond the city walls at the dark forested hills
beyond and wondered what his master could possibly want with this
place. Five members of the Lawless stood behind him, awaiting his
orders. They all wore a simple robe of black sackcloth tied at the waist
with a length of plain rope. Their foreheads, now concealed beneath

heavy hoods despite the heat of the day, all bore the mark of the Lawless, a single blue, coiled snake.

Lisnor's hood, unlike the others, hung loosely at his back. He often went about without covering his head simply because of the enjoyment he experienced at seeing the shock it caused in others. His head was completely shaved with the exception of along shock of red hair hanging from the center of the back of his head. The rest of his head was covered in horrible purple scars, with several piercings from which hung silver rings.

"Prepare to go to shore, we will be anchoring soon," Lisnor spoke without emotion. "I will go ahead to make sure all is ready for the master."

Upon their arrival in the bay, several small boats began racing toward them, each vying to be the first to offer their transport services. While many of the inhabitants of Perginton fled the city to more remote regions, there were always those who hoped to profit no matter who ruled over them. Lisnor signaled one of these boatmen to come alongside the ship. The boatman was eager to offer his services and could not stop talking.

"There you go, sir! You picked the best of the lot, and that's no idle tale. I'll see you t'shore in the shake of a stick. Yes, sir." He tilted his head and winked, ignoring Lisnor's awful looks. "Yes, sir." He nodded as though it was an obvious fact.

The boatman smelled of sour sweat mixed with fish guts, and Lisnor turned his nose away. It always perturbed him when his looks failed to cause the desired level of intimidation in the people he encountered.

The small boat moved off toward the docks with excellent speed as promised. Upon their arrival a short time later, the boatman jumped up and made his way toward the ladder that led up to the dock with an agile quickness. He took his hat off, freeing several shocks of white, wispy hair to blow in the wind. He bowed slightly as if to reinforce the good nature of his service. Lisnor noticed the man's other hand was extended, open palm upward. He began climbing the ladder without any offer of payment for the boatman's service. The old man's hand reached up and caught Lisnor by the shoulder.

"Pardon me, sire. But perhaps if you could show but a small appreciation for my excellent service?" The man issued a friendly smile while looking up under big bushy eyebrows.

Lisnor froze at the man's touch. Cold hatred crossed his twisted face as he slowly turned back toward the boatman. His hand flashed upward with a wicked-looking blade produced from beneath a fold in his robe, and before the poor man even knew what went wrong, Lisnor's blade was buried to its hilt just under his ribs. He swatted at the handle, gasping for air as he tried to speak. Lisnor stepped in closer and watched the man's eyes with a newfound eagerness as they emptied of life. Then he pushed him over the edge of the boat into the dark waters and began climbing to the docks above.

Malen was seated on the king's throne when several members of the Lawless brought Peleg before him in chains as ordered. Lanthir stood off to the side in rigid silence. Lisnor stood close by at Malen's left hand. Peleg was surprisingly clean and well groomed, and Malen raised a slightly quizzical eyebrow.

"Why, Peleg, it appears you have not suffered overly much during your captivity." Malen glanced sideways at Lanthir, who continued to look straight ahead.

"By *what right* have you committed these crimes against my people?" Peleg demanded. His voice shook with the rage he felt, and his face was red.

"By what right?" Malen repeated the question as though it never occurred to him before. "Well, I suppose by the simple right of having the *power* to do so. Anyway," he continued with a dismissive gesture, "I need to know what lies beneath your palace."

Peleg appeared confused. He glanced over at Lanthir for explanation. Malen nodded to one of his servants. The man promptly slapped Peleg so hard he was flung to the floor. Lanthir started a little but regained his rigidity.

"There is a stone map of sorts here, somewhere," Malen continued. "I simply want you to tell me where it is." Malen held out his hand as though he were trying to be reasonable. Peleg was pulled roughly back to his knees. Blood trickled from his nose and lips. He glared at Malen.

"You're mad!" he spat before turning his face back toward Lanthir. "Is *this* what you serve now?" There was contempt in his voice.

Lanthir shifted uneasily but still said nothing.

Malen laughed out loud. "Lisnor, I have no further use for this man." He pointed at Peleg. "Bring me all the palace servants. I will find what I seek."

As Lisnor's men dragged Peleg out of the throne room, Lanthir turned abruptly and walked out a side door, an expression of disgust on his face. Malen silently watched him go.

True to his word, it did not take Malen long to discover the entrance to the lower levels of the palace. It was not even hidden, and as Malen soon discovered, there was no reason for it to be so. There were many storage rooms, but unlike Malen's palace in Illyrium, there were no dungeons or treasure rooms to speak of. What Malen found only served to reinforce his low opinion of the place in general.

There was something about this one small room, however. It was at the far end of one of the passages. There was nothing special about it other than it appeared to be ancient in origin. While none of the other passages or rooms were new by any standard, this room was much older. It was small and square, and Malen could barely stand up straight. The walls of the room were rough-hewn rock, chiseled by some blunt instrument long ago.

Malen ordered everything in the room emptied, which was completed in a relatively short period of time. But nothing was found.

There were no carvings, no hidden openings, not even a clue. It was just an empty, cold, damp room. Malen's frustration was growing. He felt a suffocating panic rising in the center of his chest. If he could not find the stone map, the Garden of the Aletae would remain lost to him.

One of the men clearing the room approached Malen. "It looks like an empty room, my lord."

The man spoke the obvious conclusion without noticing the growing look of fury on Malen's face. Before the man could react, Malen grabbed him by the scruff of the neck with both hands and flung him headfirst into the wall. The hapless worker collapsed in a heap. Malen, however, caught his breath with astonishment. The man's head actually cracked the wall, and a slight breeze could be felt coming through the newly opened fissure. Malen's response was immediate and very nearly uncontrolled in his renewed hope of discovery.

"Smash it down!" he shrieked.

His men fell over themselves in their attempt to comply with the order. A hole in the wall large enough for a man to climb through was quickly opened. The worker who was smashed into the wall now sat up groaning as he rubbed his head. Malen peered through the hole with a lantern. There was another passageway on the other side. He carefully climbed through the dark opening, accompanied only by Lisnor and the other members of the Lawless. Cobwebs adorned the walls. The floor was covered in dust and moss. This place had not been visited in ages by anything but vermin and insects. By its appearance, it had been intentionally blocked off and then forgotten long ago.

Malen could hardly contain his excitement. This had to be it. The map was here and he would find it. Then nothing would stand in his way. He would have unlimited power and the crown jewel of immortality. He could not help but smile. Today he would find the connecting clue to the search that began so long ago, and he relished the thought in every detail.

He crept down the ancient corridor, careful not to miss anything in his eagerness. It was not long before he found himself standing in another room, much larger than the first. Malen held his lantern up high above his head. The ceiling of this room stood several arms' lengths higher than he could reach. Here and there, portions of painted tiles still covered the floor and walls. In the center of the room was a circular break in the floor tile. Short benches carved out of stone surrounded the spot.

Malen ordered his servants to bring torches. He handed his lantern to Lisnor and motioned him closer. In the center of the circular opening were irregular shapes and bumps. Lisnor held out both lanterns as Malen bent down low to examine the open section of floor. Malen let his hands run across the stone as though he caressed something of great value. This was it! He could feel adrenaline pulsing through his heart. It was a map carved into the very bedrock floor of the chamber. It was big enough to require four large steps to cross from one side to the other.

The map was divided into three sections, separated by small ridges of stone left to serve as a careful outline of each. The first of the sections was simple in its design. There were three elements. A small, flat, raised portion in a roughly elongated shape—*almost like a bean*, Malen considered—sat somewhat adjacent to the left of a long, flat, raised portion that disappeared into the edge of the map. Finally, an even smaller but more rounded, raised portion was situated beneath the bean-shaped object, but more to the right.

Malen carefully considered the stone carvings before moving to the next section at the bottom of the map. Unlike the first part, this area contained visible human figures and chiseled words. There was also an interesting variation in the small stone ridge that separated it out from the other two sections above. It had become as wide as a hand's breadth and gave the impression it served as a ceiling or roof over the figures carved beneath it. There was a large figure of a king seated upon a throne with his head bent slightly as though asleep. Around his throne danced what appeared to be young maidens. A flat portion beneath the figures contained a text written in the ancient language of the Tharusians, which Malen knew well enough. He hungrily rubbed his hands together as he looked toward the final section, located in the upper right-hand portion of the circular map.

This part was again altogether different from the other sections. There was a city at the bottom of the carving with a harbor facing west and many trees carved to the north and east. In the upper portion of the forest was what appeared to be a mountain with a dark opening at its base. Smaller text dotted the map in various locations. Many of the smaller sections of text appeared to be directions. Malen guessed they led to the mountain featured at the top of the map.

A larger portion of text also appeared underneath the city. It immediately caught Malen's eye. He had seen it before and already translated it once. It read,

Beware the northern forest reach, where in the darkness daunting death sleeps.
In Escalon's ancient prison hole, ancient demons there we keep.
The emerald amulet holds at bay, those unholy dogs of the Aletae.

Malen spent the remaining part of the day translating the other script located in the second portion of the stone map. He was meticulous in his deciphering. Finishing the script and sitting back to review his work with deep satisfaction, he ran a hand through his hair in an attempt to calm his building excitement. It was worded as a warning.

To he who would seek Tir nan Og, the land of palaces, the isle of Ogygia, where youth reigns, yes where youth reigns, and wealth does abound. There sleeps Cronus of the Neteru, the watchers from the sky. He sleeps and waits beneath the darkness, held... (or embraced—Malen was not familiar with this particular word) *...by the plant. The golden age of the Aletae is darkness to men, darkness to men. There death grows in the garden.*

Malen's heart beat fast as he read and reread the inscription. It was a dire warning to be sure. But what of that! Smaller-minded men may have reason to fear, but not Malen. Not he who could harness such knowledge and turn it to his advantage. To him it was pure delight.

He continued looking over the map. The upper left portion was obviously a bird's-eye view of landmasses. The bean-shaped portion resembled the island of Tharrus; and the flat wide area, the coastline of Illyrium; but what was this third smaller landmass to the southeast of Tharrus? Although there were no markings or script of any kind on this part of the map, Malen knew it was the location of the Garden of the Aletae. He bent down to get a better look and placed his now trembling hand outside the circular map for more support as he leaned in closer. Quite suddenly his hand slipped as some sort of stone plate shifted beneath it. Malen jerked back. He called for more light, and Lisnor, who was always close by, instinctively obeyed.

It was a secret panel not seen in the dim lighting. He reached down and slid the flat stone plate over to one side. The light from Lisnor's lantern glinted green off an object concealed under the plate.

"The emerald amulet," Malen whispered, "it holds at bay..." He reached down and gently picked up a heavy gold chain from which dangled a large, green gemstone of unusual size and beauty. He turned it over and blew off the accumulated dust. On the back of the gold setting were words clearly different from those of the ancient Tharusian language. These words were the same as those Malen encountered many years ago in the Book of Knowledge. He stood briskly, placed the golden chain over his head, and turned to Lisnor, who was starring at the amulet with a curious gleam in his eye.

"Lisnor, prepare the Lawless and have our reluctant friend Lanthir make ready his men. I will require an escort. We journey to the northern forest called Escalon." Malen's voice carried an exultant note.

He turned to walk back down the ancient stone corridor, but paused. "And Lisnor, the workmen who know of this room must never speak of it."

"Yes, master, I will see it done." Lisnor bowed his head and smiled with understanding as he considered the men they had pressed into labor. He would take pleasure in this task and make sure it was not too quickly accomplished.

Battle Plans

Archimere sat on a crudely made chair with his arms crossed over his chest. His eyes were cast downward as he leaned backward and contemplated their next move. Several others sat across the small fire.

"I say we jes' pick em off one b' one! Hit 'n' run." It was Mr. Bonfire who spoke. When no one agreed, he grunted like a boar rooting in the dirt.

"We can't just sit here and wait for something to happen. Every day we wait they brutalize the people more." The young man named Rafe spoke.

"Hmmpf!" Mr. Bonfire, who was obviously not impressed with Rafe's input, spit into the fire.

The sound of soft singing came to them. Valentus, who sat with the group waiting and listening to their talk, now turned his head in the direction of the music. Alenia sat on a blanket spread across the grass, singing to the other women and a few of the children. The sound of the water falling over the rock cliff lightly filled the background. All talk of going on raids failed to interest Valentus any more. He could think of little else than the beauty of the song and its singer. The music was building to its crescendo when one of the sentries abruptly appeared out of the surrounding forest.

"Lord Archimere!" The man paused to catch his breath.

"What's wrong, Zeb?" Concern furrowed the faces of the men surrounding the campfire. Zeb was one of the outpost sentries charged with watching the paths closer to their camp.

"There are soldiers just to the south, moving in this direction."

"How many?" Archimere's demeanor became serious.

"Twenty," Zeb responded definitively.

"Good. Well, it appears our question has been answered for us," Archimere said with a sudden smile. "Gather the men. Tell them to dress for stealth. Tonight we pay the invaders a visit." The men moved quickly away in several directions, leaving Archimere and Valentus alone at the fire.

Archimere looked up at the setting sun on the horizon, shielding his eyes. "The light will be gone soon," he said. "Whatever happens tonight, stay close to Mr. Bonfire."

Valentus nodded and glanced back toward Alenia. She was already moving away toward her tent. He stood with a pang of disappointment and went to retrieve his weapons. Archimere was teaching him how to use a sword, but Valentus still felt awkward with it. The only thing close to a weapon that he knew how to use was a bow. It was a necessary tool for survival when tending his uncle's flocks in the wild, and although it was only used for hunting, he possessed some skill with it.

He entered his tent and found the sword Archimere gave him. Strapping it around his waist, he glanced around, not wanting to forget anything important. Other than his bedding, he owned nothing else. Patting his hand on the handle of his sword in an attempt to be reassured, Valentus turned and walked out of his tent. He came to an abrupt stop. Alenia stood directly in front of him with her eyes downcast. His heart began to pound in his chest, and he felt a sudden blush of heat around his neck. He knew he should say something, but what?

"I was just..." he began, but she interrupted.

"Valentus." She spoke with an emotion that made him feel slightly lightheaded. Her eyes rose to meet his, and Valentus thought he saw concern in them. "Please accept this gift." She held out a bow.

Valentus could tell it was costly. The handgrip was wrapped in fine leather, and the tips at both ends were silver. The length of the bow was etched with a scrolling design. It was far more than Valentus had ever owned before, let alone even touched. He swallowed hard, but he could think of nothing to say. The mere fact that she would give *him* anything was beyond his understanding.

As if in answer to his unspoken question, she said, "It is a custom to give gifts to departing warriors. Please accept these things." She held out a quiver of like design in her other hand. It was filled with arrows with scarlet red fletching. There was a silver band around the top and bottom of the quiver. Across the silver band were etched words that circled around the open end.

"What does it say?" he asked.

"It is the ancient language of our people. It says, *Small in Greatness*, and again *Great in smallness*." She pointed to the words as she read them. Valentus watched her finger move. It was more delicate and beautiful than anything he could imagine.

"Thank you," he said quietly.

She nodded her head in response, turned, and walked away. Valentus watched her go before realizing he was holding his breath. He did not know what true valor or bravery felt like. He was just a shepherd, nothing more. Right now, nonetheless, he believed he could defeat the enemy all by himself.

Archimere's men gathered in the center of the camp to await their orders. The advantage in the upcoming battle was theirs. There were fifty of them, all well armed, and they knew the northern forest better than the enemy. The element of surprise was theirs, and they would use it. The men were divided into five contingents of ten to allow for easier movement through the dense forest. The approximate location of the enemy was determined, and each group was given their approach.

Archimere, Mr. Bonfire, and Rafe would each lead ten men in a circling maneuver south. They would use the forest paths they knew well, even in the dark, and go around the enemy. Banton, a seasoned soldier of middle years, would lead the two remaining groups to a position directly north of the invaders' camp. They would pick a good ambush spot and wait for Archimere's signal. Valentus was assigned to the men following Mr. Bonfire.

"We will need to move quickly and quietly. The enemy will be setting up camp soon. Banton, you will wait to the north of their camp. We will attack from the south and push them to you. Take as many prisoners as possible, but let none escape." Archimere drew a rough outline of the battle plan in the dirt before the gathered men. When he finished, he stood and spoke confidently. "Strengthen your hearts men. Tonight, we will be the ones to spring the trap. Now move out."

As the men began melting away into the darkness, Valentus noticed Archimere's appraising look.

"A warrior's gift?" He indicated the bow and quiver.

"Yes." Valentus was embarrassed, but said nothing else.

Archimere continued his scrutiny in silence. All friendliness left his face. His eyes went hard and cold as though he were judging a criminal and considering what punishment was most suitable. Valentus shifted nervously.

"A gift well given. My sister has chosen well." Archimere's smile was sudden and broad. He slapped Valentus on the back and then was off to lead his men.

Archimere's words echoed in Valentus' mind: *chosen well.* Yes, but chosen what?

For all his gruffness, Mr. Bonfire could move like a cat in the woods. They traveled fast and silently across hidden deer trails. It was full night as they neared the area indicated by the sentry. The invaders would be close by. It did not take long for Mr. Bonfire to find their trail. There were, as the sentry reported, about twenty of them, and they traveled light.

A soft birdcall sounded not far to their right, and a moment later, Archimere appeared from behind a large tree. He did not speak, but he used a series of hand signals to communicate. Even a quiet human voice is out of place in the forest at night and might be heard. Mr. Bonfire watched the instructions carefully and then responded in kind. They were to move to the left and wait for Archimere's signal to attack. Rafe, who was located on Archimere's right, would do the same. The sounds of men making camp came faintly to them. Valentus could feel his anxiety growing. This was his first real fight. The thought that men might, and probably would, die still felt unreal to him. They were crawling on their bellies now, moving forward slowly. Somewhere ahead, Valentus saw a firelight flicker through the close-grown forest foliage.

The men in the camp were relatively quiet. Valentus was close enough now to see their faces and hear some of their conversation. Most of what they said, however, was subdued and could not be understood. There was no mistaking the seriousness of their enemy. Each one of them wore a hardened expression.

Mr. Bonfire, who was on the forest floor next to Valentus, appeared perplexed. At first, Valentus could see no reason why, but then it dawned on him. There were only fifteen men in this camp. They were a surly-looking bunch to be sure, but where were the others? There was no noise to the north, nor any indication anything was out of place, but Valentus knew Banton's men would be there by now. It comforted him to know they outnumbered their enemy. His hand went to the bow. Having strung it a little earlier, he still could not decide whether to use it or his sword.

The tension of not knowing when the signal to attack would come, yet knowing it would be soon, irritated Valentus. Undoubtedly, they waited until the missing enemy warriors were located. He looked up at the treetops. A bright moon shone down through the leafy bowers. To the north loomed the dark shape of an imposing, bare rock mountain. Valentus exhaled softly in an attempt to calm his nerves.

A man with flaming red hair and a well-groomed beard appeared out of the only tent in the camp. He carried himself with the ease of a leader. Sleek plaited red leather armor covered his chest, arms, and thighs. His appearance was impressive, and Valentus hoped he would not meet this warrior in the coming battle. The man spoke a few muted words to the men sitting around the campfire.

The chill of the night air was suddenly rent with the sound of an inhuman howl. Valentus just about swallowed his tongue at the hideous noise. The men in the camp jumped to their feet in unison, and their red-haired leader jerked his head toward the north from where it came. A moment of silence was followed by several more piercing howls, and then the forest to the north erupted with the din of men in mortal combat. Screams and shouts filled the air. The red-haired man pulled his sword from its sheath and called his men to arms. They began to move, but Archimere yelled the battle charge and leapt into the camp from the south.

Rafe and Mr. Bonfire both jumped up and into the battle, their men following from the right and left sides. In a hair's breadth of time, the camp erupted into the turmoil and confusion of pitched battle. Valentus, like the others, followed his leader into the camp, but as of yet still found himself outside the actual fighting. There were two of them for every one of the enemy warriors. Their adversaries, however, were not ordinary fighting men. It quickly became apparent their foes were masters of the sword, and any advantage their numbers may ordinarily have given was gone.

Valentus glanced to his right just in time to see one of his companions run through the chest by a wicked thrust. His stomach tightened into a knot and then gave way to numbness. His vision slowed as blood pounded through his ears. He looked around the camp, now boiling with battle. Several others were already facedown, lying in crumpled heaps on the cold ground. He felt strangely detached from the reality of what he was seeing. A cloud settled over his senses. He stood frozen in place, his sword hanging limply at his side, just watching as the fight swirled around him.

He saw Archimere in the center of the fray. Having killed one of the enemy soldiers already, he crossed swords with the red-haired man. The two of them were a fury of flashing blades, but neither could gain any advantage over the other. Each was a master in his own right. Valentus marveled at the sight. The red-haired man almost appeared to enjoy the battle. For a man of his size, he moved with incredible speed. Archimere, nevertheless, matched him move for move.

Valentus heard his name shouted above the din of battle. The cloud of numbness vanished, and every detail of the mortal combat became clear again. He turned to his left to see Mr. Bonfire fighting one particularly large enemy warrior. He was being pushed quickly backwards when he tripped over an exposed root and fell on his back.

Valentus jumped to his aid. His sword jutted out and parried the thrust that would have certainly killed Mr. Bonfire. The enemy warrior turned his focus to Valentus with enjoyment in his eyes. He swiftly spun around and with blinding speed slapped Valentus with his empty hand, knocking him into the air and onto his back not two paces from the campfire. Valentus's sword flew out of his hand into the thick ferns of the forest floor, and his arrows scattered across the ground. The man started for him but stopped abruptly in his tracks.

Out of the darkness, from the north side of the camp, came a living terror. The Illyrian warrior froze where he stood to stare wildly at the nightmarish creature. It was twice the size of a man and covered in thick dark hair. It screamed with a blood-curtailing cry that caused the men to cease their fighting. They all turned to look upon the monster in disbelief. A second creature jumped into the camp from the other side and knocked the red-haired man high into the air and into a tall patch of forest ferns.

Archimere turned and shouted, "Run!"

All became a confusion of screams and loud beastly snarls. The foe that stood over Valentus yelled and swung his sword at the first creature. Its reaction was immediate and devastating.

The man's arm was severed and landed not far from where Valentus lay on the ground. The creature hesitated at the nearness of the campfire, but took no notice of Valentus. It deftly circled the flames and then smashed into the fray of running men on the other side. Valentus crawled to his knees just in time to see the other monster bending over the form of Archimere.

Mr. Bonfire and Rafe hewed at the creature with their swords to no avail. Valentus searched desperately for his sword but could not find it. He remembered his bow. It was miraculously still hanging over his left shoulder. He reached for an arrow, but his quiver was empty.

Rafe was cut down by one of the creature's clawed hands. Valentus heard Mr. Bonfire yell as he lashed out at the monster. He must find something to fight with. In his desperation, his hand hit upon the fletching of one of his arrows. It was protruding from the flames of the campfire. He grabbed it and, despite the flames burning at the arrow, notched it, turned, and fired in one fluid motion. The flaming arrow hissed as it sped through the night air. It hit the creature high up in the back. There was a loud smack as it pierced the monster's hide. The thing jerked upward and let out a terrifying raspy howl before turning and crashing through the forest to the southeast. Mr. Bonfire, shocked by the creature's scream, hesitated then jumped to Archimere's aid.

Valentus, in disbelief at the success of his first arrow, grabbed for another one also protruding from the fire. He took careful aim at the second beast as it turned toward the escaping Mr. Bonfire and Archimere. He let fly, and the arrow streaked toward the beast, grazing it in the right shoulder. The hairy beast convulsed with pain, turned, and then fled back into the darkness. Archimere and Mr. Bonfire helped an injured Rafe to his feet. They turned and looked back toward Valentus. He waved to them, signaling he would guard their retreat. Glancing quickly around, he found another arrow lying in the grass and notched it, watching the darkness for any further movement. All the Illyrian warriors and many of the Tharusians lay dead on the forest floor. Nothing else moved. The chaos of moments before settled into an eerie silence. There was no sound but the crackle and sputter of the campfire.

Valentus began slowly backing into the darkness away from the firelight. He kept his arrow notched. He had felt quite brave when he was signaling Archimere and the others of his intent to cover their retreat. Now that he was alone again, he wondered what he had been thinking. The enemy could be anywhere in the darkness, not to mention there could be more of those hideous creatures. He turned while looking back toward the campsite and nearly walked right into the red-haired warrior.

My Enemy's Enemy

Alenia waited, but not patiently. She found it unbearable when those she loved went into harm's way. The strange howling sounds drifting into their camp earlier made it even more difficult to remain calm. What could make such a sound? It was a tormented noise, and it made her feel cold inside. She paced back and forth in front of the warm fire. The others were worried as well. She could see it in their eyes.

It was late, but no one went to bed. They all simply stood around the fire and waited in silence.

Alenia finally decided she could wait no longer. She was about to seek out one of the camp guards when the first of the returning warriors appeared. The men were haggard, and Alenia did not hold out much hope for good news. Several of the women quickly brought them water to drink and food enough to restore their strength. More men were straggling into camp now. Alenia held her breath as she searched their faces. Where were they?

The familiar voice of Mr. Bonfire boomed through the gathering soldiers. He was barking orders for the men to bring water when Alenia pushed her way through the gathering crowd. There was her brother stretched out on the soft turf, his eyes closed. There was blood staining his left thigh and most of the front of his shirt. His face appeared pale in the dim light.

"Oh no," Alenia said, quietly holding back her tears.

Mr. Bonfire stared back at her with a look of incomprehension, before understanding spread across his tired features. "Well, he ain't kilt, if that's what's botherin' ya. He loss som' blood, but 'll be right as rain soon e'nuf."

Alenia looked to Mr. Bonfire and then back at Archimere just in time for his eyes to flicker open. She bent to down to her brother.

"Oh, Archimere, I thought you were..." She could not bring herself to finish.

"I surely would be if not for Valentus." A man helped him sit up to drink.

"Where is he? If not for him, that thing would have had me." Archimere held his left hand up to his head and sighed. Alenia straightened back up and scanned the men still returning. Valentus was not among them. Alenia felt her throat tighten, but she held back the emotion. He would come, she told herself. He must come.

The morning came late in the dark forest, but Valentus found no sleep. Although he was a prisoner, his captor seemed to have little heart for it. The man spoke very little, but he held no apparent ill will toward Valentus. There was a nasty cut across the red-haired man's forehead, but otherwise, he appeared unwounded. He glanced at Valentus with a questioning look.

"Why did you stay when everyone else ran?" The man's voice carried a tone of confidence and was direct.

Valentus looked at him and then back to the ground as he remembered the night before. "I don't know. My friends needed help, that's all." Valentus spoke with a subdued voice.

The man hesitated, reached into a small bag at his feet, and pulled out an apple. He tossed it over to Valentus, who caught it with a slight feeling of surprise. The man pulled out another apple and began crunching into it.

"What's your name?"

"Valentus."

"Valentus." The man repeated it slowly while examining the trees all around them. "I like it. I am Lanthir, and until very recently, I was champion to the king of Illyrium." He extended his hand.

Valentus just looked at it, but he made no move to accept.

"Yes, I am your enemy." He nodded as he spoke. "I do not resent your hatred of me. It is well earned." The man's face clouded, but he continued. "Last night we began as enemies, but we ended as comrades I think."

Valentus's face must have betrayed his own lack of understanding.

"Is not the enemy of my enemy my friend?" The red-haired man named Lanthir asked by way of explanation.

Valentus did not respond.

Lanthir hesitated, took another bite of his apple, and then continued. "I was like you once, filled with ideals." He finished chewing. "But one day, I woke up and could not remember what they were." He spoke this last statement as though it filled his mouth with distaste. "Do you know the difference between you and me, Valentus? You did not need anyone to tell you what was right. I could only see the truth after my own interest came into line with it. How sorry is that?" He had become disgusted with himself.

"Anyway, things have changed." The man named Lanthir stood, stretched out his arms, and yawned. He reached down behind the pack that carried the apples and retrieved three arrows. "I found these. I believe they are yours."

Valentus was astonished. Why should this man trust him with arrows?

"You are an honorable man, Valentus, and I am no longer your enemy... for my part." He indicated the arrows again. Valentus took them and placed them in his quiver, glad to recover Alenia's gift.

"I will say good-bye." He reached out his hand one more time.

"You are leaving?" Valentus was surprised.

"Well, I doubt your friends, wherever they may be hiding, will be any more eager to welcome me than you have been, and I do not blame them. So I will go my own way. I have a new enemy and a debt to repay."

Valentus slowly took his hand. Lanthir smiled, turned, and disappeared into the dense underbrush.

The next day came and went slowly as Archimere recovered his strength, and they waited. They lost fourteen good men in the attack, including Banton. The creatures came down on his position from behind without warning. What they were and where they came from, no one knew. Some whispered the word *Sargaroth* under their breath, but they were fairytales from the distant past.

The loss of Banton and the others was taken hard. Mr. Bonfire led a small group of men back to the battle scene the next morning to see if there were any wounded, but the monsters did their work well. No sign of Valentus was found. The ground was too trampled and torn to discover any useful sign of his fate. Archimere felt the weight of responsibility. He had led the men into this battle. If he had not, they would still be alive. Of course, no one could have foreseen the creatures' attack. But it was his decision, and the men followed him. If not for Valentus, more, including himself and Mr. Bonfire, would be dead. It was becoming more and more likely Valentus had simply traded places with them, their fate becoming his.

Mr. Bonfire approached the secluded spot on the upper meadow where Archimere went for solitude. The weather was mild, and the small grove of trees swayed gently in a lazy breeze. Archimere sat on the mossy turf by the spring-fed pool. Mr. Bonfire joined him without speaking. Both were silent for some time.

"What were they?" Archimere asked without lifting his eyes from the calm, dark waters.

"Some says Sarg'roth," Mr. Bonfire said with a shrug.

"What do you say?" Archimere countered, looking directly at his friend.

"Jes that no nat'tral beast I ev'r heer'd tell of could'n be kilt by no sword." A shudder passed through his features as he continued. "That weren't no nat'tral beast."

There was silence for a space of time, while both men reflected on the events of the night before. Suddenly Archimere threw a stick into the water and stood.

"We can stay here no longer. We will return to Perginton," he spoke with decisive confidence.

Mr. Bonfire shook his head as though he thought his friend was crazy.

"I will not stay here while my king sits in a dungeon or worse," Archimere said. He turned and began walking back toward camp. "Spread the word. We will leave in the morning."

"I s'pose them that hold the city will jes' welcum us back," Mr. Bonfire blurted out.

Archimere paused while considering the problem. "We will circle around to the north of the city and enter at the secret gate. Then we will teach the enemy who the masters of Tharrus truly are."

Hunted

After Lanthir left, Valentus began the trek back to camp. Archimere and the others must think him lost or worse by now. Although this part of the forest was not familiar to him, he knew it lay to the northeast. The morning was cool, but the sun's warmth could now be felt. He walked briskly with the thought of a happy welcome. Somewhere behind him a bird sang its song and another answered.

The bright sunshine began to dull into grayness as he walked. Valentus examined the treetops high above. Not much could be seen of the sky, but it was still warm so he thought little of it. Daydreaming of the reception he might receive upon his return and of Alenia's beautiful smile, he paused to get his bearings once again. Their camp should not be far. A small, sharp ridge lay directly before him so he decided to climb it rather than going the extra distance around. If nothing else, this would provide him a better view of the surrounding forest. Being quite a bit steeper than he first believed, Valentus found himself grabbing at roots and tree trunks in an attempt to prevent a fall.

After reaching the top he wiped the dirt from his hands and looked back down. A deep fog was rolling in below, blocking the view of the valley floor. He crossed the crown of the ridge only to discover the fog completely surrounded the forest ridge. The hill now gave the odd impression of an island in a sea of clouds. Nothing could be seen of the forest floor, so knowing better than to try to find his way in such conditions, he picked a likely spot and sat down for a rest.

Valentus must have fallen asleep for when he awoke the dense fog had blanketed everything, and it took a moment to recall where he was. It was impossible to tell how long he'd slept. The view in every direction was completely veiled. The earlier warmth of the day was gone, and a wet chill filled the air. He rubbed his arms for warmth and considered what to do next.

On the one hand, he could not just sit here in this exposed position all night. Yet to wander off in this fog was unthinkable. It was a true dilemma, but one he did not have to consider long. A muted but bone-chilling howl sounded through the heavy air. It was not loud and must have been some distance away, but Valentus almost swallowed his tongue. In the fog it was difficult to tell which direction it came from. He tried to convince himself the thing was far away and could not be a real threat, but another howl smashed through his attempts at calmness.

It was closer. He turned wildly in the opposite direction and began down the other side of the hill. Half sliding and half jumping, he was at the bottom and back on the valley floor in much less time than it took to climb the hill.

His breath was coming in rasps as he crashed through the undergrowth. In what direction, he could no longer tell. The terrible sound of the beast came again, but from higher up this time. Valentus, with horrible clarity, knew it must be on top of the hill where he rested. He plunged headlong into a bramble of thorns that tore at his clothing. Heedless to the pain, he pushed through to the other side and paused to catch his breath, which now came in gasps. A prolonged howl sounded from the top of the hill, and Valentus knew his trail was discovered.

He looked around for a tree to climb, but all were too thick for any kind of a good climbing hold and there were no branches within reach. Turning, he started running again. The thickness of the forest made it near impossible to gain any speed. Trees appeared out of the heavy fog only moments before he reached them, making it difficult to avoid collisions. He splashed into cold water with a shock, tripped over an unseen rock, and fell to his hands and knees, smashing into another rock as he landed. The bubbling current of a shallow stream swept past him as a burst of sharp pain erupted from his left knee. He clumsily stumbled back to his feet and glanced furtively over his shoulder. He held still and listened for a moment. The only sound was the pounding of blood through his ears. The beast was silent. Valentus was left with the awful sensation of being hunted. Like a wild animal tracked by a relentless hunter, he desperately looked for some place to hide. Through the thick cloud of fog, Valentus could see nothing past the length of his own arm.

It came to him that he once heard water covered a person's scent. He wasn't at all sure if this was true, but he quickly decided to move further downstream before continuing his flight on the other side. Every step sent a stab of pain through his knee. Even if he wanted to continue running, he doubted whether he could.

He limped slowly down the stream. Despite his attempts to move quietly, he stumbled and splashed through the water several times more before climbing out onto the opposite bank. Now he was not only wet and cold, but he was also covered in mud. Holding his breath, he listened for any sound of pursuit. There was nothing, no sound at all. No bird calls. No squirrel's chatter. He leaned his head to the side, straining for anything he could make out. The only sound was the muted dance of the stream behind him. Instead of making Valentus feel better, the unnatural stillness only increased the sense of being stalked.

He hobbled forward a few more paces and entered a sort of forest glade or meadow. Visibility was bad, but there was no longer any undergrowth tugging at his legs, and he could not see any trees close by. The fog rolled and billowed by him even though there was no wind. He began slowly limping across the open area and then froze. A sound whispered from behind him somewhere. Something splashed lightly in the stream not faraway. Valentus felt another surge of adrenaline. He peered back through the fog but could see nothing. His hand brushed across the strap to his quiver, and he remembered his bow. He quickly strung it, notched an arrow, and then slowly continued forward, not even sure which way to go. For all he knew, the hideous beast stood directly before him, waiting.

The fog moved off to his right. He froze again. Behind and to his left, there was more movement. How many were there? To his left a dark shape loomed in the fog. It moved like a ghost, as silent as the grave. Valentus softly dropped to his knee. Why hadn't the thing taken him? Surely it could have at any time. Perhaps the fog and the water did dampen his scent. Whatever the reason, all opportunity to run was gone. If he made any noise at all, his position would be known and his doom sealed.

Valentus considered the movement he noticed to his right. It could be anything. Maybe a deer was also trying to avoid the evil creature. He continued to watch the dark outline as it moved parallel to him. The creature slowly passed his position then stopped. The fog began to lighten. *It would just be my luck*, Valentus thought. This cursed fog had prevented his escape, and now, when it might at least hide him, it began to disappear. He saw the monster's outline fairly well now. It sniffed the air for his scent. Just when Valentus thought it might give up and move away, it turned its wicked red eyes directly at him. His heart sank. Raising his bow for one last defense, Valentus pulled the string back and took sure aim. He could not miss at this distance. He released, and the arrow flew true. Cutting through the fog, it hit the monster directly in the center of its chest. Much to Valentus's dismay, however, the arrow hit the creature and shattered. The beast charged with blinding speed, and Valentus braced himself for the onslaught. But the inevitable attack never came. From the fog to his right, the shape of a man suddenly appeared.

The man was large, larger than either Archimere or the man named Lanthir. Although it was still too foggy to see him clearly, he wore a light-colored hooded cloak and carried a large sword.

The man lifted the sword in the air. It flashed as if it held lightning. The beast shrieked with pain and was gone before Valentus knew what happened. The man stood ready for any further attack for another moment, and then he turned to Valentus. He slung the large two-handed sword onto his back.

"Come." His voice was strong and carried clear authority. But Valentus noticed a note of kindness also.

The man began walking through the fog across the open glade away from the stream. Valentus, hesitating, looked back in the direction the monster fled, turned, and followed him. They walked for a good while until the fog finally began to dissipate. Valentus must have slept longer on the hilltop than he first imagined, for the day was now well spent. They climbed a gently sloping hillside covered in a carpet of green, flowing grass, and the land to the north fell away to the sea, rolling on the distant horizon. To the southwest rose the darkening line of the forest they just left.

The man stopped and turned his head toward Valentus. He wore a simple hooded cloak, which shadowed most of the features of his face from clear view. A thousand questions ran through Valentus's mind, but he remained silent. Something about this man brought him a sense of security. It was peace more than anything. He had spoken but one word, yet Valentus knew he could trust him.

Valentus's unlikely yet timely savior pointed eastward. "Do you see the camp?"

Valentus looked to where he pointed. A short stone's throw to his right was a large pile of wood and several other lumpy-looking piles.

"Yes."

"Good. Start a fire and you will be safe through the night. You will find what you need there." It sounded as if the man would be leaving.

"Are you not afraid of the beasts?" Valentus asked. Everything about this man puzzled yet intrigued him.

"Never fear evil, Valentus. Instead, fear to *do* evil."

"How do you know me?" The stranger's use of his name surprised Valentus, and at the same time, as odd as it might seem, it filled him with a feeling of importance.

"I know those I want to know me." The man's answer sounded like a riddle.

"May I know your name?"

The man was silent for a moment, but when he answered, Valentus thought he could hear the presence of a smile on his words.

"I have waited long for you to ask," he answered. The man looked back toward the western horizon, which glowed brilliant orange and red. "Valentus, it is important you do exactly as I say. You must wait here and keep the fire burning high and bright. Help will come."

Again, the man offered no explanation for his strange directives, and Valentus felt it would be disrespectful to ask for more explanation.

"As for my name, you will know me by what I do," he said.

"Will you come back?"

The man stretched out his hand and placed it on Valentus's shoulder. Immediately Valentus felt the weariness leave his body. Strength flowed through his limbs. He dropped to his knees, knowing he was in the presence of someone far greater than any mortal.

"My lord, let me come with you and serve at your side." Valentus was surprised at his own sudden outburst. He only briefly knew this man, but he was ready to swear allegiance to him. It made little sense, but Valentus knew his heart would burst if he did not speak.

"You are right to call me lord, and I accept your pledge of service." The man raised Valentus back to his feet. "Do not fear, Valentus. The battle to come will take you far from home. But know this: I have already been where you are going."

The man pointed to the east. "Remember, wait until help arrives." He pointed to the eastern ocean.

Valentus scanned the distant waters before turning back to the man. "I will..." he began, but he stopped abruptly when he realized the man was gone. He spun around, but there was no sign of him at all.

Healing

Bright sunlight flooded through an open window on the far side of the room. The rolling motion was a constant companion. The sound of men at work floated into the captain's quarters. The night lasted long and his dreams were dark, but Aedan felt strangely peaceful now as he lay upon his bed. He turned stiffly to his side and raised himself up on one elbow.

The air in the ship's cabin was surprisingly fresh. It took a few moments to remember where he was. He located the window and blinked at the intense light pouring through it. His brothers should not have let him oversleep. He tried to sit up, but a sudden lightheadedness washed over him and he sank back down.

Something stirred in the corner across the room, next to the open window. He looked to where the noise came from but could see very little through the bright light. He raised a hand to cover his brow and block some of the sun's brilliance. The figure of a woman stepped softly into the stream of light. Her golden hair dazzled with intensity. Continuing to blink, Aedan stared at the woman in disbelief, unable to speak. The rays of light poured around the lady, illuminating her slender form from behind, making her face hard to see clearly. He watched her, not knowing whether he could trust his own eyes. After all, there were no women aboard True North.

He shook his head slightly in an attempt to clear it. But rather than having the desired affect, it brought on more lightheadedness, making him close his eyes and drop his head back to his pillow. The vision before him made him wonder if he had unknowingly died and now rested in the heavenly realms. The ache in his head and weakness of his body, however, quickly convinced him he most probably still lingered upon the earth.

He let his eyes remain closed for a moment, not sure what he would see when he opened them again. The lightheadedness passed, and he slowly opened his eyes to see the woman sitting quietly on a chair next to his bed. She was younger than he guessed at first. Yet there was a strange quality about her Aedan did not normally associate with someone of her apparent youth. She was more than beautiful; she was beauty itself. Aedan stared with open amazement.

"Life has reclaimed you," she said with a quiet satisfaction.

Aedan did not respond, but he continued to watch her.

She reached over to him and gently lifted the edge of a white cloth bandage binding his left shoulder. Her fingertips slowly prodded his flesh under the cloth. She said nothing, but her expression revealed genuine relief. Aedan's skin tingled at her touch, and warmth spread through his muscles. The door to the ship's cabin opened, spilling even more of the golden daylight into the room. Martin entered, a large smile breaking across his face.

"By the Great King of heaven, it is *good* to see you awake!" His words were filled with emotion as he crossed the room and stood towering over the young woman who sat by Aedan's bed. "So how is our patient?" he asked while examining Aedan with an appraising eye.

"His life is renewed," the girl answered with a slight bow of her head, which did not go unnoticed by Aedan, who was still very much confused.

"Perhaps a little walk to test his strength would be in order," Martin mused out loud. He looked to the young woman for her response.

Aedan thought he saw a look of concern cross her features.

"Perhaps a small walk," she conceded.

The sound of her voice washed over Aedan like a healing balm. After his long, tormented sleep, the soft, caring tones of her words were welcome. Martin reached down to help Aedan up to a sitting position when he finally noticed the bewildered expression on Aedan's face.

"Oh, I *am* sorry, Aedan." He paused to indicate the young lady. "I forgot. You have not been officially introduced. The vision you see sitting before you is Aayliyah."

"Aayliyah." Aedan spoke the name softly. His voice felt weak, and it hurt a little to speak.

Martin continued. "I know it must seem strange to you, but for more than a week now, she has seldom left your side."

At this revelation, Aedan glanced quickly at Martin. "A week!" His voice felt strained to speak.

Martin simply nodded. Aedan bent his head downward in contemplation and then slowly raised his hand to his left shoulder.

"The serpent's wound?" he asked questioningly.

"Yes. You were at death's door more than once, I can tell you." Martin choked back his own rising emotion as he again considered how close Aedan came to death. "It was Aayliyah's plant and her healing touch that brought you back."

Aedan's eyes locked with hers for a moment. Martin noticed the look and Aayliyah's reaction. She quickly diverted her eyes downward with a rising blush evident in her cheeks. It only served to enhance her beauty, and Martin found it necessary to gently tap Aedan's arm to draw his attention back. It was time to attempt a bit of a walk.

Bryn stood out on the deck in the open air. It was a grand day. The sun was bright, the air warm, and the wind soft. True North's sails bulged as the ship sliced through the waves. The ship's council unanimously appointed Martin captain in Aedan's temporary absence. Whatever bothered Martin earlier was now gone. He was a man renewed in vision and strength of purpose. After their re-provisioning was completed, he ordered a course of north by northwest. They were now headed to an island Martin called Tharrus. How he knew of this place was still a mystery, but then Martin was a mysterious man.

After Bryn, Martin, Rand, and Aayliyah returned to the ship from the White City, it did not take long to finish their re-provisioning. The men who stayed on the beach during the night neither saw nor heard anything of the beasts Aayliyah called Sargaroth. As a precaution, however, Martin and Bryn made sure several large fires were kept burning through their last night.

Upon reaching Truth North, or Adoil as she called it, Aayliyah immediately took over Aedan's care with the aid of the mysterious plant. His improvement was immediate and miraculous. The deathly greenish skin pallor was replaced with a rosy pink tone, and his breathing returned to normal. Bryn knew in his heart all would be well with Aedan now. Over the next week, Aayliyah barely left his side. The plant she brought was truly powerful in its healing ability, but Bryn believed it was her presence that caused it to work so quickly.

Bryn's thoughts returned to Aayliyah. She was a beautiful girl, unlike any other he had ever met. Mystery certainly surrounded everything about her, but it was her elegance of movement and confident gentleness of spirit that made the greatest impression. Bryn's heart, however, was already given to another. She was gone, but he would never be free again. His heart felt like a stone. He saw the way

Aayliyah looked at Aedan and remembered the way Kelsi once looked at him. Bryn found his hand absently searching for the leather pouch he used to keep around his neck. All his hand found was the emptiness that continued to engulf his heart. He was glad for Aedan. Somehow the hope he found for his brother's future made the lack of any for his own less dark.

A cheer went up from a cluster of crewmen working closer to the captain's quarters. Bryn turned toward the sound. Aedan, supported by Martin and Aayliyah, stepped out of the captain's cabin and into the full sunlight. More cheers filled the air as the other crewmen joined in.

"It seems I have been shirking my duty." Aedan's voice cracked as he talked.

His brothers rushed to his side, each slapping him on the back in turn.

"Whoa, keep that up and I will have more excuses to lie in bed." Aedan coughed a little as he spoke.

Several of the men erupted in relieved laughter. Argolis swooped down from somewhere far above to land on his perching post. Aedan's attention was drawn to the bird as Martin held up a hand and addressed the men.

"A little at a time. Aedan will need to rest now. You will see him again in the morning," he said.

Several of the men wished their leader well. The mood was jubilant as Martin encouraged them to return to their various tasks. Aedan watched the men go and then turned back to his brothers.

"Bryn, Llew, will you come and speak with me for a bit? I have obviously missed a few things and am still a bit confused on a couple of points." He glanced shortly toward Aayliyah and then to his brothers. Llew gave a knowing look to Bryn, a jovial smirk lifting the corner of his mouth.

New Friends

With several more days of rest, Aedan almost completely regained his former strength. Much to his brothers' amusement, however, Aedan was hesitant to leave Aayliyah's close, monitored care. He was openly disappointed when she pronounced him fit to return to his duties as captain.

The days were sunny, and a warm breeze drove them steadily northwest. Tharrus, the island Martin was trying to find was, by his description, a fair-sized place covered in forests, hills, and mountains. Although no one was exactly sure of its location, both Martin and Aayliyah strongly believed it to be roughly northwest of their current position. With each passing day, however, Martin was beginning to fear they had somehow missed it and would have to turn back to the west.

Late one evening, Bryn was on his way to speak to Berand at the helm when he saw Martin standing on the main deck. Martin was leaning forward, resting his forearms on the smooth wooden rail as he gazed to the northwest. Bryn hesitated at first, not sure whether he should interrupt his solitude. Making his mind up, he moved quietly to where his mentor stood and leaned against the rail alongside him. A soft, balmy breeze stirred their hair. The moon was full and reflected brightly off the dark waters.

Martin spoke first. "There is something about these western waters that can make a man feel young one moment, then old and tired the next."

Bryn accepted Martin's conclusion with his usual silent contemplation. Bryn did not consider himself good at conversation, not like Aedan or Llew. When there was anything that needed doing, he was often the first to do it. But when it came to discussion or speech-making, well, he was always more than happy to leave it to his brothers.

"I remember when I was a boy, my father took me on a journey across the sea. I begged him for the opportunity, only to spend most of the voyage sick as a dog. I complained like a sorry brat." Martin chuckled at the memory. "My father did not get angry or show disappointment. Instead, he arranged for me to spend the next several months aboard the rolling deck of another ship. By the time I was allowed back onto solid ground, I had grown to love this..." Martin waved his hand toward the open sea before them.

"I have never heard you speak of your father before."

Martin continued to gaze toward the dark horizon.

"Back home there are those who say you have no father or mother." Bryn spoke with mock seriousness.

Mirth played at the corners of Martin's mouth as he shook his head. "I do not remember my mother. She died giving birth to my brother when I was very young. But my father... he was a man to be respected." Martin smiled at Bryn before looking back to the sea. "He was larger than life to me. He had the strength of a bear and yet a smile that could disarm any enemy. When he laughed, everyone laughed."

"What happened to them? Your father and brother, I mean."

"I don't know." A pained expression crossed Martin's eyes.

Just then, a shout came from one of the men on night watch. Martin and Bryn found the man, who was not far forward of where they were standing. It was Aric.

"I seen a light, m' lords."

"Show me," Martin ordered.

Aric looked again and then pointed slightly to his right. There it was, blinking in the darkness. There could be no mistake. It was a signal fire of some sort, which could mean only one thing. They had found Tharrus. Martin slapped Aric on the back with approval.

"Good eyes, man! Now go and alert the captain," he said.

Aric, grinning from ear to ear, nodded and ran toward the captain's cabin. It was not long before True North was anchored safely in the bay of what they presumed to be Tharrus. The blinking light they glimpsed was now clearly identifiable on the ridge above them as a moderately sized signal fire. It was too large to be a simple campfire. But who was the signal for? No one could have known they were coming.

Aedan quickly decided on sending a small landing party ashore. It would include himself, his two brothers, Martin, Rand, and a few of his warriors. They would go ashore in the morning to investigate and gather any available information. The men chosen for this mission were holding counsel in Aedan's quarters when a soft knock sounded on the door. Aayliyah entered quietly but with a determined expression on her face.

"I apologize for this interruption, my lords." Her words were courteous but betrayed no timidity. "I request to be included in the group going ashore." She stated her petition openly and without pretense. A moment of silence followed her request as the men looked at each other.

Aedan spoke first. "Aayliyah," he said with a note of genuine regret, "it would be too dangerous to…"

"I am not afraid," she interrupted with a subtle note of defiance.

Aedan glanced quickly to the others for help.

"Frankly, I think Aayliyah can take care of herself. I say let her come if she wants," Bryn said.

Aedan looked incredulously at Bryn and then appealed to Martin.

"I am inclined to agree with Bryn. She fended for herself on the White Isle for who knows how long, and besides, she may be able to help. She does know more about Tharrus than any of the rest of you," Martin said.

Aedan clamped his mouth shut tight as he realized he was outnumbered. He turned to look at Aayliyah. "We leave at first light," he concluded with a slight tightness in his voice. Aayliyah nodded her agreement to be ready and then abruptly smiled at him before turning toward the door. Aedan was still a bit perturbed with Bryn and Martin, but he could not help feeling the heat rise to his cheeks as he watched her go.

The sun was just beginning to burn the distant waters on the eastern horizon when the nine members of the landing party left their small boat and began climbing the ridge where the signal fire burned brightly the night before. There was no sign of the fire now, but a faint hint of smoke could be smelled intermittently on the morning breeze. It was a cloudless sky above, and the rays of the first morning light burst brilliantly across the waters and across the top of the ridge above the landing party. The ridge was larger and steeper than it first appeared from the beach. The shore party, nevertheless, made good time, reaching the top before the sun climbed a hand's breadth into the sky.

Aedan decided against a direct assent, believing it more prudent to climb around and to the left. This would allow them to approach the spot where the signal fire was seen without climbing straight up the slope in an exposed position.

At the top they found themselves in a small patch of trees and brush at the southern edge. Stopping for a brief rest, they took the opportunity to study the scene before them. The signal fire still smoldered and smoked about two hundred paces from where they waited. There were several stacks of wood and other indiscernible things around the fire circle. Nothing moved.

Aedan gave the order to move out. He sent Rand and his three warriors to circle around the top of the ridge from the west. The rest of them approached the signal fire directly from their current location. They moved slowly but deliberately toward the spot.

It did not take long to discover the place was deserted. Someone, however, was near. The remnants of a hastily abandoned breakfast still sizzled in a pan at the edge of the fire ring.

"There was only one by the sign he left," Llew concluded quietly.

There were plenty of shoe prints about the area, but they all looked to be the same size and dimension. Aedan nodded his agreement. Llew pointed toward a single set of tracks leading away toward a small grouping of boulders to the north of the camp. The ground was sparsely covered with grass and weeds, but the turf was soft enough to reveal the slight imprints to those who knew what to look for. Whoever the prints belonged to must have watched them ascend the ridge, and he probably now watched them from the rocks. Aedan signaled to the others to be ready.

"We saw your signal fire from our ship. We mean no one harm," Aedan yelled out toward the direction of the rocks. There was no response.

Aedan looked to Aayliyah. "It may be our reluctant host will feel safer knowing a woman is in our company," he said with a tone of apology.

Aayliyah agreed. "We have come in answer to your beacon," she called out.

The sound of her voice made Aedan's stomach ache slightly as they waited for a response. After a brief moment, the figure of a young man stepped from behind the rocks. He was a youth of average height, dressed in simple clothes caked in dry mud and torn in various places. All in all, he looked to have fallen on difficult times. The young man came closer, but then he saw Rand and his warriors approaching from the west. His reaction was swift as he raised his bow and notched an arrow. Aedan quickly raised his hands to stop Rand's advance and then turned back to the young man.

"They are our men. We did not know what awaited us here and wanted to be cautious. They will do you no harm," he quickly explained.

The young man hesitated before lowering his bow into a ready position.

"Who are you?" he asked.

His dialect of speech was slightly strange but still of the same language spoken by most of the inhabitants of the lands in the western seas, including the Emerald Isle.

"We are travelers from the islands to the east across the sea," Aedan answered simply.

"To what purpose was your signal fire?" Martin asked.

The young man hesitated again. "Well, I'm not sure exactly, but I think it was for you."

Aedan looked to his brothers and Martin with a puzzled expression.

"But how could you have known we were coming? We don't even know your name," Aedan asked.

"My name is Valentus, and I didn't exactly. I was told to wait for help coming from the eastern sea. I don't know much more than that," the young man replied as he put down his bow and came to sit on the ground near the fire ring. Aedan and the others joined Valentus, telling their names as they sat down.

"Perhaps you should tell us your story," Martin encouraged the young man.

It took some time to tell, but before he finished, Valentus had recounted his entire journey from the tending of his uncle's flocks to his flight from the evil unknown beast and his being saved by a mysterious hooded man in the fog not two days ago. Martin and Llew both took particular interest in the description of the man.

"And he suggested help might come from the eastern sea?" Martin challenged.

Valentus snapped his head around. "He told me it *would* come, and I believed him. There is a difference you know."

"But why did you believe him? What did he look like?" Martin asked with a building excitement.

"I…" Valentus hesitantly glanced from one of his new companions to the other, not sure how to answer. "I never actually saw his face. He wore a white hooded cloak and kept his face covered by the hood. It was more the sound of his voice that made me believe him." He looked back to Martin, convinced they would all think him crazy. Llew followed the exchange intently, but he remained quiet.

Martin, on the other hand, continued with enthusiasm. "Yes. I believe you *have* seen the hooded man."

"Martin, you speak as if you know who he is talking about?" Llew suddenly questioned, a searching expression in his eyes.

"I too once met a man dressed in a white hooded cloak. A long time ago, when I was a young man, before I came into the service of your father, Llew. He is the one who directed me to the Emerald Isle. He told me where I would find the truth I sought, and I also *believed* him. He is no ordinary man." Martin looked back at Valentus with a knowing look on his face.

The others said nothing, but they followed the exchange with questioning looks, trying to understand the best they could. Llew was about to ask another question when one of Rand's warriors stood and pointed to the western forest line.

"A heavy fog is approaching," he warned.

Valentus spoke. "The beast will come with it. We must go now," he spoke with an urgent but unafraid tone.

There was not a cloud in the sky above, but still, the dark fog rolled toward them.

"It is the fog of the Sargaroth. Valentus is right. We must leave," Aayliyah agreed.

Their descent to the beach took much less time than their climb to the beacon fire. As they put their boat to oar, a primeval howl sounded high on the ridge above. Under the powerful arms of the warriors, the oars plowed through the water in unison. It took little time to reach True North. After everyone was back on deck, Aedan called a meeting of the ship's council. As they moved toward his quarters, he turned toward Valentus, who was standing quite awkwardly off to the side, and signaled for him to join them. He then turned toward Aayliyah, who was already moving off to her quarters.

"Aayliyah, wait!" Aedan took three quick steps toward her. "Will you join us?"

"It is not my place." She smiled softly and turned to go. Aedan quickly reached out and gently caught her arm. It was the most delicate thing that he ever touched. She turned and looked back into his eyes.

"You may be able to provide valuable insight. The others want you to attend." He paused and thought better of his statement. "*I* want you to attend."

She searched his eyes as though she weighed the truth of what he said. After a moment, she suddenly lightened her gaze and smiled softly. "Yes, of course. If you think it would help, I will come."

It did not take long for the council to decide on a course of action. Martin quickly pointed out, based on Valentus's story, that Perginton was the next logical destination. Valentus objected, reminding them the city was conquered and occupied by the enemy from Illyrium.

Martin explained, "I understand your point Valentus, but it is for this very purpose we have come. To find out how and where our help is needed. I believe we can best do that by visiting Perginton. Besides, we are foreigners from a distant land. I doubt the invaders would consider us enemies outright. In any case, they will first be curious, and that will give us valuable time to weigh the circumstances and form a plan."

The others agreed, and Aedan dismissed the council, giving Berand orders to set sail around the north horn of Tharrus. According to Valentus, they would find Perginton on the western side of the island.

Perginton

The morning was cloudy and dark when True North dropped anchor in the harbor beneath the walls of Perginton. A black wall of cloud moved across the sky from the southwest. It rumbled with deep groaning thunder. The bay was completely empty but for a few small boats moored to the docks. Aedan, Martin, Bryn, Llew, and Valentus all stood at the ship's rail and scanned the waterfront for any sign of what welcome awaited them. No one could be seen.

"Strange. Very strange," Martin mused.

"Where is everyone?" Llew asked.

"They are here. We just can't see them," Aedan concluded. "See, just there." He pointed toward a small building just below the walls of the city. The vague dark outline of what could have been a person disappeared around the corner.

"Are they afraid of us?" Rand asked after joining the others at the rail.

"That, or they have set a trap for us," Martin replied without removing his gaze from the city.

"Well, there is only one way to find out." Aedan's jaw was set with determination. "Rand, prepare ten warriors to embark with us. The rest will stay here and guard True North."

Rand nodded and moved off.

Aedan turned toward Valentus. "Will you join us?"

The new young friend inclined his head in assent.

"Good. We need to proceed with caution. Martin may be right. Based on what you have told us, this enemy is clever but not honorable. We will play the part of foreign emissaries, but we will go well armed."

Aayliyah was not to be included in the mission this time. And although Aedan was ready for an argument, she simply agreed and spoke a blessing of safe return over the men. Her words were soothing and yet, at the same time, stirred courage for the task at hand. She was a woman who could have easily inspired an empire. Instead, she was content in her service to others. Aedan marveled at the strength of her grace. A small part of him was already sorry she could not accompany them ashore. Yet relief washed over the rest of him knowing she would not be in harm's way.

A short time later, two shore boats were in the water of Perginton Bay, plying their oars under the growing darkness of the pending storm.

Large, cold droplets of rain smashed into the water all around them. The angry clouds now directly above flashed with great bolts of lightening. As of yet, the wind had not reached them. The boats moved alongside the docks, and the landing party quickly made their way up the ladders. Still, no one moved to greet or challenge them. The rain began falling harder. Despite the threatening weather, they did not quicken their pace. Rather, they moved with a growing sense of wariness. Something was not right here. Even a conquered city should have some life.

It was a long walk to the front gates of the city. They were broken and burned from the battle Valentus described. Evidence of the recent destruction was everywhere to be seen. The bodies of those fallen in battle were gone, but a smell still clung to the field, and several of the men covered their noses as they passed inside the gates. The city was completely silent, except for the noise of the growing wind and rain.

Aedan turned to Valentus. "Which way to the palace?"

Embarrassment crossed Valentus's face. "I… I haven't actually been inside the city before," he said a bit sheepishly.

Aedan nodded in understanding and turned toward Martin. "What do you think, Martin?"

"It is that way, toward the northeastern quarter of the city. The road we are on will lead us there." Martin pointed to where a prominent hill, covered in larger buildings, rose in prominence. Aedan, Bryn, and Llew all looked at Martin with an expression of surprise. He knew this place. There were more questions of Martin's connection to these lands, but their need to be watchful for hidden danger swallowed everything else up. All questions would have to wait.

For the most part, it was a clean and grand city, or was until recently. Although they saw no one as they walked, signs of occupation and recent looting were everywhere. Here and there, broken furniture, old pots, torn clothing, and garbage littered the entrances of several buildings. The road through the city was wide and well made of cut gray blocks. After a short time, they came to one section where the road was mostly blocked by a large pile of burned books. The pile was large enough to force them to skirt its edges.

"Why would anyone want to destroy these books?" asked one of the younger warriors named Riordan.

"Perhaps someone does not like to read?" joked one of his fellow warriors named Cian.

"Or perhaps they did not want anyone else to read what they *already* read," Martin commented as he stopped, bent down, and examined one partially burned book. Only a portion of the badly damaged book's title could be made out. It read, *Selected Tales of Tharusian H...*

The sky above intensified its rumblings, and the rain began to fall harder. Water pooled around the blocks and ran toward the sides of the road, cascading down into cleverly designed gutters and then disappearing into some unseen drainage system. This city was no backwater village made of huts and squalor. Everywhere they looked the evidence of order and solid construction met their eyes. It may not have been what some would call a beautiful city, but it was well built.

Lightening flashed across the darkened morning sky. A loud crash of thunder followed a few heartbeats later. The group picked up their pace, having no desire to face the full fury of the approaching storm. By the time they reached the large building identified by Martin to be the palace, the wind began whipping the cold rain pellets at the men with a newfound fury. Led by Martin, they quickly entered the main gate of the palace, which was still intact but unlocked. Shutting the door behind them, the men closed out the raging sound of the wind and breathed a small sigh of relief.

"Find some torches," Aedan instructed the warriors.

A clattering noise echoed through one of the hallways to their right. The men turned as one toward the sound, ready for anything. All but the storm outside went quiet.

"It is certain someone still remains," Martin concluded quietly.

"Or some*thing*," Valentus added in.

The others slowly looked at him. He was silent up to this point. And although none of them knew much about him, they all recognized a certain quality he possessed. If his earlier account was true, he had already faced the Sargaroth and survived. Everything he said concerning Perginton was certainly true. Now he was suggesting a possibility none of them had yet considered. They all watched as Valentus sniffed the air. A look of distaste covered his features. It did not take long for the rest of the men to notice the lingering, putrid smell. It was something like rotting flesh mixed with dung. The young warrior named Riordan snorted his displeasure with the unclean scent.

"Whoever these invaders are, they stink!" he replied shortly.

"I have smelled this stench before," Rand concluded, narrowing his eyes.

"Yes, in the jungle on the White Isle." Martin paused. "When the Sargaroth were near." He spoke these last words more quietly.

None of the men relished the thought of one of these beasts lurking somewhere nearby, especially with the ever darkening skies outside and the growing noise of the storm. They all heard Bryn, Martin, and Rand's description of their encounter with the Sargaroth on the White Isle. Aayliyah's descriptions only served to make the beasts more terrifying.

The warriors who searched for a torch now stood tensely wary of the unknown. Bryn noticed their hesitation. He stepped past the nearest warrior, a rather large-boned youth named Cian, and cleared his throat.

"I thought you knew, Cian, the only thing the beast seems to fear is light." He paused to take in the effect of his words.

Many of the warriors chosen for this journey were young, without wives or families. The king did not wish to see families unnecessarily separated for any large period of time without great need. The younger warriors, on the other hand, were all too eager for adventure and glory. They were inexperienced to be sure, but each one was selected based upon the skill they excelled in. When those chosen received their invitation to join the quest, not one of them turned it down. It was the opportunity of a lifetime.

They had all experienced the battle with the sea serpent, a creature that made each of them quake with fear. Based on the stories, however, these Sargaroth were far worse. When Aayliyah was asked about them, she recounted an ancient story of her ancestor Ram and how he battled this demon beast of the Aletae. If swords and spears could not pierce their hide, how could anyone fight it?

Cian looked at Bryn and swallowed slowly. His eyes betrayed the apprehension warring inside him. Water dripped down his forehead and into his eyes, causing him to nervously wipe his sleeve across his face. It was clear he did not understand Bryn's meaning.

"The torches. The beast doesn't like the *light*," Bryn emphasized loud enough for the rest of the young men to also hear.

Cian turned and hurried toward the corner of the entry room where torches were normally kept in such a building. Several others quickly followed his lead. It did not take long before a dozen torches blazed with light. The palace, for whatever reason, did not suffer the same deprivations from looting inflicted on so much of the rest of the city. Large tapestries still hung on the walls along with many other Tharusian artifacts. The room where they stood was a spacious rectangular entry with a large double door directly in front of them and hallways leading off to each side. A row of carved benches and chairs lined each of the walls.

"The throne room is this way," Martin indicated.

He opened the large double door. A long, wide hallway flanked with doors to the left yawned before them. The men slowly followed Martin into the darkened hall as firelight from the torches flickered off the walls and ceiling. At regular intervals along the right side of the hall were large tapestries hanging down in a strange limp fashion. Aedan moved toward one of them, lifted the corner up slightly, and then yanked it down in one jerking motion. It pulled free and fell to the hallway floor. The dull light of the darkened cloudy day outside gave added illumination to the hallway.

"Windows?" Rand questioned. "They are all windows."

"Yes, if memory serves, there is a small open-air courtyard at the center of the palace on this side. It provided better light for many of the interior rooms of the palace," Martin said.

"But why would anyone take the time to cover them with these heavy tapestries?" Rand continued.

"*They* do not like the light," Llew spoke quietly, but with emphasis, repeating Bryn's earlier comment.

At that moment a long flash of lightening lit up the hallway, long enough for them to see several deep, elongated slash marks across the opposite wall high above their heads. The gashes were as long as one of the torches they carried and deep enough to actually groove the solid stone blocks of the wall. Martin pointed to the remaining tapestries.

"Take them down. Take them all down." He began pulling at the nearest one.

The others moved quickly to help, and in a few short moments, five good-sized windows were uncovered. The gray light of the stormy skies outside made it easier to see inside the hall. Martin silently drew his sword and motioned for the others to follow. The sound of swords being pulled from their leather sheaths whispered softly as the men approached the throne room with all the wariness of an animal knowing it has become the hunter's prey.

The doors leading to the throne room stood partly ajar, lending to the feeling that someone or something wanted them to enter. Aedan and

Martin cautiously stepped through the open doorway, followed by Bryn and Llew. Except for the illumination from their torches, the room was completely dark. Any windows inside the throne room must have also been covered over. The rest of the men moved in behind them, followed lastly by Rand who acted as a rear guard. They spread out into a tight circle as they moved forward. The throne itself stood at the opposite end of the room. From what they could see, it was not overly lavish but simpler in its design. It appeared to be made of a carved wood and partly covered in fine padded leather.

All around the room's edge stood thick round columns. Their torch light cast heavy black shadows off the pillars onto the outer wall. The storm outside went quiet, leaving the men feeling even more on edge. It was now too silent. One of the warriors shifted his feet nervously across the floor, making more noise than he intended.

Martin, who was closest to the throne, turned to his left and froze as he peered into the deep shadows of the outer rim of the room. Leaning slightly forward to listen, he pointed toward the nearest column, motioning for the others to be ready. Just then the large, dark figure of a man stepped from behind the throne, not two arms' lengths to the right of Martin, placing the cold sharp edge of a blade neatly at the base of his throat.

"Stand right where you are," he spoke evenly. "I would hate for any misunderstandings to arise."

Cian, not far behind Martin, took a step closer to the man who was still mostly covered in shadows. Llew quickly held his arm up in front of the eager young warrior. Martin shifted his eyes back to the right, but otherwise, he did not move.

"You have us at a disadvantage," Aedan replied in a cautious yet not unfriendly tone. "We are ambassadors from the Emerald Isle, across the seas to the east. We intend no harm to the people of this place."

"Yet you make yourself free to enter without leave," the man said. His voice held no malice but openly challenged Aedan's explanation. "It has been my experience that foreign dignitaries knock first and do not come with swords drawn." Though the features of his face could still not be seen, the irony in his voice could easily be heard.

"We found the city in ruins and the doors to the palace open. I doubt you would not have been equally as cautious in your investigation. Besides, we still do not know who it is that now welcomes us at the end of a sword. A single sword, I might point out." Aedan's tone matched that of the unknown man.

"Fair enough," he replied simply, and then he turned his head to the side and said, "Let's welcome our visitors properly."

There was a shout from the other side of the room, and thirty dark figures stepped as one from the shadows and pillars all around the room. Some bore spears, others swords, and some carried bows notched with arrows. The large man who appeared first lowered his sword from Martin's throat.

"You see, there are more of us ready to properly welcome you, if that is what you wish."

A shorter and wider man, located on the other side of the room, spoke up.

"We gunna talk all mornin!" It was not meant as a question, and the man started moving forward with his sword drawn.

"Stand ready!" Rand called to his warriors, who quickly reformed their defensive circle and prepared to fight.

Valentus jumped from the circle, waving his hands high. "No! Stop!" he yelled.

The short wide man held up his hand. "What's th' matter? Ain't you gunna fight?" He sounded genuinely disappointed.

"I've always wanted to box your ears, Mr. Bonfire, but I will pass for the moment." A smile could plainly be heard in Valentus's voice.

Reunion

"Light the torches!" The man who stood behind Martin issued the order. There was a note of urgency in his voice. A short moment later, the torches blazed all around the throne room. A throng of men dressed in the shabby clothes of forest dwellers pressed in tightly around Valentus, slapping him on the back and talking excitedly. Their leader was as large, if not more so, than he appeared in the dark.

The men of the Emerald Isle all stood quietly, trying to work out what had just happened. These men not only knew Valentus but also welcomed him. Even the man called Mr. Bonfire wore something akin to a smile on his face.

"Where have you been?" the large man asked, a look of relief on his face.

"It's a long story," an embarrassed Valentus answered, who appeared uncomfortable at being the center of so much attention.

"Archimere, this is Aedan of the Emerald Isle." Valentus turned and indicated Aedan who still stood with his sword in hand at the head of his men. "Aedan, this is Archimere, our leader." He indicated the large man.

The two men stepped closer to each other for a quick appraisal.

After a brief moment, the man named Archimere spoke first. "I am sorry for the poor welcome, but as you can see from the city outside, we have good reason to feel distrusting of foreigners."

Aedan nodded his acceptance of the apology. "Any good leader would have done the same," he agreed.

Valentus interrupted. "But how did you come to be here, in the city I mean, and where are the people of Perginton?"

"We entered by the secret gate yesterday morning to find the city as you see it. We would know nothing more than you, if not for the dying man we found. He had been tortured and left to die. When we discovered him, he clung to life by a mere thread. Although he could barely speak, he told us of a demon brought into the city by the Illyrian invaders. What he described must be the same beast that attacked us in the forest. The remnant of people still remaining in the city fled in horror to the smaller settlements in the south. Before he died, he spoke of a man with a scarred face who forced him, and some others, to excavate the lower passageway. They were then tortured, and only he survived. He crawled as far as he could and then waited." Archimere stopped speaking.

"Waited? Waited for what?" the warrior named Cian asked.

Archimere looked in the direction of the young warrior. "To tell his story." Archimere paused reflectively. "We buried him and the others yesterday evening."

Archimere continued. "We found nothing more of the demon creature. It must have escaped back into the forests."

"What about the king?" Valentus asked.

The features of Archimere's face clouded. "Executed." He hesitated before continuing. "Along with his whole family." He let his head drop down in weariness.

"And you claim these invaders were men of Illyrium?" Martin asked.

Archimere's features flashed anger as he snapped his head back toward Martin. "I need make no *claim* when the evidence is not in question. It *was* the army of Illyrium that wrought such carnage on our land, and if it takes the rest of my days, I will see justice upon King Malen." He spoke low and evenly.

Martin's countenance visibly changed. Llew and Bryn glanced at each other with questioning concern.

"Martin, is all well?" Llew asked.

Martin did not answer right away. Instead he glared intently back at Archimere with a newfound intensity. "How long has Malen been king of Illyrium?" His voice was strained and tight.

A peel of thunder crashed somewhere outside. Archimere just stared blankly back at Martin as though he did not comprehended the question.

"How *long*?" Martin spoke with a stern authority.

Archimere's eyes narrowed as he weighed Martin's changed demeanor. This man from the east held a strange interest in the affairs of Illyrium. "Just over two years," he replied, offering no further explanation.

"What of King Pharin and his son?" Martin now bore a pained expression.

"They died. So we were told." Archimere shrugged, still examining Martin with careful assessment.

Martin turned abruptly and walked out of the throne room. Aedan, Bryn, and Llew watched him go in silence while the men of Tharrus continued their eager discussion with Valentus.

A short time later, Archimere turned back toward Aedan. He cast one last look of appraisal and then thrust his arm outward. "I have already greeted you as required, but now I extend my friendship. Valentus has told us of your aid to him and somewhat of your intentions. Any friend of his is a friend of mine, for my part." Archimere's smile was genuine as he spoke.

It was now Aedan's turn to consider the character of the man before him. After a moment, he reached out and clasped Archimere's extended forearm with his own. "Friendship is rare in this world of men. I am honored to find another worthy of it," he responded.

Archimere was well pleased with Aedan's words and slapped him on the back with a good-natured laugh. The men of Tharrus, as though receiving a secret signal, turned as one and began greeting the men of the Emerald Isle. The tensions that were ripe only moments earlier now melted away in relief, the silence replaced with noisy jests. None were louder than the man Valentus called Mr. Bonfire who was robustly hooting and repeatedly slapping Valentus on the back.

Bryn turned toward the doors leading away from the throne room. There was no sign of Martin. He motioned back to Aedan, who was still speaking with Archimere, indicating his intent to check on Martin. Aedan nodded his understanding as Bryn moved toward the hallway. He glanced back toward the throne room, surprised at how quickly things could change. One moment they were ready to fight and kill each other, and the next they greeted each other as brothers. Oftentimes the most significant events hinged upon the smallest of details. What if they hadn't seen Valentus's signal fire? What if Valentus was not with them in the throne room? The outcome would have been very different. Bryn cringed at the thought.

He walked down the hall and back into the building's main entry room. There was no sign of Martin, so he continued on out the door. A spitting rain still fell from the darkened sky above. It was softer than earlier. The storm was moving to the east. The muted rumblings of lightening could still be heard in the distance. Far off on the western horizon, a bright strip of blue sky was visible. Martin stood only a few paces from the doorway. He wore an expression unusual for him. It was an angry determination. Martin's demeanor quickly changed when he saw Bryn.

"Yes, I suppose it was rude of me to walk out on our reluctant hosts," Martin concluded as though he could read the question on Bryn's face.

"Is all well? News of this King Malen upset you."

"Yes, it is true. I once knew Malen, but he was *no king* back then."

Martin continued to speak as he and Bryn slowly walked back toward the throne room.

"Illyrium was my home, but that was along time ago. Much appears to have changed since then."

Bryn thought he detected sadness in Martin's voice.

They reentered the throne room to find it largely empty. The Tharusians left by some door cleverly hidden behind the throne itself, and their own men were moving slowly toward the spot, disappearing one by one behind a section of the wall that looked entirely flat and continuous from where Bryn and Martin stood.

Llew approached them. "Archimere has invited us to share the midday meal with them. They apparently occupy one of the nearby buildings. Aedan asked me to wait for you."

The building, which appeared to be a sort of residence attached to the palace, was not far. They entered the medium-sized structure into an open room with a ceiling that yawned two floors above them. It was a bare room with no seating or decorations of any kind. Although it was solid and clean, there was nothing about it that indicated comfort or luxury.

Archimere asked them to wait while he and Mr. Bonfire explained things to the rest of their people. The remainder of Archimere's men quietly disappeared in several directions, moving off to other predetermined posts or tasks while, at Archimere's request, Valentus stayed with Aedan and the others. His friendship with both groups of men unwittingly made him a sort of ambassador.

It was quiet while they waited. The warriors from the Emerald Isle shifted clumsily on their feet. They were trained to fight, not stand on ceremony or act as emissaries to foreign peoples. Martin noticed their discomfort and, in an attempt at distraction, commented on how this building was most likely filled with apartments used by the palace servants. They did not have long to wait before a curious group of women and children, still making up their minds about their new visitors, began gathering on the balcony above them. Most of the smaller children still clung closely to their mother's skirts, only revealing their small, dirt-smudged faces. Lines of tension creased the faces of the women who still watched with distrust.

"They do not look happy to see us," Cian, who stood toward the front of the warriors, spoke under his breath.

"Do you blame them? They have seen their share of treachery and heartache from foreigners in recent days," Llew responded. It was not a rebuke; just a simple conclusion.

The silent tension was broken when a young woman with long, dark, braided hair appeared at the balcony rail. She was beautiful with fair skin. Hastily she scanned the faces of their group, as if hoping to find someone specific.

"Valentus!" The name burst from her lips with trembling excitement. She left the balcony and moved quickly down the side stairs until reaching the bottom. There were tears streaming freely down the young woman's face as she unabashedly threw her slender arms around Valentus' neck.

"I knew you would come back," she whispered with quiet conviction.

Valentus's cheeks burned crimson red as he returned her embrace, glancing backward at Aedan and the others who were heartily enjoying the display. As if on cue, the rest of the women still standing on the balcony erupted in happy laughter and handclapping. Archimere and Mr. Bonfire appeared at the balcony and burst into laughter, slapping each other on the back. Mr. Bonfire was hooting so loudly he sent himself into a fit of coughing and almost fell over the balcony rail. Even the men of the Emerald Isle could not help themselves; they joined in the celebratory noisemaking. A few even gave Valentus the victory whoop. It was the most embarrassed, and happy, Valentus had ever been.

The festive atmosphere continued as they were ushered into another room where the meal was served. The food wasn't fancy but consisted of plenty of good meat and trays piled with steaming vegetables. That day, a deep and lasting friendship was forged between the people of Tharrus and the men of the Emerald Isle. If only for a brief moment, the losses suffered by the Tharusians were forgotten.

Allies

The merriment continued long after the feast finished. Shadows grew across the city outside before Aedan stood to announce their need to depart. His announcement was met with the usual good-natured groans and complaints that follow most merrymaking. He located Llew and asked him to make sure all their men were accounted for and ready to return to True North.

"Where's Martin?" Aedan asked.

"He excused himself at the end of the meal. I have not seen him since," Llew answered.

Just then, Martin entered at the far side of the room. He made his way to Aedan's side and whispered something in his ear. Aedan looked intently back at Martin and simply nodded his assent. Bryn and Llew sitting close by exchanged interested glances.

"Martin has found something," Aedan said quietly and then turned back toward Archimere, who now stood listening as well. "Archimere, your men were good enough to take Martin to the lower passageway for examination."

"Yes, he asked me earlier. Why? Did he find something important?" Archimere looked suddenly concerned.

"Yes, and Martin believes it may reveal the motive behind Illyrium's attack on Perginton."

Archimere's face went cold. "Show me," he said flatly.

Aedan instructed Rand and the rest of their warriors to return to the ship and prepare for departure. Archimere, Aedan, Bryn, and Llew all followed Martin back to the palace. The stairway leading to the lower passages was not hidden or disguised in any way. In fact, there was nothing remarkable at all about the staircase. Torches already lit the way down its two flights of steps. At their bottom was a single hallway with storage rooms accessible every ten to fifteen steps. Again, there was nothing unusual or grand about any of them.

Archimere paused at the entrance to one of these rooms. "Here is where we found the men murdered," he spoke with distaste upon his tongue.

After a brief moment of silence, they continued down the hall, following Martin until he stopped in front of the very last room at the end of the passage. They entered the room, which was already lit with several torches. This room was different from all the rest. It was much older and cut from the very bedrock foundation beneath the palace. It was completely empty, except for a pile of broken rocks on the side opposite them. A black hole gaped in the portion of wall above the heap of rubble.

"Hand me that torch, Bryn," Martin instructed as he began climbing through the hole in the wall.

On the other side of the wall was another passageway. Again, it was obviously much older than the one behind them. It did not take long for the men to climb through the break in the wall and continue following Martin. They could clearly see a flickering light further down the ancient hall. It glowed eerily yellow in the dark underground hall like the lurid eye of an evil beast. They continued toward the light until the passageway opened into a much larger room. Several torches burned in a circle about its center. Martin continued toward the circle of torches and then pointed downward toward the floor.

"It is here," he concluded. His voice died quickly in the muted air of the chamber. The others all looked blankly at the floor, which was smashed in several places. Piles of crushed rock and dirt littered the area, which was lower then the rest of the floor around them. Aedan bent down low to examine the smashed portion of floor but said nothing.

"It is just an old crumbled floor," Archimere concluded.

"That is what I thought as well," Martin replied, pausing briefly before continuing. "Until I found the hammers against the wall over there. This circular portion of the floor was intentionally broken up quite recently."

"Why would they do that?" Archimere asked with narrowed eyes.

"Why would anyone burn piles of books written on the history of Tharrus?" Martin asked in answer to his question.

"To keep others from discovering what they already found," Llew concluded.

"Look at these small markings in this section," Aedan interrupted, pointing to an undamaged section of the floor. "These are letters and words if I have not missed my guess."

"If they are, I have never seen anything like them before," Llew said.

Martin nodded with a knowing look. "Aedan and Llew are correct. They are words, very ancient words, of a language very few today can read. Although most of the words are damaged, I believe I can translate a few of them. See here." Martin pointed to a spot slightly to his left. "I think I can make out this phrase." He squinted at the words but said nothing.

"Well, what does it say?" Archimere's curiosity got the better of him.

"There death grows in the garden. The White Isle..." Apprehension passed over Martin's features.

"Is that it?" Archimere wondered out loud. "Perhaps this is news better given to the women who tend the gardens," he continued with a slightly jesting tone.

Martin turned to the others, his face ashen in the dull light. There was no mirth in his features. "It is the Garden of the Aletae he seeks."

The others still looked at Martin with uncomprehending faces.

"This Garden is no ordinary place." Martin responded. "I have read of such a place before, long ago. If I am right, its plants contain such evil that if unleashed they could destroy the world. I thought it was just a myth, until I met Aayliyah, and"—he turned to look directly at Bryn—"Bryn actually met the Aletae."

An involuntary shiver passed down Bryn's spine as the memory of his brief yet harrowing experience in the underground hall returned to him. He knew nothing of this garden Martin spoke of, but he would not soon forget his encounter with the Aletae.

Aedan looked to Bryn and then back at Martin. "The White Isle? Aayliyah's Isle?"

Martin nodded.

"But does this Malen know how to find it?" Llew asked.

"Yes." Martin waved his arm to encompass the smashed portion of the floor. "He has a map."

"What must we do to stop him?" Llew spoke the question in all their minds.

"We must return to the White Isle," Aedan replied quietly, still kneeling on the broken ground.

Archimere, who was following the exchange with keen interest, spoke as he reached his arm out to Aedan. "I will be ready to leave within the hour. My people have suffered a great wrong, and I can ask no more from them. But it is because of this same great evil that I must come with you. I give you my pledge, and I will aid you in all I can," he concluded as though the matter was settled.

Martin, Aedan, Bryn, and Llew exchanged amused looks. They had known this Tharusian for less than a day, but they already thought of him as their sword brother. Aedan reached up and grabbed the extended arm, and Archimere smiled as he pulled him back to his feet.

It took little time for Archimere's men to ready themselves and say their good-byes. Fifteen men of Tharrus, including Archimere, Valentus, and Mr. Bonfire, joined Martin, Aedan, Bryn, and Llew on the steps of the palace. The remaining Tharusians also came to give them a proper warrior's send-off. Valentus scanned those gathered. His heart sank. The one person he hoped most to see was nowhere to be found. Archimere noticed his fallen countenance. He reached over and placed his hand on Valentus's shoulder with an understanding look.

"Do not worry, Valentus. She will come," he said.

Archimere turned to a tall, lanky Tharusian who stood at the front of those who gathered to say good-bye. He was an older man whose eyes expressed a keen level of understanding.

"Marcus, I leave you in charge. I know you will lead them well. Send out word that the invader is gone. The people will come when the news is received. Much will need to be done to rid this place of the Illyrian filth."

Marcus bowed his head. "When should we expect your return, my lord?"

Archimere hesitated before answering.

"Marcus, I have done what I could to protect our people, but I am no king. A new king will need to be chosen, but it is not a thing best accomplished quickly." Archimere turned his attention to the rest of the

Tharusians. "If I do not return before the change of seasons, gather the people and choose a new king."

Archimere grasped Marcus's forearm in a parting farewell and turned to leave. Just then, Alenia emerged dressed as though she were about to go riding. She pulled a medium-sized trunk behind her.

"Alenia!" Valentus blurted out her name and then stood with his mouth open. He could think of nothing else to say.

Archimere's initial look of surprise turned to one of mild amusement. He knew his sister well enough to know her intent.

"Are you planning a trip?" he said.

Alenia let go of the trunk and stood up straight with a look of defiance. "Do not pretend ignorance, brother. It makes you appear simple. You know my mind is made up," she said with a pleasant yet determined expression.

Archimere's amusement changed to an equally determined stance. "Now look here, Alenia, there is no place for a woman on this journey." His face took on a stern demeanor.

Valentus shifted uncomfortably. Alenia, on the other hand, was completely undaunted.

"Dear brother, your concern is as it should be. However..." She paused before letting her eyes settle on Aedan. "I believe there is already a woman on board your ship and a woman alone among so many men is a far greater problem." Her smile was pleasant but confident.

Archimere looked at his new friends with an expression of doubt. Aedan glanced quickly to Martin and his brothers for aid, but he found them no help at all.

"I'm afraid it is quite true," Aedan shrugged apologetically.

Archimere knew all too well that he was already beaten. He turned back to Alenia. "All right then, but you will stay away from any danger."

"Of course. I will be in no more danger than when I followed you into the forest," she said as she lowered her head in a nod.

Archimere rolled his eyes and turned back to Aedan, indicating the matter was concluded. Together the group of men and one woman marched through the littered streets of Perginton and down toward the docks.

An Uneasy Truce

T rue North could plainly be seen resting at anchor in the harbor. The last rays of the sun poured across the waters of the western sea and outlined the ship in a red light highlighted with gold. Several of Archimere's men commented on the setting sun's magnificence and unrivaled beauty. For the first time in many months, they felt the joy of normal conversation. They talked freely and with light hearts as they passed by the first of the boathouses on the dock. These wooden shacks, once busy workhouses, now stood dark and abandoned in a long row stretching down the dock.

The men continued toward the ladders leading down to the transport boats. Normally, they would have signaled the ship and waited for transport, but abandoned boats littered the docks everywhere.

Ten paces before they reached the first ladder, a large man stepped abruptly from the boathouse directly in front of them. He wore fine leather armor and carried a champion's sword at his side. His red hair and beard were messy and gave him the appearance of someone who had spent too many nights in the forest. He held his hands out to show no ill intent, but said nothing. Archimere's sword came to his hand with a singular fluid motion.

"Wait!" Valentus shouted. "I know this man," he said.

"So do I," Archimere answered. "He led the attack on us in the forest. I crossed swords with him. He escaped once, but not again."

Valentus jumped between the red-haired man and Archimere.

"I *also* counted him my enemy, and perhaps he is. But for some reason he helped me in the forest." Valentus looked from the red-haired man back to Archimere as he spoke.

Archimere continued to hold his sword at the ready, but he made no further move. The rest of the Tharusians shifted uneasily behind him. A strong breeze whipped through the red-haired man's cloak, causing it to flap around one of his upraised arms. Still, he stood completely motionless, making no move to defend against Archimere's threatening stance.

Aedan, who stood next to Archimere, spoke. "This man, enemy or not, has obviously come to talk, not fight. We should at least hear what he has to say before deciding what is to be done with him."

Archimere glanced quickly to Aedan, still not happy with any decision keeping him from finishing what began in the forest. "You are right," he concluded after a moment more. "I will hear what he has to say."

Although Archimere's words conceded the point, neither the set of his jaw nor the position of his sword changed. Aedan nodded to Valentus, who then turned back to the red-haired man.

"This is Archimere, ah…" He paused shortly, trying to decide what title to give him. "Leader of Tharrus. And this is Aedan, prince of the Emerald Isle." He glanced sideways at the two men and shifted a little uncomfortably, not sure whether he should say anything else. "This man's name is Lanthir," he added.

Aedan and Archimere watched Lanthir with a cautious silence. The red-bearded man continued to stand still a few moments longer before slowly and deliberately lowering his arms.

"It is true," he spoke clearly. "I was the leader of the Illyrian army that conquered you."

His unfortunate use of the word *conquered* nearly started a riot among Archimere's men. The sound of swords being unsheathed was followed by loud angry challenges.

"Conquered, is it? Let me teach this foreigner whose island he stands upon!" shouted a rather large, brusque fellow with a long black beard named Rolden.

Archimere held up his hand to stop the commotion before it could get out of hand.

"We will hear him out," he said and then turned back to Lanthir with hardness in his eyes that Valentus had never seen there before. "It would be good for you to remember that those who stand before you are far from conquered." His voice was tight as he spoke.

Lanthir glanced at the men around him and then gracefully inclined his head in agreement.

"I misspoke. Forgive me," he began again. "My only point is that it is right for you to hate me as your enemy. We attacked you without provocation or justification, and for that, I am ashamed. I do not ask for your friendship. Only a fool seeks what cannot be found. For what little it matters, I spoke against the attack on your people, but the king of Illyrium takes no counsel but his own. It was he that loosed the demons of the forest against both you and my men. Of my men, I alone survived. Now he is as much my enemy as he is yours." Lanthir paused, trying to discern what effect his words were having.

Archimere still held his sword in his hand, but it no longer pointed menacingly toward Lanthir. The rest of the men stood stone-faced without expression.

"What do you seek from us?" Archimere asked, the tension in his voice being replaced by caution.

"There is only one way for me to obtain justice for my men. Malen will pay with his life, but unfortunately, he has already sailed for Illyrium. Even I could not swim that far, so I seek passage on the ship waiting in the harbor." Although his words were bold, there was no arrogance in Lanthir's voice.

Mr. Bonfire, standing behind Archimere let out a loud "Hmpf" sound before speaking. "Why don' we jus invite him to a partee!" he sneered under his breath.

"If it were up to me, you would be in chains right now. But it is not my ship." Archimere turned toward Aedan. "We have pledged our support to the men of the Emerald Isle." Archimere continued. "It is Aedan's decision to make."

Aedan silently appraised Lanthir with dark brown eyes that betrayed no emotion. Another strong gust of wind whipped across the dock as Lanthir shifted his position to face Aedan directly. He had already resigned himself to his chosen course and would follow wherever it led.

From somewhere directly behind Aedan, someone placed a hand on his shoulder. Aedan turned just enough to see Martin, who strangely wore his hood over his head, concealing his face.

"Yes, Martin, what is your counsel?" Aedan asked with a bewildered expression at Martin's odd covert behavior.

"I ask that you grant this man's request," Martin whispered.

Concern passed over Aedan's brow. "He could be a spy, working in league with the king of Illyrium."

"Look in his eyes again. You will find no lie there," Martin quietly urged.

Aedan looked hard into Lanthir's eyes before speaking. "I grant your request, but we do not sail to Illyrium. Your former master sails to the south. Join us if you will."

Lanthir inclined his head. "You have my thanks, Prince Aedan," he said sincerely.

"It is not to me you owe your thanks," Aedan replied while indicating Martin, who still concealed his face under his hood.

Lanthir silently tilted his head toward the hooded man in acknowledgment. Martin simply turned and walked to the ladder and began climbing down to the boat below. Aedan, still watching Lanthir, held out his hand by way of invitation toward the ladder. After Lanthir disappeared over the edge of the dock, Aedan, his brothers, and Archimere followed.

Valentus turned toward Alenia only to find her gazing directly at him. Her face radiated in a way that made him a bit weak inside. She walked over to the top of the ladder, passing near enough for him to smell the sweet fragrance of her hair. He quickly reached over to give her a hand as she prepared to climb down. Bending forward, the pendant he wore around his neck fell out of his shirt to dangle in the open air, attracting Alenia's eye. It was not large, but she could see what appeared to be a plant flanked by a sword. Valentus noticed her curious expression.

"It belonged to my father. It is all I have left of him," he said.

She smiled. "My brother is blessed to have you at his side."

At her compliment, Valentus felt a rush of elation burn through his chest, which just as quickly disappeared when he turned to find a grinning Mr. Bonfire waiting directly behind him.

Return to the White Isle

T he voyage south from Tharrus was as uneventful as could be hoped for. Alenia and Aayliyah quickly became close friends and were rarely apart. Their presence aboard True North brought with it a certain kind of pleasantness not normally found among sailors. The men, of course, were now on their best conduct. The rough behavior often arising when men are alone for lengthy periods of time magically transformed into polite conversation and gentile manners.

Lanthir, on the other hand, remained entirely to himself. Each night, he slept under the stars in an open corner of the main deck. He never joined the others for meals, but heartily ate whatever food was given him.

After the crew finished each meal, Valentus would bring him a plate of food. He was the only one even to attempt conversation with Lanthir, which never ended up being more than a few awkward spoken pleasantries. The rest of the men remained wary, watching him with vigilant suspicion. There were always at least three warriors somewhere nearby to keep a close eye on the Illyrian warlord. If this treatment bothered Lanthir in any way, he never showed it. Rather, for his part, he was perfectly content to simply be left alone. The days were warm and the nights balmy. So Lanthir merely rested and waited for the battle he hoped would come.

As the sun slid beneath the horizon ten days from Tharrus, land was sighted. The White Isle rose from the dark waters of the western sea just to their south. Bryn, Martin, and Llew watched from the rail as True North drew closer. The island looked different from its northern approach. There were none of the long, white sandy beaches seen on the eastern side during their first landing. Here, the jungle came directly down to the shoreline broken with craggy ravines and rocky cliffs.

It did not take long before the crash of the waves against the rocks ahead could be heard. Aedan gave Berand the order to set a course parallel to the coastline. The light was rapidly fading in tonight, making it difficult to spot dangerous rocks. It was prudent to keep their distance in the dark. They would wait for morning light before drawing any closer.

Martin pointed slightly off to their right. The rocky shoreline opened into a much broader bay. Spreading out and up from the bay into the rift valley beyond stood the White City itself. The twilight gave the ancient ruins a menacing face. Silence descended over the men all across the deck. An involuntary shiver ran slowly down Bryn's spine at the memory of his encounter with the Aletae. An icy coldness spread across his throat where the woman, or whatever she was, had gripped him, lifting him off his feet. He instinctively raised a hand to his neck and rubbed the spot.

"It looks so lonely now," Aayliyah's soft voice came from behind where Martin, Bryn, and Llew watched.

They parted, making way for her to join them at the rail. Despite knowing her only a short time, she was now one of them and they respected her. She was not given to many words, but when she did speak, it was worth listening to. Her words carried insight and instilled whatever virtue was most needed.

"How long did you live there alone?" Llew asked, wincing slightly at the thought of anyone alone in the ominous ruined city.

The call of a bird sounded behind them, and they turned to see Argolis sitting on his perching post not far behind them. It almost seemed as though the bird understood the question.

"I was never really alone," she replied reflectively. "Argolis was with me."

Llew was not satisfied. "But what of your family? Your parents, I mean. Surely you were not always alone?" He paused briefly. "Were there never any others?"

Aayliyah smiled at Llew's questions. Even in the dying light, the warmth of her smile made their spirits rise. Although Martin and Bryn said nothing, they closely followed the conversation.

"My father was guardian before me. He and my mother lived with me there in the White City until the flames of their spirits were called home. There were others, but they also left when I was very young. One was brother to my father. I was told the mantle of guardianship should have fallen to him, but he refused it." Aayliyah paused deep in thought.

"My father told me his brother never recovered from the loss of his wife. She died giving birth to their son. He was a babe when they left with the others. I do not remember much of them, only that they left." She finished speaking and leaned her elbows on the flat of the rail, looking out at the ruined city she once called home.

A footfall sounded behind them, and they turned to see Valentus approaching with Alenia at his side.

Valentus spoke to Martin. "I have seen to Lanthir's meal. He still insists on sleeping on the open deck."

"Thank you, Valentus. For now, it is probably better that way," Martin responded.

Bryn and Llew exchanged a questioning look with each other. Martin was taking great pains to keep his distance from Lanthir, yet he always questioned Valentus on his interactions with the man. While Valentus did not see anything strange in this, the brothers knew there was a reason behind the unusual behavior of their mentor. Whatever it was, they also knew it would stay hidden until Martin decided otherwise.

Just then, one of the crewmen approached with a message from Aedan requesting their presence. Bryn could not help notice Aayliyah's eyes move quickly to where Aedan stood at the helm. His hand felt absently for the small leather pouch that used to hang around his neck. Remembering it was gone, his mouth turned down slightly at the edges. He was glad for his brother, and Valentus for that matter, but he could not help feeling his own emptiness inside increase. He slowly joined the group as they made there way to the helm.

Aedan awaited them with a solemn look of determination. Archimere and Rand stood next to him. He pointed toward the far side of the harbor.

"A ship. It's hard to see, but it is there, just beyond the final approach," he said.

"They would have to be blind not to have seen us," Llew said.

"Yes," Archimere agreed. "But how could they know our purpose? Your ship is certainly not like any known in these waters. So why should we be anything but simple wayfarers coming in for harborage?"

Martin lifted his hand to Archimere's shoulder. "Malen does not take chances. No, he will not care what our purpose is here. He will act to protect the one thing he now cares most about."

"What is that?" Valentus questioned.

"The garden." Martin answered directly.

The last of the twilight finally vanished as the shroud of night blanketed the White City beyond and the entire bay before them. There would be no moon tonight.

"Aayliyah, if we were to circle further to the west, is the ruined city approachable through the jungle?" Aedan asked.

"Yes, but the way is difficult and the jungle cannot be traveled by night. There are many Sargaroth."

Her answer did not dispel any of their fears. Every one of them had already guessed as much. However, they would have to wait for the morning light to land on the White Isle. None of them relished the idea of battling through the dense jungle foliage, but at least an approach from the west might go unmarked.

Aedan gave the order, and True North slid back out to sea. They would circle more to the west of the island before landing. The men were instructed to make as little noise as possible. Even small sounds would travel far across the waters on the quiet, still night air. And even though the enemy already knew of their arrival, Aedan was hopeful to keep the direction of their departure a secret.

Once True North was clear of the island, Berand navigated further to the west, while those going ashore in the morning went to their bunks for whatever sleep they could find. Although none of the men liked the idea of Aayliyah being part of the landing party, all of them understood the need for her knowledge of the island. Alenia, on the other hand, and much to her frustration, was not to be included.

The early morning hours before the sunrise were refreshing and cool as True North came into sight of the White Island once more. It was peaceful and quiet as four shore boats were lowered into the calm waters and began moving toward the dark ribbon of coastline. Somewhere high above, the cry of an eagle sounded as Argolis disappeared in the direction of the island. Only the waves breaking on the sandy shoreline and the gentle dipping of their oars could be heard. The gray light before dawn gave a lurid quality to the black line of jungle looming straight ahead in a long, forbidding wall.

Aayliyah, who sat in the lead boat with Martin, Bryn, and a handful of warriors, pointed further to the south where there was a rounding break in the straight shoreline. They adjusted direction and were soon entering the mouth of a large river. It was a long stone's-throw in width and meandered further south toward the large, white-capped mountains in the distance. It was not long before Aayliyah directed them toward a smaller tributary branching off the main river to the north.

The first golden rays of sunshine began pouring over the river as the first of the shore boats slid smoothly into the mouth of the side tributary. The smaller river was deep but narrow, forcing them to travel in a line, one behind the other. Llew, Rand, and a third of their warriors manned the second boat. Aedan, Valentus, and Lanthir, along with more warriors, filled the third. Archimere and his Tharrusians followed closely in the last boat.

Upon entering the tributary, they soon breached the jungle walls and exchanged the bright light of the morning sun for the dull green illumination and dark shadows of the heavy canopy high above. It was hot and humid behind the thick veil of foliage, and the cool wind of the open water vanished. Somewhere in the distance, an odd-sounding bird echoed its call through the dense undergrowth, and another answered in the distance. This was a strange and exotic world, and every sound brought to mind wild and foreboding images. Every man among them keenly watched the surrounding jungle for any sign of danger.

They passed by a spot where the small river branched to their left, but Aayliyah indicated with hand motions to continue straight on.

Speaking in low, quiet tones, Martin asked Aayliyah how close she thought they were to the White City.

"Soon we will leave the boats," she answered. "It is not far from there, but the way is slow and the jungle dangerous."

Martin nodded his understanding, and Bryn continued scanning the river ahead, for what he was not sure. Something tugged at the corners of his senses. The heavy air was full of odd and curious noises, but it was not any sound that bothered him. It was, instead, an uncanny feeling of approaching danger.

An Unexpected Enemy

B ryn carefully stood to his feet. A sharp bend in the small river could be seen not far ahead. He leaned forward, attempting to see around it to the other side. The jungle growth along the banks, however, was too thick and high to allow any real view. He signaled the others to hold back while his lead boat rounded the bend. The possibility of an ambush was ever present, and Bryn knew it would not be wise for them to group too closely together.

They rounded the turn only to find all was quiet. Bryn still could not shake the uneasiness growing in his mind. He turned and looked at Martin and Aayliyah. They both scanned the overgrown riverbanks, but he said nothing. Bryn waited a moment longer, and then he whistled his all-clear signal to the other boats. Looking further down the channel, he noticed it narrowed even more. He turned just as the second boat came around the bend. Llew, Rand, and the men under their command could easily be seen. They were alert and ready for anything. Bryn motioned the two warriors holding the oars in his boat to continue forward.

The banks of the river grew higher as the channel narrowed. It was not long before Bryn could almost reach out and touch the steep-cut side with his hand. The densely growing jungle vines and ferns began overhanging the channel in a tangled mess. Large, thick green leaves stretched out over the banks and covered the surface of the water with an opaque darkness. It gave the impression of entering into a burrowed tunnel. The last shore boat rounded the bend and came into view just before those with Bryn entered under the low hanging canopy of leaves and vines.

Those in the lead were able to move along well enough for a short time, but soon the tangled foliage became so thick it hung down close to the water's surface. Their boat slowed to almost a complete stop. Several of the men stood and began pushing the green foliage aside, while those with oars shoved them into the soft dirt of the river's bank and slowly pushed the boat forward.

They continued to struggle through the tangled mess, every so often catching a glimpse of the boat behind as it also pushed its way through. The going was slow, but they were making small gains as they crept forward. Bryn looked over his shoulder at Aayliyah and Martin on the bench directly behind him. They did not appear concerned, but something continued to nag at Bryn. His right hand instinctively came to rest on the pommel of his sword. He scanned the dense foliage all around them with careful scrutiny, but no threat could be found. He slowly exhaled, allowing himself to relax a little. This side of the island was different from the paths he traveled during his first visit. There was something here, some unknown factor or presence that made him tense. He wiped the sweat from his brow and tried to peer through the confused undergrowth ahead, but could see nothing beyond the front of their boat.

Cian, who sat near the back, let out a muffled cry. Bryn snapped his head around. The young warrior held something out in his left hand. It was black and squirmed against his grip. Angry disgust crossed Cian's features as he threw it from him into the brush.

"What was that?" Bryn asked.

Martin turned back toward Bryn. "It looked like an ant!" He spoke with some surprise.

Cian shook his hand back and forth. "I have never seen an ant that was bigger than my hand before. It just about took my finger off at the knuckle," he said.

Aayliyah looked on with apprehension. She turned to Martin and Bryn. "We *must* move quicker," she stated with emphasis.

"Why? What do you know?" Martin asked.

"There is not much time. We must move faster!" Although she answered quietly, there was no mistaking her urgency. Bryn ordered the two warriors with the oars to double their efforts. He yelled a warning back to the nearest boat as he pulled his sword and carefully began slashing at the foliage in front of them.

A cry of pain sounded from where they believed Llew's boat to be located. Bryn stopped cutting and looked back into the green mess of vines. Another muffled shout could be heard. The men stopped trying to move the boat and simply listened. Riordan leaned forward and sharply slapped Cian on the back, causing him to jerk with surprise.

"What did you do that for? I just about fell off my bench!" Cian hissed back.

"Don't worry, Cian, it was just a *very* large fly," Riordan spoke with mock seriousness and then laughed under his breath.

Cian angrily swung his hand back at Riordan, causing another burst of muffled laughter.

"It was as large as your head, I tell you!" Cian spat.

"Silence!" Martin ordered quietly.

Bryn returned to cutting vines, and the boat started moving forward again, but it was not long before another ant even larger than the first one crawled down one of the hanging fern leaves. The closest warrior quickly slapped it into the dark water. Three more of the monstrous creatures dropped into the boat, sending the men into a brief moment of chaos as they fought to stomp and kill them. Again, the boat slowed to an almost complete stop as the men peered into the surrounding fauna.

Bryn was about to begin pulling the boat again, when Martin spoke. "Wait! Do you hear that?"

After a short pause, Cian responded, "I do not hear anything but the buzzing of insects."

Martin held up his hand for silence as he cocked his head slightly to the right. "It grows closer. A sort of clicking sound."

"They are coming! We must hurry or it will be too late!" Aayliyah said with uncharacteristic fear in her voice.

Nothing more needed to be said to the men. They began working with renewed fervor as the thought of what Aayliyah meant by "they" filled their minds with motivation. Several of the oversized black ants appeared at the tops of the ferns and began dropping into the boat. Shouts and the sounds of struggle came to them through the green, leafy, tangled mess. It was from the direction of Llew's boat.

A large ant dropped onto Bryn's head, and his reaction was instant. He grabbed the wicked thing and threw it into the dark water, its pinching jaws aggressively snapping at him the whole time. He looked upward toward the bank to his right. The jungle vines and leaves looked strangely liquid, as though flowing with black mud. The dismay at what he knew it must be filled his chest with a surge of adrenaline. Aayliyah muffled a scream. Bryn turned back toward her to find Martin working fast to keep the grotesque creatures away, but there were more and more of them dropping into the boat. It would not be long before these black devils simply overcame them by sheer numbers. The clicking sound rose to a near roar. Bryn quickly redoubled his efforts, trying by sheer might to pull them to freedom and safety. Ants crawled up his legs and on his back now. A particularly large one with wicked pinchers bit right through his clothes and into the flesh of his shoulder. He growled out in anger, but ignored the gnawing pain and kept pulling and yanking them forward. And then, as quickly as they had entered the narrow overgrown channel, their boat slid past the last of the vines into the open mouth of a small jungle lake.

Bryn quickly grabbed the large ant biting into the flesh of his shoulder and snapped it in half. He glanced quickly back to the overgrown channel. Both sides were now swarming with the strange, black, undulating movement. He could hear the screams of the men in Llew's boat. His stomach turned slightly at the thought of what he knew he was about to do. He turned to Martin, who was still helping rid their boat of ants.

"Martin, if it is safe, wait for us on the other side of the lake," he stated simply and then put his foot on the edge of the boat and dove headfirst into the water.

It did not take long to swim back to the mouth of the channel. The clicking noise once again grew to a disturbing level. The ants boiled all around the banks and the jungle growth, but they stayed away from the water surface. Bryn kept his head low in the water and swam another ten body-lengths before seeing the bow of Llew's boat.

It was as he expected, a bloody battlefield still being fought upon. The men were nearly overcome, and the small vessel danced with a struggle between life and death. Llew stood at the front of the boat, still fighting against the overhanging vines in an attempt to move his boat forward. He was covered with the black demons. Bryn knew there was only one chance for escape. He yelled for them to get into the water.

Disbelief covered Llew's face when he located his brother. He jerked in pain and slapped at the ants that were biting into the uncovered flesh on his neck. He yelled to his men just as one of them was lifted off of his feet by several columns of ants forming an interlinking chain of sorts with their bodies. The man screamed in horror as he struggled in vain to escape. Rand, who was closest, slashed out with his dagger. Hacking through the black columns, the man fell back into the boat.

Llew feverishly began pushing the men near him into the dark, murky water. Hundreds of ants dropped into the boat and onto Rand and Llew. Several more black columns of ants formed instantly and lifted Llew off of his feet. Rand tried to rush to his aid, but another line of ants suddenly pulled at his left shoulder, causing him to lose his balance. He stumbled on the bench in front of him and tumbled over the side. The single column of ants was not strong enough to hold his weight, and he plunged into the water.

Bryn searched desperately for some way to aid his brother, but he was just too far. Blood ran down Llew's face. The sword that was still in his hand flashed through the ants, dropping him to his knees amongst the swarming black mass in the boat. Llew forced himself to his feet, agony twisting his features, and threw himself over the back of the boat into the water.

The rest of the men were already swimming and struggling to be free of the hideous jungle trap. Black ropes made of living ants began forming from the hanging foliage. They stretched downward toward the escaping men like growing vines. The water became a confusion of splashing black foam as the men struggled to escape the hungry jaws of the menacing creatures.

Martin and those in the lead boat waited a safe distance out into the lake. They watched the scene unfolding before them in horror. It was hard to imagine how anything could survive inside the swirling black mass. One of the men pointed toward the dark opening of the narrow river channel.

"I see them! Two men, right there in the water!" It was Riordan speaking excitedly.

In another moment, several more heads could be seen. One after another, they slowly swam toward the boat, exhausted from their ordeal. Several of the men from Martin's boat climbed over the side and into the lake to make room for the wounded warriors as they were hauled up out of the water.

Martin and Aayliyah strained to locate Bryn and Llew. All the other men, including Rand, were miraculously accounted for. They were in rough shape but thankful to be alive.

"I *saw* Llew jump into the water. In the confusion… I lost sight of them, but they were both *right* behind me," Rand searched the water as he spoke. When he realized they were nowhere to be seen, he began climbing back over the side of the small boat. The warriors next to him grabbed a hold of his arms and wouldn't let go. It was an impossible rescue.

Martin sat in stunned silence as the black horde continued to pillage everything in sight. They sat there for a long time. Yet no one emerged from the channel. Too much time had passed and Martin knew it, but he was unable to force himself to turn away. Aayliyah put a gentle hand on his forearm. He turned slowly to her.

"Dark comes early to the jungle, and there is still far to go. They are strong. If there is a way for them, they will find it and follow us to the city," she said softly.

Martin noticed a tear roll down her check as she looked away from him. He turned his head back, still searching the water. Numbness crept into his mind as the constant clicking sounds of the ants continued to fill the air around them. He searched the faces of the men sitting in the boat. They were weary and bleeding, but not one of them would hesitate to face the ants again if they believed Bryn and Llew lived. But Martin knew it would be a futile and deadly decision. Still, he hesitated.

There was no sign of the other two shore boats, but Rand believed Aedan and Archimere were warned before coming too close to the danger. Yet their location and fate remained unknown. Before leaving True North, Aayliyah had drawn a rough map of the island. Their plan was simple: go to the White city and if anyone became separated they should do the same. Thus, Martin knew Aedan and the others would find a different route.

The surface of the jungle lake was darkening in the dying light. Soon there would be other dangers lurking and *hunting* in the jungle around them. With the darkness would come the Sargaroth. Martin looked back at Aayliyah, but she avoided his eyes. He swallowed the lump in his throat and gave the order to continue on to the other side of the lake. Rand looked up quickly as if to protest, but he was silenced by the pain in Martin's eyes. He turned back toward the swirling black mass and knew it was the only decision that could be made. As they slowly rowed away, against all hope, Martin breathed a soft plea to the High King of heaven for Bryn and Llew.

The White City was dazzling in the red and orange light of the late-day sun. Its rays poured over the top of the tropical forest into the valley rift where the city lay. The jungle behind looked dark in comparison as Martin, Aayliyah, and the men with them descended the long stairway from the cliff top above. No one spoke as they entered the city. The loss of their beloved princes still burned deeply.

They passed through a large stone archway, and Aayliyah bent down and plucked a small branch from one of the green plants growing around it. Martin recognized it as the same plant that had healed Aedan. She silently indicated to the others that they should do the same. Most of the men just looked back at her without comprehension. Martin bent down and slowly broke off a sprig of the plant, the Plant of Truth as she called it. It was quite ordinary in appearance to the casual observer, but it took on a strange fantastical luminescence when held up closer to the eye. He placed it into his waist belt and instructed the others to do so as well.

"It is a talisman against this evil place," he said with a sad but deliberate tone.

The street they followed came to a place where it intersected with another stone-paved roadway leading north and south. The city to the south rose higher and higher, filling the rift valley with thousands of white stone buildings. To the north lay the harbor. The valley ground fell away from them in that direction, allowing a clear view of the enemy's ship. But instead of one ship, as originally presumed, they could see at least six bulky vessels anchored close to the docks. These ships could easily have transported a small army.

Martin stood still, quietly assessing their situation. Without turning away from the harbor, he asked Aayliyah where Aedan and the others would likely enter the city.

"They must approach more from the south. I know a bridge that stretches from the jungle to the city, but I have never been in the jungle to the south. When I was very young, my parents warned me it was an evil place." There was concern in her voice.

Martin turned away from the northern harbor view and walked up the south stone road toward the higher part of the city.

Webs

Aedan searched the canopy above, trying to decide where the sun stood. It took them most of the morning to find another branch of the river leading in the direction of the White City. There was hardness in his eyes as he turned back to surveying the jungle below the small rise where he and his men now rested. They left the boats behind after finding a trailhead.

It was actually an old road, paved with white blocks of cut stone. It must have been grand at one time. Now the jungle hid most of it, leaving only enough room for two men to walk side by side. Aedan was anxious to move on, but he knew the men needed a rest. It was hot and humid, and they would need their strength today.

Giving the order to reverse course away from the ant horde was perhaps the hardest thing Aedan had ever done. He could not help reliving the dreadful morning in every detail, trying to find some hope the others survived. Fear nagged at his stomach. He forced down thoughts of Aayliyah. His brothers and Martin would give their lives to protect her, of that he was sure. But some things cannot be defeated.

When the ant army first attacked, Aedan and Archimere's boats still sat some distance from the overgrown channel. They were waiting for a signal that the others had made it through the tangled section of the channel. Aedan knew they would need at least two of their boats in order to return to True North and did not want to see all of them unnecessarily damaged should the channel prove unpassable.

The attack came so fast there was no time to react. Before Aedan even realized what was happening, the huge ants swarmed the tangled mess hanging over the channel and built bridges out of their own bodies across the water toward his boat. It was a strange sight to behold as the black lines of ant bridges grew thicker and longer over the riverway. As if by magic, they came across the narrow channel toward them by the hundreds and thousands. It was dreadfully amazing to witness. The sheer speed and determination of these creatures defied all reason.

The only choice left to Aedan was to order the two remaining boats to return to the larger river. If they stayed any longer, it would have been their doom. As it was, several of the long, black ant bridges nearly reached them, and other ants began racing over the bodies of their comrades to the attack. He could not see Llew or Bryn's boats, but he desperately hoped they made it through the tangled mess in time.

Aedan continued surveying the jungle below as he whispered a prayer to the Lord of heaven. Did he hear the prayers of men? His father believed so. But the growing knot in Aedan's gut betrayed his own lack of faith.

"I believe they made it," a voice came from behind him.

Valentus stood close by. He spoke quiet enough so the others would not hear. Aedan searched Valentus's face. There was no doubt or falseness in him. His belief was real enough, but how could he be so sure?

"I have been trying to convince myself of that very thing," Aedan said, betraying his own doubt.

Valentus lifted his foot up onto a rock and rested his arms across his knee. There was a certain quality about this young man. Even though he was often enough unsure of himself, he never shied away from doing what he knew was right. Aedan had come to trust him in the short time of their friendship.

"There was a time, back in the fog on Tharrus, when I too should have died. But a man came out of nowhere and delivered me. I believe He still watches over those who do His work. It is true we all must die sometime, but I know the others are alive," Valentus said.

"How?" Aedan asked, taken back by Valentus's calm assurance.

Valentus thought for a moment. "Because I feel it here." He placed his hand over his chest. "And because I remember the man who saved me." He paused momentarily. "When I consider whether they have come to harm, I feel His presence."

Both of them silently resumed their watch over the jungle. It was not long before Archimere approached to let Aedan know the men were rested and eager to move on. Lanthir sat off to one side, not far away. He still kept to himself for the most part, rarely saying anything, but always watching. When Aedan issued the order to move out, he noticed Lanthir watching him. There was curiosity in his eyes. Aedan acknowledged him with a slight nod and then turned to lead the men down the old road.

They walked for another two hours through the humid heat, sweat running freely down their faces to sting their eyes. Aedan wiped his brow and looked ahead. A structure loomed before them. It was misplaced in the thick jungle. The block road led directly past its front. It was a ruined stone building, circular in shape with no roof. Cut stone and fluted pillars stood all around its perimeter. The jungle grew densely right up to its walls, but the remaining stone kept it somewhat free of vines. It was clear enough of undergrowth to allow the men to sit and rest comfortably. Aedan gave the order to stop.

Other broken structures could be seen in the jungle, but they were almost completely covered by the voracious plants. Aedan guessed this place must have been a sort of outpost of the White City. He walked inside the ruined building through a large, open archway. Several stone benches lined the walls of the circular chamber inside. But for some rather large webs lurking in the high up corners, the rest of the chamber was empty. Aedan wondered what people had once made this island their home.

Whoever they were, they had lived their lives here, raised families, and pursued their own hopes and dreams. It was obvious this place was built to last, but as he looked around at the crumbling stone, he knew time brings all things down to decay. Whoever these people were, good or bad, they disappeared long ago and now only the jungle remained.

It was a melancholy place, and Aedan hoped his life would leave something more enduring than what he saw around him. What was it his father used to tell him and his brothers when they were young? He paused to remember, and then it came to him. He said they should work hard, but remember that of all the grand things men build, only love lasted forever. The memory of his father brought a fresh hope to his spirit.

He took one last look over the interior of the building. Another archway opened on the other side of the room. He walked over, and it opened out to the jungle on the other side. The ring of pillars continued around the perimeter on this side as well. He looked out over the jungle scene before him and froze. The expression on his face went cold as he realized what he was seeing.

He turned and ran back to where his men waited on the other side of the building. Archimere leaned with his back against one of the pillars near the archway. Aedan placed his hand on Archimere's shoulder and with more calmness than he now felt asked him to come. Archimere sensed the urgency in Aedan's features and followed him back into the building. Aedan led Archimere to the other side and silently pointed toward the jungle. The two men stood stock still for a moment as incomprehension engulfed their minds.

Webs stretched from the stone pillars to the nearby trees. These webs were different from those inside the building, which were old and better called cobwebs. These were freshly spun webs, not only massive in their dimensions, but each individual web strand was as thick as a man's thumb. Archimere's eyes widened at the scene before them. Webs as far as they could see. It was a virtual city of webs so thick that the jungle appeared to be covered by a shroud. Hundreds of dark tunnel openings gaped out of the web city. None of the webs' makers were visible, but neither man liked to consider what could have made these. The ant army was terrible, but this sight filled their minds with a new depth of dread.

"From the frying pan into the fire," a voice said from behind them. "I would have preferred to face the ants." They turned to find Lanthir staring up at the webs.

The three men backed slowly away from the sight and began quietly getting the others ready to move on. Each man was silently signaled with the sign for danger and the need for stealth. None of them fully understood why, until they moved out past the end of the building where they could see into the jungle beyond. No further explanations were needed. Each man cringed internally at the sight, but they made no sound as they moved off behind their leaders.

Valentus walked behind Archimere and next to Mr. Bonfire. Although he remained sure in his belief that the others had made it through the ants, he kept a careful watch on the webs to their right and did not feel quite as confident about his own future. The screeching sound of a large bird made the men freeze in their tracks. High up in one of the nearby webs, a great-sized, multi-colored bird struggled with the sticky web he was caught in. The more the creature struggled, the more it became trapped.

The men all stood still watching the bird's plight. Before any of them even knew what they were seeing, a large spider ran from its nearby tunnel and was on top of the unfortunate bird. The spider was dark in color with a body built for speed. Thick black hair stuck off its body and legs like a porcupine. It quickly wrapped its prize up in a silk shroud and left it to hang, disappearing slowly back into its hole.

Valentus slowly released his breath and glanced around at the rest of the men. Not too few of them wore ashen faces. He wondered if he looked as frightened as he felt. Aedan motioned with his hands for them to continue on. They slowly and deliberately moved off down the stone road, which, much to their relief, led westward away from the spider city. After walking for another hour, the men began to talk again. They spoke in hushed tones at first, but as the distance from the last of the webs grew, so did their spirits. Before long, they had all but forgotten the danger behind them. The further north they traveled, the ancient stone road widened somewhat, and the temperature eased a little.

Somewhere high above the thick canopy, the clouds must have covered the sun. Even though it was still relatively early in the day, it became suddenly dark and gloomy in the jungle below. The men once again grew wary of the high walls of jungle fern that flanked them on both sides. Something about the lack of light made everything appear more menacing. Of course there were a myriad of creeping things and small creatures roaming the jungle floor. With each movement they rustled the large ferns, giving rise to more than one false alarm among the men.

Aedan walked at the head of the column. If Aayliyah's map of the island was accurate, the White City should not be much farther to the north. He guessed their altered route would bring them in from the south. The others, if all was well, should have already reached the western entrance to the city. He turned and signaled for the men to maintain silence. He did not want to alert the enemy to their approach.

He turned back to walking when the scream of one of the men split the dense jungle air. His breath caught inside his throat as he jerked toward the sound. The men at the rear of the line were in complete chaos. Aedan ordered those in front into a defensive position and ran to discover what happened. Archimere, Mr. Bonfire, and Valentus were already there and stood poised with swords drawn.

"What happened?" Aedan asked between clenched teeth.

Archimere indicated toward the stone blocks at the edge of the path with anger in his eyes. He did not speak, but continued to hold his sword at the ready. A large smudge of blood was scraped over the area, and a few of the ferns were broken off at their bases.

"Did anyone see what happened?" Aedan asked the nearest of the Tharusians.

Several of them looked as though they were poised to flee. Fear twisted their features. Most of them did not even think to pull out their swords. Aedan grabbed the nearest man by the arm. The man jerked sharply in reaction. Aedan waited for his full attention.

"What did you see?" he asked in a calm voice.

The man glanced back toward the ever-darkening wall of jungle. "Marcion was dead before we even knew the thing was there," the man said in a voice strained with grief.

"What did this?" Aedan continued, pulling the man's attention back to his question.

The Tharusian swallowed hard and looked back to Aedan. "It was so swift. I saw something black... *I don't know what...* then it was gone."

Aedan released the man and turned to Archimere.

"I and my men will go after him." Archimere quickly concluded.

Aedan shook his head. "Your man is beyond all help. No one could have survived that amount of blood loss. He is already dead. If you go out there"—he pointed with his sword toward the jungle beyond—"you too would soon be dead. No, we must get to the White City before darkness falls."

Archimere was about to protest when Mr. Bonfire pointed back down the roadway they'd just come.

"What th' brat's britches is that?" he spat off to the side.

The rest of them turned their attention back down the path. Something large and black sat on the old road where it last turned to the left. It was roughly half the height of a man, but it spread out as wide as the road itself. In the clouded light, it almost looked like a pile of tree branches sticking out of a fallen log. The thing, whatever it was, stood completely still. But for the fact that it was not there a moment ago, it could have easily been mistaken for just another part of the tangled jungle.

Without taking his eyes from the object, Aedan deliberately pulled out his sword, cocked his head slightly to his right, and spoke in an even tone to Archimere, Mr. Bonfire, and Valentus.

"Get the men out of here."

At first those closest just looked back at him with hesitation. The dark object on the road behind them suddenly moved ahead and then stopped again. The large ferns somewhere off to their left also moved. Aedan snapped his head back toward his men.

"Run!" he yelled.

It took another painfully long moment for the men at the head of the column to fully grasp the order. Those at the rear, however, already having witnessed the attack on their friend, needed no further explanation. They pushed into the men in front of them, causing a brief but confused collision. The giant black spider was now clearly inching forward one leg at a time. It suddenly jerked forward again and then stopped, almost as though it was trying to get them to turn and run. Aedan made himself ready for the attack he knew would come. He guessed there was at least one more spider to the left, waiting somewhere behind the thick fern wall. At the present, however, he was more concerned with the one he could see.

"High King of heaven, come to our aid now," he whispered under his breath.

Someone stepped up beside him. Aedan turned to see Archimere. He held a spear retrieved from one of his men. The two of them would guard the rear of the retreat. None of their men liked the thought of retreat. But there was nothing to be gained by being slaughtered on the road. The column of warriors was too vulnerable from the sides, and they all knew it. These creatures were impossibly fast and could attack from the dense jungle wall at point-blank range.

Holding the long, shafted spear out in front of him in a ready position, Archimere took a deep breath and let it out slowly. The dark outline of the creature remained completely still for another moment, and then it jerked into a run with such swiftness that they involuntarily stepped backwards in surprise before regaining their resolve. The fading light only served to enhance the thing's blinding speed. Covered by shadows, the movements of the charging creature were blurred in growing darkness.

Archimere thrust out his spear just in time to stop the creature's charge and prevent them both from being trampled. Their attacker abruptly halted and lifted its front legs high into the air above them. Its fangs flashed with savagery, and its wide squat shape took on a new menacing size as it reared up onto its back legs to more than double its height. Archimere jabbed his spear at the spider's underside, but it deftly backed out of reach and then flashed out with one of its front legs, knocking him off his feet and into the air. The spear flew out of Archimere's hands and clattered onto the road behind him.

Aedan jumped at the spider, shouting and flashing his sword with a flurry. It backed away from Archimere and turned to face Aedan. Instead of attacking, however, the thing backed slowly away, shrinking back down onto all its many legs. Aedan, puzzled at the spider's actions, took a guarded step closer.

The ferns directly to the left of where he stood parted to reveal another large spider, also black in color. Aedan saw it from the edge of his sight, but there was nothing he could do. It had him neatly trapped. Archimere, still on his back, reached to pull out his sword, but he was not in a position to defend against this new spider. Aedan attempted to twist toward it, but before he could complete even half of the needed rotation, it was on him. Its bristle-covered legs grabbed him over the shoulders and yanked him backward off his feet toward the jungle wall. He fought to swing his sword, but could find no target.

Just as he hit the first of the ferns, the spider jerked violently, throwing him back to the ground. It collapsed and stood again with a strange jerking motion only to fall again and collapse inward upon itself with revolting convulsions. The dark wooden shaft of a spear protruded from its body. Lanthir stood defiantly on the jungle road behind him. His face burned hot with the intensity of battle. He wiped the sweat from his brow and bowed his head to Aedan, and then he picked up Archimere's spear and ran at the other spider. It reared onto its back legs again, but Lanthir charged in without hesitation and rammed the spear's tip deep into its underside. The thing screeched in agony as it tried to fight back, but Archimere and Aedan were on it with their swords, stabbing deep into its black body. Dark liquid spurted and oozed from the wounds as it jerked backwards in convulsions onto the old road, its legs collapsing inward just like the other spider. The once impossibly large monster shriveled into little more than a shell.

The three men stood in tired silence, ready for whatever else might come. Some distance off in the jungle, behind where the first spider originally appeared, came a disconcerting sound. Something, perhaps many things, were crashing through the dense jungle undergrowth toward them. The three men turned and ran back down the road toward the city they hoped was near.

Escape

Not far ahead the jungle road turned more to the north, rising steeply up the side of a densely covered ridge. The three men did not stop running until they reached its crest. They paused there to catch their breath. From were they stood, there was a wide view of the jungle floor behind them. The noise of approach continued to grow louder, and now, as they looked down behind them, they understood why. Hundreds of giant black spiders charged through the tall, green foliage.

Although much of their actual bodies were obscured below the large green ferns, there was no question as to what they were. Their battle must have alerted the entire spider village to their presence.

"Well, do we stay and fight?" Lanthir asked with a tone suggesting he liked the odds.

Archimere looked across at Lanthir and then back to Aedan with disbelief. It seemed to Aedan that admiration also played at the corners of the Tharusian's eyes.

"Not that it wouldn't be a battle to be remembered, but we should save ourselves for the enemy we came to find," Aedan responded.

At that moment, a particularly large spider jumped from the ferns at the base of the ridge, landing a mere fifty paces from the crest. The movement was so sudden, Aedan and Archimere turned as one and sprinted across the top of the ridge in the opposite direction. Lanthir hesitated. He watched the spider come closer, then with a slight look of disappointment turned away with the agility of a cat and followed his companions. Spiders were now pouring over the top of the ridge with an eager ferocity. The larger spider in the lead was only twenty paces behind now and gaining.

Ahead, the road turned sharply to the right, and Aedan and Archimere disappeared around the corner ahead of Lanthir. The road ended abruptly at a small stone courtyard that was completely hedged in by thick foliage on all sides. Back toward the north, however, a small opening broke the continuous thick, green wall. Not far beyond the break, the supports of a footbridge could be seen.

Aedan and Archimere darted through the opening. Lanthir turned to follow when a brownish spider with red markings suddenly sprang from the undergrowth on the south side of the courtyard. Its head was covered with evil eyes that watched him with greedy hunger. He considered whether to make a stand, but just as quickly saw the foolishness of any such thought. The spider lunged at him, slashing with a long thorn-like protrusion. Lanthir dove backwards just in time to avoid being impaled. Rolling once, he was up and diving through the opening and onto the bridge. Aedan and Archimere reached for him, but he was already up and urging them forward.

The bridge, only wide enough for two men to walk side by side, spanned a deep canyon rift between the jungle and the White City. A fast-moving river, broken by several dramatic waterfalls, rushed far below them.

They were halfway across before they paused to look back. The bridge was too narrow for the abnormally large spiders to cross it, and the distance was too far for them to jump. The three men breathed a quiet sigh of relief and turned away. Out of the thick ferns crashed the large jumping spider. It flew through the air with ferocious agility and roared with a shrill grating noise. Before they could react, it landed on the bridge and knocked Lanthir onto his face. The spider's stinger slashed downward. Lanthir braced himself for the killing blow, but the stinger jerked at the last moment, hitting ineffectively into the bridge itself.

The spider appeared to lose its balance and tottered precariously. Lanthir quickly turned over to find that Archimere had severed one of its legs with which it held to the bridge. Aedan now slashed at another. The spider grabbed desperately for a better hold, but it could not support its own weight. It slipped off into the raging waters below.

Archimere reached a hand down to Lanthir, who hesitated briefly considering the hand of his enemy. Making up his mind quickly and decisively, he grasped the hand and let out a loud, deep-throated laugh. They turned and walked across the bridge and into the city where the rest of their men waited.

Bryn lay in complete darkness, wet and cold. His mind felt heavy and dull, and he couldn't recall how he came to be there. Something shifted in the darkness next to him. He carefully put his hand out in the direction of the movement and touched something solid. A soft groan came to him.

"Llew?" he spoke quietly. When there was no response, he tried again. "Can you hear me, Llew?"

He reached over and placed his hand on what he guessed was a shoulder and shook it gently. The only response was another soft groan, and Bryn shook him again.

"Where is this place? I can't see anything," a quiet, dry voice crackled back at him.

"Lay still, I think you hit your head on a rock," Bryn answered.

He fumbled his hands around him, trying to get a better understanding of where they were. They lay hard against a wall that felt like smooth rock. It curved upward and closed in just above Bryn's head.

There was water not more than an arm's length in front of him. It was some sort of hollowed-out den or cave. Bryn tried to remember how they had gotten there. The battle with the ant army began to come back to him. He wondered how much time had passed. Such things were hard to determine without the stars or daylight as a reference.

He remembered going back to help the other boat and Llew's desperate plunge into the water. In the confused jump, Llew hit his head on a rock protruding out from the bank's edge into the dark water. By the time Bryn reached him, the vicious ants were already forming rope lines toward Llew's unconscious body. There was no way to escape above the water's surface. The banks were too high. Bryn, in one last hopeless attempt, pulled Llew down into the murky black channel. In an effort to keep both of them from simply floating back up to the surface, he used the large protruding rock Llew hit his head on to hold them under the surface and out of reach. It was then he discovered the hollow space under the riverbank.

Bryn pulled Llew behind him into the black opening. His senses crawled with disgust as he forced his way past slimy underwater weeds, not knowing what might be waiting for them in the darkness. All his impulses screamed for him to return to the surface. But no matter what lurked in the black tunnel, he knew death hovered above with the ant horde. The water cave angled downward away from the river for several body lengths before abruptly opening upward. It was then he found the open-air pocket with a small rock ledge on one side.

It was no small task to pull Llew out of the water onto the ledge. Once securely on the rock shelf, Llew's body was racked with coughing and gurgling sounds. Bryn carefully leaned him over on his side until they subsided and he was quiet again, his shallow breathing assuring Bryn that he still lived and had not drowned. It was here, on the small ledge in the underwater cave, that they still lay in the darkness. Bryn remembered the fire starter he always carried with him. He felt around for anything he could use for fuel. There was nothing on the ledge within reach.

"Lay still, Llew. I am going to crawl forward a little to see if there is anything burnable farther up."

Llew agreed, his voice still weak and haggard.

Bryn inched forward. There was little room on the shelf, and he did not want to fall back into the water. He didn't relish another soaking. Instead of closing in tighter as expected, the wall of the small air pocket felt as though it receded away from the small ledge. In the darkness, it gave the feeling of a vast openness before him. He fought down the feeling of alarm and reached further in the darkness, hoping to find some dry wood. He could no longer feel the hard rock ledge and realized too late that he had overextended his reach. His heart came into his throat as he jerked over the sharp edge, clawing at the blackness in a futile attempt to right himself. His stomach tightened as the awful realization that he was falling into total darkness engulfed him.

Bryn hit the ground hard. The underground floor, instead of hard rock, thankfully felt more like sand. He rolled over and shook his head. He must have fallen a little more than his own height. Thankful to be alive, he patted his hand around and hit upon a small pile of dry sticks some rat or mouse gathered for a nest. It did not take him long to start a fire. With the small amount of light coming from it, he could make out some larger sticks in a corner not far away. He gathered them and built up the fire. Hearing a shuffling noise from back up on the ledge, Bryn looked up as Llew's face appeared.

"I see you have found the light," he said dryly.

"How are you feeling?"

"My head feels like someone used it for a drum. But other than that, I am glad not to be ant food."

Llew slowly lowered his legs over the edge and dropped down to join Bryn. The firelight flickered against the walls of the small cavern around them. It was smooth-looking, as though fast-moving water had often washed past them, giving an almost polished effect. Here and there, large sections of the wall sparkled with some sort of quartz or crystalline rock.

Looking around, Llew spoke with a note of irony. "If my head did not hurt so much and there weren't large man-eating ants above us, I could like this place. Anyway, what of the others? What happened?"

"I believe they escaped the ants. There was a lake not far from the spot of the attack. I know not of Aedan and those behind you."

"I do not think they entered the tangled channel. They must have returned to the river to find another way."

"This fire won't last long. We better look around while we can still see," Bryn commented.

The cave was not large, but it narrowed quickly in the opposite direction away from where they believed the river above was located. The light from the small fire was not bright enough to see anything beyond vague outlines. Llew tore the sleeves off his tunic, found a thicker branch, and began tying the cloth tightly in a bunch to its end. When he finished, he held it to the fire. The flames slowly caught and engulfed it. He held it up above their heads, making several higher veins of crystal rock dance with color. Bryn looked blankly at his younger brother for a moment, slightly embarrassed that he had not thought of this first. A few moments later, they were both exploring the length of the cavern with two brightly burning torches.

The cavern narrowed considerably but did not end. A corridor-like channel branched off and continued directly away from the rock ledge. Not far down the passage, it began sloping downward and then turned sharply to the left. Based upon the location of the river behind them, they guessed they were headed north toward the White City. Light-colored sand covered the floor of the passage, helping reflect the small light of their torches. Like the walls in the cavern, the narrow tunnel was water-worn and smooth.

"Some ancient underground river must have flowed here once," Llew said.

Bryn stopped and put his hand on Llew's shoulder.

"These torches will not last much longer. If we go too far, we might end up crawling back to the river through the dark."

Llew hesitated, looking both ways. "You are right, but something ahead pulls at me."

Reluctance weighed heavy on Bryn's mind. It surprised him. Normally, it would have taken a team of wild horses to stop him from going on. What held him back? At first, he thought it was just a desire to be cautious. After all, they did not even know if this underground passage actually led anywhere. They might waste hours wandering only to return to the river.

"Just a little further. We can always use our tunics for the torches. They are dry enough now," Llew urged.

Bryn looked at the torches. The tightly wound cloth was still burning, but not as brightly as before. Something ahead also pulled at *him*. Perhaps this was the source of his misgiving.

"All right. We will continue, but we must return to the river if the passage does not turn back toward the surface soon."

Underground Discovery

T he passage way did not turn back toward the surface but continued in its downward descent. Bryn and Llew decided to use only one torch at a time in order to conserve their cloth. They could not see as well as before, but a little light was better than none. The water-cut tunnel narrowed and widened several times before they came to another larger cavern. They could not see across it, but could sense its expansiveness by the way their voices echoed. The air was cool, and the muted sound of water falling onto rocks came from somewhere ahead in the darkness.

Bryn, who held up the torch, stayed close to the wall as they walked. He looked back toward the entry of the small, water-worn passageway.

"We must not stray too far from the tunnel or we may not be able to find it again. Who knows how many others might lead off from such a large chamber?" he said.

"Just a little further," Llew urged. He held his unlit torch to Bryn's and rekindled the flame.

Now that both torches were burning, they could see farther ahead. Several large boulders blocked the way nearest the wall to their left. They carefully maneuvered their way around, finding it more open further out into the cavern. The sound of falling water grew louder, and they soon came upon a dark ribbon snaking across the floor. By the sound it made, they knew it must be water. The black river was too wide to jump across, so they followed its edge for a time. The muted sound of the waterfall abruptly changed. It was like a door opened, and the sound came to them directly. Llew who was walking in front, stopped suddenly.

"What is it?" Bryn asked.

Llew held his torch farther out as Bryn stepped forward. The dark line of water ended in complete darkness, and a cool breeze hit them in the face as though it came directly out of the ground at their feet. Llew picked up a rock and tossed it into the darkness. They waited, but no sound came back to them. Both of the brothers backed up slowly and began retracing their steps back to the cavern wall.

"Do you see something over there?" Llew asked as they walked.

Bryn stopped and looked across the river, but he did not see anything unusual. "I see nothing but more rocks on the floor."

"That's it!" Llew exclaimed. "Why can we see over there when our torches barely light the way here?"

This had not occurred to Bryn, who again felt a slight irritation at his oversight. There was a narrow portion of the cavern floor across the river that glowed with a silvery light. It was still quite hard to see, but they should not have been able to see anything at all. They continued forward, considering how they might crossover the river to investigate. They could swim, but they might lose their torches. And the prospect of floating toward the waterfall in complete darkness and plunging into the black chasm left both of them feeling a little queasy.

A large boulder blocked their immediate path, so they went around it. On the other side, there was an open area among several larger boulders, where stood a small stone bridge.

"Where did that come from?" a puzzled Llew asked.

Bryn examined the bridge as though it was not real. "We probably missed it in the darkness," he answered unconvincingly.

Two large torches protruded from holders on each rail of the bridge. Llew held what remained of his barely burning cloth to the torch nearest him. The fire easily caught and the torch flamed up, throwing significant light around them. The torches must have been soaked in tar and left to harden for a long period of time. Bryn lit the remaining torch, doubling the illuminating light. They stepped slowly onto the bridge and tested its soundness. It felt solid, so they crossed over. Two more torches waited on the other side. Llew reached to retrieve them, but Bryn put out his hand, stopping him. The ground underneath them was no longer the living rock of the cavern floor, but cut blocks of a stone glowing with a strange luminescence. Bryn swallowed hard.

"I do not think we will need those going forward. They will be more helpful left here, if we need to come back this way," he said.

The glowing blocks formed a clear road across the floor and through the boulders. Between the torches and the glowing pathway, the walking became much easier. It did not take long to reach the other side of the cavern. The luminescent road led directly to a tunnel large enough for three horses to ride abreast with ease. The walls, ceiling, and floor were all lined with the strange, glowing blocks, making the torches unnecessary for the moment.

They put them out and left them at the cavern's entrance. The broad tunnel led straight away at an incline. Not far from the entrance, however, a smaller branch turned sharply to the right. Llew turned to follow it. Bryn followed him, but he breathed a heavy sigh of frustration with his younger brother's desire to explore. Now was not the time for it. They came to another dark opening and stood contemplating whether to continue. A cold breeze brushed against their faces, and they could once again hear the distant sound of falling water.

"That must open onto the cavern," Llew said as he started toward it.

Bryn held back a moment longer as a strange feeling washed over him. It was as if something summoned him forward. The feeling was not new, and he felt slightly sick to his stomach at the strange sensation. The face of the white king sitting on his underground throne flashed across his memory.

"I do not think we should go this way," he said as Llew disappeared through the dark opening.

The knot in Bryn's stomach returned as he reluctantly followed Llew. They found themselves standing on a sort of large balcony. A short wall of white stone surrounded its outer perimeter. They walked up to the wall and looked out into the darkness. The cavern air was noticeably cooler.

"What do you think is out there?" Llew asked. He spoke with excitement.

Bryn turned away and glanced back at the entrance to the tunnel. "Nothing good, I can assure you."

Llew turned to examine Bryn's face with a questioning look.

"This is the realm of the Aletae. I think I would rather return to the jungle river and face the ants than run into them again," Bryn said with an ironic tone.

They turned back toward the tunnel opening without further comment, but as they drew closer, Llew noticed something reflecting silver on the cavern wall. Upon closer examination, it appeared to be a lantern made of silver metal, similar to the ones Bryn saw on his first visit to the White City. Llew reached up and felt to the side of the lantern.

"There is a lever here. I wonder..." He did not finish his thought.

Llew pulled the lever, and the lantern began to shine with a bright silvery glow. A brief moment passed, and another lantern began to glow further down the cavern wall. Then, as if in a tightly choreographed dance, small silver lights began glowing one after another in all directions. A short time later, the vast cavern was awash in silver light. They could see the flat area they had just crossed, and a sheer cliff that fell into a broad chasm beneath it. Small, pale, silvery stone buildings could be seen covering the floor of the chasm. In the very center of the rift, the light reflected with an odd metallic cadence, almost as though it was undulating back and forth.

"That area in the middle, it almost looks like it is moving," Llew said.

The silver lights, which were still being triggered by some unseen mechanism, began crossing over the area in a straight line until reaching its middle. The lanterns then began corkscrewing in a collapsing circle.

"I think it's a lake, and that lighted line must be a bridge," Bryn guessed.

"Then that smaller circle in the middle is an island. There must be an entire city down there," Llew spoke with astonishment as he leaned further over the wall.

It was a truly amazing sight to behold in its grandeur. The silver light continued to grow brighter until the island and its surrounding dark waters could easily be made out. The island was not flat, but it rose from the black water to what must have been a significant height.

"We should try to find a way out of here," Bryn stated impatiently, trying to fight down his growing concern. He had barely escaped the Aletae before and did not wish to test himself again. Even now he could hear their call echoing through his mind.

Llew did not respond but remained silent. Bryn turned to him with a questioning look. Llew stood enraptured at the sight before them, staring wide-eyed at the rock island.

"Do you see the silver colored tree in the middle? It smells with such a sweet aroma!" Llew almost sang the words, speaking to no one in particular.

Bryn squinted his eyes toward the island. He could see what looked possibly like a tree, but could make out no such details. He certainly could not smell any sweet aromas. A flash of worry washed quickly over him, remembering the visions of glory that filled his mind during his confrontation with the Aletae.

"Llew, we must go now!" he spoke forcefully.

Llew did not respond. Bryn reached up quickly and grabbed Llew's shoulder with a little more force than he intended. His brother's reaction was instantaneous. Slashing his fist backwards, he caught Bryn full in the jaw. The force astonished Bryn, who was thrown hard to the balcony floor.

"You would do well to let me be," he snarled with ferocious animosity.

Bryn never knew his younger brother to be given to anger, let alone hatred. But he could not mistake the hate filling his features now. Llew reached down and picked up a jagged rock that must have fallen from the cavern's roof some time ago. He gripped it like a weapon, and his face clouded over with dark malice.

"You will *not* keep me from it!"

Bryn held out his hand in a gesture of goodwill.

"Llew, it's me, Bryn. I wish you no harm."

Bryn tried to stand slowly, but Llew slashed downward with the rock just missing him. Bryn swept his brother's legs out from underneath him with a quick swing of his foot, and Llew fell hard onto his back, hitting his head on the balcony floor. Bryn retrieved his feet quickly, but Llew lay where he fell. He moaned and rolled over, holding his head. When he sat back up, his eyes looked clear once more.

"What happened?" he asked with a puzzled expression.

"You fell and hit your head, *again*." Bryn smiled.

"Did I hit you?" Remembrance flooded over Llew's face with uneasiness. "The tree. It…" He left the thought unfinished.

"I know," Bryn said, and then looked back toward the tunnel. "We must find a way out of here."

Shadows from the Past

Martin lifted his eyes to the jungle rimming the cliff walls above. The sun was already beneath the horizon with night fast approaching. His heart was heavy at the unknown fate of Bryn and Llew. He knew any hope left for their survival was a shadow at best. Bryn would never have stopped trying to save his brother, no matter what the odds were. Martin would have happily joined them in their fate, but for his responsibility to Aayliyah.

He surveyed the rising city before them. Malen was here somewhere, but finding him would prove difficult. The White City was larger than even Hilgreen and offered a hundred places large enough to hide a small army. The thought of Malen gave rise to sudden anger that surged up from his gut. Malen was the author of all the evil they suffered, and he would pay. By what device he had usurped the throne of Illyrium, Martin did not know. But that it involved betrayal he was sure. A quiet whisper in Martin's heart gave warning against allowing his anger to become hatred. He shook his head in an attempt to clear his thoughts.

Turning to Aayliyah next to him, he thought to ask her more about the Book of Stories Bryn found in the underground passage.

"Aayliyah…" He paused, her name still on his lips.

Her face was pale, and concern played on her features.

"Is everything all right?" he asked, abandoning his earlier question.

Her eyes furtively glanced around the square they now rested in as though desperately searching for something important.

"Something is wrong," she said, her voice trembling slightly.

Martin glanced quickly around the square, but he could see nothing amiss. "Are you sure? I see nothing wrong."

"The Plant…It is *gone*!" She swallowed hard on the last word.

It took a moment for Martin to realize the importance of her statement. The plant, the one she had called the Plant of Truth, the same that had healed Aedan, was the only thing keeping the Aletae locked in their underground prison. If it was gone, so was the barrier restraining them from escaping back into the world of men.

"Could you be mistaking this square for another?" he asked doubtfully.

"They grow in *all* places of rest within the city. If it is gone from here, someone removed it," she concluded quickly.

Martin stood and began examining the square. The surrounding grassy area was covered with small spots of torn sod where a plant was recently pulled out by its roots. He wondered why Malen would destroy it. He could not possibly have discovered its unique healing power yet. And even if he had, why destroy it? He would be more likely to attempt to harness its power.

Martin looked back at Aayliyah, who was already walking briskly toward the north of the square. He took several fast steps to catch her, but the ground under his feet began to shake. It only lasted an instant, but it was strong enough to unsettle his balance.

Aayliyah looked back at Martin with fear in her eyes.

"Find the others. I must save the plant," she said and then turned and ran out of the square.

Martin took a few more steps and then stopped. Everything in him wanted to follow her, but he could not leave his men, and he knew Aedan and the others were somewhere to the south. Aayliyah vanished from sight as he stood watching. This was her city after all, and Martin would have no hope of catching or finding her now. He turned back to Rand and the others who stood looking on.

"We must move to the south and find Aedan," he instructed evenly as his hand felt for the sprig they each placed in their belt. "Keep your eyes open for any more of these plants," he spoke calmly to the men, despite the apprehension growing inside him.

They walked southward and passed by several more resting squares. Each location revealed the same conclusion. The Plants of Truth were gone, torn out by the roots, and carried away. Two more quakes shook the ground under their feet. They were not far from where Aedan and the others should be, but darkness was descending fast and the way becoming more difficult. As the last of the light vanished, they came to a white stone bridge spanning a large, black fissure in the valley floor. Martin scanned the other side for any sign of the enemy's presence. A small silver light flickered from a slightly elevated position. He was quietly indicating to the others the need for stealth when little lights began flickering on all around them. The trap was cleverly and patiently prepared. Malen's men must have seen them earlier and picked this spot to wait, knowing it would be dark before Martin's group reached it.

There was an immediate swishing sound as Rand and his warriors pulled their swords from their sheaths. No order was needed. They quickly backed into a defensive position facing away from the bridge and the chasm it crossed. The sound of soft foot falls came from behind them as a group of heavily armored men also approached across the bridge from the south.

"I assure you, it would be foolish to resist. There are well-trained archers on the balconies of all the surrounding buildings. Even in this darkness, you would not last long," the voice said with confident arrogance. The speaker approached with the group of soldiers crossing the bridge. "You will drop your weapons and follow me or face immediate death." There was no bluff in his voice.

Martin spoke quietly to Rand. "Rand, do as he says. We must trust the others are still free and their presence unknown."

In the darkness, Martin could not see the frown he knew would be on Rand's face. This veteran of many battles would not lightly surrender in any circumstance. When Rand did not move to lower his sword, Martin added, "Now is *not* the time to challenge, but trust me, it will come soon."

There was another brief moment of hesitation before Rand threw down his sword and instructed the others to do so as well. The loud clattering sound demonstrated the warriors' displeasure with the order. Each man was quickly searched and forced to follow the enemy across the bridge. Martin fell into line toward the rear of his men. Although he was fairly sure Malen was not one of their captors, the fact that they would soon be brought before him was clear. His heart beat faster at the thought of the inevitable meeting. They were led through the winding streets for some time before coming to another large courtyard where they were ordered to sit.

Their uncomfortable vigil lasted all night. The morning light was long in coming, and sleep proved difficult to find. Several earthquakes shook the city early before the dawn. With the rising sun, its rays burst across the valley rift, turning the tops of the white buildings into liquid gold once more. Martin looked down at the plant he carried in his belt. It still appeared as healthy and living as the moment he plucked it from the plant.

He knew that with the morning light Malen would also, most likely, come. Although it was true Malen would not bother himself with anything he considered demeaning or trivial, he would also never trust anyone else to complete a task he considered sensitive. The presence of men from across the eastern ocean would be an important mystery, and Martin knew Malen would not rely on anyone but himself to solve it.

Almost in direct answer to his thoughts, they were ordered to stand. Martin positioned himself behind several of the men and gently raised his hood to cover his features. Malen walked out from the doorway of the largest mansion facing the courtyard directly across from them. He wore an expression of curiosity and walked slow and deliberately toward them. He was quickly joined by one of the enemy warriors wearing an insignia of high rank. The man was quite large and walked with a noticeable swagger. His face betrayed a streak of cruelty and brought to mind an old boar with broken tusks.

Malen appraised each of the captives and their clothing before speaking. His eyes lingered on Martin for the space of a breath and then moved on.

"Well, you are certainly not from Illyrium or Tharrus by the look of your dress." He sounded as if the conclusion bored him slightly. He continued. "But why are you here? That is the only question I care about." He spoke now as though he were a teacher trying to impart a valuable lesson to his pupils.

Martin cringed at the sound and nearness of his voice, but he held still, trying not to draw unwanted attention.

"Which of you is the leader?" Malen questioned.

Rand stepped forward without hesitation. "I am their captain," he stated in an even tone.

Malen considered him for a moment. "Well, I am sure you are, but you are not the *leader* here, are you?" he concluded with a condescending expression.

"You." He pointed at Martin while looking at him. "Come here."

Martin stood unmoved.

An expression of irritation crossed Malen's face. He turned to the pig-faced man. "If he is does not move, kill that last man on the end." He pointed at Cian.

The enemy warrior immediately pulled out his sword and started walking toward the large-boned youth with a malicious grin. Cian, his mouth set in defiance, tightened his stance and waited to defend himself, with his bare hands if necessary. Before the large enemy could act, however, Martin stepped forward.

"That will not be necessary. I will answer your questions," Martin spoke in a low tone.

"Of course you will," Malen responded with arrogance, trying to cover the slight apprehension he felt at the sound of the hooded man's voice. He did not know why, but anxiety was rising in the pit of his stomach. He could not isolate what it was that bothered him about this man. He scrutinized him carefully before continuing. In his experience, acting too quickly in any matter could lead to an unwanted outcome.

"Your dress is foreign. Where do you come from?"

"From far to the east, across the ocean. We are ambassadors of the king of the Emerald Isle," Martin answered.

The tension in Malen's gut increased, and cold sweat broke across his brow. They were from the east. Images of the great bird of light from his nightmares flashed suddenly across his mind's eye. He forced down the fear awakened by the memory and continued his questions.

"What is your name?"

"I am called Martin."

The name meant nothing to Malen, but the sound of the man's voice continued nagging at the edges of his mind. It was familiar, like a remembrance from the distant past. He cupped his hands behind his back and paced back and forth in front of Martin, searching his memory. He considered what he knew of the Emerald Isle. His search for knowledge had brought him to the furthest reaches of the east, but never to this Emerald Isle. What could these men want here? How could they have known of the White Isle? Who did they really represent? Was this king of the Emerald Isle a threat to Malen? All these questions must be answered, and as Malen looked over the men before him, he knew only the hooded man held the answers.

"Why do you wear a hood?"

Martin stood silent. Even though many years had passed since their last meeting, Malen would surely not have forgotten the face of his own nephew. Malen nodded to the large, boar-faced man. He walked over, grabbed the hood with his thick meaty hands, and roughly yanked it back off Martin's head. Martin immediately took a step forward toward Malen, his amber eyes flashing with defiance.

Malen's face went pale, and he took an involuntary step backward. His eyes were wide and round as he stared at the face of his nephew. The strength and vitality drained from his features.

"It cannot be," he whispered under his breath. "Pharigant?" He spoke with a voice that suggested he did not believe what he saw was real. He opened his mouth to speak once more, but then stopped, turned, and walked quickly back into the mansion.

Prince of the White City

Aedan watched the enemy standing guard over Martin and the others. He sat hidden on the upper balcony of a building that stood on higher ground not far away. They first discovered their friends about midday. It did not take Aedan long to decide on a plan to free them. It was simple enough. When it came to battle, Aedan's father taught him the simple approach was often the most effective. There were only a dozen guards or so, but Aedan knew more would be nearby.

He sent Archimere and his Tharusians along with half of his own men in a flanking move to search them out. Archimere was to neutralize as many as possible and then secure the approach from the northwest. Once Archimere signaled, Aedan would act. He and his remaining men would merely walk into the courtyard and openly confront the guards. With their attention drawn to him, Archimere's approach from behind might just go unnoticed.

Aedan searched the huddled group of captives once more. He still could not find Bryn, Llew, or Aayliyah. They should have been with Martin, and their absence filled him with alarm. The nightmarish scene of the ant army flooded back into his mind, and his guts began to ache. He forced down the anxiety rising up into his chest, telling himself that they must have avoided capture. He had to stay focused.

The sun was in the right position now. The afternoon was becoming early evening, and the bright disc stood low on the western horizon. Its brilliance, along with the angle it now shone into the White City's rift valley, would make it difficult for anyone to see clearly in the direction of Archimere's approach. Aedan shielded his eyes from its brightness. A small, quick flash of light flickered to the northwest. There was a short pause, and then it came again. It was Archimere's signal. Aedan crawled back from the edge of the balcony and made his way quickly down to the first floor of the building where he had left Valentus, Lanthir, and the handful of his remaining men.

"Archimere is in place…" Aedan began but stopped. He searched his men and then turned toward Valentus. "Where is Lanthir?"

Valentus glanced quickly around the room as though the answer was just as much a puzzle to him. "He was here, only just moments ago."

Aedan sent the young warrior named Riordan to search the building. He soon returned with a frown on his face. "He is gone! He *will* betray our plans to the enemy." Riordan spoke the conclusion they all feared.

"No, I do not believe so," Aedan answered with careful consideration. "He came here to fight a different battle. His vengeance is foresworn for this Malen, and I believe he means to fulfill it personally. Nevertheless, we must be even more careful now. Be on your guard. If our plan fails, wait for daylight and make for the eastern coast. Berand will be waiting there with True North."

They moved out quietly, watchful for any traps that may await them. All was quiet. Apparently, the enemy did not expect trouble from the direction of their approach, so focused were they on the harbor to the north. Aedan raised his hand as they neared the edge of the last building obstructing their view of the courtyard where the prisoners were held. He scanned the faces of the men with him. They were ready. He took a deep breath and stepped confidently from the edge of the building onto the stone street leading to the courtyard. He strode forward with long intentional strides, never doubting his men were close behind.

Aedan was no more than five paces from the first of the Illyrian guards when the man finally noticed him. His head snapped to attention at the realization of what he was seeing. He quickly leveled the long spear he carried toward Aedan and angrily called to his fellow guards. By the time Aedan and his men reached the man, all the remaining guards had swiftly formed into a defensive position behind their leader. Aedan smiled largely and raised his hands in greeting.

"Welcome to my city!" He spoke with all the largeness of a king. "If I had known to expect you, I would have prepared a proper welcome." His greeting created the desired effect. Confusion swept through the enemy warriors.

"Who are you?" their leader spat, a large man with a nose that looked more like a snout than anything else. He spoke nervously, a look of suspicion narrowing his eyes.

Aedan, careful not to look in the direction of Archimere's approach, saw movement across the courtyard. "I am Aedan, Prince of the White City." He spoke without hesitation, his own demeanor taking on the air of an insulted dignitary. "*I* should ask you, who come to *my* city unbidden and unannounced, the same question." His eyes clouded with darkness, fury playing at the edges of his mouth.

The man appeared befuddled at the response. Clearly, he was not prepared to handle a diplomatic crisis. The guards standing at attention shuffled their feet nervously. A noise came from somewhere behind them, and as they started to turn toward the sound, the captives jumped to their feet and began making a noisy protest of their treatment. The distraction was just enough to draw the attention of the Illyrians. Two guards closest to them quickly leveled their spears and began barking orders to be quiet and sit back down.

Aedan, taking full advantage of the momentary confusion, pushed aside the leader's spear shaft, and in one fluid motion pulled out his own sword, its point coming to rest a hair's breadth from the man's throat. Valentus and the few others with Aedan all followed his lead. The man sucked in his breath and held perfectly still, his eyes focused intently on the point of Aedan's sword.

One of the Illyrian guards standing nearest to him leveled his spear menacingly. "There are only a few of you!" he spat and took a step closer. The point of Aedan's sword pressed in closer to the leader's throat.

The man swallowed hard. "Don't do it, Nester! He'll kill me." He spoke as a man already defeated, his voice trembling with fear.

"You know King Malen will have my hide on his wall if I don't..."

Before the man could finish his statement, a rush of feet came from around the fountain behind the guards. Archimere, Mr. Bonfire, and the rest of their men charged without warning, smashing into the back rank of the enemy guards, knocking many of them to the ground before they could react. Those still on their feet turned with their spears, only to realize their attackers were already in too close for longer weapons to do any good. The battle was over before it had started. Aedan's plan had worked.

Mr. Bonfire wore an expression of disgust as though he was sorely disappointed the battle had not involved more fighting. But his expression quickly changed to one of enjoyment as he was charged with the task of tying up the guards with the ropes that bound his friends, a chore he handled with all the eagerness of a hungry man invited to a banquet table. Aedan moved immediately to join Martin, who stood talking to Archimere and Valentus.

"Hail! Prince of the White City." Although Archimere spoke it in jest, there was a note of admiration in the tone.

"Where are Aayliyah, Bryn, and Llew?" Aedan asked, feeling slightly out of breath due to the anxiety that again rose up into his lungs for fear of what the answer might be.

Martin turned to face him. "Aayliyah is fine." He put his hands up, hoping to dissuade Aedan's fear. An expression of relief moved across Aedan's face, but then refroze when he realized there had been no mention of his brothers.

"And my brothers?"

Martin looked from Aedan to Archimere, and then to Valentus. "In truth, I do not know. Bryn went back to give Llew's boat aid during the ant attack." He paused and swallowed hard. "Neither came out." He then added quickly, "But my heart tells me they simply found a different way."

"A different way?" Aedan asked, shocked at the news. "What are you saying? What other way could there have been?"

"I do not know," Martin admitted, letting his breath out. "I only know that you should not be here either. The sea serpent's poison should have claimed your life, but the Master found a way for you. He will find a path for your brothers as well. I know this here." He placed his hand over his chest. Aedan's eyes became vacant as he stared hard at the white, stone-paved blocks under his feet.

At that moment a strange sound floated down into the courtyard. It sounded like someone clapping hands together slowly. Aedan glanced around the courtyard. He noticed Martin starring upward over his shoulder, a look of anger mixed with determination in his eyes. Aedan spun around to find one single man standing on the balcony of a building adjacent to the courtyard. The man was well dressed but not in what anyone would call ornate clothes. He wore the golden circlet of a king on his head.

"Well done! Well done indeed. I couldn't have done better myself," the man said, but then stopped as though considering something for the first time. "No, no. I am sure I probably could have, but that is not the point. You have done better than expected. However, that imbecile I placed in charge of my men certainly made your task much easier." He placed both of his hands on the rail and surveyed the scene before him as though he had won a great victory. "It did take a little *longer* than expected." He concluded with a smug grimace.

"We have your men," Aedan said. "Those around the perimeter have been captured as well. Come down and we will discuss terms of—"

"Do you really think I am that stupid?" Malen interrupted with a flash of anger.

Aedan paused before answering and said, "You have my pledge that you will not be harmed if you surrender now."

Malen burst into a fit of laughter, slapping his hand on the balcony rail. "Oh really, Pharigant? I don't know who this young buffoon thinks he is or where you have been these many years, but I thought *you* were smarter than this." He waved his hand at Aedan, who looked at Martin with a questioning look. If Aedan was bothered by the insult, he did not show it.

Martin stepped forward. "Malen, we need to talk."

"Talk!" Again, anger flashed across his face. "About *what* I wonder?" He tapped his finger against his lips while holding his elbow in his hand in mock consideration. "Perhaps we should discuss why you are *not* dead. Or"—he feigned thoughtfulness—"why your brother murdered your father, only to leave the throne of Illyrium to me." A slight smirk turned up the edge of his mouth. "Or so that is what the accusation was anyway. I, for one, could hardly bring myself to believe such a thing of Serigant. But then again, some people would do *anything* for power." He smiled maliciously. "No, we will discuss something rather more important, I think. Why are you here?" His expression went cold.

Martin exchanged looks with Aedan before answering. "We have come as emissaries of the king of the Emerald Isle far across the eastern ocean."

"*Emissaries?*" Malen paused. "Do you take me for a fool? You stand here with your Tharusian rabble and expect me to believe you are nothing more than emissaries from some distant land." It was not a question.

He continued. "Many years may have passed, but do not forget that I know you, Pharigant. There was a time you may have come close to matching me, if only for a short time. But I have discovered knowledge beyond your wildest dreams. You could not even begin to understand the powers I now possess." Malen's face glowed with exultant pride, fringed with irritation.

Martin's expression showed no signs of give. "The knowledge you possess has little real value."

The direct confidence of Martin's answer unnerved Malen.

"Lisnor!" he all but screamed. "Bring out our guests."

A man dressed in a simple black robe with a long, ugly scar twisting across the whole of his face appeared at the edge of the balcony, pulling a rope tied to the neck of two people whose hands were also tied. Two more men dressed in the same black robes appeared behind the captives and pushed them forward. Berand's face was clearly visible. It was bruised and bloody. Behind him was a much smaller figure. The ugly man grabbed and yanked the smaller person into open sight. It was Alenia.

There was a commotion in the men behind Aedan and Martin. They turned to find Archimere and Valentus with their weapons ready. "Enough talk," Archimere said. "Let us take them here and now."

Malen laughed before abruptly contorting his features with annoyance again. "Do you think so little of me as to presume I have not defended my position? I *knew* of your movements from the first moment you entered this city." He sneered at them. "Your lack of respect is beginning to upset me. Lisnor!" He barked the command without turning his head and held up his hand.

The man with the ugly scar produced a wicked-looking knife from a fold in his robe and pressed it hard to Alenia's throat. Alenia gasped, and Valentus yelled out her name as he tried to push past Martin.

"Wait!" Martin spoke sharply to Malen while holding Valentus back. Malen hesitated, his hand hovering in the air.

"I *know* why you are here. I know of the Garden of the Aletae. I also know of the plant that gives life and have already seen its power," Martin said.

The statement had its desired effect. Malen was visibly shaken by the revelation. He turned his hand downward toward the man called Lisnor, who promptly lowered his blade from Alenia's neck. Malen's face went white. Not only did Martin know of the Garden, but he also knew of the Plant of Life. If his claim to have already experienced its power was true, everything would change. Malen stood completely still, frozen in contemplation of the horrible possibility that his old pupil, Pharigant, not only came back from the dead but also surpassed Malen's own knowledge. The thought unnerved him greatly. What else did his long-lost nephew know?

Malen's brow wrinkled with frustration at this new development. Everything had gone exactly as planned until now. Malen was on the verge of discovering the hidden location of the Garden of the Aletae. It was somewhere close by, and it would not take him long to find it. He had found many other secret things while walking the paths of the dead, and this would be no different. But Pharigant's reappearance continued to nag at his confidence just the way his nightmares had done earlier. It did not escape his attention that Pharigant reappeared from across the ocean *to the east*, just as the great bird of light in his night terrors. It was a development he had not foreseen, and it gave rise to doubts in his mind.

He looked down at Pharigant. A mixture of emotion flooded over him once more. They were teacher and pupil long ago. They had sought knowledge together and were of one mind in that pursuit…if Pharigant had not disappeared. Who knows what they might have accomplished? The thought caught in Malen's gut. It made him angry that such an idea would even suggest itself. He had never needed help from anyone, least of all Pharigant. There was only room for one at the top, and Pharigant would have to be removed. But first, Malen needed to discover what he really knew about the Garden.

Malen reached to his side and pulled up a horn, blowing two sharp, quick blasts. As the sound died away, it was replaced with the reverberation of many feet pounding the solid-block roadways all around the courtyard. A hundred well-armed warriors poured into the courtyard from every direction, quickly surrounding the men of the Emerald Isle and their Tharusian allies.

"I think you have learned a valuable lesson, *Prince* of the White City." Malen spoke directly to Aedan with condescending scorn. Turning to his lieutenant, he said, "Bind them all"—he paused—"and bring me the one they call *Martin*."

The Deception of
Lawlessness

Malen sat across the small table looking at the man who had once been his pupil, the son of his older brother. His hands were crossed in contemplation. What could his presence mean? How *could* he be here? It was as though Malen now looked into the face of a ghost, yet the strength displayed in Pharigant's features were not that of any apparition. His sudden reappearance greatly troubled Malen's mind. He was little more than a memory for so long, and now, here he sat in the flesh.

Malen decided he would take no risk with Pharigant. Despite his earlier boasting, he knew the potential threat his nephew could represent.

Lisnor and two members of the Lawless stood behind the captive with malicious jeers on their faces.

"Master," Lisnor spoke while looking down at Martin, "tell me what you want to know, and I will take pleasure in extracting it from him."

Malen was irritated by the interruption of his thoughts. He stood up and walked methodically around the edge of the table to stand next to Lisnor. He paused suddenly brought his fist up with surprising speed, connecting with the side of Lisnor's face. Lisnor stumbled to his knees, spitting blood from his mouth with a hiss.

"Did I *ask* for your counsel?" Malen took a deep breath to regain his composure.

He walked in a semicircle around the other members of the Lawless, and they shrank back out of fear and awe at his nearness. A new thought entered Malen's mind, and he resumed his seat in front of Martin.

"Pharigant"—he laughed suddenly and held out his hands—"you have been away too long my old friend. *Much* has happened in your absence. I..." He paused with a look of consideration. "Yes, I have changed. I have discovered powers you could not possibly imagine exist. You may know something about what it is I seek." Here he waived his hand around generally to indicate the island and city. "I suppose I might have been disappointed had you not. You always were an excellent thinker." He stood once more and turned his back to Martin. "Perhaps our desires are more similar than we realize. Much *good* can come from this place. Think of the suffering caused by the petty bickering of little kings, the wars, poverty, and hunger." He suddenly spun around to face Martin. "What if there *were* no more divisions? What if there was only *one* king? Think of the peace that would come to the world!" Malen's face glowed with the vision in his mind. "With you at my side, Pharigant, we could make it happen."

Malen did not notice the shock that passed over Lisnor's face. Somewhere in the twisted cold blackness of Lisnor's heart, he had always desired to please Malen, like a pupil wants to impress his teacher. At times, he even considered him as a sort of father figure, always believing *he* would succeed Malen. He looked down at the man his master called Pharigant and hated him. He let his mind fill with the cruel thoughts of torture and suffering he would inflict on this new rival until, quite abruptly, another thought entered his mind: the Aletae.

He discovered them the first night of their arrival. Or perhaps it was more correct to say, the Aletae discovered him. He had been exploring for any clue as to the location of the Garden until long after sunset when he heard a woman call his name. It did not take him long to find the underground passages and the lady. She was a woman of great beauty and desirability. He followed her to a large hall where a stone king sat enthroned. Lisnor thought him more a god than a king.

The woman then showed Lisnor what he could become. *He* would be a hero and second only to this new god. He relished in the memory of it once more. No one had ever loved or shown care for Lisnor, yet the woman in the underground hall worshiped him. She promised him much, if he only did one thing for her: destroy the strange-looking plants that covered the city. There was something about these plants Lisnor didn't like, but it was a small task. The woman instructed him to tell no one of their secret meeting, and now he found himself glad he had not informed Malen. Perhaps *he* would become the master. Perhaps *he* could be a hero that all worshiped and dreaded.

Martin looked at Malen for some time without responding. He was bleeding from the corner of his mouth where one of the Lawless had struck him earlier. Reaching up and wiping the blood away with his sleeve, he considered what he might say to his uncle. He could tell him of the better way he had found and of the Lord of heaven who reveals Truth, something far stronger than mere knowledge. But he knew it would receive nothing but scorn from Malen. The proud cannot hear the truth until humility has had its way.

"Peace is easily spoken of, but not so simply accomplished," Martin responded.

"There are ways." Malen sat back down and looked at Martin with narrowed eyes. "I have done it before. You see, I already have one of the Garden's plants. I call it the Ice Thorn. It took years to mature, but its power to persuade was well worth the waiting. You may know of the Garden and the Plant of Life, but only I have the knowledge and power necessary to bend them to my will. With your help, there is nothing I could not accomplish through the secrets of the Aletae. Imagine what wonders might await if you pledged yourself to me."

"Did you offer the same thing to Serigant after you murdered my father? The plant will not grant what you seek." As Martin spoke, Malen's expression went cold. Martin continued. "Yes, the plant is life because Truth is life. You must first seek Truth before the life of the plant can mean anything for you. You speak of peace, but peace without freedom is just another word for slavery."

"Enough!" Malen's face twisted with angry hatred. "The Truth!" he spat. "I will *have* the power of the Life Plant, and of all of the Garden. *You* force my hand." Malen lifted his finger to a man by a back door. Alenia and Berand were pushed into the room.

"I'm sorry m' lord," Berand sputtered through split lips. "We were surprised during the night watch. They've *taken* True North!" One of the Lawless hit him in the gut before he could continue, and he doubled over in pain.

Alenia stood silent, but Martin could see the obvious defiance in her eyes.

"Have they harmed you?" Martin asked.

She flashed a look at Malen. "No, but they took the ship and stole Aayliyah's book," she spoke quickly.

Malen wore an expression of enjoyment at the scene before him. He perked up at Alenia's mention of Aayliyah's book. "Oh yes! The book." He turned and walked to a shelf behind where he stood. When he turned back around, he carried the ornately carved and decorated wooden box that Bryn had found in the underground passage on their first visit. "Fortunately, I had plenty of time to look this over while waiting for your slow-witted men to attempt their piteous rescue. The language is old, but not that of the Aletae. It is an ancient form of our own language. At first I found little to no value in its moral teachings, ethical stories, and warnings about *truth*." This last word seemed to stick on his tongue. "But then, I did find *something* of interest. Here at the back."

He opened the book and set it down in front of Martin. He pulled out a small, tattered leather manuscript and began to unfold it. He started to read its content out loud. "The lineage of Ram, Guardian of the Plant and Lord of the White City." He paused and looked up with unveiled excitement. "Here is what caught my attention." Martin could not help but lean in for a closer look himself.

"Right here at the bottom. It says something *quite* interesting. It tells of a small pendant that is passed down from one guardian to the next. Here is a rendering of it." Malen pointed to the bottom right-hand corner of the manuscript and to a drawing of a small pendant simple in design. The image of a small plant with round berry-like objects intertwined the hilt of a sword. Around the blade appeared to be something like a flame.

"I am curious about this woman, Aayliyah," Malen said. "She intrigues me. From the babblings of this girl"—he pointed at Alenia without looking at her—"it would seem there is still *someone* left of your company that I have not met. This is her book, not yours. Isn't that correct, Pharigant?"

Martin's face did not betray his anxiety. "You have no idea of the forces you are playing with Malen," he responded. "The Aletae do *not* serve others!"

"The *Aletae*?" Malen asked with a curious expression. "They have been gone for centuries. Even I cannot raise the dead, yet. But who knows, after I find their Garden, perhaps even that will be within my reach."

"The Aletae do not die! They are not like you and me. They are not human," Martin said, remembering Bryn's description of the woman and her stone king. Then he looked directly into Malen's eyes. "You and I, Malen, we *will* die."

Malen hesitated. Martin's words stung, but he would not let his old pupil get the better of him. "Where is the woman called Aayilyah?" he asked with a cold warning in his tone.

Martin said nothing.

"Bring the two prisoners here," Malen spoke to his wicked servants called the Lawless. They roughly jerked Alenia and Berand over to the table and forced them both into chairs. Malen pulled out a long, bladed knife with a razor-sharp edge on both sides. He examined it as though looking for some flaw.

"Where is the girl?" he asked Martin one more time.

"You will not find what you—" Martin began, but Malen's hand flicked out with lightening speed and drove the point of the knife right through the back of Berand's hand, pinning it to the wooden table.

Berand cried out briefly with the shock of it. Alenia went white in the face, but she remained quiet.

"Shall we try this one last time!" Malen shouted then nodded to the Lawless standing behind Berand. The man forced Berand's other hand onto the table.

"Aayliyah is no longer with us." Martin spoke quickly. "She..."He paused shortly while looking at Alenia. "She *escaped* into the jungle, and we could not find her again."

Malen had not expected this answer. His perplexed expression, however, was quickly replaced with one of satisfaction. "If you had said anything else, I would not have believed you." He paused, and then abruptly reached over and yanked the dagger from Berand's hand. Berand grunted, sweat running down his ashen face, but he did not lose his composure.

"Escaped? I see. You were *using* the girl to find the Garden for yourself. You worried me at first, Pharigant." Malen smiled. "All your put-on *piety* and talk of Truth. I see now you have not changed much. Good! Perhaps you and I may even find a way to join our paths."

Martin's mouth curled up slightly at the edge, giving an impression of agreement with the possibility.

At that moment, one of the Illyrian warriors entered the room. "My lord." He inclined his head before continuing. "The men have found something. You will want to see it. It is not far."

Malen stood and quickly ordered the prisoners returned to the others. He was about to leave the room when he paused and turned back. "No, I think you should come with me, Pharigant. This may be of interest to you. But before we leave, I have one little detail to see to."

Martin feigned his appreciation and stood to follow. He glanced back at Berand, who indicated with his eyes that he understood Martin's deception. But when Martin's eyes fell on Alenia, he was surprised to find her staring at the picture of the pendant in Aayliyah's book. She wore a strange expression of recognition. Martin, not wanting to draw attention to her, turned quickly and followed Malen.

They walked down the stairs to the bottom floor and through some doors to a room at the back of the building. The space was completely dark. Thick, heavy fabric drapes hung over all the windows, much like what Martin had encountered in the king's palace on Tharrus. Malen walked over to one of the windows toward the far side of the room and lifted a small corner of one of the drapes. It let in just enough light for Martin to see clearly around the room. It was completely empty. Malen walked over to another door near where he stood and slowly opened it. He stepped back and watched as though he waited for someone or thing to come out.

Martin squinted his eyes and looked toward the black opening in the doorway. At first he could see nothing. Then, as though materializing out of thin air, the dark shape of something enormous began to emerge. Malen quickly reached under the collar of his cloak and pulled out a large, round object about the size of a walnut that hung by a chain around his neck.

"Come closer," Malen said. The creature had to stoop to get under the doorway. It was enormous and terrible to behold. Martin's insides twisted sharply as he realized what it was that stood before them. The Sargaroth's eyes were blood-red, and his entire body was covered in long, twisted hair.

"There is a woman hiding in this city that has escaped from us. Find her and bring her to me alive. Kill anyone that may be with her, but do not harm my men. It will be dark soon. Gather the others and go." Malen spoke as though the beast could understand him.

"It will be done," the monster answered. Martin was not prepared to hear the thing actually speak. Its voice was deep and dark, and the very sound of it made his insides crawl with fear. The Sargaroth turned and disappeared back into the darkened room.

The Dark City

L lew pushed on the door, but it would not give. He bent down a little, put his shoulder to it, and pushed with all his strength. Still it did not budge.

"It's as I feared," Bryn replied from behind him. "Locked from the other side, just like the entrance to the underground I found on my first visit."

"Do you still have your dagger?" Llew asked.

Bryn patted his waist belt until he felt the hard, smooth leather handle. "Here." He handed the knife to Llew, who began digging into the wood around the door's handle. It was solid and hard and would be no easy task, especially in the darkness of the small building where they now stood. The soft glow of silvery light emanating from the strange blocks down below the stairway provided just enough illumination. The two brothers took turns hacking into the hardened wooden door for what felt like several hours before a small beam of gray light could be seen. Llew just began his shift when he heard what sounded like a soft voice from the other side of the door.

"Did you hear that?" he asked Bryn excitedly.

"Hear what?"

"I thought I heard someone speaking outside just now."

They both listened quietly for some time in silence before hearing it again. It was barely audible, but clearly a woman's voice.

"Hello! Is anyone there?" Llew shouted back. "We are locked in. Can you unlock the door?" he asked hopefully. When no immediate answer was forthcoming, he added, "It's Llew and Bryn."

"Wait," the small voice spoke back, followed by silence once more.

Nothing happened for some time, and the brothers began thinking the person just left them. The scraping sound of a large key being forced into an old lock renewed their hope. The handle turned hard, and the door slowly swung open. The light was gray and the day almost gone. Standing there before them was Aayliyah. Relief flooded her features.

"You are alive!" she exclaimed while throwing her arms around both of their necks at once.

"Yes, yes we are," Llew answered, clearing his throat with slight awkwardness.

She looked behind them at the dark opening to the underground city. A puzzled expression crossed her eyes and mouth. "How did you get down there? And how did you escape the ant army? I believed you were…" She could not bring herself to finish the thought.

"It's a long story. But first we must find out where the others are," Bryn answered.

A distant, low-throated howl echoed down from the jungle above the cliff walls. Aayliyah's head turned swiftly in the direction of the sound.

"We must be quick." The tone of her voice became serious. "Nothing keeps the Sargaroth at bay this night. The lamps have remained unlit since I left. We must prepare a place of safety for the night. There is not much time left." She turned and hurried down the nearest road.

Bryn and Llew followed hard after her. The gray light was failing fast, and the thought that nothing would keep the Sargaroth out of the city after last light spurred them on with a newfound energy. Aayliyah approached a small courtyard that looked strangely familiar to Bryn. These courtyards all looked similar, but if he had not missed his guess, she led them to the same place he, Martin, and Rand had stayed in on their first visit. They followed her into the manor house and up three flights of stairs to the roof. A small garden grew at the center of the space. Wooden benches circled the garden, and lamps stood around the roof's perimeter. Aayliyah quickly began lighting the lanterns. Finally, she shut the heavy door to the rooftop garden and locked it with a heavy silver chain that hung there.

"What of the others?" Bryn asked.

"They have been captured," Aayliyah answered quietly. "We cannot help them tonight, but I will show you in the morning."

"Why were you not with them?" Llew questioned.

"I was with them until I discovered the enemy was destroying the Plant of Truth. The Plant must be protected at all cost. It has been my sacred duty for as along as I have been guardian. Only the Plant keeps the Aletae in their underground prison. If it were to be completely destroyed, they would once again rule the world as they did in days of old." Aayliyah paused to tend to one of the unique plants growing in the small garden. Bryn recognized it as the same plant Argolis had brought them aboard True North.

"You were wise to plant a hidden garden for additional protection," Bryn commented.

Aayliyah's lips parted in a sad smile. "It was my father's idea. He knew this time would come." As she finished speaking, the building began to shake and groan underneath their feet. It was another quake, and it lasted longer than before.

"I hope that doesn't continue all night," Llew said.

"They are getting stronger. You may not have felt them underground, but the island has been shaken several times since our return," Aayliyah answered. "The White Isle is dying, for its life is tied to the life of the plant."

"What do you mean?" Llew asked with a look of concern.

"The Book of Stories, recovered by Bryn, tells of how my forefather, Ram of the Flame, defeated the Sargaroth once he had discovered the secret of their weakness. The story, however, did not end with the defeat of the Sargaroth. Their masters, the Aletae, used many other terrible weapons against them. From their knowledge of evil, the Aletae had planted a garden where each plant's fruit gave them the power to enslave humanity. Many of the plants caused pestilence wherever they grew. Some caused madness. But of all the plants, none were as powerful as the Silver Tree that sat at the Garden's center. It had the power to give knowledge, and knowledge without goodness leads to lawlessness and death. Ram's people were all but overcome when the hooded man appeared to him and delivered the Plant of Truth."

At the mention of the hooded man, Llew suddenly snapped his head back toward Aayliyah. "Did you say a *hooded* man?"

"Yes, he came to Ram when hope had once again been lost. But the Plant of Truth, once taking root in the soil of any land, destroys the evil works of the Aletae's garden. Once it was planted here on this island, it drove the Aletae down into their underground city. Here, where the evil was the greatest, the Plant took such deep root that now to remove it will mean the death of the island." Aayliyah paused before concluding, "So the Book of Stories warns. Very few of the Plants of Truth now remain. Time is running out."

Llew quietly reflected on their experience in the underground caverns before speaking. "I do not know about the Garden, but the Silver Tree is more than just dangerous. It is *deceptively* beautiful."

Aayliyah wore an expression of amazement. "You have *seen* the Tree!"

Llew glanced to Bryn, who appeared not to be paying much attention at the moment, and then turned back to Aayliyah. "Well, we *sort* of stumbled onto it by accident. You must have been there many times?"

"No," she answered simply. "I have never seen it."

Bryn stood with his back to the others, searching the rooftop garden for a moment. He then walked over to one of the wooden benches, picked it up, and smashed it against the stone tiles under his feet. He repeated this action several more times before prying the broken wooden pieces of the bench apart. He turned to find Llew and Aayliyah staring at him.

"If Sargaroth will be hunting in the city tonight, I would just as soon have something we can use as weapons against them. And since fire seems to scare them..." he said in answer to the questioning looks on their faces.

Llew nodded his appreciation of the suggestion and began bashing one of the other benches against the hard surface. After dismantling all the benches, they picked out several of the longer pieces of wood and gathered the remaining smaller shards into a single pile. The darkness of the night was already upon them by the time they finished, and a small blaze danced in the gathered wood. They placed the ends of the longer pieces into the fire before sitting back to rest. Several hours of darkness passed by quietly and they began to tire of their vigil.

Bryn was just about to suggest they take turns sleeping when a long, piercing howl sounded not far away, echoing off the many stone buildings in the city around them. It was an awful sound that filled their stomachs with dread and banished every thought of rest. Another creature answered from somewhere nearby. In mere moments the air was filled with the unearthly noise. It was the sound a pack of predators makes when closing in on a kill. It grew louder and higher in the ferocity of its pitch and then abruptly went silent.

"They are here!" Aayliyah whispered.

Bryn noticed movement from the corner of his eye. Turning his head, he saw one of the lamps begin flickering. At first, it did not seem important until he realized there was no wind, not even a soft breeze. The lamp's flame flickered lightly and then began to dim. Bryn's eyes narrowed as he scrutinized the flame.

"That lamp, the one right there," he said. "What's wrong with it?"

Aayliyah stood up and moved closer. Llew reached out and put his hand to her shoulder. "If you do not mind, I would feel better if you did not move any closer to the edge of the roof." She nodded with gratefulness and sat back down.

Instead, Llew moved past her and toward the lantern. The once bright flame flickered a few more times and then went out. He reached and touched the base of the metal stand. Pulling his hand back, he rubbed two fingers together.

"The oil has leaked out." He examined it closer. "There is a crack. Here." Llew pointed to the bottom of the lamp base where what appeared to be a tube entered.

"It must have been the quake," Bryn said.

The two lanterns nearest the one that had just gone out began flickering and dimming. In mere moments both were dark. Bryn and Llew quickly examined the remaining four lanterns. None were damaged, and their flames continued to burn brightly. Breathing a sigh of relief, they turned back toward Aayliyah. She still sat near the edge of the small garden with her back toward the darkened section of the roof wall. Both of them froze, their eyes fixed on something beyond her.

She noticed the sudden expression of concern on their faces. "Bryn? Llew? What is it?" Her voice went cold.

Neither answered, but both carefully began edging their way toward the small, smoldering fire they had made of the bench wood. Their eyes remained fixed on their target as they bent to the fire. Aayliyah slowly turned her head to the side. Something crouched just beyond the garden in the black spot between the darkened lanterns. It was hunched low down to the roof floor, not ten paces from where she sat, poised as though ready to spring upon its prey. It made no noise. She locked eyes with it and muffled a scream with her hand. It sprang toward her in that instant with a deafening roar.

Bryn was there. Sliding on his knees, he pushed her out of the way and held out the burning end of a small plank. It caught the creature in the chest and slid down its underbelly, hissing and crackling with a strange metallic sound. The monster screamed in tortured pain as it knocked Bryn onto his back and flung itself against the far wall, breaking one of the working lanterns. Oil spilled over its dark hide and caught on fire. Everywhere the fire touched, the creature's hide melted like water. Its red eyes opened wide with horrible fear and desperation. Convulsing in the torment of death, it flung itself over the side of the wall and into the darkness below.

Bryn crawled over to make sure Aayliyah was unharmed. Two more Sargaroth crawled over the darkened portion of the wall not more than five arms' lengths from them. They moved slowly and deliberately in an attempt to avoid the light. Bryn reached for his torch only to find it had gone out and now only smoldered.

Llew yelled a battle cry and charged at them with a burning board in each of his hands. The creatures turned on him with snapping jaws, ready to slash out with their deadly claws, but they hesitated at the nearness of the flames. He shoved the torch in his left hand at the nearest Sargaroth's face while throwing the one in his right hand like a knife at the second monster. It sizzled through the cool night air, spinning end over end until hitting its mark. The burning end of the wooden shaft stuck right into the Sargaroth's gaping maw. Both creatures disappeared over the roof's edge in a flash. More horrible screams filled the night air. Llew's remaining torch began to smolder. The bench wood was not dry enough to keep a steady flame.

Bryn pulled out the sword Aayliyah had given him earlier. A soft glimmer of light shimmered from the blade. Llew was about to comment on it when he felt a blast of warm, steamy breath on the back of his neck. Bryn's eyes widened. With no time to think, Bryn tossed the sword toward him, and Llew reached out, caught it, and swung it around in one fluid motion. The blade sliced through the creature's neck with little resistance as it came over the wall. The head rolled onto the roof floor while the body fell back into the night.

Llew stood transfixed by the sight of the blade in his hands. The dark blood of the Sargaroth hissed as it ran off its edges. The metal now danced with a white light streaked with red lines and flashes. Bryn approached with an expression of amazement. He was about to speak, but the building began to shake again. The intensity of the quake grew and shook everything with such ferocity that all three of them fell to the roof 's floor on their hands and knees. Llew lost his grip on the sword, and it clanged down against the stone blocks.

The quake ended as quickly as it had come. The three of them sat back up slowly. Bryn reached over and picked up the Sword of Ram, which still danced with the mesmerizing lights. He turned its blade over and examined it closely.

Aayliyah stood up and moved toward Bryn. "My father told me the story of Ram of the Flame and the strange power of his sword, but never have I seen it like this." She spoke with awe and held out her hand toward the dancing lights, running her fingers along the tapered length of its blade. "It is cool."

Llew stepped toward the remaining lanterns. "These will not last much longer." He concluded with resignation before looking toward the darkened sky. "Morning is still at least three hours away."

The last three lights were flickering and dimming, damaged by the last quake. "Aayliyah!" He turned abruptly. "Where does the oil come from?"

She paused as though the question was confusing. "The oil?"

"Yes, the oil that burns in these lamps. Where does it come from? These supply tubes must come from somewhere close by." There was urgency in his voice. He stepped over and placed his hand on the metallic tube at the base of the nearest lamp for emphasis.

"There are reservoirs in the lower levels of each building. It was part of my task to keep them full for the buildings I used and for the outer lamps."

Bryn handed the sword to Llew and picked up two more lightly burning bench boards. "Show me," he said to Aayliyah. "Llew, you stay here with the sword and guard this place. It maybe our last hope of surviving this night."

The building was even darker in the lower levels, and the two barely burning boards provided little to no illumination. Aayliyah, nevertheless, moved with agility and speed, knowing the layout of the building by memory. The front doors of the main level were still shut tightly and locked from the inside. They moved quickly to a back room and opened a door with a short stairway leading down into a cellar-type room. It was not large, but it contained a deep stone vat that shimmered when the light of the flame came close.

They quickly surveyed the contents of the room. Several large containers sat in the corner beside the vat. They filled them and started back for the roof. When they reached the top of the first flight of stairs, something large bumped up against the front doors and the chain that locked them jingled. Bryn stopped and turned to look back at the doors; his heart felt as though it had skipped a beat. He watched for a second and then the doors shook with a loud, smashing sound. The Sargaroth were back. The doors shook several more times and began to come loose at the hinges before Bryn turned back and ran to catch up with Aayliyah.

They reached the roof just in time to see Llew desperately swinging Ram's sword in a wide arch as three Sargaroth circled him. The sword flashed with bright lights and sparks as it cut the air close to the enemy. Bryn's reaction was immediate. He took one of his jars and threw it with an arching motion, splashing oil over the nearest two monsters. Reaching down, he placed the now smoldering end of one of his boards in the coals of the small fire. The flame leapt up, and he tossed it at the closest Sargaroth. The beast ignited in a burst. It roared with agony while colliding into the second oil-coated Sargaroth in its attempt to escape the torment. The flames that danced on the hide of the first creature jumped to the second. They both vanished over the side of the building wall amidst the horrible sounds of their tortured screams. Llew made an end of the third one with a quick well-placed thrust into its chest. The unearthly sounds of dying Sargaroth filled the air for a short while longer before the night went completely still.

"I do not think those that remain will risk the light of the sword again tonight," Aayliyah spoke softly into the hushed silence. "Ram of the Flame has arisen and they are afraid."

The Gates of Cronus

T he Illyrian soldier was right. It was not far, almost under their very noses. They walked past one row of stone buildings and then turned toward a rock outcropping that jutted upwards the height of three large manor houses. At its base, overgrown with vines, stood two enormous stone doors. It was the largest gate that Martin had ever seen. An ominous feeling filled him with misgiving.

A dozen Illyrian soldiers worked quickly at clearing off the vines and overgrowth. The large stone doors were truly magnificent. An image of a single tree was carved into their stone face. It was centered to follow the middle line of the gate. The tree's branches were full of large leaves and heavy laden with a kind of fruit that hung in large clusters. It was rather beautiful in an artistic sense. Martin examined the gate carefully. What was it that made his insides go cold? There was nothing besides the fact that it was barred from the outside that should cause such a feeling. Yet everything about this place felt wrong, and his heart began to pound harder.

He glanced toward the ground around the base of the gate. The turf was broken in small, round spots. Malen was so focused on the gate itself that he had not noticed. A thought entered Martin's mind. Martin quickly felt the area of his belt where he had placed a sprig of the Plant of Truth at Aayliyah's earlier prompting. It was still there.

"Do you know these words?" Malen pointed to the large letters cut into the giant capstone that ran across the top of the gate.

Martin analyzed them carefully. "It is the ancient language of the Aletae," he answered. "It says these are the Gates of Cronus." Speaking the name aloud gave Martin's tongue a bitter taste. Now he understood the misgiving that came upon him. Cronus was said to be of the Neteru, the watchers in the sky, who long ago left their celestial dwelling and came to the world of men. It was he who had spawned the unholy Aletae. The realization of who the real enemy was behind their enemy made Martin's heart begin to beat faster. How could they fight against this... this thing... this inhuman being from the stars?

Malen watched Martin carefully before speaking. "Yes, as I suspected you have not forgotten my training. Good." He turned to his men. "Bring ropes! I want these doors opened within the hour."

At that moment the ground began to shake again. The intensity of the quake did not soften as before, but it continued to increase until the men began falling to their hands and knees. A loud and strange noise filled the air around them. It sounded like the earth itself was groaning, like two great pieces of iron forcibly yet slowly grinding against each other. In some ways it reminded Martin of the sound of a battle horn, deep yet piercing in its effect. The shaking of the ground stopped, but the unearthly screeching continued to ebb and flow. The Illyrian soldiers around Martin all quickly regained their feet, but they now stood starring at the sky all around them. The strange sound continued until it not only filled the men's ears but also crept into their souls. Several of the men involuntarily began placing their hands over their ears in an attempt to stop it.

Malen, unlike the others, stood with an expression of pure rapture on his face, his arms hanging limply at his side. His gaze was steadfastly fixed upon the gates directly in front of them. It did not take Martin long to discover the reason for Malen's fixation. The Gates of Cronus had opened an arm's span in width during the quake. The heavy wooden beam that barred it from the outside lay broken on the ground in front of them. That alone, however, was not the reason for Malen's enraptured visage. For standing in the middle of the opening was one of the most radiantly beautiful women Martin had ever laid eyes upon. She was taller than most and wore a beautiful shimmering, bluish gray garment that hung down to the ground. Her shoulders were bare, and a delicate silver chain hung around her neck with a large blue sapphire faceted at its apex. Her hair was as black as midnight and flowed past her shoulders in long, wavy locks.

The cold sensation that gripped Martin's insides when first coming to this gate now intensified and grew into outright fear. Bryn's experience with the Aletae flooded back into his mind. The deceptive beauty of this woman warred against what Martin knew to be right in his heart, and it alarmed him. She said nothing but just stood and looked directly into Malen's eyes. It was as if she didn't notice the rest of them. Martin was thankful for that small blessing, for he knew that anyone her gaze fell upon would be lucky indeed to avoid her trap. Martin was a little to the left of where Malen stood. From that angle, he could only see the side of his uncle's face, but the pure delight on it could not be mistaken.

"I can see it!" Malen spoke suddenly. His voice was uncharacteristically filled with emotion. "The Garden! It is more beautiful than I could have imagined," he said in a wistful whisper.

Martin could only guess that the woman was filling Malen's mind with the same kind of visions of greatness that Bryn had experienced. He took a step closer to Malen, thinking to bring him back to reality when he first noticed the man called Lisnor standing a little to the other side of Malen. Lisnor did not wear an expression of delight or joy of any kind. Rather, a dark jealousy brooded in his features.

Martin stopped where he stood. An answer to the mystery of why Malen would destroy the Plant of Truth without first attempting to harness its power now occurred to him. It was simple. Malen had *not* ordered the Plant's destruction nor did he most likely even know about it. Martin hesitated as he pondered this new information. The expression Lisnor wore was deeper than mere jealousy. It was outright hatred, and not for the woman. Lisnor stared directly at Malen. Revelation flooded into Martin's mind. Lisnor must have already met the Aletae. Perhaps he too had experienced the same enticing visions of greatness. It would explain the expression he now wore. Something the Emerald King told Martin long ago echoed into his memory. If you are patient in war, the enemy will often enough divide and destroy themselves.

The woman raised her arms toward Malen. They were bare to the shoulder and almost as white as the stones of the city. She beckoned him to come. She did not speak, but Martin had the feeling she did not need to. What happened next took Martin completely by surprise.

Two more women, similar in appearance, stepped from the black opening of the gateway. One of them fixed her gaze on the man named Lisnor, while the other turned directly toward Martin. His mind was immediately filled with images of crowds singing his praises. He was a great man of wisdom with knowledge beyond reckoning, a prophet the people clamored to hear and worship. His heart soared high inside himself with exaltation. A vague warning nagged at the corners of his conscience, but he could not remember what it was he should be afraid of. He struggled to recall it, but he could not. The woman was there by his side, adoring him. She placed her arm around him and her hand onto his cheek. Her touch sent a thrill through his senses.

"Come with me," she whispered in his ear. "I will lead you to wisdom and power beyond all imagining."

She began to walk away, urging him to follow her. He took one step. But before he could continue, the figure of a man stepped abruptly from out of nowhere to stand directly in front of him. The man's features were completely covered by a light-colored hood.

"Martin!" the hooded man said. His tone was commanding but not harsh. The false visions that were filling Martin's mind immediately vanished. He could think clearly once more. The hooded man held up a flowering green sprig in his right hand. Martin reached out and received it. He looked down at it and recognized it immediately as the same sprig he kept in his belt. The warning that tugged at his conscience earlier now became clear again. The woman was of the Aletae, and her visions, although fearfully realistic, were false paths to death. Martin looked back up to thank the hooded man, but he was already gone. The woman, however, still called to him as though she hadn't seen the hooded man.

Martin approached the woman. She held her hand out to him once again with an alluring smile parting her lips. Martin looked at her hand and reached up and placed the green sprig into it. The woman's smile vanished, and a tormented expression spread across her features.

"*What have you done?*" she screeched with a sudden convulsion racking her body. She jerked backward and shielded her face with her other hand as though trying to hide from the plant. The woman continued to shake in a strange, unnatural manner until her white skin began to turn gray and crack. It began in her hand, which still held the plant sprig, but spread quickly over her whole body. Her voice went quiet, and she stood completely still as though frozen in her strange, twisted posture. The two other women looked on in terror, and then fled back into the dark opening of the gate.

Malen stood completely still, watching the unfolding scene in silent contemplation. His mind had also obviously been freed of all false visions. Yet he showed no signs of anger at this development. In fact, he appeared even more excited than he was upon his first discovery of the woman. Martin followed his gaze back to the frozen woman and her extended hand. The plant still sat in the very spot he had placed it, but its appearance had been transformed. The greenness of the plant shimmered. It actually glowed with a beautiful but soft radiance. Malen stepped closer. There was a building anticipation and greed in his eyes.

"It is the Plant of Life!" he spoke with amazement. "I have found it."

"It is *not* what you think!" Martin spoke loudly, trying to distract Malen. But his words had no effect. Malen reached for the plant.

"*Wait!*" Martin shouted. He feared the plant would affect Malen the same as it had the woman. And as much as he wanted to see Malen punished for his crimes, he had not yet abandoned all hope for him. He was, after all, his uncle.

Malen, however, deftly cupped the plant into his hand and cradled it as though it were a delicate babe. He appeared to be wholly unaffected by its touch. The plant apparently had no openly harmful affect on humans, however evil. The glow of the plant began to subside the moment it left the woman's hand. It soon returned to the ordinary appearance of a simple plant sprig.

Malen turned it over and examined it closely, as though memorizing it in every detail. It was beautiful to be sure. But even more than that, it was powerful. He had just witnessed its ability to take the life of one as powerful as the Aletae, but could it also grant life? Anything powerful enough to take life could, most assuredly and when used correctly, give life. Malen had seen the principal at work before. Of course, never on this dramatic level, but the principal was the same. The difference between a deadly poison and a healing potion is often just the manner of use.

He held the plant up to the light of the sun. It looked ordinary enough now, but it was possibly the key to dealing with the Aletae. The Garden would be his now. The foolish woman had filled his mind with a vision of the very thing he was seeking, and now, with this plant in his control, not even the Aletae could get in his way.

"Lisnor!" Malen spoke without looking at his servant. "Bring ten of the prisoners and enough men to guard them. Include the girl. Where we are going we may find a use for them." He looked suddenly at Martin. "And bind his hands."

"I *thought* we had an arrangement!" Martin spat as several Illyrian warriors restrained him.

"We did," Malen answered. He then added with a grimace, "But things have changed. Haven't they?"

A Sacrifice

After entering through the Gates of Cronus and traveling for what felt like several hours down the underground road, the captives were finally allowed a short rest. They were given no food or drink, but were thankful for the break.

Martin, who was kept close to Malen, was now forced to sit down with the other captives. He quickly surveyed who had been brought along. Aedan, Archimere, Mr. Bonfire, and Valentus sat toward the front of the group with Alenia protectively nestled in between them. Rand, Cian, Riordan, and two of the younger Tharusian soldiers were directly behind.

"Are you all right, Martin?" Aedan asked quietly.

"Yes, but listen carefully, we might not have much time to talk." The others nodded their understanding. "The men with me when we entered the city all placed sprigs of Aayliyah's plant in their belts. Do they still have them?"

Aedan looked to Rand for his answer. Rand felt around his belt and then carefully held the small green sprig up. It appeared as healthy as the moment it had been plucked. Martin quickly motioned for him to keep it hidden. Cian and Riordan also indicated they still had theirs.

"Now listen. The plant is deadly to the Aletae, and I am afraid that we have not seen the last of them. Have the men divide up the sprigs, so all of you have a piece."

Martin noticed the guard assigned to watch him approaching. He made ready to stand, but felt something being pressed into his hand, which was tied behind his back. It was a small piece of the plant. He looked back to see Aedan nod his head. He bent his head slightly with an answer of appreciation and then rejoined the guard. They continued their march downward into the heart of the island. No torches were needed to light the way. The entire underground roadway was lined with a kind of block that glowed a silvery light. It was not bright, but they could all see well enough.

They came to several places where the tunnel branched indifferent directions, but Malen appeared confident in his decision each time.

"How do you know which way to go?" a curious Martin asked.

Malen examined Martin with a look of cool disdain. "Do you think I am weak-minded?" he asked with irritation. "The Aletae may control others with their petty visions of heroism, but I used it to search *her* mind. In trying to manipulate me, she opened herself to my control. It was not difficult." There was pride in his last words.

"And is it not possible she also has searched *your* mind? Perhaps she has led you into a trap," Martin responded.

Malen nodded toward Lisnor, whose hand immediately snaked out and caught Martin solidly in the jaw. He stumbled to his knees, involuntarily losing his grip on the small twig in his hand. He quickly tried to cover it with his knee, but it was too late. Malen reached down and picked it up.

"Of course. I should have guessed. You would not have limited yourself to just one piece of such a powerful weapon." He turned to one of his men. "Search them all. I want every piece of this plant, no matter how small, brought to me!"

It did not take the Illyrian soldiers much time to find the remaining sprigs. Malen placed them in a pouch that hung from his belt. A cruel smile crossed his face. "Thank you, Pharigant! I should be well set now. Come, the Garden is just ahead."

They walked down another short length of tunnel until a black opening gaped before them. There were no gates, just the blackness of the underground cavern that awaited them on the other side of the opening. The group stopped, as very little could be seen of what lay ahead. Malen, however, signaled for Lisnor, the captain of his guard, and a dozen Illyrian soldiers to bring Martin. They entered a smaller branch of the tunnel leading off to the left and upward. They followed this smaller branch a short while until it ended at a doorway that opened onto a large balcony. A cool breeze hit their faces when they passed through the doorway, and the distant roar of falling water could be heard.

Malen turned to the wall on his right and pulled down a lever. The action triggered a long train of silvery lights to be lit in spectacular fashion. It was an amazing sight to behold. A vast cavern lit by silver light. An entire city lay before them, made up of small and large structures of the same white stone used in the city above. They appeared, however, more like monuments than dwellings. Malen ran to the edge of the balcony and pointed to the middle of the expansive cavern.

"There it is!" he spoke excitedly. "The Garden! It is just as I saw it!"

Surrounded by a black, glassy lake, the Garden was built high upon an ancient rock that rose up out of its dark depths. Stone colonnades lined its edges and wound up its various levels. No details could be seen from this distance, but Malen acted as though every detail were clear to him.

"The tree! It is even more beautiful than I envisioned." Malen rubbed his hands together in greedy anticipation.

Martin walked closer, squinting his eyes in an attempt to see further. "I can see the island and the lighted pillars, but I see no tree. It is too far." Martin concluded quietly.

Lisnor grabbed his arm and, with a snarl, yanked him back away from the balcony's edge. As he was pulled backward, Martin caught a glimpse of something large moving in the darkness of the valley below, not a large object, but rather a large area of movement, like many things moving together. He waited for Lisnor's attention to be drawn back toward the Garden before letting his eyes drift back to the area. It was down and to their right and appeared to be higher and more level than the rest of the vast cavern before them. In fact, if Martin was not wrong, it was just beyond the opening where the rest of the men now waited below.

Strangely enough, the silvery lamps lighted much of the area but did not actually seem to diminish the darkness. Large boulders and even a few smaller bridges could easily be made out, but whatever moved out beyond was covered in darkness. Almost as though it wore the darkness as a cloak. There was something about this silvery light. It allowed you to see, but did not banish the darkness. This struck Martin as odd. It was not the darkness of shadows untouched by the light, but rather that the silvery light coexisted with the darkness in some sort of odd allegiance.

Malen turned from the balcony's edge and walked through the balcony door back down the passage. Martin examined the area one more time before being forced to follow. The strange movement had stopped. They walked back down the side tunnel and met up with the others. Malen, followed by their entire group, immediately continued through the black opening into the cavern beyond.

Once through the black opening, Martin was surprised to find it was light enough to see. Malen turned to their left and began walking along the cavern's wall and downward. Martin hesitated long enough to scan the flat area in front of them and to the right of where Malen now descended. Everything within a distance often to fifteen steps could be easily seen, but beyond was an area of complete darkness. This would not have been strange except for the fact that rocks and bridges farther away could still be made out. It left the sinking sensation in Martin's gut that something, or many things, waited in the unnatural black. But what did they wait for?

The Illyrian captain standing near Martin also peered into the dark with hesitancy. Recovering himself, he roughly slapped Martin's shoulder, indicating he was to follow.

Barely visible from the cavern entrance, the underground road descended down from the higher ledge into the chasm. It led directly to the large black lake that spanned the cavern floor. The monument-like buildings lined the terraced shoreline. The roar of a large waterfall continued to rise as they circled to the far side of the lake. From the balcony high above, the lighted bridge appeared small and thin, but the realization of its grandeur now struck Martin. Five full-sized wagons could have crossed it side by side.

Malen, despite the difficulty of their long walk, appeared to increase in energy as they crossed the bridge toward the dark rock island. About midway across the wide bridge, Martin glanced down toward the glassy black water below. A large, serpentine body, as thick as a man, arched in and out of the water in an undulating motion. Several more of the same creatures disturbed the water around the bridge. It was as though they were quietly gathering in anticipation of being fed.

The road narrowed and wound back and forth as it climbed the height of the black rock. Two silver lamps stood adjacent to each of the white stone colonnades lining the road. So far, there was no sign of any living plant, only black rock glistening with wetness from the fine mist that now permeated the air from the large waterfall. It was a steep climb, but Malen never slowed his pace. As they neared the top of the jutting rock, they turned one last bend in the road to find themselves standing under a primitive stone arch and looking upon a truly amazing scene.

The top of the black rock was somewhat flat, except for the very center where a smaller rock jutted up the height of a man. At the very pinnacle of the smaller rock grew a large tree. It was ancient in its appearance and spread its green branches out to the sides. Large clusters of fruit grew in abundance, hanging heavily from the branches. A beautifully sweet aroma permeated the air. Perhaps the most amazing thing of all was the tree itself glowed with the same kind of silvery light that filled this underground world. The glow was beautiful, but it lacked any sense of warmth that came from real light.

Martin gazed upon the fruit. He'd never seen anything like it. It was purplish-red in color, and each individual piece was plump and round, giving the impression that each one was full to bursting with goodness and satisfaction. It held an alluring quality, something that pulled at your senses and called to you, tempting you to come and taste. Martin took a short step closer when the image of the hooded man flooded back into his mind's eye. He shook off the growing spell of temptation and quickly looked around the Garden, surprised to find no other plants of any kind. As he examined the rather bareness of the rock, he noted the men all wore an expression he could best describe as unsatisfied hunger. They all stared steadily at the tree. He searched from face to face until his eyes fell upon Aedan. No hungry expression could be seen there. Instead, Aedan's eyes narrowed and his mouth turned slightly downward. He was not looking at the tree but off to the side.

Not ten paces to the left of the tree stood a stone table. It was the length of a tall man and appeared to be cut from the black rock itself. Channeled grooves where chiseled into the top, running from the center to the sides. A shallow channel was also cut in the black rock at the base. It circled the entire table and met on the side closest to the tree and ran to a shallow depression near the base of the tree's roots. In the bottom of the depression were several black holes. The table was simple in design, but the dark feeling he experienced when seeing the Gates of Cronus returned.

"Do you like my tree?" The voice was deep and resounding in its tone but cold in its impression. Martin glanced quickly around to discover who had spoken. Off to the right of the tree was a dark area, much like the darkly shrouded part of the flats above the lake. Martin hadn't notice it before, so focused was he on the grandeur of the tree. The voice definitely came from that spot, but nothing could be seen.

Suddenly, the darkness lifted as though a dark cloak had been removed. An enormous creature sat upon a large, white, throne-like chair. The person sitting there was like a man, but much too large with skin as white as the stone of the city above. He wore a beautiful golden crown. The throne and the king who sat upon it sparkled as they reflected the silver light of the tree.

Martin swallowed hard. He knew he stood in the presence of Cronus himself. Not one of the Aletae, but their father. He was one of the Neteru, the watchers from the sky, who had disobeyed the Creator by descending to the earth and teaching wickedness to men.

"The fruit of the tree is delightful, and you are *hungry*. Are you not? One bite will give you the strength of the gods, and their knowledge as well," the unearthly creature said.

Malen remained silent, but Martin noticed his hand hovered near the sack containing the Plant of Truth twigs. Despite the abrupt appearance of Cronus, Malen was not unnerved in the least. It was as though he had anticipated it.

The king stood from his throne. "Has my champion finally come?" He looked directly at Malen. "I will give you the power of the Garden!" He raised his left arm into the air and spoke an unintelligible word. A ball of silver light appeared in his hand. He spoke a few more strange words and then flung the ball into the branches of the tree. What happened next amazed them all. Streams of light danced from the tree and shot across the dark cavern toward each one of the stone buildings. They all began to glow, revealing their true nature. Each building, as far as the eye could see, contained an exotic and very large plant or tree, each one more beautiful than the next. It suddenly occurred to Martin that the rock island was not the Garden. It was just the center. The whole chasm was the Garden.

Questions flooded into Martin's mind. He wondered what each plant had the power to do. He felt a quiet warning in his heart to turn away as he gazed at the garden. It began to nag at him. He knew what appeared to be innocent curiosity often was just the first step in falling prey to wickedness. He fought down the desire to know and turned back toward the king.

"Have you brought a sacrifice?" The creature addressed Malen.

"I have brought many," Malen answered, waving his hand at the captives.

It now occurred to Martin why they'd been brought along. Malen must have seen the need for a sacrifice, a human sacrifice, when searching the Aletae woman's mind. Alarm made his heart beat faster. He had to think of something. But what could they do? They had no weapons. Their hands were bound, and they were hopelessly outnumbered by their Illyrian captors.

The king of the White City held out his hand toward the stone table. "I accept your offering."

Martin thought he saw eagerness in the king's eyes. Malen pointed to Valentus. Illyrian soldiers grabbed him roughly and began dragging him toward the stone table. He struggled against them with all his strength, but did not cry out.

Alenia cried out in fear. Martin looked around desperately for some way to save him. Lisnor approached the table and produced the wickedly curved knife he had held to Alenia's throat earlier. Several of the prisoners, including Archimere, shouted for Valentus to be released. They fought against their captors only to be beaten down. Mr. Bonfire head butted two soldiers and sent them flying to the hard rock ground, but he was eventually subdued by a heavy club to the head. Alenia turned her head away with tears flowing freely.

"Malen!" Martin shouted. "You *cannot* do this! You *need* not do this. Use the Plant of Truth," he implored.

"That was always your trouble, Pharigant. You were too *weak* to use others for your own gain. Look around you! This is paradise and I will not *lose* it." Malen nodded to Lisnor.

Valentus was forced flat against the table, his hands tied to an iron ring protruding from its top. Lisnor stood over the young man and looked toward the Neteru king with true adoration. His hand raised the blade slowly into the air and hovered for an instant. The rest of the men renewed their struggle against their Illyrian guards, but to no avail. Lisnor turned his attention from the king back to Valentus. His expression changed from adoration to brutality as he inhaled deeply. Valentus, realizing his struggle was in vain, let his breath out slowly. He readied himself for the wicked blow. Time stood still as he turned away from his executioner. Lisnor's evil twisted face was not the last thing he wished to see.

He turned toward Alenia. Her body shook with sobs. He closed his eyes, forcing the darkness of this moment from his mind. Instead, he saw Alenia standing on the stage, singing once more. He felt the cool night breeze of the midsummer's fair ruffle his hair and heard her beautiful voice carrying clear to his heart. As though from a distance, he heard someone scream, felt a sharp quick pain, and all went silent.

Hidden in Plain Sight

The captives all stood in silent disbelief. It had happened so fast. The reality of it was hard to accept. The knife hovered above Valentus, and then it plunged toward his heart with blinding speed. Except it never found its mark. From out of nowhere, a piece of black rock sung through the air, hitting Lisnor square on the side of the head. He dropped like a sack of flour. The knife missed Valentus only by the barest of margins. Unfortunately, after hitting Lisnor, the rock bounced off only to land squarely on Valentus, rendering him unconscious as well.

They all stood dumfounded. Where had the rock come from?

"I wouldn't move if I were you," a familiar voice spoke.

Lanthir, wearing the ordinary uniform of an Illyrian soldier, stood behind Malen with a knife to his ribs. How he'd accomplished joining their ranks and remaining hidden in plain sight for so long was a complete mystery.

"As much as I would like to finish this here and now, I need you to tell your men to lower their weapons and untie my friends." Lanthir's tone was threatening. He stood at a slight angle to Malen, careful not to turn his back on the imposing figure of Cronus.

Malen stood frozen in a moment of indecision. He had clearly *not* foreseen this development. The knife dug slightly deeper into his ribs, encouraging him to speak with more haste.

"Lay down your weapons!" Malen's angry but hasty command was followed by the clatter of metal against rock as the Illyrians threw down their weapons.

It did not take long for the prisoners' bonds to be untied. Archimere and Alenia rushed to Valentus's aid. Aedan directed the others to quickly gather the discarded weaponry. There were too many Illyrians to effectively guard them all, but at least they would be disarmed. Valentus was revived and helped to a sitting position on the edge of the table. He appeared no worse for the wear, but was a bit confused as to whether he was actually alive or not. As he leaned forward off the edge of the table, the small pendant he kept on a chain around his neck fell from the folds of his shirt to hang freely in the air.

The inhuman being named Cronus, who until now stood unmoved, suddenly jerked forward. He glared at the pendant with unmasked fury. He pointed at Valentus, and as though on cue, nine female Aletae stepped from the shadows at either side of his throne. They no longer bore any resemblance to anything anyone would consider beautiful. Their appearance was, however, quite menacing. A head taller than any of the men, they hissed and snapped as they closed in toward Valentus. Those with weapons jumped in front, ready to defend.

Aedan held his sword out toward one of them, but to his dismay, the female creature ripped it out of his hand before he could even react. Another of the Aletae grabbed Cian by the front of his cloak, picked him off the ground, and threw him to his back.

Lanthir, still keeping an eye on the monstrous king, reached his hand deftly into the pouch hanging from Malen's belt and pulled out a handful of the green, leafy twigs. In a quick arching motion, he flung them over the Aletaen's heads. The effect was immediate and devastating. Their sharp, piercing screams filled the cold air of the cavern until they went silent. Only two of them escaped direct contact with the plant. The king also cried out, turned and fled back down the path toward the bridge, disappearing into darkness. The two remaining Aletae followed hard after him. The others were frozen into stone like the woman Martin encountered at the gates above.

Through all of this, Malen remained perfectly still with Lanthir's blade pressed sensitively to his side.

Martin walked swiftly to Valentus and examined the pendant. It was an exact match to the seal of the Guardian in the Book of Stories. The question was how did Valentus come by it?

Alenia, who still held her arm protectively around Valentus, noticed Malen glaring at the pendant. Not liking the look in his eyes, she reached out and tucked it back under Valentus's shirt. The black rock island began to vibrate under their feet, and aloud cracking noise echoed through the chasm. The ground did not shake like the other quakes. Instead, it felt more like it was pulsating. The cracking noise ended only to be replaced by the same unnerving, grinding, moaning noise that filled the air at the Gates of Cronus.

In the growing apprehension of what the menacing sound meant, no one noticed that Lisnor had regained his consciousness *and* his knife. He slowly stood with one target in mind. He would give Cronus the desired sacrifice and become his champion. He came one step closer to Valentus before raising the wicked blade above the back of his victim. Lanthir was the only one who saw the danger. With no time to think, he took the knife he held to Malen's ribs and flung it at Lisnor. The throw was rushed, but it sunk deep into Lisnor's left shoulder, causing him to scream out in pain. Martin and the others all turned just in time to see Lisnor drop his own blade and run off into the darkness toward the bridge.

They turned back to give Lanthir the praise he deserved only to find him standing with an odd, vacant expression on his face. Malen stepped back suddenly to reveal the small dagger in his own hand. It dripped with a thick dark substance. A deep-red stain began to grow on the front and side of Lanthir's shirt. He stumbled forward and fell to his knees, coughing up blood. He turned his head to look at Malen's face, which jeered in exaltation.

Malen sprung toward the silver tree and grabbed one of the clusters of fruit from a low-hanging branch.

At that moment, the hideous grating noise returned. It grew louder and louder until it began to hurt their ears. Somewhere across the cavern, a large rock fell from the cavern's roof and crashed into the lake's black water. The Illyrian soldiers panicked and began running for the bridge. Malen used the commotion to join in the escape with the others. There were simply too many of them to be stopped.

Martin, Aedan, and the others all rushed to Lanthir's side. He began to fall forward, but Archimere was there and caught him.

"Is Valentus safe?" Lanthir asked.

"Yes. You saved him. *Twice!*" Archimere answered.

Lanthir glanced furtively toward Archimere's face. "You were the best man. Never before has anyone bested me with a sword. But you..." he coughed.

"That is not the way I remember it. It hurts me to admit it, but I found more than my match in you," Archimere answered honestly.

"Ahhh, but you kept your honor. That is the difference of a true warrior." Lanthir continued. "I would have been your friend in a different life."

"My enemy's enemy *is* my friend," Archimere said, gently placing his hand over Lanthir's heart. "I am sorry it has taken this for me to trust you."

"You were right to hate me," Lanthir said with a weakening smile. "It was I who destroyed your people."

"No. It was Malen who did that!" Martin answered as he bent down closer.

"It *really* is you, Pharigant! I thought I saw you before. In the tunnels… with Malen." A fit of coughing racked his body. "I would have given you justice, if I could have. Now it is up to you to free Serigant." Lanthir's face was white in the silvery light, and his voice was growing quiet.

"*Serigant* is alive? Where?" Martin's tone became urgent.

"The pit of voices," he whispered faintly. "Ask him…" He struggled for air. "To forgive me?" Lanthir breathed once more and then slumped back limply.

Archimere gently laid Lanthir back to the ground. They straightened his limbs and placed his sword on his chest. A loud, cracking noise in the roof of the cavern above boomed through the air. A second loud snap made them know it was time to leave. They turned away from their fallen friend and toward the only path off the rock. Running down the curving pathway above the bridge, they could see the Illyrians below them had already reached it. Another loud thundering crack sounded, and a black jagged rock the size of twenty men fractured from its position on the roof above. It fell directly onto the middle of the bridge, smashing and twisting it to bits.

The Illyrians paused only briefly before their fear drove them into the black water. Without the bridge, swimming the lake was the only escape. The first of them reached the midway mark before disappearing below the surface. A second one vanished before the others realized something was not right. The sight of several long, shiny, black, snake-like bodies in the water brought the others to panic. Before long, the black water had transformed into a frothy chaos filled with screams of terror.

Martin stopped those following him and pointed to the right of where the bridge had been. "We will cross over there."

"Do you think it safe?" a horrified Alenia asked.

"Don't worry. I think *now* would be the safest time." He pointed at the unfortunate Illyrians. "Every creature in this lake will be drawn to that commotion."

The men placed Alenia in the middle of their number to better protect her, and then they waded into the lake. They tried not to stir the water, but jagged rocks lined its floor, making it difficult to avoid stumbling. Alenia hit her foot against a larger rock and plunged forward into the bone-chilling water, making a large, splashing sound. They all stopped and examined the length of lake between them and the frenzy taking place near the ruined bridge. There seemed to be no movement in their direction.

"Swim quickly, but quietly!" Martin warned them as they reached the deeper water.

Once they reached the middle of the lake, Riordan, who was near the front of the group, let out a yelp and jerked to a stop suddenly, sending a good-sized ripple through the water.

"What's wrong?" Cian, who swam next to him, asked tensely.

"Something large just bumped into me," Riordan answered with an unsettled voice.

"Are you all right?" Aedan asked.

"I think so."

"Good. Then keep swimming. But quietly!" Aedan said.

Cian looked at his friend with a chastising annoyance. Riordan glanced sheepishly around before starting to swim again. They swam another ten body lengths before Cian also jerked to a stop and grunted in alarm. They all stopped swimming and went perfectly still. A black, cylindrical body arched out of the water not two arms' lengths from Cian. It was as thick as a full-grown man, and its length must have been great by the length of time it took to disappear back under the dark surface. Several more surfaced to the side and appeared to be heading right for them.

Cian and Riordan turned to attempt escape.

"Stop! Move only enough to stay afloat," Aedan ordered.

Despite wearing an expression that suggested such a move was unreasonable, the two young warriors obeyed. The large, snakelike creatures disappeared directly under them. The small group all held their breath for a long, uncomfortable moment before seeing the creatures resurface on their far side, heading for the now dwindling disturbance by the bridge. Each of them breathed a sigh of relief and then quietly continued on to the shore.

They climbed out on the other side only to see Malen, his captain, and a handful of Illyrians running up the incline toward the cavern's entrance. Few of them survived the black water, and there was already little remaining evidence of the disaster. The dark lake surface returned to its black glassy reflection, and silence once more descended. The small group followed their enemy upon to the level flats above the chasm. Several more chunks of ceiling could be heard falling somewhere across the vast darkness.

Martin searched the flat area opposite the entrance. The unusual darkness he had seen when they first entered still lingered. It hid something, but Martin had no desire to discover what it might be. He half turned away when a large figure stepped from the shadowed area to stand not fifty paces from them. It was Cronus. His face was filled with dark hatred and his eyes with menace. He opened his mouth and let out a roar that was more animal than human-sounding. Those with Martin all turned apprehensively toward the sound, almost not wanting to discover its source.

The king's visage had openly changed. He no longer wore the aloof dignity of a king on his throne. His eyes blazed red, and as the hideous sound of his roar diminished, the veil of darkness lifted. Martin's eyes widened at the sight. Fifty or more Sargaroth stood poised and ready to strike at their master's command. Hot, steamy breaths came from them as they breathed, in exhilarating anticipation of the kill.

Martin stood frozen in place. A hand grabbed his shoulder from behind.

"Martin! Now would be a good time," Aedan spoke in urgency.

They both spun on their heels and ran for the cavern entrance. Alenia and the rest of the men were already disappearing into the tunnel. A loud, prolonged roar filled their ears with dread. Martin glanced over his shoulder as he ran. Terror pulsed through his veins. The tunnel was not far away, but the Sargaroth were coming and they could not be outrun. They were almost upon them. Martin knew reaching the tunnel would not protect them. The silver light of the blocks didn't bother the Sargaroth like the light of fire or sun. He crossed the threshold into the tunnel, and his fear was replaced by calm. Martin stopped in his tracks. He knew what had to be done.

"Lead the others to safety!" he shouted to Aedan as he turned to meet the enemy.

There were so many of them! It was a strange sensation just to stand and watch them come. It was as though he was someone else watching his own demise. The evil creatures appeared to gain in size and ferocity as the ground between them vanished. He clenched his teeth, waiting for the inevitable deathblow to come. His death, he hoped, would give the others precious time to escape to the light above.

Everything around him slowed to an almost dream-like state. A sense of peace enveloped his heart. It surprised him because it was fear and terror he expected as he stood to face the death that hurled toward him. Instead, he laughed out loud. What was there to fear? Death? He had already accepted it many times before in battle. Should he fear it now? He raised the Illyrian spear in his hands high above his head to honor the Creator God he'd chosen to serve. He closed his eyes and remembered how the Emerald King spoke of the one true God and how rest had finally come to his soul.

They were almost upon him now. What a strange way to die, in this place of darkness. He always believed it would be under the light of a cloudless sky. He braced himself with the Illyrian spear he now carried. It would be over quick, of that he was sure. And then they were on him.

A Happy Reunion

The expected impact did not come. Someone rushed passed him on his right side and then on his left. It was the most unexpected sight he could have imagined. Bryn and Llew stood between him and the army of Sargaroth. Llew waved two burning torches at the enemy, while Bryn held a sword that burned brightly with some sort of internal flame. It was beyond all hope. They were not only alive, but now stood between him and sure death. Tears streamed freely down his face with the joy of the sight.

Somewhere behind the swarming Sargaroth, Martin could hear the terrible and unnatural roar of the king of the Aletae. He prepared to join Bryn and Llew, but then noticed something on the ground by his feet. It was a single leaf of the Plant of Truth. He picked it up as a thought came to him, and he smiled. Placing it onto the tip of his spear, he closed his eyes and threw it with all his might. It disappeared into the darkness of the cavern air and Martin thought he saw a glint of silver light flash off its metal point as Cronus, with fierceness, rushed toward Bryn and Llew.

A split second later, the wooden shaft of the spear protruded from the king of the Aletae's right eye. He screamed in horror, clawing at his eye, and fled back down the road to the island. Aedan and Archimere rushed forward, each carrying a bucket filled with an oily liquid. They showered it above the heads of the Sargaroth. Llew then threw one of his torches into their midst. Flames roared high into the air above their heads, followed by the deep panicked screams of the Sargaroth.

Aedan, Bryn, Llew, Archimere, and Martin ran back up the tunnel to rejoin their friends. It was a long way, but the thought of pure daylight and fresh air urged them on until their lungs burned with the effort. They found the others waiting at the Gates of Cronus, and the gray light of the early dawn was a welcome sight. The sun would appear soon. Aayliyah stood and rushed to meet them. Relief crossed Aedan's face at the sight of her.

She was more beautiful than he had even remembered. Suddenly his tongue became heavy and clumsy. He could find nothing to say. His time on the island left him dirty and not so good-smelling, a fact he suddenly became all too aware of. Aayliyah gave him a curious appraisal then flung herself into his arms. He slowly tightened them around her delicate frame. There he stood until the ground began to shake under their feet. Another earthquake increased its intensity and then finally began to diminish. The rock cliff above the gates began to pop and crack loudly, letting them know they had already stayed too long.

Quickly, they made their way to where the rest of their men remained captive. It was not far, and they found them still bound but completely abandoned. Apparently, the captain of the guard had returned without Malen and ordered his men to retreat with him toward the city docks. It did not take long to free the others and begin making their own way to the harbor where Berand believed the Illyrians anchored True North. As they left the courtyard, Martin stopped and turned back toward the manor house Malen used as a headquarters. Something was bothering him.

"I have to know," he said in answer to the others' questioning looks. "Do not wait. Get the men back to the ship. I will meet you at the harbor."

Malen stood in the upper room of the stone building, considering his next move. He had instructed his captain to go and execute the remaining prisoners. If Pharigant or any of his friends ever made it out of the cavern, he would make sure there was no help waiting for them. What was taking the pig-faced idiot so long? There was much to do, and he could not stand to waste even a moment.

A loud crashing boom from the mountains behind the city roused him from his contemplation. He'd grown used to the earthquakes. They would rage for a time, but then subside as they always did. Malen felt the pouch at his side, and the large form of the fruit inside caused a pulse of excitement to shoot through his chest. He would not eat this fruit. He had a better purpose. Instead, he would return to Illyrium and use it to plant his own silver tree, a tree that granted knowledge. It would finally be his. And after Pharigant's men were out of the way, he would return to the Garden below with all his warriors and take whatever else he wanted. And he would want it all. Only the Aletae would be in his way. He patted the second leather pouch hanging at his side and heard the crunch of the few remaining twigs of the plant of life. They would not be hard to deal with.

The sound of someone walking in the hallway came to him. He turned, expecting to see the ugly features of his captain, but he was taken aback to see Pharigant standing in the doorway.

"Well. You *are* full of surprises." He sneered. "I should have killed you when I had the chance."

"The island is dying, Malen. Your men have abandoned you. Surrender yourself and I will—"

"You will *what?*" Malen spat in anger. "The Garden is within my grasp, and I will not leave it now!"

The ground began to shake violently, throwing them both to the floor. Martin reached his hand to the nearby table in order to steady himself. Aayliyah's Book of Stories was there, within reach. He quickly recovered it as he stood back to his feet. Malen, however, was gone. A door was ajar near where he had stood a moment before.

"Is all well?" a familiar voice said from behind him. Turning, Martin saw Bryn and Llew standing in the doorway.

Martin nodded his head in answer. "Come, we must leave this place quickly. I do not think we have long." He glanced toward the spot he last saw his uncle. "Malen has sealed his own fate."

Martin, Bryn, and Llew caught up with the others halfway to the harbor. Aayliyah had insisted on stopping to retrieve three large pots containing the Plant of Truth.

"These are the last of the plants," she said sadly. "I will not see them perish with this island."

Their progress slowed considerably as the pots were heavy and awkward to carry. Several more large quakes shook the island before they stood on the docks looking at True North anchored a short distance away. It filled their hearts with hope to see it. Several Illyrian ships also remained but appeared to be abandoned. They took three shore boats moored nearby and immediately made for True North. The loud screech of a strange wailing noise they had heard earlier began filling the air once more. The island appeared to be shaking violently, but in their boats they could not feel it. Several large waves in rapid progression, however, came close to capsizing them. A large white tower crashed down into a cloud of dust that billowed outward, followed by several of the larger buildings. The small group boarded True North and made a hasty search for their crew.

They were found locked in the hold below the main deck, hungry but none the worse for their trouble. The distant sound of a thundering boom vibrated the entire ship as they freed the sailors. They all ran out onto the upper deck just in time to see one of the mountains toward the far end of the island disappear.

"Raise sail!" Aedan commanded. "Let us leave this place."

Malen smiled as he walked out onto the balcony that over looked the harbor to the north. Perhaps he had overestimated Pharigant. Let him flee with all the others. None of them understood what power waited in the caverns beneath the city. Eager anticipation flooded his mind as he once again considered the possibilities that were now real.

The quakes were growing in strength, but he would not let that stop him. He gazed up at the jungle rim to the east. A sliver of the sun was just cresting above the horizon. He almost looked away before noticing something moving in the eastern sky. He watched it a little longer. It appeared to be a large bird of some kind and was flying directly toward him. The first rays of the rising sun were red and made the bird appear to glow in scarlet light. His stomach began to tighten. Surely the bird would find a perch, or change directions soon. It continued on directly toward him. As it came closer, it grew in size and the brightening light of the sun illuminated it in a magnificent fashion. Images of the nightmarish bird of prey that tortured his sleep so many times before flashed through his mind's eye.

Malen's heart beat faster. He squinted in an attempt to see it better. He tried to convince himself that it was just an ordinary bird. He raised his hands to shield his eyes from the growing brightness of the sun. The bird became impossibly large and as red as blood. Panic flooded over him, and he tried to turn and flee, but the terrible thing was already on him. He heard the piercing cry of the bird and fell to the stone floor of the balcony. As he looked up in terror, out of the blinding light, he saw the bird's dagger-like talons sweeping down at his face. It was the last thing he ever saw.

The sails bulged under a strong wind as True North sped across the tops of the waves. It felt good to be in the open sea air once more. Several more booms raced across the waters to them. They sounded much like thunder when lightening hits too close.

"The island!" one of the sailors shouted.

They all rushed to the rail to be met by a long series of booms and cracking noises that dwarfed all the previous ones. The far south part of the island appeared to be rising up into the sky and the city by the harbor descending into the bay. It hung this way for a while before it began sliding like a plate into the waters of the harbor. Everyone aboard True North stared in speechless amazement. After beginning its slide, half of the island, including the whole of the White City, vanished beneath the ocean.

When two-thirds of the island had slipped beneath the waters to the north, the remaining raised portion of the island slapped back down into the water and vanished with a roar. A gigantic white wave raced away from the area to the south. A few moments later, multiple rings of large waves hit True North, surging them far to the north. Many of them fell to the deck with the force of the initial impact. Martin and Aayliyah were the first ones back to the railing. Nothing remained except white foam with large bubbles erupting periodically.

Homecoming

Martin, Aedan, Bryn, and Llew all ran down the long, narrow corridors of Ryathidon, the ruling fortress of Illyrium. Martin knew of the Pit of Voices and the stories of its effect on the mind. He raced beyond hope that his brother still lived. It had been a long time, and he searched deep into his memory to remember the way to the pit. It took longer than he hoped, but he found the secret door and rushed down the descending stairs. Aedan, Bryn, and Llew had to fly to keep up with him.

They reached the bottom, and Martin lifted the heavy black iron lever that served as a latch. The door swung open. All was dark on the other side. Martin used his torch to light several other torches in a barrel by the door. They held the torches up high to better search the room. They could see the iron grate in the middle, but all was silent. They walked towards it.

"This is the place. The Pit of Voices," Martin said.

There was anxiety in his voice, and he hesitated. Aedan, Bryn, and Llew stepped forward and pried up the iron grate. Aedan went first and encouraged Martin to follow him. Bryn and Llew followed behind. Never before had they experienced such blackness, not even in the underground city of the Aletae. They stood at the bottom of the stone stairs and surveyed the room, their attention immediately drawn to the black fissure-like crack in the far corner.

"I don't like the look or feel of that," Aedan said.

"Over here!" an excited Llew spoke.

Their lights reflected off a small bundled mass of clothes and hair against the far wall. They all rushed to the spot.

"Serigant! Can you hear me, Serigant?" Martin's voice carried a level of anxiety that the brothers had never heard before.

There was no response or movement. Martin worked at moving the long, matted, dirty hair from his brother's eyes. He placed his ear down by the hair-covered face.

"He still breathes!" Hope returned to Martin's voice.

They tried to stand Serigant up, but his legs were too weak, and he collapsed back into Martin's arms. Serigant moved his head slightly as though waking from a long sleep.

"Is that you, Pharigant? I have died then." He spoke with peaceful resolution.

"No, you are as alive as I am!"

The iron grate above slammed back down into place, and the sound of chains being locked came to them. They set Serigant carefully back down and rushed to investigate. Sitting in a chair not far from the opening was the twisted face of Lisnor. He wore a triumphant, arrogant expression. Standing over him was the hulking form of the keeper of the Pit.

"It was not difficult to know this would be the first place you would come and the best place to wait for you. You see Ranf here? Take a good look. He will be the only face outside yourselves that you will ever see again."

Martin moved quickly up to the grate and held the torch up so that his face could be seen. "Ranf, do you remember me? I am the king's son! You serve the king. *Remember*, Ranf."

Lisnor shook his head and laughed. "Malen is the king. Ranf serves Malen."

"Malen is dead, Lisnor. The island is gone. It sank beneath the ocean and took Malen with it." Martin turned back to Ranf. "I am the king now."

Ranf did not move, and Martin had given up hope when Ranf suddenly reached down, grabbed Lisnor by the scruff of the neck, placed him on the stone floor, and sat on him.

"What are you doing?" Lisnor screeched in anger.

Ranf ignored him, bent down, and laid hold of the chain and unlocked it with his key. He then lifted up the heavy grate as though it were as light as a feather. Martin and Aedan grabbed Serigant and dragged him out of the pit. After they were all out, Ranf stood once more, grabbed Lisnor, and tossed him easily down the stairs and into the pit. Lisnor's curses filled the dank air as the grate was closed once more.

"Do you have some water and food?" Martin asked Ranf, who nodded and lifted a leather satchel he carried over his shoulder. They placed the drink to Serigant's mouth, and he coughed, but he came awake once more.

"It *is* you, Pharigant," he whispered with a voice hoarse from lack of use. "I have dreamed of this day, but I did not think it would ever really come."

Lisnor's cursing suddenly went silent. "What was that?" he asked loudly. "Something is down here!" He spoke with true fear in his voice. And then his shrill scream filled the air. "They're taking me! Help me!"

Bryn walked over to the grate and held the torch down low. Lisnor's loud protests and demands for help went silent. Bryn searched for him but could see no one. Llew helped him open the grate, and the two of them descended a few steps of the stairs. Bryn bent down and examined something on the rock. And then he held the torch higher to examine the rest of the pit. He nodded to Llew and then slowly backed up the stairs without turning their backs to the black fissure in the floor.

"What is his problem? Tell him we would not leave anyone down there. He will see the mercy Serigant did not," Martin instructed, but then he noticed the strange look in Bryn and Llew's faces. "What?" he asked.

"He is *not* there," Bryn answered in bewilderment.

"What do you mean?" Aedan asked.

"The only thing we could find was what looked like..." Llew paused and looked at Bryn for confirmation.

"What did you find?" urged Martin.

"Deep scratches in the grime of the floor. Leading all the way to the large crack, and then nothing," Bryn answered.

It was a ghastly end for anyone, but nothing could be done, and none of them would risk exploration of the fissure for one who had chosen his own course.

A week had gone by since their arrival. Serigant was healing well, but he remained weak. It would take time to regain his full strength. It was an outright miracle he had not lost his mind in the pit. No one had ever lasted as long as he did. His first command after coming fully to himself was that the Pit of Voices be filled in and buried forever. He, of course, offered the throne to Martin as the elder brother and rightful heir. Martin, however, refused. He had relinquished that right long ago and only wished to continue on the path he had chosen. He would remain with Aedan, Bryn, and Llew and return with them to the Emerald Isle.

One final thread of evil remained to be severed. They hunted for the Ice Thorn planted by Malen. Without him, the thorn had no master, but as long as it continued to grow, it would be a threat. Knowing his uncle, Martin knew it would be somewhere close enough to receive Malen's own personal care. It took several days, but it was found in a secret side lawn surrounded by high hedges, completely invisible from every vantage point, but one. Martin was searching Malen's chamber for clues when he paused to lookout the western window in tired frustration. There, directly below the window, sat a simple square garden devoid of anything but a large, ugly, gnarled tree.

They tried to cut it down, but all their attempts ended in painful wounds from its thorns. It became clear to all that this tree was ready and able to defend itself. Furthermore, anyone who came within the confines of the small garden area would leave with a splitting headache. It was Aayliyah who offered the solution. She suggested that the only effective weapon against an offspring of the Garden of the Aletae was the Plant of Truth. So they planted one of the three remaining plants next to the Ice Thorn. When they returned the next morning, the Ice Thorn was completely shriveled and cracked down the middle. The Plant of Truth, on the other hand, had grown to more than three times its original size.

With the successful defeat of their last enemy, the time came for the men of the Emerald Isle to return home, and King Serigant called for a feast in their honor. It was a joyous time of loud music and heaping mounds of food of every kind. But there was sadness in the approaching departure as well. They had gained new friendships and forged the deep bond that comes with being sword brothers. Archimere, Valentus, Alenia, and the other Tharusians would accompany them as far as Tharrus where their journey would finally part paths. None of them liked the thought of the inevitable farewell that must come, but Tharrus was a broken kingdom that would require much healing.

Valentus was quiet through much of the feasting. Through all their adventures, he had found a new purpose and a place amongst his new friends. That was ending now. What awaited him on Tharrus? Perhaps the sheep would still be there. The thought did nothing to quell his mood. How could he ever return to his simple life again? But what choice did he have? He sat staring into his cup until someone slapped his back sharply.

Mr. Bonfire stood behind him, grinning down through his stained teeth. "Yer bein' asked fer boy." He pointed toward a group standing around King Serigant.

Valentus approached and would have remained behind the backs of those standing in a circle, but for Mr. Bonfire bearing another one of his grins and shoving Valentus through the perimeter of people. His cheeks flushed with the unwanted attention.

"Valentus, isn't it?" King Serigant said in a jovial tone.

"It is with great pride that I introduce the Guardian of the Plant to you." Archimere bowed down with true grace.

Valentus, not sure what was going on, assumed he was either the focus of a jest, or that Archimere had indulged a little too much in the frothy ale that flowed throughout the hall. Aayliyah stood next to Martin and Serigant, but their expressions were serious.

Aayliyah stepped forward toward Valentus. "I have been told that you wear a unique pendant around your neck. May I see it?"

Valentus glanced suspiciously around the circle of faces, but he reached slowly for the one possession he had from the father he never knew. Aayliyah examined it closely with ever widening eyes.

"It is *true*!" she exclaimed. "It *is* Ram's pendant." She searched Valentus's face as though it was the first time she had seen him. After an exhaustive inquisition, her eyes filled with tears. "How could I have not seen the likeness before? You have my own father's bearing." She threw her arms around him in an emotional embrace. "You are my cousin, the true heir of Ram."

Bryn approached next. He waited for Aayliyah to step back. He held his sword across his palms. "This sword was given to me by Aayliyah, but I believe you are its rightful master. May it serve you well. Especially if one of those Sargaroth ever show up again," he said with a twinkle in his eye.

The crowd burst into laughter as a flood of well-wishers surrounded an uncomfortable Valentus, slapping his back and cheering his good fortune. Silence descended abruptly, and Valentus, not sure what had happened, turned around to discover what had so subdued the enthusiastic crowd.

Alenia stood at the entrance to the hall. She was a vision of beauty that made Valentus's mouth drop slightly. She wore a glimmering green dress that sparkled in the firelight, and her dark hair hung in large curls down over her white shoulders. She walked slowly but deliberately toward Valentus, stopping at an arm's length from him. Her eyes met his, and he swallowed hard. She held her hand out, palm upward. It held a golden ring. Valentus just stared at it, not knowing what it meant.

Archimere stepped up next to Valentus. "I believe the Lady is making a claim. Do you dispute the claim being made?" he asked seriously.

"What?" Valentus glanced furtively at Archimere.

"The ring, man. It means she has claimed you as her husband. Do you dispute the claim?" He explained the Tharrusian tradition.

"*Husband?*" Valentus was dumfounded as to what he should do. "But I have nothing to give her. I... I could not provide for her."

Archimere's eyes narrowed. "What trick is this?" he asked in mock anger. "Do you deny being the nephew of the lord of one of the largest estates on the whole island of Tharrus?"

"Well, no, I suppose not, but—"

"Well nothing. With the unfortunate death of your uncle and his immediate heirs in the battle of Perginton, I fear you are the only heir left." Archimere rested his argument and waited for Valentus's response.

"Heir? Do you mean to suggest that I own my uncles' estate?" The thought never occurred to Valentus.

"Not to restate the obvious, but my sister's claim remains unresolved."

Valentus glanced around the crowd one last time and then back into Alenia's eyes. He reached out, took the ring, and proclaimed a little louder than intended that he approved. The crowd once again erupted into loud, rousing cheers, and the men picked Valentus up off his feet and carried him to another corner of the room to celebrate. The feast was coming to a close when Serigant and Martin called Aedan, Bryn, and Llew to them. The look on Martin's face was somewhat serious for the surrounding celebration.

"Merchants from somewhere to the northeast arrived earlier today seeking a market for their trade." He looked briefly at Bryn before continuing. "They brought several gifts to Serigant, hoping to establish goodwill." He hesitated before continuing, glancing once more toward Bryn.

"If you have something to tell me," Bryn said, "I would like to hear it."

Martin reached his hand over to Bryn. "They gave my brother this."

He dropped something heavy into Bryn's hand. Bryn examined it carefully. His face went white, and he began to sweat.

"Well, what is it?" Llew asked.

Bryn handed it to Aedan, turned, and walked from the room. Aedan turned it over several times before recognition crossed his features.

"It's Lord Rovian's seal. A ring that only he wore." Llew's expression showed that he still did not understand its significance.

"Kelsi was Lord Rovian's daughter. She was with him when his ship was lost at sea."

Llew took the seal and held it up to the light. "But how did these merchants come to have it?"

Martin stood up and looked to the spot they last saw Bryn. "How indeed?"

Israel Cooley won his race

and went home to be with his King and Savior

on the night of April 19, 2019.